Nova Terra: Titan

Seth Ring

Nova Terra: Titan
Copyright 2018 by Seth Ring.

1st Edition

TABLE OF CONTENTS

CHAPTER ONE

It had been a long and mentally trying day for Xavier filled with the normal medical tests and his overprotective aunt trying to do everything for him, but the end was in sight. Same old, same old. The hum of his massive motorized wheelchair and the squeak of his aunt's shoes on the polished floor lulled him into a strange state of detachment. He had been down this hall so many times that it had become rote.

Lurking behind his aunt were six silent bodyguards. Xavier suspected they wouldn't make any noise if they tap-danced across broken glass - ever present, silent watchers whose eyes never stopped evaluating everything around them for threats.

He had lived with his aunt since he could remember. After all these years the permanent, unsmiling, besuited bodyguards had become a familiar part of the background. So much so that Xavier almost didn't notice when the guards opened the doors in front of him, checking for threats before they entered.

It wasn't like he couldn't open the doors and walk through the hospital by himself. He could, but the tendency for his skin to split open when he moved without his wheelchair and the tremendous pressure his bulk put on his bones kept him sitting still.

Thankfully, there was some light at the end of the tunnel. After years of theories on what was wrong with him, the doctors thought that they had finally figured out a fix for his condition. As the elevator headed down to one of the basement floors for his final checks, Xavier couldn't help but be hopeful.

A chime announced the arrival at their floor, and the soft hiss of the doors snapped Xavier out of his reverie. The long, neutral hall stretched out into the distance. Pale pastels, intended to be soothing, presented the promise of tedium and wasted time. The bland hall was currently full, as a man in a delivery uniform struggled to push a massive crate down the corridor.

At a touch from his aunt, Xavier's massive wheelchair hummed out of the elevator and down the hall, the large wheels squeaking against the hospital tile. Xavier looked up at the 8-foot ceiling, thankful that he was sitting. At least sitting down, he did not have to duck. Silver linings, right?

A nurse coming toward the elevator squeezed past the delivery man with a wheeled bed. Appreciating the soft curve of her backside, the delivery man leaned out for a second look as she passed him. Blocked by the large crate that was in his way, he leaned out to the side, causing his precariously balanced load to shift forward. Twisting to the side, the box began to topple toward the bed.

The nurse heard the scrape of the box as it shifted and only had time for a gasp before it came crashing down. In a desperate attempt to shield her patient, she threw herself across the bed and closed her eyes, bracing herself for the pain she knew was coming.

Yet the impending crash never came, and a couple seconds later she opened her eyes in confusion, looking up. And up. And up. Met with the sight of the largest person she had ever seen casually holding the massive crate, she stared in open-eyed amazement at the giant who had saved her.

Dark hair cropped short above a massive face with a rugged brow and a strong jaw gave the intimation of attractiveness, yet the ideal was ruined by the skin that stretched across his cheekbones, pulling back on the corners of his eyes, nose, and mouth, creating a grotesque caricature of superman. Just bigger. Much, much bigger.

The giant smiled at her and she smiled back, lost in the surreal situation until rapid splashes of red blood snapped her out of her dazed state.

"Oh, you're bleeding!" she mumbled, still half in shock as she watched blood rain down from the giant hand that gripped the edge of the box to join a pool of blood that was beginning to form around his feet.

"Well, would you look at that?" responded Xavier, his deep bass voice echoing through the corridor as the bodyguards swarmed forward.

Twenty minutes later, Xavier sat next to his aunt while a nurse finished taking care of his wound.

"Always the hero," Julia teased, poking at his broad shoulder. "You should have left it up to the guards rather than hurting yourself."

"You've taught me better than that," Xavier said with a slight smile.

Soon the doctor arrived and sat down next to Julia, handing her a large stack of papers. Xavier stayed in his wheelchair to avoid towering over the other two or breaking a chair. His hand had been bandaged to prevent additional blood loss, and a nurse had finished taking a blood sample to run some more tests. Holding his bandaged hand to keep the bleeding from starting again, Xavier looked at the doctor with some interest. Rather than the normal boring tests, it seemed from the doctor's expression that something new was going to happen, and whatever it was, it would be a welcome break from the monotony of his normal routine.

Ever since he was little, and his condition was discovered, Xavier had been stuck in the same routine. Sitting, studying, slow Taijiquan exercises, and doctor's tests. The school and Taijiquan practice were not so bad, but after so many years the sitting and doctor's exams were starting to wear on him. There was very little excitement in his life, a fact that made him hyper-aware of any changes. Speaking of changes, his aunt had been trying to hide something from him, a birthday present most likely, and Xavier wondered if the visit today something had to do with it.

The doctor looked at Xavier and his aunt, Julia Lee, pushing his glasses back on his nose. As Xavier's only surviving relative, Julia still had custody of Xavier until he turned 18 in two years, though no one looking at Xavier's 8' 9" frame would ever imagine he was only 16 years old.

After many years of testing and treatment that yielded no results, a fringe researcher had come up with an idea to help, and through cooperation with the Horizon facility, the doctor was here to suggest it.

Going over the information again with Julia and Xavier, the doctor explained, "Even though we've talked through this exhaustively, Ms. Lee, I still have to take Xavier through the process for the sake of both our legal rights."

"Xavier," the doctor turned to look at the giant boy. "If you choose to proceed, you will be undergoing a new type of nanodermatology treatment that is being referred to as CNB, Cutaneous Nanite Bonding. It is a new treatment that has been pioneered by a medical research facility in Switzerland. While it has not been cleared for general use, you have been approved to receive the treatment because it was developed using your body as a model. We've been aware of this treatment for a couple years but have been hesitant to suggest it because of your accelerated growth rate. Your tests over the last year have shown a significant decrease in growth so it became an option."

Taking a deep breath, the doctor looked between Xavier and his aunt. "The only catch is that the treatment will take some time. Due to your higher-than-average mass we are estimating that it will take at least two years. During that period, you will need to be in suspended animation the whole time. I know it is a lot to take in, but how does all this sound? Do you have any questions or concerns?"

"It is a bit overwhelming, truthfully." It took Xavier a couple moments to process before his deep voice rumbled out. "So, I'm going to be dead to the world, out for two years?"

"Ah, not quite," The doctor jumped to his feet and grabbed a stack of papers from a cupboard, handing them to Xavier. "Suspended animation is a bit different from what you see in the movies. The classic example is someone frozen in ice for some time and then thawed out later, right? That is not what we are talking about. With the advent of Nova Terra, technology has developed to the point where we can take an individual's mind to a new world, leaving their body behind for a short period of time.

"In order to facilitate longer periods of uninterrupted gameplay, Horizon, the company that makes Nova Terra, has developed what they call 'extended suspension' through the use of special game pods that monitor the health of the user and provide nutrition, muscle stimulation, and waste removal. Think of it as an extended vacation from your body."

"You'll be playing a game for two years straight," Julia cut in. "That amounts to 14 years due to the time dilation. A single hour in the real world is equivalent to seven hours in Nova Terra."

"Wait, so I'm going to be 30 when I get out?" Xavier asked, horrified.

"No, no," the doctor laughed, waving his hands. "You will be 18. Only two actual years will have passed. It is a pretty interesting phenomenon when you think about it, but it is completely natural. In the real world, it is called being in a Flow state, where time seems to shrink or stretch based on the activity you are doing. Nova Terra keeps you in a constant Flow state, stretching time so that you experience seven times as much as you would in the outside world."

"That does not seem safe at all."

"It is, though. The human brain is a magnificent thing, and we have almost thirty years of research and study that demonstrate no side effects from this. You do not need to worry."

Xavier was a bright kid, so he was particularly concerned about the possible impact of prolonged immersion on his brain. Despite his youth, he had finished primary and secondary school years ago and had even completed two degrees, one in Business Management and another in Urban Planning. After all, what else is there to do besides school when you could not move about?

It was a shame that, despite his smarts, he was unable to live as a normal person. Xavier had long dreamed of being able to see the new worlds that virtual reality had begun to offer, which made this idea immediately attractive. Xavier glanced at his aunt, who was watching him, trying to guess his feelings about this.

Xavier couldn't help himself and let a smile spread across his face. Up to this point, his life had been tedious. It wasn't as if he lacked for anything, no it was the opposite. There was no struggle, no effort needed. If he wanted something, and it wasn't bad for his health, then his doting aunt bought it for him.

Forget the fact that he was many times richer than she was, she wouldn't even let him use the absurd amount of money his parents had left him. Hemmed in and coddled by all who met him, the thing he wanted the most was freedom, and the idea of being in an adventure game like Nova Terra was an amazing opportunity to get that freedom.

Julia Lee gave a small sigh of relief. She knew her nephew well and it was obvious that Xavier was excited about this idea. After a few more minutes of talking some of the details through, she nodded at the doctor. Xavier would be sent into the game where he would spend the next two years of real time while the treatment worked to repair his body.

The papers signed, and a date set for the following week, Xavier and Julia made their way out of the hospital and toward the massive all-terrain vehicle that they drove. However, as soon as they exited the hospital doors, the flash of lights announced the gathering of paparazzi that seemed to follow Julia around like gnats.

"Ms. Lee, Ms. Lee, is it true that you are engaged?"

"Ms. Lee, what are your thoughts on the rising energy costs?"

"Ms. Lee, you are being accused of setting up a hostile takeover of DeHauser Energy. Do you have any comments on that?"

Their security was expecting it, and it wasn't long before they were able to force their way through to the car. Pushing past the crowding reporters, the leader of the security team opened the butterfly door of their vehicle and pulled down the ramp before guiding Xavier's chair up into the car and into its place where it locked in.

"Thanks, Henry," Xavier nodded at the guard.

"Of course, Master Xavier," the guard responded, his stern face breaking into a smile. All of Julia's employees adored their giant charge. Glancing back at the paparazzi pushing against the rest of the security team, Henry grimaced. "Sorry about all the noise, sir. Next time we'll use the private entrance."

"It's not a problem, Henry. The pictures are good for my aunt's publicity."

Julia, a drop-dead gorgeous blonde with a figure that even gods would kill for, was the most eligible bachelorette in the world, helped, of course, by the fact that she was also a minority shareholder and the CEO of Atlas, the largest energy company in the world. Rich, smart and beautiful, it was no wonder that the tabloids followed her like puppies. Seeing her grumble, Xavier couldn't hold in his smile.

Most of the ride home was spent discussing Xavier's coming immersion. Julia had played Nova Terra since its release and was well established. Combined with the fact that the majority of her business was done in the virtual city of Fantasia, Julia was well versed with virtual reality.

"Xavier, you should join me when you get into Nova Terra. This game is not the same as other games, and it takes a lot of work to get established." Julia flipped her hair over her shoulder.

"Come on, you know that work is the last thing I'm afraid of," replied Xavier with a smile.

"I know, I know. But you don't understand how different it is. It is not like any MMO that you have ever played. There is no grinding, no leveling up, no health bars or anything like that. It's pretty much real life and it's as dangerous. To some extent, it is like the wild west. Untamed and lawless. Unless you have the strength to protect yourself, you are at the mercy of other players."

"What about quests and storylines?" asked Xavier. "Don't games have to have a story?"

"They practically don't exist," grumbled Julia. "Normal games have level progression; Nova Terra only has mastery. There are no experience points or anything of the sort. Want to learn to fight with a sword? Start practicing. Want to learn magic? Figure it out. There is no system assist or any sort of auto-targeting. The same is true of storylines. At least, there isn't a 'story' that anyone has discovered. The game has history, but there is no final boss."

"Wait, then what do you do?"

"You do what you want to do. You can do anything. You can live in a city and make shoes for NPCs. You can join a pioneering expedition and settle a wilderness town. You can hunt monsters and slay dragons. Well, not that last one. At least, no one has been able to yet. We're working on it, though."

"You've been playing for a long time, right? What have you been doing?" asked Xavier. He knew his aunt played Nova Terra, but they had never talked about it since he wasn't able to participate, and she didn't want to make him jealous.

"Oh man, let me tell you! We have the best mercenary corps in the entire game. Prettiest, too," replied Julia with a smug look. "But this illustrates my point. It took me four years in real time to build up the Society of Roses. That is almost 30 years in Nova Terra! You can't step into the game and expect to make quick progress.

"First I had to establish the group and then gather players. I mean, it took countless years for everyone to train to the point where they were good enough at fighting to complete the missions! And that is not even considering our reputation as a group. We only managed to get a permit to build our headquarters in the capital a year ago. If you take the time dilation into account, it took us 21 years in game. 21 years of calculated moves and hard work.

"We had to work our way up, managing our relationships with other groups and the powers in the world. Nova Terra is not like a game where each NPC has a couple quests and lines of dialogue. They all have their own lives; to the point that you could accept a quest and then come back and find that the person who gave it to you went and died. Or started a new business. Or got married or had a kid. At the end of the day, Nova Terra is another world. And like the real world, life moves along without you. If you're serious about going it alone, you'd better be prepared to work for what you want. If you put in the time and effort, you will be okay. Nothing of value is going to come easy, but everything is achievable."

Furrowing his brow, Xavier thought for a minute, his eyes drifting across the scenery outside his window.

"Then where is the fun? Isn't the point of a game to provide entertainment? If Nova Terra is so hard, how is that different than real life? There must be something about it that draws people in. I mean, almost 70% of the world plays."

"Oh, don't get me wrong. It is fun. Really fun. It isn't as uncomfortable as real life. Like, you don't sweat no matter how hot you get. Everyone's hair looks great no matter how much you have been running. It is like life, but with most of the uncomfortable and inconvenient parts edited out. But Nova Terra is more than that. When it first came out, it was a game, but when they built Fantasia it became as important as the real world."

"Fantasia? You mean the city? Isn't Fantasia in Nova Terra?"

"Not quite. It sits parallel to it. So, you can hop back and forth. Think same universe, different planet. I do almost all my business there because of the time dilation. That is the only way I have time to play." Julia smirked. "Almost everyone in the business world uses Fantasia to handle their business and Nova Terra to relax."

CHAPTER TWO

Seeing the large smile on his aunt's face as she talked about Nova Terra, Xavier couldn't help but think back over the many years he had lived with her. She had gained custody of him from birth after a tragic accident took the lives of his parents. Julia, only nineteen at the time, had stepped up to play the part of both mother and father to him. Not to mention, Julia had taken on a leadership role in his parents' multi-million-dollar energy corporation.

Xavier hadn't even made it to the hospital to be born when a drunk driver turned his parents' joy at the coming birth of their first child to a nightmare. His parents had survived long enough to be brought back to the hospital emergency room, but both passed away during surgery. Miraculously, Xavier survived both the crash and the emergency c-section that followed. His aunt rushed to the hospital only to find her sister and brother-in-law dead.

Xavier had grown at a furious rate, dwarfing other children of similar age. His bones and muscles grew so strong and dense that he was walking by the time he was two months old and was almost four feet tall by the time he was one. This astounding growth left the pediatricians who were monitoring him dumbfounded. His ever-increasing diet fueled his rapid growth, and the doctors could only attribute it to some unknown form of gigantism.

As he got older, he began having problems. His bones, organs, and skin struggled to keep up with his massive frame. Almost daily his skin would stretch and split, leaving bloody trails across his body as his skin cells tried to duplicate. Despite his abnormal strength and the size of his bones, gravity began to prove too much for him. Facing this difficult situation, the doctors were at a complete loss, trying one failed treatment after another.

For the past sixteen years, Xavier had gone in and out of hospitals around the world, trying every conceivable method to solve the issue with his body. His aunt, who had proved to be a successful businesswoman in her own right, had spared no expense. She wasted a veritable fortune on treatment and research no matter how obscure.

In this unprecedented case, Xavier's muscles and bones were almost 32 times stronger than normal, allowing him to move his 840-pound body like a regular sized person. However, even though Xavier's body was much stronger than was reasonable for someone with his condition, far surpassing the limits of normal humans, his weight still caused him to struggle to support his body.

In fact, by standing to his feet, he easily broke the World's Strongest Man deadlift record. Unfortunately, the pressure of gravity on his bones had caused numerous stress fractures in his hips and legs over the years, and, by the age of eight, Xavier had found himself unable to walk without a mechanized brace.

To complicate his situation, his medical condition caused him to be threatened by the danger of literally ripping through his own skin. The result of his massive musculature meant that any sudden action would cause his skin to tear open, accompanied of course by lots of blood and pain. Careful movement was still possible, and through technological aids like his electric wheelchair and his mechanized brace, his life could have a modicum of normalcy.

After getting home, Julia got him settled in his room and reminded him that his Taijiquan instructor was going to be coming in half an hour. While he waited, Xavier opened his computer to do some research. From what he knew already, Nova Terra was a gamer's dream, but it differed from many of the games that existed previously.

"Information on Nova Terra," Xavier said, watching the computer create a virtual library for him. Seeing the huge amount of information still streaming in, he narrowed the search. "Basic game information." Soon he had a manageable amount of information in front of him, and he began to browse.

No visible stats, no damage counters, the game was touted as the first true alternate reality. If you could do something in the real world, you could do it in Nova Terra. The ads boasted unlimited freedom, restricted only by ability and resources. Judging by the variety of posts on the message boards, it wasn't an overstatement to say that you could do anything in Nova Terra so long as it did not fall into the category of certain criminal acts.

Xavier had not even scratched the surface of the information on the game when a knock at his door let him know that his instructor had arrived. Clicking open the door from his computer, he moved to the edge of his massive chair and grabbed his robotic frame. Strapping his legs into the supports he pushed a button on the side of his chair, and with a hydraulic hiss, his chair pushed him up into a standing position.

Standing at five feet tall, Ms. Chen was dainty, with short hair and a gentle looking face. Although he was almost twice her size and countless times her weight, Xavier greeted her with the utmost respect. She had been teaching him for many years and was more of a grandmother to him than a teacher. The fact that he had once watched her completely thrash ten of his aunt's best bodyguards at the same time helped, as well.

"Hello, sifu." Xavier greeted his teacher, his mechanized brace helping him bow slightly.

"Hello, child. Julia informed me that you will be leaving us soon. Then we better get all the practice in that we can. First stance."

"Only for a few years. Supposedly, when I get back out of Nova

Terra, I will not need this brace anymore."

With the assistance of the mechanical frame, Xavier was able to move through each of the stances that they had been working on. He had been doing Taijiquan for almost 11 years, but the nature of his condition had made progress rather hard. He tried passing from stance to stance smoothly, focusing on his breathing, relaxing his body to avoid stiffness and gathering his strength in anticipation of each of the moves.

"You'll still probably be as clumsy as an elephant," grumped Ms. Chen, pushing him to correct his stance.

There was always a slight clumsiness that could not be overcome due to the mechanical frame, but overall, Ms. Chen was satisfied with his efforts. After two hours of careful practice, she climbed up on Xavier's massive chair to give him a kiss on the forehead.

Since he was rather sweaty, Xavier moved to his bathroom after saying goodbye to his teacher. He had designed his personal living space, so he didn't have to duck as he walked through the door and into the massive shower. Peeling off his sweaty clothes, he showered and got changed. Each one of his actions was focused and deliberate. The more he thought about living in a world free of the danger of hurting himself with a simple movement, the more excited he became.

The days passed slowly, too slowly for Xavier; whose anticipation grew every hour. Thankfully, there were tests to do to make sure nothing would go wrong with the immersion process, otherwise he might have gone crazy. As the day got closer his regular routine was interrupted as the hospital set up his pod and had him try it out.

For Xavier, who had never enjoyed the opportunity to pursue life the way others were able to because of his physical condition, Nova Terra promised a level of normalcy he had only dreamed of. While swords and magic and dragons were not normal, at least he could experience them the same way as everyone else.

Sitting next to the floor-to-ceiling window in his room, Xavier looked over the well-manicured lawn and neatly pruned trees that dotted the southern side of the estate. For years, he had been trapped. Trapped by his body, trapped by the perfection of a life where everything was handled for him. It was almost time to break free.

The day before his immersion, Xavier accompanied Julia to the Atlas headquarters to complete the final paperwork. Because he was a major shareholder in Atlas, they held a board meeting to explain his situation and set up the procedures for decision making while he was in Nova Terra.

"This paperwork is a drag," Julia complained, flexing her cramped hand. "If I have to sign another paper my hand will fall off. You sure generate a lot of paperwork for someone going into a game. I can't wait till you are finally in Nova Terra. Then I might finally get some time off."

"Then you'll finally have time to go on dates with one of the hundred guys who called you yesterday," countered Xavier with a straight face, earning himself a scowl.

"Forget it. I am too busy making my guild the number one guild in the world."

"Oh yeah? How close are you?"

"We are doing pretty well." Julia sighed. "There are a lot of good players in Nova Terra and, unfortunately, they play together. We rank in the top ten, though the rankings tend to fluctuate a good bit. Considering the restrictions on our guild, I am quite proud of what we have achieved."

"What sort of restrictions?"

"Well, we only accept women into the guild, and we are a pure mercenary corps, which means we do not take on anything that isn't a mercenary job." Seeing her nephew's confused look, Julia smiled. "There are many things that a guild can do in Nova Terra. We handle requests from other players and NPCs. Other guilds might trade in luxury goods or sell production items in a store.

"Some even hunt for rare creatures or explore the game. With how large Nova Terra is, people haven't even scratched the surface of the game. According to the rumors floating around, there is an entire storyline that we have not activated yet. But that is a rumor at this point. With all the different things that we could choose to do in Nova Terra, we have decided to focus on mercenary jobs.

"While we might take on a job to guard a merchant caravan or a bunch of miners, we won't run our own caravan or do the digging for ore ourselves. We do have a production branch, but we use everything they produce ourselves. Because we restrict ourselves to a specific kind of work, it is a bit harder for us to expand than guilds with a diversified portfolio."

"That makes sense, I guess. All those restrictions are self-imposed, right? What made you decide to play that way?"

"That is an old story," Julia paused to tuck a stray hair behind her ear. "About thirty years ago, I was in another guild, but the leader was a total jerk, so I quit. When I quit, a bunch of the other ladies quit, as well. We wanted to show him that we could make a guild that was even better than his."

"Thirty years ago? That would have made you, what? Four years old?"

"No, thirty years ago in the game. This was four years ago in real life."

"Right. Time dilation. So, what happened to the old guild?"

"They ended up disbanding about three years ago, after we crushed them in a tournament. When we left, we took a good chunk of their core players and the three best player versus player casters in the game. PvP combat is a huge part of the game, so losing us crippled their ability to compete with the top tier guilds. Most guilds solve their problems through duels or team fights, so after we left, they suffered. All the other guilds started to pick on them. I mean, we did too, but we actually had a reason.

"After they collapsed, we continued to grow as we found other players like us. I don't think there was ever an official conversation about it, the rules formed naturally based on what we are all interested in. I mean, there are only sixty of us. So, it isn't like we are one of the big guilds. Sixty players is a nice size because we can split into squads of eleven. Ten mercenaries and one officer. We have five total squads with five players in our production division. The five officers are our guild officers, as well. Overall we have a neat little family."

"It sounds like it." Xavier could tell how proud his aunt was by the huge smile on her face as she talked about her guild.

The intercom buzzed, and Julia's secretary informed them that the lawyers had arrived to handle the final paperwork for the medical treatment. It did not take long for the documents to get filed with Atlas' lawyers, and after finalizing the documents for his immersion, there was nothing left for Xavier to do but wait. Waiting suited Xavier fine - after all, he felt like he had been waiting for his whole life. He would leave the business stuff to his aunt while he got ready for adventure.

The last two days passed, the time of immersion arrived, and his tearful aunt brought him to the hospital. The whole ride over she fretted and tried to convince him to immediately contact her when he got into the game. With a high mastery character and a fully formed guild, she could help him get used to the game in the shortest time possible - an offer that Xavier immediately rejected, of course.

"I want to play by myself at first. You know, take my time and explore. I have 14 years, for goodness sake. At the very least, I want a year on my own. Plus, your guild doesn't allow men, so I can't join anyway."

"Believe me, Xavier, the game isn't easy. Especially in the beginning. We have tons of experienced players who can teach you the ropes. Plus, the girls have always wanted to meet you! I am positive that they would make an exception for you, if you wanted to join. Like I said, it is not an official rule or anything like that. It just ended up that way."

"I'm sure all the ladies in your guild are very nice, but I would like to spend some time on my own," Xavier said, suppressing a shudder. Thinking about being surrounded by innumerable women like his aunt made his skin crawl. He loved her dearly, but one overprotective, clingy aunt was more than enough.

Unable to move him from this position no matter how much she threatened or cajoled him, Julia finally huffed and let it be, but only after extracting a promise that he would at least call her within the first year. A year in the game was only a bit more than a month and a half in real time anyway. The game had a video chat feature that would allow them to connect easily, and Julia went over how to use it with Xavier three times to make sure he understood.

A few hours later, Xavier had been prepared by the staff and was about to enter his custom-built pod. Bending down was awkward with his braces, but Xavier bore with the discomfort so that his aunt could give him a hug. Xavier consoled her in his slow, deep voice. "Don't worry, Aunt Julia, I can still communicate with you and the doctors while in Nova, so I will be sure to let them know if anything is a problem. Think of this like boarding school. Plus, I will see you soon in game."

Straightening back up, Xavier stepped over to the massive pod and watched his aunt leave the room. Looking around for his last view of the real world for the next two years, he shed his hospital gown, proving to the curious nurses that he was indeed proportional all over, and lay down in the pod, which began to fill up with a nanite-infused gel from the large nanite colony on the wall.

Twice the size of a traditional full-immersion pod, the device that had been customized for Xavier was quite impressive. Housing better processing power, multiple power system fail-safes, a state of the art monitoring suite and every other feature one could imagine apart from a mini-bar, the pod had cost a pretty penny, but Julia, ever business minded, had worked out a special deal with Horizon to provide special state-of-the-art backup batteries that Atlas had developed for their pods in exchange for this custom built pod.

Almost instantly the strong anesthetic put him under, and he fell into a deep sleep. Outside the pod, the doctor was glaring at the curious nurses while keeping one eye on the controls for the pod. It had taken almost three years of experimentation to come up with a mixture of anesthetic that was strong enough to put Xavier out without shutting his organs down, so the doctor paid special attention to the pod's vital sign indicators to make sure there were no problems.

"Good luck, young man," the doctor whispered as he headed off to settle his next patient.

CHAPTER THREE

It wasn't his first time in virtual reality, so the deep darkness with the calming blue loading bar came as no surprise to Xavier. In fact, it made his heart beat all the faster. Well, his proverbial heart at least.

The world Xavier loaded into was a soft white color stretching endlessly in all directions. Lacking a body, Xavier floated around for a couple seconds before a gentle cough indicated that there was someone behind him. Turning his attention to face the figure of an unnaturally beautiful woman clad in a shimmering blue dress, Xavier would have smiled if he had a mouth with which to do so.

"Hello, traveler. I am Myst, your guide to the world of Nova Terra. As this is your first time logging into Nova Terra, I will take you through the tutorial. During this tutorial, we will work together to create a personal avatar for you to use during your stay in Nova Terra. Please be aware of a couple of restrictions on this avatar. First, you cannot swap your gender. Second, you are limited to a 20% overall change in your appearance. Third, your physical stats will be generated based on a full body scan and a few minor tests and initially will be linked to your real-life body's condition. Do you have any questions, traveler?"

"Uh...yeah. What stats are available?" Xavier had done as much as he could to prepare for this chance to play Nova Terra, but there was surprisingly little information outside the game.

"That is a great question, traveler. There are a few stats that you can see by saying Status. Please do so, and I will explain each."

After saying "status", a simple blue window popped up in front of Xavier.

Name: [None]	Race: [None]
Health: [N/A]	Mana: [N/A]
Titles: [None]	Conditions: [None]

"Thank you, traveler. As you can see from your status, you currently have nothing filled in. Once we begin the process of creating your avatar, many of those fields will be filled. Apart from your name, which is the final choice you will make before you begin your journey in Nova Terra, you will be presented with a number of race choices as well as a series of tests based on the result of your body scan. All six of the main races are available except in extreme cases, and some rare races are locked unless you meet specific qualifications."

Without taking a breath, Myst continued, "Your max health and max mana will display in your status, as will your titles and any uncommon conditions, however, the rest of your stats will be hidden, as that would ruin the immersive experience. That said, I can still tell you about the basic stats. Strength governs how strong your avatar is as well as how much damage you do when using a melee weapon. Dexterity governs your avatar's coordination and speed in addition to how much ranged projectile damage your character does.

"Constitution is your avatar's ability to take damage as well as your endurance and damage resistance. Intelligence will govern how fast your mana pool recharges and how quickly you can process information. Wisdom is your avatar's ability to make good choices and relate to other people. Finally, Charisma will govern how well other people relate to your avatar. Please note that there are hidden stats, as well, that you will have to discover on your own. Do you have any other questions, traveler?"

Xavier thought for a moment before responding. "How does my Intelligence going up change my perception of the game? I mean, how does the game simulate a person getting smarter?"

Myst stood still for a moment and then shivered, her perfect face taking on a slightly more human look. "That is a great question, traveler. The computer controller in your pod has been fitted with a completely non-invasive system assist that will slow your perception of the game's time to allow you more time to think as well as several system assists that will help you do specific things like math or recalling information. Do you have any other questions, traveler?"

"Yes. How do I increase stats if I cannot see them? And what about skills? I don't see a spot for them."

"That is a great question, traveler. As you may be aware, there are no levels to speak of in Nova Terra. Instead, as you acquire skill and practice various activities, you will find yourself increasing in proficiency. To have an idea of where a player stands in comparison to others, they will need to compare their abilities, as in real life. There are a near infinite number of tasks that can grant you increased proficiency through training like gaining titles, skill at completing tasks, finding hidden stats, the rank of monsters you kill, and quests you complete. Think of each of these things as mini-games that have been optimized to help you gain mastery of various tasks.

"You might think of titles as a count of the things you have done in your adventures. Gaining a title is as simple as cooking your first meal to as complex as slaying a dragon and saving a princess. Completing some tasks will grant you specific bonuses while others will add to your reputation. In addition, there are some rewards, called advancements, that come with specific ability or skill increases based on your race. Additionally, please note that biological changes in your body will also be factored when you log in, which is why regular exercise is recommended for every player.

"In short, skills are handled the same way they are in the real world. While skill levels are hidden in order to increase immersion, the more you do something, the better you will be at it. Do you have any other questions, traveler?"

"Wait, then I have to manually do and learn everything?"

"That is a great question, traveler. That is partially correct. To increase your proficiency in a skill, you must use it repeatedly, like in real life. The learning time will, however, be shorter than the real world, and the more you practice, the more the system will assist you. Otherwise, you must master skills on your own. Do you have any other questions, traveler?"

"So, apart from the six fields in my status, I can't see anything else about my progress?" asked Xavier, confused.

"That is a great question, traveler. That is incorrect, you will also be able to see quests, access an inventory, and contact the administrators. Nova Terra is not, however, a virtual reality game; rather it is a brand-new world. It may be helpful for you if you think of Nova Terra as the real world with a few convenient advantages. Do you have any other questions, traveler?"

Thinking for a second, Xavier shook his head, "No, thanks. I am ready to start creating my avatar."

"Excellent. Please wait while I complete your full scan and set up your base point." A moment passed as Myst took out a small device and waved it toward Xavier.

The white landscape blurred, and Xavier found himself in a modern-looking exercise facility. Machines of various kinds dotted the room, and music played in the background. For a brief moment, Xavier even thought he had returned to the real world. It was only when he realized that he was still disembodied that the feeling faded.

"Please enter the Fitness Assessment Android in front of you."

Myst pointed with her clipboard at the human-shaped robot standing in the middle of the room.

A thought sent Xavier floating toward the robot. As soon as he got close, there was a brief flash of darkness, and the eyes of the robot flickered to life. He looked down at the small, slim form of the robot with a mental frown. This new body was, at most, six feet tall and felt strange. It was as if his limbs were tied and no matter how much he wanted to; he couldn't stretch.

"Thank you, traveler. I will now adjust your Fitness Assessment Android to the correct size. Please move each of your limbs when I ask you to." Walking around behind him, Myst adjusted something on her pad and Xavier soon found himself much more comfortable.

The change in perspective was disorienting, but after a couple moments, he got more familiar with this new body. Standing, he very slowly lifted his right hand to examine it. The robot was thinner than his real body and felt much lighter as well.

"How does this body feel, traveler?"

"It's okay. A little lighter than my real body. I sort of feel like I am in water," commented Xavier, wiggling his fingers.

"Please wait while I recalibrate your weight, traveler." Myst fiddled with her pad once again. As she moved sliders around, Xavier felt the familiar sense of heaviness settle on him. While it still was not as intense as the feeling in the real world, at least he didn't feel like he was going to float away.

Once the adjustment was done, Myst directed him to an area along one of the walls. A short track stretched along the wall with pillars set at regular intervals on both sides. Directing him to stand at one end, Myst told him to move down the track as fast as he could once the indicator light went on. After he finished, there was a short, pregnant pause.

"Thank you, traveler," Myst said in her sweet voice, a slight trace of confusion in her words. "May I ask why you walked down the track? I only ask because your physical statistics indicate that you could have completed the track much more quickly, if you chose to."

Wait, running? Xavier felt blood rush to his face as he was overcome with embarrassment. Though, could he be blamed for his mistake? The last sixteen years of his life had been spent moving carefully and deliberately. It was no longer a conscious decision but an inbuilt reaction. If he needed to move, he did so with caution. If he didn't, he kept his body as still as possible.

"Oh. Hmmm. Right." Xavier tried to cover his embarrassment by coughing. "Can I try again?"

"Of course, traveler. You can try the assessment as many times as you need in order to feel comfortable in your avatar," said Myst. "Apart from the look, this avatar will feel the same as your in-game avatar. The primary function of these tests is to make sure you feel comfortable in your new body."

"Oh?" Xavier looked around at all the different machines. "Okay, awesome. Let's try this running thing again."

As he walked back to the starting line, Xavier made a conscious effort to lengthen his steps. No one understood the concept of effective incremental change better than he did. For his next attempt, he walked the course again, focusing on stretching his legs out to their full stride. The feeling of taking a full step without experiencing the ripping feeling of his skin breaking open was at first strange, quickly turning almost euphoric.

After walking the course ten times, Xavier was able to break into a slow jog. He had jogged and even run when he was younger, so it was not a completely foreign movement to him. But it had been years. It was obvious from his awkward movements that he lacked practice.

"Hardness to softness, let go of stiffness. Hardness to softness." Repeating this mantra in his mind, Xavier focused on sensing the stiff, hard areas of his body as he jogged back and forth on the track. Taijiquan focused on dissolving stiffness in the practitioner's body in order to create softness, which proved to be a big help as Xavier got used to running.

Like a machine, Xavier moved back and forth on the track.

Sometimes jogging, sometimes walking, sometimes breaking into a sprint for a couple steps. He soon lost track of how many times he moved back and forth, but he had no intention of stopping. After feeling trapped in his own skin for so long, the unfettered movement was almost like a drug to him.

At first, the most he could do was a few jogging steps as he walked back and forth. It was as if there was a mental block that slowed him down instinctively. That didn't last too long, and soon he was able to jog the whole distance. After jogging back and forth twenty times, Xavier paused and stretched himself out. His muscles felt fatigued, but he was by no means tired. Still, it felt good to stretch.

Once he finished stretching, he moved to the starting line again and resumed his jogging, this time concentrating on breaking into a run for a few steps in the middle of the track. Unfortunately, the track was short, and his long legs took him to the end in only a dozen steps.

"Excuse me, Myst?" Xavier paused from his running. "Do you have a longer track? I feel like this one is too short. I can't really run on it."

Myst, seeing that the track was too short for him, adjusted something on her pad. The wall at the end of the track shot off into the distance as the room stretched. Once the straight track was a mile long, Myst stopped the wall and smiled at Xavier.

"Thanks." Excited by the long, open space in front of him, Xavier took off, speeding up as he progressed. Soon he was pounding down the track, his long stride sending him down the track at a fantastic rate. At a full-blown sprint, his stride was only a bit under twelve feet long, causing the impression that he was devouring the distance.

Despite the building fatigue, Xavier could not stop running. He had heard about the phenomenon of the 'runner's high' and had seen his aunt running a lot, but, for him, it was different. As he flew down the track and back again over and over, one feeling dominated the rest. Freedom. The pain and fatigue that started to build in his legs, the breaths that grew more difficult, all of that was crushed beneath an overwhelming sense of lightness.

For more than a decade, he had been shackled by his body, unable to express himself through any significant motion. So, when he began to cut loose and run, it was like a dam bursting. All his pent-up feelings poured out in an unstoppable tide, forcing his legs to move. Almost completely absorbed in his frantic run, there was a very small part of Xavier that was thankful that his body was a robotic one. Otherwise, he would be bawling as he ran.

The exercise room was well lit, and Myst showed no impatience, waiting until Xavier exhausted himself completely. Unsure of how long had passed, Xavier lay panting on the ground, completely spent from his mad dashes back and forth. At some point, the ends of the track had connected, creating a giant loop around the room so that he did not have to turn around, but Xavier hadn't noticed until he finally collapsed and was once more aware of his surroundings.

CHAPTER FOUR

"Thank you for completing the running test, traveler," Myst said, producing a small device that looked like a phone. "Please wait for a moment while I calibrate your results." Myst waved the device toward Xavier, who felt strength flooding through his body. Within a few seconds, his body felt revitalized and full of energy! Oblivious to Xavier's curious stare, Myst input some numbers into her pad and then escorted him over to a large pile of stones that had appeared in the middle of the giant room.

"Traveler, this next test is to determine the upper limit of your strength. Please select a rock and move it to the ring on the ground over there. You may repeat this action as many times as you want within sixty seconds."

Nodding to himself, Xavier stretched his arms a bit and looked at the ring that was about four steps away from the pile. A regular person might have trouble moving even one of the large boulders that sat in the pile, especially considering that what would take Xavier four steps would take them twelve at the least. Xavier rested a hand on a particularly large stone, looking at Myst, who had pulled a stopwatch out of thin air.

"You may begin, traveler," said Myst with a smile.

Taking a deep breath, Xavier squared his body up with the rock, bent his knees and lifted, promptly falling over.

'What the...' laying on his back on the ground Xavier stared at the large stone in his hands, wondering if it was made of Styrofoam or something like that. He had braced himself to pick it up, but the stone was so light that he had put way more strength into pulling it up than he needed, losing his balance and falling over!

"Um, Myst?" Xavier said, holding the rock with one hand as he pushed himself to his feet. "There is something wrong with your rocks."

"Traveler, would you like to abort the current test?"

"Uh, yeah, sure." Xavier tossed the rock to the ground, watching in total confusion as it landed with an earth-shaking thump. The large stone acted like it was heavy while it was on the ground, but as soon as Xavier applied any force to it, the stone seemed to float! Testing an even larger stone, Xavier found the same to be true. No matter how big the object and how heavy it appeared to be, Xavier could lift it with absolute ease. "Myst, what is going on?"

Myst paused for a moment before shivering, almost as if she reset.

Then another moment passed as Myst shivered again. Waving her device once more, she stared intently at it and then frowned. The frown came and went so fast that Xavier almost thought he imagined it as the now happy Myst pushed some buttons on the device and waved a hand.

"Traveler, it seems that your strength currently exceeds the traditional metric, making it impossible to categorize. As a result, the anti-burden feature of Nova Terra activates every time you lift an object. Please wait while we re-calibrate the test."

The rocks began to disappear one by one, and a series of massive logs appeared in their place. The logs, unlike the stones before them, were all the same size, but each had its weight written on the side.

"Please attempt to lift each log, traveler." Myst pointed to the lightest log which read 100 kg.

If a kilogram was 2.20462 pounds, 100 kilograms would come out to 220.462 pounds, a weight that Xavier would not have any trouble with, even in the real world. His limit was closer to 230 kilograms or just over 500 pounds.

Approaching the first log, Xavier grabbed the two handles set in the middle of the log and heaved it up. Like the rocks he lifted, Xavier could barely feel the weight at all. Apart from brief feedback when he first began to move the object that indicated it had weight to it, there was nothing. It was like lifting a piece of paper.

"How strange, it is almost like the game is compensating for the weight once I prove I can pick it up," thought Xavier.

The next few logs were the same, and Xavier soon came to the 200 kg log. This was close to his lifting limit in the real world, but so far, he had not felt even the slightest amount of weight from the logs he had been lifting. Planting his feet, Xavier grasped the handles of the 200 kg log and lifted. Unlike the rest of the logs, this one felt heavier, though by no means was it heavy. Tossing it to the ground, Xavier's brow furrowed. Despite being heavier, the 200 kg log still felt like it was only a couple pounds in his hands.

'I can't be that strong.' he thought to himself.

"Traveler," Myst interrupted Xavier's thoughts, "please lift the log at the very end."

Looking down the line of logs, Xavier saw the log she was pointing to. It looked no different than the other logs apart from the 5000-kilogram weight written on the side. Quick mental math put it at 11,023.11 pounds, over five and a half tons! Xavier's first reaction was to laugh. Who in their right mind would try to lift that much weight? If the log rolled on him it would crush him! But then the strange reality he was experiencing settled on him, and he began to wonder.

So far none of the weights he had lifted were a challenge in any way. Maybe the 5000 kg log was the same? Now curious, Xavier walked over to the log and rested his hand on it.

"Only one way to find out, I guess," Xavier thought, squaring up with the log. Placing his hands on the log's handles, Xavier took a deep breath, his massive fingers curling around them. Immediately, Xavier could feel the difference. The massive weight resisted his pull the way he expected it to and already he could feel himself fighting gravity.

With a low roar, Xavier yanked upwards, his massive legs sinking down into the dirt. It was heavy. Probably, the heaviest thing Xavier had ever lifted! For the briefest moment Xavier was unsure if he could lift the log more than an inch or two off the ground but then his competitive spirit burst to life in his chest and the rest of his body engaged, straining upwards.

A massive burst of strength suffused his muscles, and Xavier pulled the log up to his waist. He had seen bodybuilders lift large weights up over their head in a smooth motion using technique, but Xavier had no idea how to do that. Still, through brute force, he curled the log up from his waist to his chin, his arms and legs beginning to quiver. Panting, Xavier gritted his teeth and powered through, shoving the log up in the air over his head and holding it for a moment before jumping backward, letting go.

With a tremendous bang, the five-ton log smashed into the ground, leaving a large dent where it landed. Xavier clenched his fist in victory, a surge of satisfaction running through him. That was five full tons! After taking a moment to savor his accomplishment, he turned to look at Myst, who was staring at him, her eyes wide in complete shock.

"Well done, traveler," stammered Myst after she recovered. "You have set a new world strength record! The previous world record of greatest weight was held by Paul Edward Anderson who lifted 2,850 kilograms in a back lift. You have beaten his record by 175%. Would you like to record your name so future generations know what you have done?"

"Hmm? Record my name? Is that like a leaderboard or something?"

"Yes, traveler. We record the names of those who complete monumental tasks so that all might know of their might and glory."

"Oh." Xavier thought for a moment before shaking his head. "Nah, I'd rather not. I'm playing this game to get out of the spotlight, not in it. The last thing I need is my name on a public list."

"Very well, traveler, I'll keep your name anonymous when we enter the new record."

"Thanks. Now, can you explain what is going on with these weights? Why are some so light compared to others? It feels like the weight disappears when I lift them up off the floor. Well, except for that one." Xavier said, his eyes resting on the various logs he had lifted.

"That is a great question, traveler." Myst took a deep breath. "To understand the specifics of how strength and weight work in Nova Terra we must first examine the way strength and weight work in the real world. After all, Nova Terra is designed to mirror the real world without some of the inconveniences that exist in reality. This interaction can be understood with a simple example. Imagine we have two individuals. Both individuals are adults of average physical ability.

"The first person is equipped with metal armor, a sword, shield, and a pack of supplies. The gear he is currently wearing weighs approximately 25 kilograms. The second person is wearing light clothing. Each person begins to walk around a track. Given the extra weight that the first person is carrying, they will expend twice the amount of energy as the second, unencumbered person.

"Consider what would happen if they walk for two hours. Both will be tired, but the individual who has worn the armor will be more fatigued than his companion. Now, imagine that at the end of the two hours of walking, you asked them to each complete an obstacle course and participate in a life-threatening fight. It is obvious that the second individual will perform better than the first because they have more energy.

"During the early test of Nova Terra, players reported that even walking to task locations with all the equipment they needed to complete those tasks was too tiring. This resulted in an abysmal completion rate. The solution that we came up with was to implement the anti-burden feature. Nova Terra measures your weight and strength and drastically reduces the weight of items that fall below a specific threshold. This allows an average individual to carry approximately four times the normal amount of weight they could carry in the real world without experiencing the burden and fatigue that they normally would.

"Additionally, the weight of any items above that threshold are adjusted based on the strength of the individual and the amount of mastery they show in a particular area. Otherwise, there would be no way for a small or slight person to wield a greatsword or draw a non-composite bow. Since Nova Terra boasts the freedom to play as you want, we wanted smaller races not to be disadvantaged in this area."

"Huh, that makes sense, I guess," Xavier mused. "It would be a drag to carry tons of weight around all the time. But there is no way I would be able to pick up a ton outside of this game. Aren't you artificially boosting my strength? I thought the game didn't do that?"

"That is a great question, traveler. I'm still processing why you are able to lift so much weight. While there are races that boost the strength of the player, no racial bonuses have been applied to you at this moment. Your strength is an approximation of reality based on physics, your size, quality and quantity of muscles, strength of tendons, bone density, and a number of other factors. All of which were entered via scan when you first entered." Looking as puzzled as Xavier, Myst clicked around her pad for a couple minutes before shaking her head.

"I see no anomalies in your scan. According to the data we have compiled, this is your approximate strength in a situation where your body has no prior damage. It is worth noting that your bones in the real world have millions of fractures and would not be able to support anywhere near this level of weight without shattering. But should you ever find yourself healthy, you would be able to exhibit this level of strength without issue."

For a moment, silence reigned as Xavier tried to get his mind around what Myst was saying. So, if he was healthy in the real world, he would be able to lift five and a half tons? Did that mean that after he got out of the pod, he would have that level of strength? Unable to believe it, Xavier shook his head. Regardless, he wasn't even close to healthy, so it didn't matter one bit.

"Please browse the list of races available in Nova Terra while your scan is being completed," Myst said, breaking Xavier out of his thoughts.

"Aren't there more tests for me to do?" Asked Xavier.

"I do not have any additional tests that would present you with a reasonable challenge, traveler. Your physical state is too far outside the anticipated values for any of the tests we have ready to be effective. Thus, I am giving you the option to browse the races while we wait for your scores to be compiled."

A large window filled with different races opened up in front of Xavier. Seeing that the six basic races were there as well as a button to scroll down, he started browsing all of the options. Humans, Elves, Dwarves, Halflings, Beastkin, and Demonkin made up the basic six races that occupied the world. Each had a racial advantage in the form of a proclivity to a subset of skills as well as a unique starting area. Further down the list were a number of Half races that would allow him to combine the various main races for a price. There were also new races like Seafolk, Feyfolk, Undead and many other fantasy creatures.

Each race came with various strengths and weaknesses, though in all cases, they were small adjustments on the player's natural abilities. If you were a strong, fit person in real life, you might be slightly stronger by choosing a dwarf or slightly weaker if you chose an elf. But if you were overweight in real life, that would be reflected in your character in the game. That is why people were encouraged to work on themselves outside the game with regularity. After all, any advantage a person possessed in real life could be carried over to the game.

And this was true for everything, not just level of fitness.

Influence could be brought into the game through the recruitment of other players, money could be brought in through the massive cash shop and the city of Fantasia, and knowledge was applicable due to how closely the game resembled reality. As Xavier scanned the races, he began to realize that choosing a race was a key part in developing a character who could take advantage of the myriad possibilities the game presented, by leveraging the one thing that all players brought to the game equally - their individual playing style.

CHAPTER FIVE

A full ten minutes went by as Xavier browsed the list with no movement from Myst. Finally, she shivered and spoke to Xavier with an uncharacteristically flat tone. "Your scan has been completed and your race choice has been assigned. Please select your race from the following list."

Available Races:
Titan

The window in front of Xavier refreshed, and he couldn't help but blink at it. Gone were all the choices he had been browsing, and in their place a single entry stood by itself. Confused, Xavier looked for a scroll button. Unable to find one, he asked Myst where his choices were. In the same flat voice, Myst said, "Your assigned race choice is displayed in the list. Please select your race."

"But there is only one race," protested Xavier.

"Your assigned race choice is displayed in the list. Please select your race," responded Myst.

"But what about the basic races! Don't I get to pick one of them?"

"That is a great question, traveler. No. Due to the results of your physical scan, there are no available playable races that fit within the allowance for adjustments to an alternate reality body. Due to the psychological damage that could be done to you when experiencing the difference in dimensionality between your real body and your alternate reality body, you cannot be assigned any race currently playable by player characters. Due to this, the system has chosen a race from within the lore that matches your physiological characteristics and has made the necessary adjustments, so you can play as this race. Your assigned race choice is displayed in the list. Please select your race."

"Wait, you made a race for me?"

"That is a great question, traveler. No. We adjusted an existing NPC race so as to prevent the balance of the game from being broken and are allowing you and any other player who meets the requirements to play that race. Your assigned race choice is displayed in the list. Please select your race."

"Okay... I guess I'll choose my race from the list," Xavier said sarcastically as he looked more closely at the single race that had been made available for him.

Titan. Even the name sent a twinge of disgust through him. He was playing this game in part to get away from the disadvantages of his massive size, and the game hadn't even started before he was reminded of it! And what was with locking him out of the other options? Sighing in frustration, Xavier decided to just get through the tutorial. The game representatives and the doctor would be hearing about this as soon as he got out, that was for sure.

Clicking on the Titan, another screen popped up describing the race in more detail as well as displaying the various abilities of the race.

Titan - Unique

Now lost in the mist of time, this ancient race once ruled the world, rivaled only by the great Dragons. Long-lived and immensely strong, the Titans were masters of almost anything they put their hand to and created a far-reaching empire that is still ruled by the Elemental Giants. Little else is known about the Titans, and further information must be unlocked through discoveries in game.

Racial Requirements	
Titan's Strength: To unlock this race a player must have the strength of a titan.	Titan's Endurance: To unlock this race a player must have the constitution of a titan.

Accept Race	
Yes	No

Wait a second. This can't be right," Xavier said. "How do I have the strength and endurance of a titan? I haven't even started playing!"

"That is a great question, traveler." Myst stopped talking and stared at him.

"Uh. Something must be wrong. May I talk to an administrator or something?"

"That is a great question, traveler. There are no errors. Your body is anomalous, meaning that it deviates from what is standard, normal, or expected. As such, what is standard, normal, or expected cannot be used, and a new standard must be developed. Far from being at a disadvantage, you will likely find yourself the utter envy of all the other players. You are countless times stronger than even the strongest player, you have an excellent reaction time, and you have no noticeable mental impairment. Just because you are different and fall outside the norm does not mean there is something wrong." Myst fell silent again, continuing to stare.

"Argh! Fine!" Hitting the 'accept race' button, a large mirror replaced the race screen, and Xavier was faced with an eight foot, nine-inch tall giant, complete with leather and fur clothing and a massive sword and shield. The only thing that separated the image from being the perfect example of a ferocious fantasy barbarian was that it was his own face that stared back at him.

Selecting a couple options on the side, Xavier was able to see what he would look like in different types of medieval fantasy clothing, including wizard robes and a blacksmith's leathers. While not the most handsome, Xavier was passably good looking when his skin wasn't all stretched out, though his size was so shocking to most people that his looks rarely registered. Still, it was a bit strange for Xavier to see this version of himself. He had often avoided mirrors in the real world due to their frustrating reminder of his ugly situation. The rugged strength of the face before him was a welcome sight.

Thoroughly annoyed at this whole process, Xavier tried to use the available slider to make himself as short as possible but was only able to reduce his height to 8' 5", a measly 4" below his regular height.

"Please be aware that no additional changes are available due to your avatar already being adjusted by 20%," Myst's flat voice commented. "Would you like to accept these changes or reset your avatar?" Grousing in his heart about the limits that Nova Terra put on changing one's self when creating a character, Xavier reset his character and tried modifying some of the giant's other features, only to find himself coming back to the maximum height setting.

Looking over the powerful and imposing figure in front of him, Xavier mused that maybe it wasn't so bad to be tall. The fact that the game let him pick up a unique race went far toward mollifying his frustration, and it wasn't like being large was new to him. After all, he had spent his whole life towering over those around him. Thinking more deeply about it, not being able to see over other people's heads would be quite strange. He set his height to his real-life height and added some barbaric looking tattoos across his left arm and chest.

"That doesn't look too bad," Xavier thought, accepting the changes. Instantly, the robotic body that currently housed him twisted and grew, the metallic skin tone softening and changing to a dark tan. His shoulders broadened, and his chest widened as his height shot up another foot, leaving him towering over Myst.

Flexing his fingers and clenching his fist, Xavier could feel the power in them. Power that his hands in the real world lacked. There was a solidity about this body that his body in the real world didn't have, a weightiness as if this body was somehow more real. Jumping in place, Xavier felt no discomfort whatsoever. Instead, he felt strong and powerful, as though he could take on the world.

"Thank you, traveler. Due to your race selection, your starting location has been locked. When you arrive at your starting location, you will be prompted to select your name. Once you have entered the game you will encounter many different situations and challenges that will require you to use your wits and strength to overcome. There is much to discover in Nova Terra, including quests, specialized classes, and secret treasure. Please enjoy your stay in Nova Terra!"

As the world of white faded away, Xavier found himself in a small stone room with a magic circle in the center. Standing at the door was a guard who stepped forward with a clipboard and said in a nervous tone as he looked up at Xavier's towering bulk, "Ho, traveler. Please write your name for the record."

Mulling over his name choice for a moment, Xavier wrote "Thorn" in the available space. After receiving a small package that included five pieces of bread, each barely big enough for a single bite, five equally small water skins, and five copper coins, he ducked through the door and into a bustling medieval city complete with cobblestone streets.

Welcome to Nova Terra

Welcome, traveler! In order to get your adventure started, please see one of the secretaries at Berum's city hall to receive your first quest.

The long cobblestone street, easily two carts wide, stretched to his right and left, and the colorfully painted wooden buildings that rose on either side presented a charming picture. Hawkers called from their storefronts, trying to attract the attention of the crowds that raced by. Players, easy to spot by their determined movements toward their respective destinations mixed in with the slower, less deliberate townsfolk NPCs who went about their daily lives, unaware of the incongruity between the players and themselves.

Xavier, no, Thorn, was astounded at how realistic everything was and could have been convinced it was reality if not for the box of text hovering in the middle of his vision. Dismissing it with a thought, he joined the flow of players. Despite standing a full two feet above the rest of the crowd, the players were far too preoccupied with their own tasks to pay attention to him. Plagued his whole life by the stares of others, a profound sense of relief swept over him as he looked around at the crowds hurrying by while paying him little to no attention.

In fact, despite his height, there were many other players that stood out far more than Thorn, who was dressed in the simple beginner clothing. Fanciful armor covered a myriad of races streaming by, giving full testament to the claim that Nova Terra was a place of diversity. Graceful elves stalked down the road, brushing past human warriors in massive plate mail armor. Short but wide dwarves cut a determined path through the crowds while equally short halflings slipped through like tiny fish.

Even more interesting were the odd Tigerkin that dotted the crowds or the Birdkin wheeling lazily overhead. Many of the more exotic races could not be seen, since they were more region specific. Demonkin were entirely missing from the city. From the research that he had done, it seemed that Humans and Demonkin formed the two main races of Nova Terra. Each race was part of an empire occupying approximately half of the continent.

It was the friction between these two empires that formed the primary conflict in Nova Terra, with the other races allying themselves with the two main races. Berum, the city where Thorn had spawned, was in the north-west, far from the front lines of the Human and Demonkin conflict. The far north of Angoril was a frozen land of tundra, ice-covered mountains rising like dragon's teeth into the sky. Berum was located on a long chain of mountains that started in the far north, skirted the steppes and flowed all the way down to the Midlands along the western coast.

Deep forests and tall mountains marked the landscape around Berum, and the local population consisted of hardy human pioneers and taciturn dwarves who preferred to stay in their mountain fortresses.

After spending several minutes looking over the pop-ups that explained how to use his inventory and the limited number of other game features, Thorn decided to spend some time wandering around the city where he had started. Starting points in Nova Terra were based on a variety of factors and were divided into three different categories: rural, urban, and military. Anyone who spawned in a small town was considered to have a rural start while those who first spawned in a city had urban starts. Starting in a military fort was rare but had been known to happen, especially when the player had a military history in the real world.

Surprisingly, Nova Terra was quite adept at identifying what a new player was familiar with and using that knowledge to ease them into this new world. There had been some hubbub when Nova Terra launched because people were concerned that the system was reading the player's memories, but Horizon's public demonstrations to the contrary put them at ease.

Looking at his in-game map display, he saw the city he had arrived in, Berum, in the north-west of Angoril, the primary continent in Nova Terra. Even though the game had been out for a number of years, no one had managed to explore the entirety of

Angoril, and many a guild was still focused on trying to map out the massive land. Angoril was roughly divided into eight sections, four in the north and four in the south.

From what he had read about Nova Terra, it seemed that each of these sections was a duchy, ruled by an appointed duke. In the center of the northern half of the continent, residing in the floating city that graced most of the advertisements for the game, was the Imperial city where the Human Emperor held court. Mirroring this, the Demonkin capital was located in the center of the southern duchies. But, rather than floating, the Imperial city of the Demonkin occupied the inside of a massive pit.

The southern and northern ends of the continent were temperate and had rotating seasons, but the four central duchies were closer to a tropical environment.

Apart from the continent of Angoril, there were three smaller continents that had been introduced in various patches, and each had a different theme. Rasyn, off Angoril's eastern coast, was styled after Japan's Tokugawa period. To the north lay Gerund, a Viking themed location that housed numerous barbarian clans while to the south was Moa'techa, the Mayan themed empire. Each of the smaller continents was also dominated by a specific race.

Thorn spent almost an hour walking around and taking in all the new sights and sounds of the city. It wasn't until he heard someone complaining about the rate of loot drops that he even remembered this was a game. The sights and smells were mesmerizing to someone who had been closeted his whole life. Brought out of his daze by the reminder, Thorn decided to check where he stood before he made a plan of action.

"Status."

Name: [Thorn]	Race: [Titan]
Health: [100%]	Mana: [100%]

Titles: [None]	Conditions: [None]

Racial Traits	
Titan's Strength: Increased resistance to mind-affecting conditions	Titan's Endurance: Increased resistance to physical conditions

Titan's Strength and Titan's Endurance were excellent. Both were defensive abilities and complimented his massive innate strength. Extra resistance to anything was excellent as far as Thorn was concerned. After all, the more defenses the better.

CHAPTER SIX

"Uh, sir?" a polite cough brought Thorn back to the present. Tugging gently on Thorn's sleeve was an intimidated city guard whose nervous companion was behind him, clutching a wooden nightstick.

"Yes?"

"Um. Would you, uh, mind moving, uh, to the side of the street?" stammered the guard, pointing to the side. "You. Er. You're kind of blocking the traffic."

"Oh man, I am so sorry!" Thorn exclaimed. He had been so engrossed in his status that he hadn't realized that he was standing in the middle of a street, a long queue of carts bunched up behind him. While they could have squeezed by, the sight of his 8' 9" frame had scared the drivers enough that they called over a guard to deal with the giant.

"No, no," reassured the guard. "It is no problem at all."

Stepping to the side, Thorn took the opportunity to ask the guard some questions. "I'm new to Berum and was a bit lost. Could you point me toward the town hall? I need to see someone for my starting quest."

"Uh, you are a traveler? Sheesh." Relieved, the guard put a hand to his chest. "I thought you were one of those barbarian frost giants. You had me worried there for a minute."

"Frost giants?"

"Yeah. They're huge like you, but people say they have terrible tempers. I heard one of them got mad and froze a whole city full of people. Everyone in the city, dead, just like that. Anyway, city hall? No problem."

After getting directions, Thorn left the guards and made his way to the large building that dominated the center of the Public district. Berum was split into four main sections, each focused on a particular grouping of businesses.

The North district was residential and had the largest number of restaurants and businesses for entertainment. To the east of the city center was the Public district, where most business was conducted, based around city hall, while to the south was the Canal district, which was where all the goods going in and out of the city passed. The western part of Berum was called the Forge district, where the businesses that had to do with crafting were located.

City hall was a large, multi-story stone affair that gave the impression of a beehive as uniformed clerks ran around, this way and that. Players streamed in and out as well, eager to hand in their quests and get their rewards. Thorn made his way up the steps, ducking his head to pass through the door. Players instinctively moved around him, looking at him with curiosity. The guards, however, grew nervous as Thorn's shadow fell over them.

Ignoring the guards who were readying their spears, Thorn passed by them into the spacious main hall, taking in the marble floors and pillars with glee. Thorn loved buildings that had enough space for him to stand. In fact, because of that, he had spent quite a bit of time studying architecture. He had always held the ambition of creating living spaces customized to his personal needs. A big smile on his face, he walked over to one of the secretaries who was staring at him wide-eyed.

"Hello, I'm Thorn. A new traveler. I was told I could get my first quest here?"

"Uh, yeah." Spellbound, the secretary, a pretty brunette with a button nose and deep dimples had to look almost straight up to look Thorn in the eyes.

With a chuckle, Thorn crouched, reveling in his freedom of movement. In the outside world, this simple movement would have ended with bloody cuts in his skin and lots of pain. Nova Terra was different, and Thorn was free to move as he wanted. Crouching brought them almost eye to eye, a position much more comfortable for the secretary.

"You are big." Still stunned, the secretary couldn't seem to get past Thorn's size. She stared at the hand he had rested on the edge of her desk. It was easily twice the size of hers.

"I am," agreed Thorn, amused as always by the sheer unbelief on her face. "So... about that quest?"

"Hm, oh, right. Oh, I'm sorry, you surprised me," the secretary stammered, embarrassed by her staring. Straightening herself out, she launched into the standard announcement for the first quest. "Welcome to Berum, traveler. Please hold for a moment while I scan you in. Once I've done that, I'll get you the opening quest."

Welcome to Berum
Welcome, traveler! You have arrived in Berum and are ready to start your grand adventure. To begin, visit the following places: Edgar's Emporium Training Hall City Library McCarthy Farm

After agreeing to the quest, Thorn thanked the secretary and strolled out past the worried guards, giving them a friendly nod on his way. Before he had started the game, Thorn had been nervous about all of the social interactions that he was going to be forced into; after all, most of his life had been spent alone. Thankfully, his friendly and cheerful disposition seemed to serve him well, and, so far, it had not been an issue.

Opening his map display, Thorn realized that each of the places that the first quest had him going was in a different section of the city. Obviously, the point of the quest was to get him used to the area. Though, if he had known that, he wouldn't have spent two hours wandering around the town. His random stroll had taken him by all of the locations he needed to visit except for the McCarthy Farm, which was located right outside the city.

Retracing his steps, Thorn headed off to his first destination, the City Library. Located in the northern district near some of the upscale neighborhoods, the City Library looked similar to City Hall. Much of the architecture in Berum was similar, and the buildings, comprised of large stone blocks, gave a sense of longevity and stability. Unfortunately, Thorn still had to duck when going in.

The library was split into three floors, with a large open courtyard in the middle, covered by a stained-glass roof, creating a charming picture in the streaming sunlight. Players stood or sat in various library nooks, browsing through books they had taken off the shelves. Seeing that there was a central desk, Thorn headed that way, only to experience a repeat of his interaction with the secretary at City Hall.

"Hello, I'm a new traveler and this is my first time here at the library."

"Wow, you are big," said the wide-eyed elf after a moment of stunned staring.

"Uh, yeah. So, can I get a library card or something?"

"Library card? Oh, right. Yes, yes." Pulling out some forms from underneath the desk, the librarian helped Thorn register himself, explaining the rules and regulations as he did so.

"You can borrow a single book at a time but only for a week at a time. Once that week is up, the book will automatically be returned to the library through the enchantment on the back. While at the library, you can read as many books as you would like, and if you want to return them, stack them on the return table. Make sure you don't leave anything in the books like bookmarks, as they will be returned with the book as well.

"The three different library floors each contain different sorts of books. On the bottom floor, you will find histories, biographies, and books about the different races. The second floor consists of crafting, job-specific, and how-to books. The third floor is comprised of an eclectic mix of various ancient tomes and books in other languages.

"If you are having any trouble finding a book, you can use the scrying stones located throughout the library to search by title, author, or subject." Pausing to scan the form that Thorn had completed, the librarian filed it away and then brought out a flyer. "We also offer accredited classes through NTU. They can be taken here in Nova Terra or in Fantasia where we have a campus. If you are interested in a class or a full degree you can sign up here at the desk. We accept in-game currency or universal credits."

"I heard that degrees can transfer from the outside world, is that right?" asked Thorn.

"Oh yes. So long as the program was accredited, you can apply any degree to receive an equivalent in-game title. Would you like to apply a degree now?"

"No, I'm good for now," replied Thorn, looking around at all the books. Reading was one of his favorite things to do, but now was not the time for that. In this new world where he could move, he didn't want to spend his time cooped up inside.

Leaving the library, Thorn headed for his next location, the Training Hall. It was located in the Forge District near a large collection of smoke-belching smithies. The Training Hall comprised of a large open parade ground and a large gymnasium-style building located next to the city barracks. Inside the parade ground, a large group of local NPCs were running through sword training while a couple travelers smacked furiously at some scarecrows.

"Ho, traveler, are you here to unlock your true potential?" boomed a voice as Thorn entered the hall. Turning his head, he saw a man coming toward him dressed in a simple leather sleeveless shirt and brown pants. A large, thick metal studded belt with matching bracers and boots completed the classic look of the warrior trainer. "I can teach you to be the best warrior this world has ever seen! As long as you can pay, of course." This last sentence was quite a bit quieter.

"Ah, you offer classes? What do they cost?"

"Haha! Of course I do! Best warrior training this side of the East Empire's gladiator pits! The cost is 10 silver every three days for basic training, 50 silver for intermediate and 1 gold for advanced. You have to pay for a week at a time, and if you quit, I keep the money!" The large man tried to look down on Thorn, a task made difficult by the fact that he was a good two feet shorter.

"If you are interested, step up, and I'll test you. This part is free," said the trainer, walking over to a clear spot in the yard. Everyone else stopped what they were doing and looked over. Hamm, the trainer, would regularly invite people up to "train" for a fee, and then beat them black and blue in the name of testing before sending them to practice their basics.

"Here, take this," Hamm tossed Thorn a practice sword while he readied his own. "Now, I want you to attack."

Holding the sword that looked more like a dagger in Thorn's massive hands, he swung it a couple of times before looking over at Hamm and moving toward him.

"Wait, wait! Not me, don't attack me!" babbled Hamm while backing away from Thorn, his face white and his hands shaking. "Attack that dummy, over there. Actually, attack that one." Hamm pointed to a training dummy farther down the line made of a strange black metal.

Shrugging, Thorn turned to go over to the other dummy as Hamm gulped in relief. Just now, when Thorn had swung his sword through the air, his arm moved so fast it almost disappeared. Though not close, Hamm could still feel the shockwave the training sword made as it whipped through the air! He had no desire to get hit by that. Even if he blocked it, a strike with that much force would break his arm! How strong was this huge traveler anyway?

Squaring up with the training dummy, Thorn concentrated. He had never used a real sword before, but he figured it was the same as the wooden practice swords he had used, right? The faster you swing the more force should be generated. Taking a deep breath, Thorn twisted his waist and, drawing the sword behind his shoulder, swung hard at the training dummy's side. His sword blurred through the air and impacted into the side of the dummy with a boom, snapping the blade into pieces and breaking the dummy off its stand!

Amidst the silence that blanketed the training hall, Hamm walked forward to examine the ruined dummy. The side of the metal reinforced body had been crushed in on itself as the force of the sword slammed into it. As far as he could tell, the cutting edge of the blade had been angled wrong and had not actually cut into the now-ruined dummy. Rather, Thorn had used brute force, crushing the dummy's splintered wooden side and bending the metal bands beyond repair.

This strength was far beyond what any normal traveler should be able to generate, making Hamm extra thankful that he had not tried to receive the blow himself. He could only imagine what would have happened to him if Thorn had aimed that swing his way. Out of the corner of his eye, he could see Thorn, who was examining the now busted training sword. He shivered at the thought of being on the receiving end of that swing. Aware that everyone in the building was watching him, anger overtook his embarrassment.

"I said attack it, not destroy it!" blustered Hamm, only to be met with quizzical looks from everyone who was standing around watching. Realizing how stupid he sounded, he stomped over and yelled to hide his embarrassment, "And what sort of warrior breaks their weapon like that? If you were surrounded by enemies and your sword broke, what would you do then?"

"Ummm...I could..."

"Yeah, that's what I thought!" interrupted Hamm, tossing Thorn the other practice sword. "Try again, but this time, no breaking the weapon!" And so began one of the strangest training sessions in the history of Nova Terra. Next to a growing pile of broken practice swords, Hamm yelled and blustered, berating Thorn for swinging too hard and damaging his weapon.

He yelled, "Power is fine, and speed even better, but the warrior's most powerful advantage is based in control! Swing with speed, hit with power, but control your force, don't let it control you!" Nearby, a couple of other native trainers stood watching, grins on their faces as Hamm got more and more frustrated at the inhumanly strong traveler

who was making a mess of the training yard.

CHAPTER SEVEN

"Hey Hamm, didn't you say there wasn't a traveler you couldn't teach the sword to in a day? How is this one getting on?" mocked one of the other trainers, earning a laugh from the others and a glare from Hamm.

"Shut it, Markus! He is coming along fine!" snapped Hamm.

His brow furrowing, Hamm stomped off, accompanied by the laughs of the other trainers. He returned a couple minutes later, dragging a massive box. With a grunt, he kicked it over, and a massive quantity of real swords in all shapes and sizes poured from the top.

"Markus is right, curse him. You are so strong you need something heavy enough that you can feel its weight to learn control. See if any of these work for you," Hamm said to Thorn, who began to root through the pile. There were short swords, long swords, bastard swords, broadswords, massive claymores and even a couple of naginata, but none of the swords felt heavy in Thorn's hands. He was so strong that even the heavy iron broadswords felt weightless to him.

Shaking his head at Hamm, Thorn said, "Sorry, none of these are any heavier than the practice swords."

"Well, you are going to have to get used to them. After all, pure force will only take you so far in a fight."

"Are you talking about softness?"

"Softness?" sneered Hamm, "Why would you want to be soft? I'm talking about flexibility! You are strong but using that strength all the time will fatigue you! You need to be able to relax your body and then apply your strength where you need it!"

"Right, like softness transitioning to hardness. Explosive strength," nodded Thorn, oblivious to Hamm's growing rage. Thorn picked out the largest blade he could find, a massive great sword that was a full six feet long. Despite the fact that it was designed with fantasy in mind, it looked like a normal long sword. The blade was not as flexible as the Taijiquan swords he had practiced his forms with, but it would work for a demonstration.

Holding the hilt in a reverse grip with his left hand, Thorn brought his hands together in a salute before sinking into the first stance. His countless hours of practice made the motion a natural one. Sinking into a horse stance, he shifted two steps to the front and then rotated into a bow stance, pushing his right hand out toward the front while blocking on his left side with his blade. Rotating his right wrist, he turned his body, cutting with the end of the blade and deflecting with his hand. As he continued his slow kata, he could hear the snorts of disdain from Hamm and the mocking chuckles from the others watching.

Yet, as he continued the Taijiquan forms, the snorting lessened. The longer he watched Thorn's forms, the less ridiculous Hamm found them. Despite the slow speed and gentle motions, Hamm could tell that Thorn's absurd strength was waiting to burst forth. Imagining himself on the end of one of those excruciatingly slow stabs, Hamm couldn't help but feel himself breaking out in a sweat.

Not everyone felt the same way, though. A large human warrior who had been looking on from the side spat on the ground. Hoisting his large sword to his shoulder, he walked in front of Thorn, forcing the giant to stop his kata.

"Oi, big boy. Anyone can pretend they know something about

fighting, but real men fight!" the big warrior bellowed, grinning. "Or are you too scared for an actual fight?"

The brief nervousness that Thorn had felt when the man first walked up evaporated into excitement, and he looked at Hamm with a burning gaze. A chance to try actual combat with a body that worked? Thorn couldn't be more willing! In fact, his excitement was so palpable that the big warrior took a step back, caution floating through his mind.

"Is there a ring we could use to spar?" Thorn asked Hamm, who pointed to a spot along the back wall where there was a square sparring ring.

Walking over to the sparring ring, Thorn was about to step inside the lines when a prompt popped up in front of him.

Fighting Ring
All warriors need to hone their techniques through mortal combat. Enter the fighting ring to prove yourself a warrior!
Players will respawn upon death with no penalties
All wounds caused in the ring will heal upon exit
No City penalties for fighting

Accepting the prompt asking if he wanted to duel, Thorn stepped over the line and walked to one corner of the ring, excitement burning in his heart. While Thorn had never experienced actual combat before, he was quite familiar with blood and pain, so the thought of fighting with real swords held no fear for him. Besides, this was a game, right? No matter how realistic the experience, it wasn't like he was going to get injured.

Seeing Thorn so excited, the big warrior was much less confident in himself. He had watched Thorn's slow moves in disdain, but Thorn's reaction to his challenge was unlike what he had envisioned. Normally the biggest guy around, Thorn's 8' 9" height had made the warrior feel uncomfortable, and like most people who rely on their size to assert dominance, his solution was to try direct confrontation. But, despite Thorn's quiet, reserved, and respectful attitude, the giant seemed all too eager to take on his challenge.

As the two squared up to each other, they presented a contrasting picture. The warrior stood at 6' 6", 265 pounds of solid muscle. Studded leather armor covered his body, and a two-handed claymore hung from his back while a small metal shield rested on his belt. Numerous scars covered his arms; a small scar running across his left eyebrow gave him a dangerous look.

Across from him, Thorn was simply massive. Standing more than two feet taller than the warrior he faced, Thorn was twice as wide in the shoulders. The beginner clothing that he was wearing only highlighted the massive muscles of his legs, arms, and chest. His hand engulfed the pommel of the great sword like a kitchen knife, despite the fact that it was almost as large as his opponent. His face, though wide and rugged, had a certain peacefulness that seemed incongruous with the idea that he was about to engage in a bloody fight.

Settling into his stance, Thorn's body exuded a relaxed air, as though he was resting while his opponent hopped up and down a couple times to get his muscles engaged. Hamm, who had followed them over, waved for the crowd to be quiet and checked to see if both players were ready. Getting the okay, he waved his hand.

"Start!"

With a low roar, the big warrior dashed forward, his claymore held in two hands. As he was about to reach Thorn's range, he jumped to Thorn's left and delivered a vicious cut with his blade! Caught off guard by the strong attack, Thorn froze for a moment before his instincts kicked in. Stepping back, Thorn's body seemed to collapse into itself, and the claymore slid past his chest with less than an inch to spare.

Sensing the incoming follow up, Thorn reversed his energy,

flowing back toward his opponent. Switching his sword to a reverse grip to guard against the backswing, his shoulder blasted forward toward his opponent's chest! The big warrior had landed from his sideways movement, and his sword extended to his left, putting him off balance as he tried to retreat. Despite the awkwardness of his position, the warrior was an experienced fighter and managed to draw his small shield and get it between Thorn's shoulder and his chest at the last second!

With a loud thump, Thorn and the warrior collided, sending the large warrior stumbling backward. Not missing a beat, Thorn, who had not shifted from the impact, stepped forward. Switching from a reverse grip to a forward grip, he thrust his sword out so fast the blade seemed to disappear.

Desperately warding off the strike with his buckler, the big warrior continued moving backward, unable to catch his balance. Each successive stab put extreme pressure on him. Just when he thought he would be able to get his feet under him, Thorn pivoted, whipping a massive leg out in a sweep!

Unable to dodge in time, the big warrior hit the ground with a bone-jarring slam. Stunned by the fall, he could do nothing but watch as Thorn transitioned right back into a stab, planting his blade right next to the warrior's throat!

"I give up!" squeaked the warrior. His face was pale as he stared with horrified eyes at the blade that had sunk into the stone floor.

Grinning, Thorn suppressed a shout of excitement. Leaving his sword stuck in the floor, he picked up the big warrior and put him on his feet, dusting him off.

"Thanks for the fight! I'm Thorn, what's your name?"

"Uh...Bi...Big M... Mac. Mac. You can call me Mac."

"Nice to meet you, Mac. Thanks for sparring with me. Want to try again?"

"No, no, I'm all good," said Big Mac, backing up. "I better rest."

"No problem," said Thorn, pulling his sword out of the ground. "Let me know if you want to try again!"

Watching the terrified warrior leave the ring, Hamm shook his head. Thorn's moves were smooth, powerful, and well-practiced, but it was evident that he was woefully short on actual combat experience. Stepping into the ring, Hamm coughed to get Thorn's attention.

"Hmph. Do you still want someone to spar with, kid?"

"Yes, sir! If you are available."

"It's been a while since I last fought, so pardon me if I'm a bit rusty," said Hamm, pulling out a saber and shield from nowhere and doing a quick stretch.

Off to the side, the other trainers rolled their eyes at this line, muttering, "Been a while? Then why did you come back yesterday covered in bandit blood?"

This time Thorn made the first move, stepping forward and striking down with an overhead chop. Hamm deflected the blow smoothly while closing the distance and striking with his saber at Thorn's right foot, forcing him to step back. Hamm continued to advance, stepping inside Thorn's range, making it difficult for the giant to swing his large sword. Unable to create space, Thorn tried to force Hamm back with a body check. Nonplussed, Hamm blocked the blow with his shield, using the deflected force to spin around behind Thorn and deliver a slash to his hamstring.

The sharp, stinging pain told Thorn that he was in a lot of trouble if he didn't get away, so he slid one of his legs back and rotated his torso, striking with his arm. Because he was so close, Hamm wasn't able to dodge the blow and flew backward. Rolling out of the fall, Hamm bounced to his feet and dashed back toward Thorn, saber swinging.

Trading blows back and forth, it became clear that Hamm was much more skilled than Thorn. Within minutes, Thorn's body was covered in bloody gashes from the saber. Watching the scene, the crowd winced every time Hamm added a new cut to his massive opponent. Despite the cuts, Thorn was having a great time. The cuts were painful but looked much worse than they actually felt. Thanks to the pain reduction that Nova Terra employed, they felt much more like an insect bite than an actual cut, allowing Thorn to ignore them.

Hamm, however, was getting frustrated. Most of the time players would give up once he showed them how much better he was, but Thorn seemed to be indomitable. Finally, fed up with Thorn's lack of awareness, Hamm's form blurred. Dashing forward, he slid passed Thorn's guard, his saber coming to rest on Thorn's neck.

Stepping back and admitting defeat, Thorn grinned at the sword trainer. Clasping his hands together, he bowed to show his respect as he would when he trained with his *sifu*, Ms. Chen.

"Thank you for your instruction."

"You are a pretty incredible first-timer," Hamm said, shaking his head. "You're a machine. Where'd you learn those moves?"

"My master taught me. It is called Taijiquan straight sword, or Jian. Taijiquan is a primarily barehanded system of martial arts that also uses saber, sword, and spear."

"Well, it has a pretty strong base," admitted Hamm, wiping the sweat from his forehead. "But it is quite apparent that you do not have much experience actually fighting. Unfortunately, that means that we don't have much for you here." Taking a moment to gesture toward the other trainers, he continued. "Most of what we do is teaching new travelers how to fight in the first place. That means teaching them the basic forms of fighting. Most travelers come to this world with fear and a major aversion to violence. Our job is to break them of it and instruct them in the basic way of using various weapons. You don't fit that bill, since you already have those basics pretty much mastered."

"Oi, Hamm!" A dwarf clutching a pipe in his teeth pushed his way through the crowd, his meaty hand tucked into his broad leather belt. "You may not have anything to teach him, but that doesn't mean I don't!"

"This is Dovon. He teaches grappling," Hamm said with a sigh.

"M'boy, I saw your match! Quite impressive it was, too. But what do ya do when you are without a sword, eh? I can train you up so that all them muscles won't be for show, eh? Look at these tendons, Hamm, perfect for a grappler, and those knuckles! Exactly what ya need for a solid punch. Boy, you're with me now, I won't take no for an answer!" Stepping forward, Dovon latched onto Thorn's wrist and tried to pull him away from the ring but found himself unable to move Thorn even an inch.

Rather than becoming dispirited, Dovon grabbed one of Thorn's hands, examining it. After a long moment, he moved to the other hand and then to Thorn's arms and legs.

"Holy Terra, boy. I take back what I said. These muscles are not for show at all. What on earth did your mom feed you to turn you into such a monster? Eh, doesn't matter. Come on, come on, I'm going to show you how real men fight." But before he could pull Thorn away, a slim elf maid stepped in front of him, a knife dancing through her fingers.

CHAPTER EIGHT

"Dovon, leave him be. He already knows how close combat works. He needs more experience, like Hamm said. What he needs are long-range attacks," said the elf maid with an evil smile. "And that is my purview."

"Back off, leaf head," growled the dwarf, cracking his knuckles.

"No, you back off, shorty," said the elf, in no way intimidated. Her eyes narrowed. "Or how about I tell your missus where you were this past Tuesday?"

Face blanching, Dovon dropped his hands and put on his best smile, immediately stepping out of the elf's way.

"Anyone else fancy themselves this boy's teacher?" Seeing that none of the other trainers stepped up to challenge her, the elf chuckled. "Hello, Thorn, I am Janus Fairgoode. I specialize in projectiles. Mostly bows, but I do dabble in other thrown weapons, as well. If it's made for fighting at a distance and isn't magic, then I'm your gal. I teach lessons at the same price as Hamm."

"Thanks, but I don't actually have money to pay for lessons. I only started playing today, so I stopped by to check things out and complete my starter quest," said Thorn.

Ignoring dumbfounded expressions on the crowd's faces, Thorn waved goodbye and strode quickly away. Down the street, he suddenly realized the sword that Hamm had lent him was still in his hand. He turned around to return it, but when he got close to the door, he could hear Janus' high-pitched voice yelling, so he decided to return it later.

It wasn't marked as a stolen item, so he stuck it in his inventory. Nova Terra's inventory system worked much like inventories worked in other games. It was a subspace where the character could store almost anything that they possessed.

Checking his quest, he saw that he still needed to go to Edgar's Emporium and the McCarthy Farm. Edgar's Emporium was in the southern district, also known as the Market District, where the majority of the trade goods came into the city. A large shop, Edgar's Emporium sold everything an adventurer could need. However, five copper coins weren't enough to buy much of anything, so Thorn didn't stay long.

The currency of Nova Terra was pretty simple, with ten copper making up a silver, one hundred silver making up a gold, and one thousand gold making up a platinum. UCs or Universal Credits, the currency of the real world, were also usable, but the exchange rate fluctuated based on how many people were trying to buy gold.

That left only the McCarthy Farm. McCarthy Farm was outside the city to the south-west, sprawling over rolling hills. At the entrance to the farm, an NPC was handing out a quest to kill some rats that had been raiding the farm's fields. After accepting it, Thorn walked over to the nearby fields only to stop and stare in amazement.

Players were dashing this way and that, each trying to land a killing blow on the pests as soon as they spawned. No sooner had a rodent appeared than a mass of players would surge toward it. Shrieking and hooting, they tried to land a blow on it before the unfortunate creature vanished back into the code. Shouts of "kill stealer" and loud swearing were everywhere. Unsure of what to do, Thorn stood in place. He was so engrossed in this new scene that he barely felt it when someone ran straight into him and tumbled to the ground.

"Oh, excuse me," said Thorn, instinctively concerned for the girl who had landed on the ground.

"No, no, my fault. Haha, I should be watching where I'm going!" said the redheaded girl, scrambling to pick up her witch's hat before she jumped up and dashed off again.

Bemused, Thorn could only watch as she sped off. With a shake of his head, he backed up and started walking out of the yard, trying to find a quiet place to kill vermin in peace. His wandering took him out of the fields where new players were slaying creatures and into a nearby forest.

Due to his physical condition, Thorn rarely left his house during his 16 years of life except to go to the hospital, so he quite enjoyed the cool quiet of the forest. Winding his way aimlessly through the trees, he cast his mind over what he knew about the game.

Nova Terra was a unique game that bragged it was more of an alternate reality than an actual game. This is why stats were hidden and the game required you to actually complete tasks to improve your skills.

When he had first heard about entering the game as a form of treatment, Thorn had become excited about the idea of being able to move as he wished. He was especially excited about being able to put his martial arts training into practice. He had played turn-based strategy and management games, as they did not need the quick movements that Real Time Strategy games and Shooters did.

But, compared to most sixteen-year-olds, Thorn was way behind when it came to familiarity with games. Then again, he was way ahead when it came to maturity. This stood him in good stead since Nova Terra was less of a game and more of an alternate reality. Plus, the idea that he could fall back on his aunt if he found himself floundering was always in the back of his head.

While Nova Terra wasn't a pay to win game, there was no denying that money and influence could give you a definite edge. The shop sold all sorts of items that could give a player an edge, and players who had the cash to spend benefited from it. Thorn was not lacking in that department, though he had not yet decided how he felt about spending money on a reality that wasn't ultimately real. Besides, there was something quite romantic about the idea of forging your own way, setting your own destiny and pulling yourself up by your bootstraps.

With his only experience fighting being the two matches that he participated in at the training hall, Thorn was looking forward to practicing in the game. Thorn, cautious by both nature and experience, recognized that he needed to learn in actual combat. A normal fight was not like a fight in the ring, where his wounds healed after it ended.

Stopping in a little clear area in the woods, Thorn settled into a horse stance and completed a few of his forms. He had always focused on very slow and steady movements, infusing strength through gentleness and control. But his body was different in Nova Terra, and with mounting excitement, Thorn began to inject more and more strength into each move. He moved faster and faster until his hands and feet were snapping through the air. Ecstatic at the feeling of moving his body freely, Thorn let loose, stepping, turning and bursting with power. Slow to fast, smoothly transferring his weight and energy.

His master, Ms. Chen, had talked a lot about Fa Jin, the energy bursting principle of Taijiquan, but Thorn had never been able to practice it himself. Instead, he had often spent hours in meditation, visualizing himself moving through his techniques, focusing power into his strikes by coordinating his whole body's movement. Engrossed in his practice, time sped by, and before he knew it, the sun was starting to set, and his stomach was starting to rumble. He sat down where he was and pulled out one of his loaves of bread.

The loaf, a reasonable size for an adult, looked tiny in his hand. With a shrug, he ate it in two bites, grumbling as he pulled out another one. Munching on the other loaf, he looked around at the trees and the soft sunlight filtering through the leaves. It was quite beautiful in this new world, and Thorn couldn't help breaking out into a huge grin.

Life was looking up. His usual routine had smashed wide open and adventure was on the horizon. Gone was his life of watching the world pass from his chair. He took a deep breath, drinking in the clean, crisp evening air. For the first time ever, he didn't have to worry that a sudden movement would have him bleeding all over. He could finally relax and enjoy the moment.

Darkness arrived, blanketing the world in a deep blue, pierced by the bright yellow of the moon. While the light from the moon was more than bright enough for Thorn to make his way through the forest, the trees' long, dark shadows stretched into each other, creating a sinister atmosphere. Though shocked at how drastically the feeling of the forest changed with the coming of night, Thorn was not particularly worried. Feeling smug, he toggled his map display and retraced his steps toward the McCarthy Farm.

Arriving at the rolling hills and green fields that marked the edge of the forest, Thorn saw that the fields were as full as before. Players were doing their very best to find the randomly spawning pests for their quest. Shrugging to himself, Thorn walked out and joined the throng.

Finding a spot in the crowd was easy, and Thorn's size worked to his advantage. Space quickly cleared around him, especially once he pulled out his sword. With the six-foot sword, Thorn had an almost ten-foot reach. A few practice swings emptied out his surroundings as other players backed up to avoid the whistling blade.

Dealing with the pests turned out to be much more difficult than Thorn anticipated. Each time a pest would spawn, the closest players would swarm over to try and kill it to get credit for the quest. The real dangers, however, were the players farther away who would shoot arrows or throw projectiles, resulting in the area around each spawning pest turning into a pincushion.

Finally, after almost three hours of frustration and not managing to get a single kill, Thorn had had enough and squatted down. Extending his large sword, he began to sweep it across his side, a few inches above ground level. Switching hands without stopping, he continued to sweep his sword back and forth, the hum of the sword cutting through the air, creating a deadly reminder to the nearby players to stay away.

After two minutes, a pest popped out of the ground, only to get bisected! Not even bothering to pick up the body, Thorn continued his swings uninterrupted. Nodding to himself in satisfaction, he checked his quest mentally, happy to see his kill count increasing. This method generated the ten pest kills he needed after a few minutes, and he stood up, stretched, and went about gathering the bodies of the rodents.

Tossing them into his inventory, Thorn walked back to the edge of the farm where he had gotten the quest. The NPC quest giver was not at his usual post, leaving Thorn confused. Seeing Thorn looking around, a friendly player informed him that the NPC was sleeping and wouldn't be out till the next day.

"Huh, I guess that makes sense," Thorn thought to himself. "If this is an alternate reality, it would be strange to assume that the NPCs were going to stand around in the same spot waiting for players. Does this mean that all the NPCs have their own lives?"

Looking around, Thorn decided to try and find a place to sleep for a bit. While the farm wasn't far from Berum, Thorn wasn't interested in going back to the town and trying to find an inn for one simple reason. What sort of inn would have a bed that was more than 8' 9" long? His bed in real life was a custom-made monstrosity that could fit a full family of five, but Thorn could not imagine he would be that lucky here in Nova Terra.

The number of players that were out and about had in no way decreased, causing Thorn to wonder what was going on. Pulling up his in-game browser, Thorn searched for information on sleeping in Nova Terra.

The result surprised him. Despite the time dilation, players often had to sleep in a semi-regular schedule in-game. This was due to the mental energy that the players were exerting during each in-game day. A player's mental energy expenditure would increase based on how tense their situation was. This meant that a player out in the wilderness fighting monsters might need to sleep every night while those who stayed in the safe cities might only need to sleep once a week.

Players could sleep in Nova Terra, but many players would sleep when they logged out, setting up their schedule so that they were in Nova Terra for five game days, and out for two. An interesting side effect of this was that the players who spent their time producing were able to keep up with the production demands of the adventurers who often had to spend a third of their game days sleeping.

Still, that did not help Thorn's current predicament, which was where to put his head down to rest. Looking around for a dark corner, Thorn found a spot by the barn and sat down. Leaning back against the wall, he instinctively began the breathing exercise that his master had taught him. It helped him calm down and manage his pain. For years, sleeping had been more of a chore than a pleasure as lying down only increased the pressure on his chest and lungs.

Concentrating on his spirit, he touched his tongue to the roof of his mouth and began to exhale in a long, continuous breath, pushing the air from his diaphragm. As he fell into the rhythm and felt his body begin to relax, Thorn wondered if the Chi that his master always talked about was real in Nova Terra.

As a fantasy setting full of fantastical creatures and ancient mysteries, Nova Terra teemed with things that would be pure myth in the real world. Even magic, a difficult and esoteric subject, had popped up in the last few years, causing fledgling mages to begin to spring up like weeds. While doing his research, Thorn had considered trying to learn magic but decided that it was not for him.

Spells, while powerful, were a total pain to cast and even more of a pain to learn. According to the little that he had read, every spell had multiple pieces that all had to be in order for the spell to work. Not only did spells require a deep understanding of the verbal command that triggered them, but also the accompanying hand gestures and sometimes physical reagents. All this seemed like too much trouble when Thorn could hit things with his sword.

Thinking of hitting things with his sword, Thorn reflected over the two fights he had experienced earlier in the day. The first fight had fit his expectation pretty well. Despite Mac's experience, Thorn's training had proven better, and he was able to win. However, the fight against Hamm had been very frustrating.

Hamm's movements were precise and seemed to anticipate Thorn's every move. In fact, he had not been able to touch him with his sword no matter how he swung it. Resolving to practice more, Thorn drifted off to sleep.

CHAPTER NINE

It was early morning when he woke up. Eating the rest of his bread, he waited for the farmer who had given him the quest to appear. Turning in the quest was simple, and Thorn collected the ten copper coins the farmer was offering for the pest corpses and walked back to Berum. The line at the gate wasn't long. Apart from some nervous looks from the guards, he got into the city without issue. Heading back to the eastern district, Thorn turned in his quest at City Hall.

Seeing his somewhat lost look, the secretary recommended that he go to the job board and look for some tasks to get himself started. Thorn, who had been wondering what to do next, thanked her and hurried off to see what other sorts of things the game had for him.

Quests in Nova Terra were different than quests in other games in that there was no physical indicator that an NPC had a quest to give. With no yellow exclamation points or question marks floating above the NPCs' heads to tell Thorn that there was something special to do, he had been a bit lost as to how to find something to do. The job board settled that.

Located outside of City Hall, the job board displayed quests issued by the NPCs of the city. It also showed tasks that players submitted to have other players complete for a fee. This worked out well for everyone because Nova Terra did not have experience points. Functionally, there was no difference between a task issued by a player and a task issued by an NPC. Not only was the board a place for tasks, but it was also a recruitment board. This allowed guilds, mercenary corps, and other groups to advertise and recruit players to work with them.

Looking over the board, Thorn found a task that suited him. The surrounding forests were being plagued by a large pack of corrupted wolves, and the city had offered a bounty on them. They were paying three copper per tail turned in. Pleased that there was no limit to the number of tails that could be submitted, Thorn headed for the forest after spending his 10 coppers on more bread.

He had never hunted anything before, so he had to rely on walking around some of the areas mentioned in the task on the job board. Thorn spent almost an entire morning wandering this way and that through the forest, looking around for some wolves. Unable to catch sight of even a single wolf, Thorn sat down to eat lunch while he considered his next move. At this rate, he would starve to death before he found his first wolf.

Opening the in-game browser, Thorn looked for information on finding wolves. There was quite a bit of information on hunting in general, and Thorn spent an enjoyable hour reading through some of it. Bookmarking a couple of pages for later reading, Thorn finally found a forum post that mentioned that the wolves around Berum were farther out in the forest than the task said. Looking at the area on the map that the post mentioned, Thorn confirmed he had not yet walked through that area.

Standing up and dusting his pants off, Thorn moved in that direction. The forest was nice, but the constant ducking to avoid the low hanging branches was getting old. So, though Thorn was still excited to get some wolves, he decided to find somewhere else to walk around. The journey wasn't too long, and Thorn arrived at the edge of the marked space within an hour.

According to the forum posts, the corrupted wolves had been

around for a while and the task that the city issued had been a pretty consistent task. To the north-west of the city, north of McCarthy Farm, was a large stand of old growth forest tucked between three large mountains. This forest was the home of the corrupted wolves; from there they spread to the north and west of the city.

There wasn't any information on where the wolves came from or how they had been corrupted, but the post had mentioned the way to differentiate a corrupted wolf from a normal wolf. Corrupted creatures, as a rule, had extended claws and fangs and red glowing eyes. Many also had streaks of black running through their fur that increased with their level of corruption.

The main feature of corrupted creatures was a complete fearlessness and a deep bloodlust that would cause them to attack with abandon as soon as they discovered prey. While this made them very hard to fight, they didn't have to be chased down like normal wolves. As he moved forward, Thorn began to see the trees thinning out and the undergrowth disappearing. After a while, he noticed that the trees were bigger, and he had much less trouble walking under them.

The forest floor here was covered in a spongy layer of composting leaves and debris from the trees, fine blades of grass poking up wherever beams of light were able to pierce the thick foliage. Thorn was walking around a large boulder when his scalp prickled, and a dark shape came barreling at him from the side. Instinctively raising his right shoulder, Thorn felt a sharp pain as a corrupted wolf's teeth ripped into his skin, forcing him to stumble backward.

Still reeling in shock from the ambush, Thorn reached out, his immense hand curling around the corrupted wolf's chest. With a grunt, he heaved the wolf off and scrambled backward until his back was against the boulder.

Three corrupted wolves appeared, low growls issuing from their throats, and began circling him, looking for a weakness. Checking his shoulder, Thorn was relieved to see that it wasn't bleeding too badly. Still, he could feel his health trickling away, so he couldn't afford to wait too long. Seeing him look down at his shoulder, the wolf on his left howled and dashed forward, its claws flashing.

This time, ready for the attack, Thorn pulled his sword out with his right hand while shifting his weight onto his right foot and snapping a sidekick at the wolf as it jumped. Feeling his foot connect, Thorn borrowed the rebounding force to drop into a squat before shifting forward into a bow stance as he cut upwards with his blade, bisecting the wolf in front of him while dodging the snapping teeth of the wolf attacking from the right.

Without even looking, he reversed his swing and lopped off the attacking wolf's head with a neat slash. Turning to face his left again, Thorn's mouth dropped open. The first wolf to attack was also dead, its head crushed by his snap kick! Releasing a big breath, Thorn patted his chest. Real combat was nerve-wracking!

Collecting the tails of the three wolves to turn in for the quest, Thorn rested for some minutes before continuing forward. The attack had come out of nowhere; Thorn's perception wasn't strong enough to spot the hiding wolves, so he wasn't sure what else he could have done. He had heard people talk about being able to sense killing intent, but Thorn had grown up in the most peaceful environment possible, so he didn't even know what killing intent would feel like.

In fact, the countless hours that Ms. Chen spent forcing him to complete his slow Taijiquan moves and the fact that this was a game were the only reasons he could fight at all. Despite how lifelike the game was, Thorn was not able to suspend his disbelief completely, giving him something of a laissez-faire attitude when it came to things like getting hurt. This allowed him to be completely fearless when facing his opponents.

Advancing, Thorn had more warning before his next fight. He caught sight of another three wolves coming over a hill. Three bloody minutes later, he had earned three more tails and a nasty bite on his leg. Fortunately for him, in Nova Terra health regeneration was closer to a game than to real life, otherwise,

Thorn would have been in a lot of trouble as the wounds built up.

After resting for a couple moments outside of combat, all of his wounds began to knit themselves back together, taking only a few minutes to heal completely. Emboldened by his two encounters, Thorn decided to speed up a bit and, covering vast amounts of ground with his enormous stride, ran into six more groups of wolves before dusk began to settle. Knowing that the thick layer of foliage would make the forest completely dark soon, Thorn decided to call it a day and head back for town.

After about forty-five minutes of walking, he made it back to Berum, picking up another three tails on the way. Over the course of the day, he had collected 27 tails, which, at 3 coppers each, came to eight silver and 1 copper. After a guard pointed him to a cheap inn, Thorn bought some dinner and went to bed. Even though he could stay up for a couple days in a row due to the time dilation, Thorn was not in any rush. After all, he had the next 14 years to do quests.

The inn was somewhat run down, but since cheap was currently the name of the game, Thorn did not care. He paid the gawking tavern owner and squeezed up the stairs to the small room he had rented. Like he had dreaded, the bed was a small single. Stripping the sheets off of it, Thorn lowered himself onto the groaning floor. Worried that the floor was going to collapse under him, he stayed as still as he could. Running through his breathing technique, more out of habit than anything else, he soon fell asleep.

At some point in the night, feeling a cold breeze, Thorn woke up. Sensing something wrong, he lay still, his eyes barely open. It took him a moment, but he made out a small figure crouched in front of the window. Dressed completely in black with a mask over its face, the figure seemed to have just come in through the slightly open window.

Reaching around in the dark, Thorn grabbed the first thing that his hand fell on. As the figure stood and snuck toward the window, Thorn hurled it at the thief!

Oberlin Danihoff, III, had been out of luck recently. Starting with that twelve-year-old kid from whom he'd tried to lift a magical tome. That kid had turned out to be an archmage of some sort, specializing in lightning. And to make a bad thing worse, the magical tome had almost eaten one of his fingers! Then it was the madman with the portal in his room who summoned some sort of eldritch horror. Ugh. He had been washing slime out of his hair for weeks.

Needless to say, his often-impeccable luck had recently been complete garbage. It was so bad, in fact, that he, the greatest thief in all of Angoril, had been reduced to scrounging for coins in a dump of an inn in the middle of bloody nowhere. Shaking his head in frustration, he continued to move forward slowly until a cold breeze blew across his back.

"I thought I latched that!" he thought, swearing to himself. A quick glance at the bed showed that it was still empty, but Oberlin was a professional, so he turned to close the window. When he got to it, he realized the latch was actually broken, explaining why it had swung open behind him. As he began to re-affix the latch, he heard a heavy creak behind him and turned his head in time to see the entire bed flying across the room at him, a gargantuan shadow monster that filled the room rising up behind it!

With an ear-piercing scream, Oberlin dove through the window in an attempt to avoid the bed hurtling toward him, all the while cursing every god he could think of.

Startled by the loud commotion, the inn's owner rushed out from the back, his nightgown askew, clutching a comically large axe. Thorn pulled the bed out from the hole he had created and looked down. The bed frame had smashed out some of the wall next to the window, allowing Thorn to squeeze his bulk out of the hole and drop to the ground next to the thief, who was on his back groaning after falling 15 feet.

Landing with a thump, Thorn watched the unresisting thief, who was muttering something about quitting this stupid game while he waited for the innkeeper to come out. The commotion, resulting from the loud smash as the bed frame impacted the wall moments after the thief dove out the window, seemed to have roused the whole inn.

Still fuzzy, Thorn was unsure of how to proceed. Before he could decide if he should find a guard or take the thief to jail himself, the innkeeper rushed out the door of the inn, his giant axe waving around him in the air. The innkeeper looked around wildly, and, upon spotting the gaping hole in his wall on the second story, let out a furious shriek!

"WHO SMASHED A HOLE IN MY WALL?!"

"Um, that was me," Thorn admitted, raising a hand.

"HOW ABOUT I SMASH A HOLE IN YOU?!" Apoplectic, the innkeeper tried to grab Thorn by the collar, but, due to the difference in height, he only managed to grab Thorn's shirt near his ribs. "YOU... you..." realizing that he was currently threatening someone twice his size who, moments before, put a massive hole in the wall, the innkeeper trailed off, deflating.

"Yeah, I'm sorry about that. I didn't realize I had grabbed the bed," said Thorn, rubbing his nose. "I was trying to scare off this thief."

"Well I'd say you succeeded," muttered Oberlin to himself, trying to push off the ground.

CHAPTER TEN

Seeing him trying to stand, Thorn grabbed Oberlin and picked him up. Setting him on his feet, he left his massive hand resting on the thief's shoulder, his fingers ready to squeeze should the thief try and make a run for it. Surprisingly, Oberlin made no attempt to free himself, seeming completely resigned to his fate.

The innkeeper, too scared to continue yelling at his giant customer, ran to the end of the street to get a city guard. While he was leaving, Oberlin looked up at the mammoth figure holding onto him and grimaced.

"Greetings, my good man. Given the dubious nature of this initial meeting, why don't we start over? I'm Oberlin Danihoff the third, last in a long line of professional swipers. Being that we are both of the non-digital variety, and you haven't lost anything, do you think you could do a chap a favor and let me scoot before the constabulary show?" Oberlin looked at Thorn with a hopeful gaze.

It took Thorn almost a full minute to understand what the slim thief was saying, but once he got it, he couldn't help but chuckle. Shaking his head, he continued to hold the thief, impervious to his babbling until the guards arrived. Once he saw the guards, Oberlin gave an explosive sigh, looking up at the sky.

Rejecting the guard's offer of having Oberlin give him compensation, Thorn expressed his desire to go back to sleep, so the guards dragged the depressed thief away with them. Over to the side, the innkeeper was staring in despair at the hole in his wall. He had been tempted to raise a fuss so that Thorn would pay for the repairs but had abandoned that plan as soon as he saw the giant.

As for Thorn? He yawned, and stretching out an arm, he grabbed the exposed floor of his second story room, pulling himself back up to squeeze through the hole. Fluffing the small pillow he had been using he lay back down on the floor of the room and was soon fast asleep. Gulping, the innkeeper swore to himself that he wouldn't be involved with this freak!

"Who climbs into a second story without jumping? Wait! Forget jumping, who does it at all?" he thought, dragging his axe back into the inn.

Thorn woke up early to bright morning light streaming through the hole he had made. Examining the damage, Thorn could see that the walls were made of plaster-reinforced wood with wooden frames around the windows. The plaster on the inside of the wall had been pulverized, and the exposed wood had been splintered beyond recognition.

After taking a good look at what was needed to fix the problem, Thorn made his way downstairs to the dining room. A quick look around confirmed that none of the rather spindly chairs would be able to hold his weight, so Thorn took a seat on the floor and waved over one of the staring waitresses.

"Morning, do you sell breakfast?"

"Yes sir," she replied, pulling out a menu for him. "It's two copper for the standard breakfast, which is two eggs, breakfast potatoes, toast, and juice."

"Excellent, I'll have six." Thorn handed the menu back. "You can scramble the eggs."

"Six, sir? Six eggs?"

"No, six of the standard breakfasts. That would be 12 eggs. Plus all the other stuff."

"Y... Yes sir," replied the waitress. Bemused, she walked into the back, returning five minutes later with a massive tray with three breakfasts stacked on it. Letting Thorn know that the rest of the food would be coming, she hurried away.

Thorn, excited to be eating something other than bread, devoured the potatoes first, before putting the eggs on the toast. Each piece of toast was polished off in two bites, and the rest of the eggs were inhaled, as well. Thorn was enjoying his juice, the plates in front of him empty, when the waitress came out to deliver the second set of food. At the sight of the empty plates, the waitress almost dropped her large tray in shock. This time she stayed in the dining room and watched in awe as Thorn shoveled the new food into his mouth as fast as the last.

Paying for his meal, Thorn heaved himself off the floor and went in search of the innkeeper. He found him outside talking to a dwarf with a thick leather apron. Thorn apologized again, and after some discussion, convinced him to not only let Thorn pay for the repairs, but to also rebuild the bed in that room into something that would fit Thorn's massive size.

That left Thorn with almost no money. So, after getting a few supplies and some food for lunch, Thorn readied his sword and headed back out to the old growth forest where he had encountered the corrupted wolves. Arriving without issue, Thorn ventured deeper into the forest.

The corrupted wolves seemed to travel in packs of three, which made them hard for a normal individual to hunt. At the same time, the low price per tail made the bounty unattractive for groups who would have to split the profits. Thorn, however, was not normal. His martial arts training, coupled with his size, made it easier for him to hunt. By lunchtime, he had a tidy pile of tails.

Noticing that the deeper he went into the forest, the greater the frequency of his encounters with the corrupted wolves, Thorn did his best to range around the outskirts of the forest while keeping a sharp lookout to make sure he did not encounter multiple groups of corrupted wolves at the same time. While he could deal with three wolves at once, he could not do so without injury. Adding another three wolves was beyond what Thorn could handle at the moment.

The next few days passed in a familiar routine. During the day, he would hunt corrupted wolves around the edge of the old growth forest. When evening came, he would make his way back to the city to turn in the quest. Seeing how willing Thorn was to pay for the wall repair and bed upgrade made the innkeeper much friendlier, and he happily continued to reserve Thorn's room for him.

Although the money was only trickling in, Thorn was content. He had no particular desire for money, so he was not worried that the task he had taken barely paid for his daily expenses. Every day he made a couple of silver that he stashed away after paying for his colossal meals and his room.

Once Thorn had been hunting corrupted wolves for a week, he decided to make another visit to the Training Hall to pay for the sword he had borrowed. Waving to the guards, he ducked into the hall. Hamm, about to start his familiar speech, saw him and brightened up.

"Hey, kid! You're back! Ready to learn how to wield that junky sword?"

"Good morning." Thorn smiled back at the friendly trainer. "Actually, I'm here to return the sword. I borrowed it last time I was here, but now I have enough money to buy one for myself."

"Wait, that is one of my swords?" Surprised, Hamm grabbed the sword from Thorn and examined it. Seeing the familiar handle but damaged blade, he shook his head in disgust. "What were you doing with it? Chopping rocks?! What did I tell you about control, kid? Look how trashed this blade is! After only a week too. Sheesh. You know, I'm starting to think you are not suited for swords."

Glancing around at the hall, empty in the early morning, he turned back to look at Thorn. "Listen, kid, you better scram before Janus gets here, unless you want to spend the next year practicing shooting arrows. She threw quite the fit that you ran off last time. But I've got a tip for you. Out in the mountains, north of the city, is a friend of mine who might have a combat style that is more suited to you. If you want to go further on the martial path, you should look him up."

As Hamm finished speaking, a notification popped up, asking Thorn if he wanted to accept a new quest. Agreeing, Thorn opened the quest details.

A Hidden Master

The martial path is long and fraught with danger. Having learned all that you can from Sword Trainer Hamm at the Berum Training Hall, you have been given the opportunity to further your training with a mysterious master who lives in the mountains to the north.

Find Master Sun

After getting rough directions from Hamm, Thorn thanked him and immediately left the Training Hall as fast as he could. Janus had reminded him of his aunt, and he was especially bad at dealing with those types. Since Hamm had recommended that Thorn not bother with a sword, he spent a couple silver on a heavy machete that came with a sheath. Then, after having the smith who was selling it add a few serrations to the thick spine and sharpen the swage, Thorn tied it onto his lower back for easy access.

The directions that Thorn had been given were not very precise, so he stopped back at the inn to let the staff know that he may be out for a couple days and to stock up on some food that he could cook in the wilderness. Thorn had never been camping before, so he was eager to try spending a couple nights out in the open. He had bought an extra-large blanket earlier in the week to cover his new bed, so he brought that along, as well.

After a quick stop at an adventurer's shop, Thorn gathered up his gear and left the city through the north gate. To the north of the city, a large plain ran up to a small, mist-covered cluster of three mountains. Bisecting the plain was a lazy, winding river, a ferry waiting to take Thorn across for a single silver.

Thorn had been in the game for a couple weeks now and was settling into his new life. While he still had no overarching goals, he could roughly sense a new drive, a new purpose, beginning to form in his heart. Tempered by his frequent fights with corrupted wolves, Thorn had found great enjoyment in hunting them.

Thanking the ferryman, Thorn jumped off the log raft and set off for the mountains. He was looking for a 'Master Sun' who was supposed to live somewhere on the second mountain. Hamm had told him that he might have to spend quite a while looking, but that did not bother Thorn one bit. The last thing he was lacking was time.

While the quest log did not give him much information to go on, Thorn was interested in what this Master Sun could teach that Hamm and the other trainers couldn't. He agreed with Hamm that the sword was not a good weapon for his size. In fact, after weeks of fighting corrupted wolves, it was pretty obvious that even his Taijiquan was not well suited for fighting, either.

Taijiquan itself was highly effective, but it had been designed to allow a lesser force to fight against a greater force. In the three weeks that he had been playing Nova Terra, Thorn had never found himself in a situation where his force was exceeded by his opponents. The longer he fought the wolves, the more he realized that he could swat them out of the air, killing them as they jumped at him. There was no need to dodge or attempt to divert the attacking energy when he could meet it and overcome it with force.

For a while, Thorn thought the solution to this would be to get a bigger, heavier sword. But even that did not seem to be optimal, as Thorn found that it was easier, albeit more dangerous, to use his hands and feet. The speed of readying a weapon could not compare to the speed of a palm strike, and his palm strikes rivaled the destructive power of a sword swing.

This realization had dawned on Thorn after a trio of corrupted wolves surprised him immediately after dispatching another group. About to collect the tails of the first group, Thorn heard a sound and looked up in time to see a large wolf bounding toward him. Instead of drawing his sword which was stuck in one of the wolf corpses next to him, Thorn instinctively swung a backhanded chop that smashed the wolf's spine and almost severed its head.

After crushing the other two wolves with a couple of punches, Thorn realized that he had actually killed these wolves faster than normal. Much faster, in fact. From that point on, he had abandoned his sword and started killing the corrupted wolves with his hands and feet, increasing his daily hunting counts.

By the time evening had arrived, he had reached the foot of the second mountain, so Thorn decided to set up camp. As the last rays of sunlight slipped over the horizon, Thorn pulled out the fire starter he had bought and tried to light a campfire. After a few failed attempts, he finally got a blaze going and sat down to enjoy a meal.

Given his total lack of cooking experience, Thorn had opted to bring pre-cooked food that he purchased from the inn. His storage space kept everything at the same state it was when it was put into his inventory, so he did not have to heat up the food again or worry about it going bad.

Thinking that it would be better to have a light meal before he set out again, Thorn pulled out a whole roasted chicken, a massive bowl of rice, two gallons of tea and a bunch of condiments, spreading them out on the ground before digging in. As he was finishing up his meal, Thorn heard a surprised exclamation from the edge of his camp.

CHAPTER ELEVEN

"Hey, you're that frea...that big guy from before!" stammered a voice, catching itself mid-sentence.

Looking up from his meal Thorn, saw the red-haired girl in the witch's hat who had run into him the first day he had arrived in Nova Terra.

"Hello," replied Thorn in response, taking her in. Dressed in open fronted cloth robes with hot pants and a belly shirt, she presented the classic look of a fantasy witch, from the pointy hat perched on her mass of red hair to the high heeled boots with a slight curve in the toe.

"Yeah, I was going back into town to drop off some skins since our bags were getting too full. Oh! I have a great idea! Come with me!" Turning back the way she had come, she grabbed Thorn by the hand and pulled him along as she dashed off. Or at least, she tried to. Pulling on him was no different than trying to pull a mountain with a tow rope. Thorn didn't move at all, and the unexpected resistance knocked her off her feet again.

Thorn quickly took a step forward and put out a hand to steady her. Taking the opportunity, the red head continued to pull him forward as she walked toward a small hill that was off to the left while Thorn, somewhat perplexed, followed. Over the top of it,

Thorn found a small group of individuals sitting around a small fire, taking care of their equipment.

The group watched them approach. As the two got close, a six-foot human who seemed to be armed like a knight moved forward to greet them while an elf in robes shifted a wand closer to hand and someone who looked like a dwarf slipped back into the darkness.

"Mina, who is this?" called out the knight, his hand tucked into his belt near his sword as he looked at the giant before him.

"Ouroboros, this is that guy I was telling you about! The huge noob I ran into a couple weeks ago in the starter field. Noob, this is my team, Ouroboros, Velin, and Jorge!" Finally letting go of his hand, Mina gestured toward the knight, the cleric and the back of the camp where the small figure had disappeared.

"Uh, hi. My name is Xa...Thorn. Um...sorry for intruding." Thorn felt quite bashful. It was his first real interaction with other players, and he wasn't sure how to handle it. Normally when people looked at him it was with fear, strange fascination or pity, but the group in front of him seemed to not care about his abnormal size.

"Nice to meet you, Thorn," said the knight, reaching out a hand. "I'm Ouroboros, the leader of our small band of misfits. By your gear, am I right to assume you only started Nova Terra a little while ago?"

"Yeah, I started a couple of weeks ago," responded Thorn, taking the offered handshake. He was thankful that the game seemed to scale his force based on his intentions, so Thorn didn't have to pay careful attention not to crush the knight's armored hand. "I just met Mina for the second time a few moments ago, and I'm not quite sure why she brought me over."

"Oh, yeah, yeah. Ouroboros, you said we needed to recruit a fifth for that mission; why don't we take Thorn here? He looks super strong, so I bet we can loot everything!" Thorn could almost see the dollar signs in her eyes as she gushed to her team.

By this point, the cleric had come over and a short figure appeared next to Thorn, revealing Jorge to be a dwarf in dark leather with a wicked-looking curved knife that he was in the process of sheathing.

"Pleased to meet you," said Jorge in a gravelly voice. "Can you carry a pack?"

"Uh, yes?" Thorn wasn't sure where this was going.

"Good." And with that, the gruff dwarf walked back to the fire, where he resumed caring for his gear.

Following the dwarf, Ouroboros invited Thorn back to the fire to share the meal they were eating, and the group sat down together while Ouroboros explained their situation. The four of them were a group of adventurers who took quests from the traveler's board. They had been thinking about taking on another quest, but it required five members. They had been discussing going back to town to see if they could find someone who would be willing to sign on with their group as a Porter.

Seeing that Thorn was unfamiliar with the term, Mina explained. It turned out that a Porter was a player who took on a special group role in Nova Terra that could be assigned by a group leader to one of the members of their party. It increased inventory space and reduced the weight of the items the porter carried, but it prevented any special movement abilities or skills from being used.

Additionally, there were some restrictions on how the Porter could use their inventory. Anything that the Porter put into their inventory from the party could only be retrieved by the group leader and was sent to the group leader when the party was disbanded, preventing the Porter from being able to run away with all the loot. The main exception was, when the porter died, they would drop all the loot they had picked up.

The quest they were about to undertake promised a fair amount of loot as well as quite a few chances to gather skins, so the group wanted to make sure they could bring everything back with them. The quest itself was something they could complete with four players and bringing along a noob to act as Porter would help the group maximize their profits. It sounded good to Thorn, as it would help him get a better understanding of the game. Plus, Ouroboros was offering to pay him two gold a day plus 5% of their total haul as compensation, so he agreed.

Pleased, Mina welcomed Thorn to the group with an overwhelming flood of words. Seeing his somewhat frantic look, Ouroboros cut in while Mina was taking a breath, ignoring her nasty glare.

"So, Thorn, why don't you tell us a bit about yourself?"

"Sure," said Thorn, nodding his head. "I started playing only a couple weeks ago, and I'm still getting used to this whole thing. This is my first time with a virtual reality game like this, but I am learning as I go. So far I've been hunting wolves for the bounty which has kept me going pretty well."

"Oh wow, so you really just started! Are you having any trouble getting used to the time dilation? When I first started, I would always forget that there was a time difference, which caused me some issues."

"It hasn't been too bad. Things seem to move at a slower pace in game than they would in real life, which helps quite a bit."

"That is true." Ouroboros nodded. "Still, loading into the game in the morning and experiencing multiple days in the game always threw me off since it was the same day when I logged out at night. I have a regulator, which helps me play more consistently."

"A regulator?" asked Thorn.

"Man, you are a noob," laughed Mina.

"Sleep regulators are devices that attach to your gaming equipment. They help you wake up and sleep on a particular schedule that minimizes your time out of the game. It lets you play while you sleep. Professional gamers use them to maximize the number of hours they can be in the game," Ouroboros explained with a smile.

"Whoa, are you all pro gamers?" asked Thorn in astonishment.

"Yup. We are part of Ragnarok."

Surprised, Thorn could not help his indrawn breath. Despite being a noob, Thorn was not entirely ignorant. Ragnarok was one of the strongest guilds in Nova Terra! Made up of elites, Ragnarok was an absolute powerhouse and held numerous records in the game. Unlike the Society of Roses, who were mercenaries, Ragnarok kept to themselves and worked to unlock the many secrets of Nova Terra.

Thorn, excited to have fallen in with guild players, began asking questions, and Ouroboros kindly humored him, chatting about Nova Terra while Mina interjected long rambling rants every time they got onto a subject that caught her fancy. Jorge, on the other hand, sat by the fire drinking out of a large mug that seemed to never run dry. The cleric, Velin, sat near Ouroboros, tossing a word in when she felt like it.

After a couple hours had passed, Velin got to her feet and excused herself, mentioning that she had to log out to eat. Deciding to give everyone a break and to resume on the next game day, Ouroboros set a time to meet, and the group of four logged out, leaving Thorn to wait out the night. While he was waiting, Thorn fished out some more food and enjoyed another meal. Once he finished, he pulled up his in-game browser and began to look through the information on parties. After having lived his entire life without much interaction with his peers, Thorn had never even thought of forming a party. He had assumed that he would go through Nova Terra the same way he went through life. Alone.

However, that wasn't really a fair assessment since people had surrounded him his whole life. His aunt had taken wonderful care of him, and he trained with his master at least once a day. Additionally, he generally got along quite well with the nurses and doctors with whom he came into contact, to say nothing of the bodyguards who followed him and his aunt around at all times.

Despite the presence of so many other people in his life outside the game, Thorn couldn't help his overwhelming feelings of being alone. One of the counselors he had talked to had aptly described it as 'feeling trapped in your own skin'. For many years, Thorn had thought that his feelings were unique because of his situation but talking with counselors had helped him understand that this feeling of loneliness in a crowd was a common thing.

Thinking about the next day's activities, Thorn could not suppress his mounting excitement about working with Mina and the others. Hunting the corrupted wolves was fun, but Thorn was determined to explore all the wonders of Nova Terra, and that meant playing well with others. About to turn in for the night, a pop-up announced that he had gotten a new message. Expecting that it was his aunt bothering him about playing together, Thorn sighed and clicked on the notification.

To his surprise, it was actually a message from his master, Ms. Chen, asking how the game was going and if his training had been helpful. His sleepiness vanishing, Thorn opened up the video chat feature and recorded a message to send to her. He explained how the Taijiquan he had learned had been helpful for the most part. However, he was running into Taijiquan moves that seemed good in practice but were not helpful because of his size.

Several times he had tried to execute a move when fighting the corrupted wolves only to completely miss because of the size difference. Taijiquan had been created with two similar sized people in mind, and as a result, he was struggling to put it into practice with his massive form. On the other hand, when it worked, it was very effective! After explaining his experiences so far in the game, Thorn asked for some advice on how to make what he already knew work against smaller, weaker enemies.

Closing off the message with a description of his interactions with Hamm, the sword trainer from the Training Hall, Thorn bowed with respect and said goodbye before clicking the send button. Due to the difference in time between the game and real life, the message had to be processed so that it wouldn't look to Ms. Chen like it was being fast forwarded.

Thorn suspected that what he needed was more practice in how to apply the techniques, but he was hoping that his master would have some good insight into how he could use the forms that were second nature to him now for effective combat.

Sending the video message to his master got Thorn thinking about the issues with his form that were brought about by his size. Many of the smaller joint manipulations and locks that he had been seeing did not work the same way for him due to how large his hands were. At the same time, he was so strong that he found he could overpower everyone else he had met in a direct contest of force.

For someone who had trained for more than ten years to employ as little force as possible in his movements, this concept was throwing him for a loop. For example, when he matched strength with the large warrior in the Training Hall, he had tried to give way to his opponent's strength in order to use his force against him, but no matter how much he gave way, his opponent simply couldn't move him.

Yet, when he exerted a force of his own, his opponent could not even begin to handle it. The same thing had happened countless times when fighting against the corrupted wolves. Moves that were designed to accept and redirect force did not work the way they were supposed to while moves that would never work for a normal person killed the corrupted wolves with ease. Palm strikes intended to deflect crushed bone instead. Granted, it was not the worst problem to have in a fight.

Having finally verbalized the problem he was having, Thorn decided to do some research on other fighting styles. Over the next nine hours, Thorn combed through the game forums and searched for other types of martial arts that favored a more direct, aggressive approach. A couple of the different styles caught his eye, and he spent some time looking them up and sorting them according to his interest.

Direct striking arts like Karate from Japan and Pencak Silat, which had been created in Indonesia, both favored sharp powerful strikes and hard offense. While both contained empty hand and weapon forms, Silat was more weapon oriented while Karate favored empty hand forms over weapon forms. Another interesting martial art out of Thailand was Muay Thai, a hard-striking art that placed special emphasis on external strengthening. While adaptive combat arts like Systema from Russia and Krav Maga from Israel were also popular, they focused more on defense and grappling, which was not Thorn's main focus.

Taijiquan was only one of the many Chinese martial arts, and at first, Thorn looked for another Chinese martial art to learn, but he realized that almost all of them were very similar to Taijiquan in their movements. Putting them aside until his master responded to his message, he looked instead for an art that he could learn on his own to maximize his attacking potential.

CHAPTER TWELVE

Thorn was still sitting by the fire looking through his in-game browser when the others returned. While it had been a full ten hours since they had logged out for Thorn, only an hour and a half had passed for them. Enough time to stretch, take a shower and grab something to eat. As for Thorn, he had been watching martial arts videos the entire time. However, before he could settle on a particular style, Mina and the others arrived at the camp. Closing the browser, he stood up to greet them, dwarfing even Ouroboros' six feet.

"Geez, you are big," Mina complained, craning her neck to look up at Thorn's face. At 5' 3", she was just over half his height and barely came up to his belly button.

"Hey, Thorn," greeted Ouroboros. "You all rested up?"

Nodding, Thorn gathered all his stuff and put out the fire.

"Excellent. We're heading to the valley now. I'll explain on the way." Leading the group, Ouroboros started outlining the task at hand. "About ten miles out, there's a small valley that is currently occupied by a few different tribes of kobolds. Normally they aren't a big issue because the tribes fight each other incessantly, but there are reports that they have united. Kobolds reproduce quickly, so they become a huge threat when they get organized.

"There have been reports of kobold Greater Shaman showing up, so we have been tasked with scouting the situation and killing the Greater Shaman. It is a five-man job, but our guild works in groups of four, so we thought it would be a good idea to bring a porter along. Oh, that reminds me. We haven't actually talked about our classes yet. I'm a Holy Guardian, Mina is an Ice Witch, Jorge is a Shadow Assassin, and Velin is a War Priestess."

"Wow, you all have classes? That is pretty impressive," commented Thorn.

Classes in Nova Terra were a rare and somewhat controversial part of the game. While the game put forth the claim that anyone could do anything in game, the ancient inheritances scattered around the land that allowed players to gain special classes were not available to everyone. These classes unlocked special abilities and paths that allowed the players who received them to grow into powerful characters.

Classes could be almost anything, and there were countless classes scattered throughout the game. Organized into three ranks, a class' strength was determined by the number of words in its name. Classes like Warrior, Priest, Mage, and Rogue were common and could be acquired through specialized statues that could be collected from difficult dungeons. Each statue could, for a price, grant the class it was associated with to any number of people.

Rarer were two-word classes like Holy Guardian, Great Sage, Ghostly Warlock, and Master Thief. Two-word classes were powerful, uncommon, and granted from a limited number of mini-statues that were given as rewards for long quest chains. Every uncommon class holder was considered an elite of the highest order, and for Mina, Ouroboros, Velin, and Jorge to all be uncommon class holders showed that not only were they professional gamers, but they were among the best.

Smirking at Thorn's starstruck expression, Jorge looked at Thorn's monstrous frame and said, "What about you? You must have picked up a crazy class to get a body like that."

"Haha," laughed Thorn, embarrassed, "I'm pretty tall in real life."

"You must be almost seven feet tall!" exclaimed the normally quiet Velin after doing some quick math.

"Ha, she thinks I made myself taller," thought Thorn. "Still, that was some quick math."

"Haha, something like that." Changing the subject Thorn, asked about their classes. "Did you all have to complete long quests to get your classes? I heard that was the only way to get uncommon classes."

"Sort of. Ouroboros and I were able to do much of our quests together, which helped the whole thing go faster," said Mina. "Jorge got his on his own while Velin got hers when she joined Ragnarok."

"Mina, that's enough," said Ouroboros, shooting her a disapproving look.

"Oops, sorry. There goes my mouth again." Covering her mouth with an exaggerated grimace, she peeked at Thorn. "I shouldn't be talking about it. Top secret information and all that."

"I'm sorry, I didn't realize it was private," said Thorn.

"No problem, it just isn't something that players go around talking about. To professional gamers, knowing someone's class is like having a guidebook to their capabilities, so you can imagine that people guard that information," replied Ouroboros with a wave. "Mina should know better. But I'm sure she would have blabbed it out even if you hadn't asked."

Sticking her tongue out at Ouroboros, Mina grabbed Velin's arm and pulled her off to the side.

"Come on, Velin, let's walk over here away from all the stupid boys."

Worried that the atmosphere was going to get awkward, Thorn asked about the size of the valley they were going to, learning that it was about three miles wide and nine miles long. That reminded Mina of something that she had wanted to talk about, so she ran back over to Thorn's side, leaving Velin rolling her eyes.

Their trip did not take long, and the valley soon came into view.

Stopping the party, Ouroboros laid out the plan.

"Based on our intel, there are six different tribes in the valley. At least three of them have a Shaman, so we will need to be aware while we are fighting them. The Greater Shaman is the main target this time, but we are not sure where he is; we'll need to flush him out. The plan is to take down the three villages with Shaman to make the Greater Shaman mad. Jorge, you are in charge of clearing the path for us. It will be a pain if we alert the main camp, so no messing around, okay? Thorn, you'll stick with Mina, Velin, and me until we engage. Once we do, stay back until we've cleared the mobs, then pick up anything that drops. Oh, do you know how to skin animals?"

"I have never skinned anything before." Thorn shook his head.

"Okay, no problem. Mina, you are in charge of skinning after we clear. Try to show Thorn how as we are going," said Ouroboros, adjusting the large shield on his arm. Finished with the plan, he nodded to Jorge. "Let's go."

As soon as the words left his mouth, the entire air of the group changed. A deep calm settled over them as they prepared to move out. Jorge slipped into the forest, while Mina, not speaking for once, stepped close to Thorn. The two of them followed Ouroboros, whose friendly demeanor had chilled, a grim expression resting on his face. The only one who seemed unchanged was Velin, who continued following quietly as she had the whole time.

Every once in a while, as they moved through the forest on the valley floor, Ouroboros would make adjustments in their direction. At first, Thorn did not recognize what was happening, but soon he realized that each time Ouroboros would make a change, a bird call would ring out. Furrowing his brows, he looked at Mina, who confirmed that the bird was actually Jorge.

Soon they began to see more evidence of Jorge's passing as they began to find fresh kobold corpses along their path. Goblin sized creatures, kobolds had a snout and ears like a dog and paws for feet. Their fur-covered skin was valuable in large enough quantity, so Mina got to work, showing Thorn how to skin them, starting from the cut that Jorge had made on their neck or in their back. Despite her normally frivolous attitude, Mina was proficient at skinning, and after a couple demonstrations, Thorn had a good grasp of the basics. They continued on like this for a while before Ouroboros called for a halt.

"There should be a village up ahead. Jorge should be back after checking it out. Mina, we're going to go with a standard assault. Velin, the Shaman will be yours to deal with. If you have any issues, shout." Turning to look at Thorn, he smiled. "Thorn, all you need to do for the assault is watch. Kobolds are quite weak on their own but can be dangerous when they get into a group. Enough of them and their teeth and claws become a problem. The Shaman is a different story, though. Shamans have an annoying poison magic that is especially dangerous, so try to stay at least 100 feet back. That should keep you out of his range."

Nodding his head to indicate that he understood, Thorn followed behind the other three, his heartbeat speeding up. So far, he had only stumbled around Nova Terra, doing whatever came up. All of his encounters with enemies were with small groups, so he was interested to see how four people could handle an entire village of monsters. Plus, there was a lot of talk about how different elite players were from regular players, so he was excited to see how they would handle a large fight like this.

At the edge of the forest, a ramshackle wooden wall appeared before the group. From what Thorn could see, the wall, which stood about five feet tall, protected a few buildings that looked more like piles of junk, and a cave entrance. Dotted here and there were poles decorated with bones and feathers, giving the village a tribal feel.

Hearing another bird call, Ouroboros nodded to the others, and then, lowering his shield, he clashed his sword into it and charged! As his sword rang on the shield, a milky white wave spread out from him, covering the party in a white sheen, and Thorn received a notification that he had been blessed with Greater Fortitude.

Ouroboros charged forward like a freight train, his metal armor shining in the morning sun. At first, Thorn was a bit confused, as they were not near the gate, but that confusion was soon cleared up as he watched Ouroboros speeding up. Lowering his body behind his shield as he reached the wall, Ouroboros gave a roar and bashed his way right through the wooden palisade!

Wood splintered and flew through the air as Ouroboros crushed his way through the wall, clearing two screeching kobolds with a casual swing of his sword. The kobolds, caught off guard, went running this way and that as Ouroboros laid into them. Mina and Velin, who had reached the destroyed wall, began to attack as well, leaving Thorn standing on the edge of the forest.

Mina, raising a wand with a shining blue gem on the end began to whisper, pointing her wand at a group of kobolds, who were blanketed in a cold, sleeting rain. As the icy sludge covered the kobolds, the heat drained out of their limbs, slowing them down. Unable to shake off the freezing spell, the kobolds began to struggle, losing more and more body heat by the second. Within a few seconds, their struggles slowed and then ceased, leaving only cold corpses.

Waving her wand toward another group, Mina continued her whispering, leaving behind nothing but bodies. Meanwhile, Velin stood in between Mina and Ouroboros, who was cutting down any kobold foolish enough to get in range of his sword. Standing there calmly, Velin seemed to be waiting for something to happen.

Thorn, watching from behind, was stunned by the efficiency of the team. Ouroboros, after crashing through the wall, had advanced until he was about twenty feet into the camp, where he now stood, holding the point against increasing waves of kobold warriors. Mina and Velin had come in after him, with Mina standing closest to the wall.

Despite their best efforts, any kobold that tried to approach from the sides was met with Mina's freezing spell, creating a natural wall of frozen bodies and ground on either side of the team. This forced the kobolds who wanted to attack to rush toward Ouroboros' position, where they were chopped into pieces by his flashing sword.

When Thorn thought that the fight would end without any climax, an angry screech rose from the mouth of the cave as a kobold with red dyed fur and countless bone totems rushed out. Or tried to. As soon as the screech sounded, Velin, who had been standing between Ouroboros and Mina, lifted her staff. Chanting, a light began to gather on the end of her staff, creating a blinding glow.

Even standing a hundred feet behind her, Thorn could feel the danger emanating from the gathering energy. Unfortunately for the kobolds, their Shaman was either too far away or not sensitive enough because he continued to rush forward, waving a wand of his own. Velin finished charging her staff and, with the last word, thrust it toward the Shaman.

From the tip of the staff, a bright beam of light the width of a tree branch shot out, cutting toward the Shaman! With a guttural growl, the Shaman activated one of his totems, covering himself with a blazing flame shield. The beam of light blasted into the shield, causing it to shake wildly. Pausing the beam for a brief second, the shield was unable to handle the strength of Velin's attack, and with a bang, it exploded in a wave of flame. Continuing forward, the beam of light struck the Shaman in the chest, instantly burning a hole right through him!

The beam of white light left a charred hole in everything it touched. Looking at the smoking trail it left, Thorn couldn't help but gulp. What a powerful spell!

'How about I don't get on her bad side,' Thorn thought to himself, throwing a glance at Velin, who was wiping a fine layer of sweat from her forehead.

After the Shaman's death, the fight ended almost abruptly as the now leaderless kobolds fell into even more disarray, rushing around in panic. Unable to see Jorge at first, Thorn was about to ask about him when he noticed a kobold on the edge of the village jerk, a gleaming knife tip protruding from its chest. As it fell to the ground, Jorge was revealed behind its back. As soon as he retrieved his knife, Jorge faded away, moving on to his next target.

"Hmmm, must be some sort of stealth ability related to his class. I wonder if it would work for me?" Thorn mused. He could imagine the chaos it would cause if he could turn invisible.

Seeing that the group was cleaning up the last of the kobolds, Thorn sprang into action, pulling some of the corpses that had no heads back from the group and beginning to skin and loot them. Having gotten used to the method that Mina had taught him, it only took a bit over an hour to process the entire village. Many of the kobold's bodies had been destroyed beyond redemption, but even so, Thorn was astounded at how fast the process went.

CHAPTER THIRTEEN

When Thorn asked Mina about it, she mentioned that, for tedious tasks like skinning, the system actually applied a bit of assistance, so that players wouldn't become bored with it. Thorn nodded to himself, thankful for the game designer's foresight. After finishing the skinning, Thorn picked up a pile of loot that Jorge had found from scrounging through the village.

"How much room do you have open, Thorn?" Ouroboros asked, getting ready to leave the destroyed village.

"I'm good. I still have 80% of my team inventory open."

"Holy Terra! Thorn, your inventory must be enormous!" gasped Mina. "How freakishly strong are you?"

"Haha, I'm not that strong, just big," said Thorn with a laugh, downplaying his ability.

"Good, that means we should be able to clear the next valley without a problem," said Ouroboros with a nod. "The next village is close by. Let's head there now. We'll take a break after we finish clearing it."

Ouroboros blew two short, sharp blasts on a whistle, and then the group moved out, leaving the ruins of the kobold village behind. As they walked along through the forest, occasionally coming across kobold corpses, courtesy of Jorge, Thorn couldn't help but be impressed by this group he had joined.

From the comfortable but focused way they proceeded, it was obvious that the group had worked together for a long time, each person fitting into their role like a well-oiled cog in an efficient machine. Each had a role and trusted the others in the group to fill their role as well. Seeing how they had crushed the village of kobolds without any trouble at all, Thorn could only marvel at the difference between this party and regular players. Elites indeed!

And to think that they were part of a guild of others like them. Shaking his head, Thorn thought to himself that this game hid some scary people! Even putting aside the terrifying white beam that Velin had shot out, Mina's deadly blizzard was equally dangerous. And that was to say nothing of Ouroboros, who held off close to two hundred kobolds, almost single-handedly blocking them and killing at least half of them!

Then there was Jorge, who had not stopped dropping kobold corpses in their path since they started. Fast, deadly, and invisible. Thorn felt a cold shiver travel down his spine. These people, though friendly on the surface, were dangerous. Very dangerous.

"Hey Thorn, what sort of class are you thinking of taking?" Mina asked, unable to stand the silence.

"Hm? Oh, class? I don't know yet," Thorn confessed after thinking for a minute. "I'd be suited to something like a tank, but I was also thinking about getting a non-combat class like a craftsman or something. I heard that there is good money in non-combat classes."

"What! How lame." Mina rolled her eyes. "Non-combat classes are so lame. Why would you want to play a game to spend all your time working?"

"Mina, without non-combat classes, you wouldn't have half your gear," Velin remarked flatly, throwing a glance at the ranting witch.

"Well, yeah. But look at Thorn's size! It would be a total waste for Thorn to not be a warrior," Mina replied, patting as high up as she could reach on Thorn's arm. "I mean, look at him! His arm is bigger than me! Can you imagine him in full Hellplate, with a Barbed Greatsword? It would be epic!"

"Hellplate?" asked Thorn.

"It's a kind of plate armor used by warriors and other offensive melee classes," said Ouroboros, sending Thorn a link to a picture in his in-game browser.

"Oh, that would look pretty impressive," said Thorn, looking at the spiked armor in the picture.

"Alright, let's continue this conversation later," Ouroboros said, pointing toward a village on the top of a hill. "Get ready for a fight. Same as last time."

Watching the group spring into action, Thorn couldn't help but be envious of their smooth cooperation. Each stepped into their role smoothly, and the result was the complete and utter destruction of the kobold village within ten minutes of the start of the fight. The only difference was that this time the kobold Shaman surprised the group by casting a spell before they spotted him, resulting in poisonous projectiles raining down from the sky.

However, even with the ambush, the team responded without missing a beat. Velin, who had been channeling energy into her staff, lifted it into the air and covered herself, Mina, and Ouroboros with a shield that deflected the falling arrows into the surrounding kobolds. At the same time, Ouroboros whistled, two long, one short and then turned back to killing the kobolds that mobbed around him.

Less than a minute later, after the arrows had stopped falling, Jorge appeared with the Shaman's head, which he tossed into the milling crowd of kobolds, sending them scrambling in terror. After they finished dealing with all of the kobolds in the village, they made camp a ways away and got ready to settle in for the night. According to the map that Ouroboros pulled out, the other village was close, so they would be able to handle it the next day and then go after the Greater Shaman.

After a peaceful night, they pressed on, and Thorn witnessed them repeat their deadly process on the last village with a Shaman.

As he was sweeping up the loot, Thorn asked why they were only bothering with the villages with a Shaman.

"Because the other villages will have no worthwhile loot," said Jorge, appearing out of nowhere.

"Exactly," confirmed Ouroboros. "Our actual goal here is to clear the Greater Shaman. We shouldn't have an issue, but we wanted to make sure that he was not able to team up with the other Shaman. As you can see, we are not afraid of numbers, but numbers and multiple casters can be a pretty serious problem."

As he finished speaking, a guttural roar echoed through the air, causing the whole group to look toward the far end of the valley.

"That's our cue," smiled Ouroboros. "Let's go end this thing."

"About time! I want to wash my hair," quipped Mina with a laugh.

Cutting through the forest in the direction of the Greater Shaman, the group abandoned all semblance of stealth. For a moment, Thorn was concerned. What if the kobolds from the three other villages that they had not cleared gathered together? He could only imagine the size of that army.

But then he remembered the sight of Mina's blizzard spell ending the lives of the kobolds en masse and mentally shrugged. It was not the first time the group had done this, so they knew what they were doing. Plus, Thorn was having a blast following them around, even if he was hiding at the back and picking up the loot. It was nice to see them in action and watch their well-practiced cooperation.

They found the Greater Shaman on a large rock at the end of the valley. Peeking out from behind some trees at the edge of the forest, they could see him berating a group of kobolds that looked a bit larger than normal, his spittle flying as he raged at them. The six kobolds he was yelling at were not only larger but much better dressed than the other kobolds they had come across in the valley so far.

"Kobold Chieftains," Mina whispered, seeing Thorn's questioning look.

"No wonder we didn't see them at the other towns," commented Velin, joining the conversation. "This might be a bit more trouble than the other fights."

"Alright, change of plans." Ouroboros cut off the conversation with a wave of his hand. "Six is a bit much for me to handle, so we'll put Mina and Velin on defense. I'll handle the Greater Shaman while Jorge helps the girls with taking down the Chieftains."

"Is there a way I can help?" asked Thorn, eager to contribute.

"Do you have a bow?" Seeing Thorn shake his head no, Ouroboros smiled. "Thanks, but we got it."

Frustrated, Thorn could only watch as the others moved forward to engage the milling kobolds. Was it the fact that he was still wearing the beginner's clothes and didn't have a visible weapon? Due to his size, Thorn had tried his best to present as non-threatening a persona as possible since most people were instinctively insecure around him as it was. In this case, it seemed to have backfired and given Ouroboros the idea that he was weak.

How very different this world was. Nova Terra was so similar to the real world that it was easy to forget that there were some very basic rules that were not the same. In the real world, society had settled the issue of crime, and resorting to violence to solve problems was unacceptable. In Nova Terra, violence was often the first and only means of settling a conflict.

This made the agreeableness that Thorn had spent so long developing worth very little in this crazy new world. While it seemed to help in his interactions with the NPCs he encountered, so far, his gentle persona had been more of a hindrance than a help when dealing with others. Seeing the team engage in combat, Thorn decided that he would find some armor and a sling for his weapon when he got back to town.

Maybe that would help toughen up his image and make the other players he encountered take him a bit more seriously. After all, how lame would it be to continue hanging around the back while other people did all the fighting?

By this point, the team had engaged the kobolds, but their formation was completely different from the last three big fights. Instead of creating his usual immovable defense, Ouroboros chanted in a strange language, summoning a blood-red aura that covered both him and his weapons. Even from all the way in the back, Thorn could feel the uncomfortable suppression the red mist caused.

'It's like being stared at by a predator!' Thorn thought to himself. 'This must be what they mean when they talk about killing intent.'

While Thorn felt a bit uncomfortable, it was obvious that the blood mist had a much larger impact on the kobolds facing Ouroboros. Many became too terrified to move, and it wasn't until the Great Shaman roared out a command and the chieftains bounded forward that the rest of the kobolds managed to recover.

As the chieftains moved, Velin stepped forward as well, waving her staff toward Ouroboros and Mina. Around each of them, a faint golden shield bloomed. Mina's looked like a regular shield spell, but when the golden shield rose around Ouroboros, it mixed with the bloody mist around him, turning a deep rose gold.

Feeling the empowerment from the shield spell, Ouroboros gave a roar and launched himself through the air, jumping an astonishing twenty feet! Flying over the charging kobold chieftains, Ouroboros was about to fall when a pillar of ice with a flat top shot up from the ground, giving him an easy place to land and jump again! This ice pillar that appeared from nowhere allowed him to propel himself all the way to the Greater Shaman, who had failed to react in time.

Lashing out with a ferocious slash, Ouroboros began a frenzied assault on the Great Shaman's magic shield. Each blow seemed to become more and more powerful, causing the green magical shield around the Great Shaman to ripple. Additionally, the blood-red mist around Ouroboros' sword seemed to be attaching itself to the green shield, corroding it.

Behind him, the six chieftains had engaged with Mina and Velin, who were at ease as they defended against the large kobolds. Mina deployed her blizzard spell, slowing down all of the surrounding kobolds while Velin summoned a bow of light and sent glimmering arrows raining down on the attacking force.

To Thorn's complete and utter amazement, this fight, which was supposed to be the hardest part of the quest, ended faster than any of the earlier fights. It took less than thirty seconds for the Great Shaman's green magic shield to fall, and once it did, Ouroboros cut him to pieces immediately.

Meanwhile, Mina's blizzard spell proved as effective as always, slowing all of the kobolds that came close to her and Velin. Any kobold that lost their ability to move soon found a golden arrow sticking out of their head or heart as Velin rapidly fired an endless stream of arrows out over the crowd.

Jorge, unlike in the other fights, actually made an appearance, producing a second curved dagger and cutting a bloody swath around the edge of the crowd of kobolds, making sure to focus on those not affected by the icy sludge Mina was summoning. Within a bit less than three minutes, the four players had cleared almost 70% of the five hundred kobolds that had been milling around, as well as the six chieftains and the Great Shaman.

Under Thorn's dumbfounded gaze, they spent another couple of minutes wiping out the remaining 30% before waving to him. Realizing that the whole mission was over, Thorn walked to the battlefield, shocked by the incredible power shown by the four elite players.

"So that is the difference between an elite player and a regular player," Thorn thought, shaking his head in amazement.

After waiting a moment for the effects of the blizzard spell to disappear, Thorn got down to skinning the massive number of kobolds that the team had taken down. The ones killed by Mina and Velin had almost perfect skins with only a single arrow hole in them. The kobolds that had been killed by Jorge and Ouroboros were unrecoverable. Jorge's victims were generally in multiple pieces and covered in long, bloody gashes. Similarly, Ouroboros' strong swings had sent the limbs of the kobolds he killed far from their bodies.

Clearing all the loot took Thorn almost two hours of non-stop work. Finally finishing up, he walked over to Ouroboros, who was talking to Velin in a low voice. Falling silent when Thorn got close, Ouroboros turned to him and smiled.

"All finished? Then let's head back. With this, the mission is done, so we can turn it in. When we get back to Berum, we can divide the loot."

Traveling back to town took less time than the trip to the valley, but the team was not in any rush, so they took it easy and spent another night in the wilderness. Before getting to town, Ouroboros changed out his gleaming full plate armor for armor made of scuffed leather and replaced his weapons with poor quality weapons. Similarly, the girls swapped out their weapons and high-quality items. Velin even produced a hat with a veil, covering her cold but beautiful face. Only Jorge didn't bother swapping out his gear, instead activating invisibility and disappearing into thin air.

"Alright, everyone ready?" Ouroboros checked over everyone. "Thorn, we don't want to draw any attention, so we are all going to split up. We'll meet at Champ's Adventuring Depot to process the loot."

CHAPTER FOURTEEN

Nodding that he understood, Thorn watched the rest of the group split up, and after waiting for a moment, he walked toward the city. Berum, like many cities, was surrounded by a large wall with guard towers placed every hundred feet. Four gates, one in each cardinal direction, controlled traffic coming in and out of the city. Thorn soon arrived at the northern gate where the guards were watching players and NPCs walking in and out.

Passing through the gate, Thorn ignored the guards' stares and made his way to the location that Ouroboros had marked on his map. Champ's was a spacious courtyard with a couple warehouses set around a large tent with the sides rolled up. Players queued by the tent, entering one at a time to have their items appraised by the NPCs.

Spotting Ouroboros by the side, Thorn queued up and waited for his turn. After about half an hour of waiting, Thorn was called in front of one of the NPCs and started removing things from his inventory to place on the table. Objects like skins could be placed into stacks and were bundled by the system, otherwise Thorn might have buried the entire tent in kobold skins. As it was, he still took out over 700 skins, causing the NPC appraiser's mouth to drop open in shock.

After that were piles of low-quality weapons, semi-rare resources dropped by the chieftains, and a couple of rare items dropped by the Shamans. The Great Shaman had only dropped a special token that Ouroboros had taken as proof that they had completed the quest, but the team had been able to recover a number of precious statues from his cave, which Thorn also took out.

The appraiser, staring in amazement at the piles of loot that Thorn pulled out of his inventory, got busy calculating and soon gave Thorn a piece of paper with a series of numbers written on it. Looking at the paper, Thorn saw that it had a neat list of all of the items that Thorn had pulled out, each with a price associated with it. If the party leader agreed, Champ's would buy those items for that price. If they did not agree, the items would be returned to the team's inventory.

Taking the list, Thorn walked to a nearby tavern, where he spotted Mina and Velin sitting with Jorge at a table. Walking over, he looked at the spindly chair for a moment before sighing and moving it to the side. Ignoring Mina, who was giggling, Thorn sat on the ground and put the list on the table.

A few minutes later, Ouroboros arrived and, after a quick look at the list, approved all of the items. With a ding, the list was replaced by a pouch of gold. The skins alone came out to an astronomical 7,000 silver, or 70 gold, while the rest of the items had been sold for over 30 gold, giving the group a total profit of 103 gold! Thorn could only shake his head at the difference. He had slaved away for weeks to make only a few silvers.

Ouroboros had agreed to pay Thorn two gold a day plus 5% of the total profit from loot, bringing Thorn's share to 13.15 gold. Ouroboros handed Thorn 14 gold and waved him off when he tried to return the difference.

"Don't worry about it, Thorn. There is no way we could have carried this much back if it wasn't for you."

Having settled the matter of money, Thorn and the others ordered food from a waitress who walked up to the table and continued to chat as they ate their food. Thorn was especially hungry and ended up spending a full ten silver on his meal, eating at least three times as much as the other three combined.

"Holy Terra, big guy!" Mina exclaimed, shaking her head and pointing to the piles of empty plates. "Aren't you afraid of getting fat? You ate more food than I would eat in a week!"

"There is a lot of me to keep up," smirked Thorn, patting his belly.

"Yeah, no kidding."

Seeing that Mina was going to launch into another verbal barrage, Velin gave Ouroboros a pointed look, causing him to swallow the food he was eating and jump into the conversation. However, his haste left him coughing, and it was only after a few minutes that he could actually get some words out.

"So, Thorn. Any plans now that the mission is done?"

"None so far," said Thorn, scratching his head. "I was thinking of looking for a class. Or I may get some weapon training. Watching you four has been eye opening, and I sort of feel like I have been wasting my time in Nova Terra so far. I was also thinking about picking up some other porter jobs since they suit me pretty well."

"That makes sense. Classes are pretty important." Velin took a small sip of her coffee before dabbing at her lips with her napkin. "They introduce some specialties and abilities that you cannot get otherwise, which can be a huge advantage. Do you have any idea of what sort of class you want to get?"

"Honestly? No idea." Thorn shook his head, playing with his cup. "I have to do some more research. Do you have any recommendations?"

Hearing Thorn's response, both Mina and Velin looked at Ouroboros, who smiled and sighed.

"Why don't I give you a basic rundown of how classes work," Ouroboros said, unable to stand the looks from the girls. Pulling out a small, three-sided pyramid from his inventory, Ouroboros placed it in the center of the table and activated it.

Instantly, they were encased in an ethereal mist, the sounds of the busy tavern fading away. Seeing Thorn's interested look, Mina jumped in to explain that it was a sound isolation pyramid that would keep other people from hearing what they were talking about.

"That's right, I meant to ask about that," said Thorn in confusion. "What is the big deal with classes being so secret?"

"It isn't just classes, it is everything, really!" replied Mina in excitement. "Haven't you noticed that all of the information in Nova Terra is suppressed? If you want to find something out, you have to actually go and look for it or find someone who knows about it! No one knows why, but actually, Eve suppresses most of the information about Nova Terra that is spread to the outside world!"

"Eve?"

"You don't even know about Eve? Man, you really are a noob!" declared Mina. "Eve is the persona of the AI that runs Nova Terra. She is the first god and is the only AI entity that can interact with the outside world. She deletes or modifies posts on the forums to prevent information from spreading."

"Whoa. I mean, that makes sense though. When I was doing research before I started, there was very little concrete information about the game."

"Yeah, no one knows why. I mean, Eve says that too much information will break the immersive aspect of Nova Terra, but there are tons of other theories about why she shuts down information."

"What about in game?" Thorn asked, leaning over the table in interest.

"Power," Ouroboros cut in, looking at Thorn with a piercing gaze.

"Power," Thorn repeated, leaning back as the group fell silent.

Power. It did not take more than a second for Thorn to understand what Ouroboros was talking about. In a world like Nova Terra, information could be said to be the most precious thing. One of the most important aspects of the game was that there were drastic differences between what players brought into the game that could not be overcome by any amount of hard work. Some things could be trained, but others were fixed.

Like Thorn himself, some players brought traits that gave them a huge advantage in the game while other players had a much humbler start. The only playing field that was completely even for all of the players when they started was knowledge. All of the players who came into the game were clean slates due to the level of control that Eve exercised on the release of information about Nova Terra.

This made every sliver of knowledge that a player got in the game worth something. The player who knew more would naturally have an advantage over a player who knew less. More knowledge translated into more opportunity, more chances for growth.

Take classes, for example. Even the most basic classes were not simple to acquire and could only be retrieved from the end of chain quests and specific dungeons. At the same time, having a basic class would allow a player to stand out from the crowds, giving them special abilities and talents that the average person could not possess, no matter how hard they worked.

And that was to say nothing of the uncommon classes. A single uncommon class could create an elite, one of the best players in the game. But getting an uncommon class was as hard as ascending to the heavens, and no one was willing to share the opportunity with others. After all, that was the same as finding a winning lottery ticket and then giving it away.

But it wasn't just classes. Information about quests, lost history, secret locations, even magic, were all protected pieces of information. Who knew if a single passage from a book on history could lead a player to a great ancient inheritance? And that was to say nothing of the practical advantages of having a class that no one else knew about or understood.

As Ouroboros related, because of the advantage that

information gave, all of the major guilds had come to a tacit understanding to keep information as tightly controlled as possible. The fewer people who knew, the fewer who could compete for the top spots in the game. As a result, many of the elite players were tight-lipped when it came to their classes and the things they knew about Nova Terra.

"That makes sense," Thorn said, after thinking it over for a moment. "Not only does an information ban allow the major guilds to control who can grow and how fast, but it also grants them persuasive power. They can say things like, 'If you join me, you will get a special class.' That way they can grow while keeping the quality of their ranks. Pretty brilliant when you think about it."

"Exactly," said Ouroboros, a flash of appreciation lighting his eyes at how quickly Thorn grasped the main concept. "Information has always been powerful, but it has taken on a new level of power here in Nova Terra, where we are all trying our best to unearth information about the game."

"So how do regular players find out information? Do they have to join a guild?"

"Sort of. There are two ways to gain information besides finding it yourself and learning it from another player." Ouroboros took a drink. "The first is by joining a guild. Every guild has its specialization, and the types of intel they have are going to be reflected by that. Guilds like ours, Ragnarok, are focused on game progression, so we have a lot of information on how to grow as players and how to complete quests. Other guilds, like The Eye of Oghma, which is focused on magic research, will be the best choice if you want to learn about magic.

"There are craftsman guilds that have unique recipes and mercenary guilds that have a huge breadth of knowledge due to the different tasks they have completed. Merchant guilds would be able to tell you the price of goods anywhere on the continent, and exploration guilds have mapped huge areas. Each guild protects their information very seriously, and one of the worst charges that a guild member can face is leaking sensitive information.

"The second way to find information is through the player guild, Avalon. Officially, its name is The Children of Avalon, but everyone calls it Avalon for short. No one knows much about them, but they seem to know everything about everyone. They are an intelligence organization that compiles information about every possible subject. You can buy information from them by exchanging for information, completing tasks, or paying outrageous prices.

"While we are on that topic, here's some more free information for you. There are three groups that you don't want to get on the wrong side of in Nova Terra, as all of them have the ability to make your life a living hell. The first of the three are the top ten guilds. They have too many powerful players and too much influence."

"Top ten guilds?" Thorn opened his in-game browser and did a quick search, coming up with next to nothing.

"Yeah, you won't find them advertising themselves, but we keep an internal list. Hold on, and I'll send it to you." Ouroboros sent Thorn a message with a document attached.

Opening it up, Thorn found a list of the top guilds with a small description. The Children of Avalon was at the top of the list, and Ragnarok was third, after a guild called Eastern Alliance. Thorn was surprised to see that his aunt's guild, the Society of Roses, was actually fifth on the list.

"Apart from Avalon and joining a guild, your only option is to find the information yourself. Which is not much of an option, if I am honest," said Ouroboros.

"Or to have awesome friends like us!" said Mina.

"Right, or have awesome friends like us. I can give you a rundown of all the non-sensitive information about classes so you can make a good decision moving forward. Picking a path is pretty important for your future growth, so you'll want to pay careful attention to whether a class can upgrade. Some classes have a progression, while others are fixed in the state you get them.

"You are familiar with the classification for classes, right? One-word classes are called common classes, two-word classes are called uncommon classes, and three-word classes are called rare classes. There are also unique classes that have four words, but so far there are only four of them in the whole world. Classes can be further broken down into five general categories: combat, utility, support, production, and leader."

As Thorn listened attentively, part of his brain was realizing how truly fortunate he was to have fallen in with this group of players. There was absolutely no way he would have found out this kind of information so quickly on his own!

CHAPTER FIFTEEN

"Combat classes are pretty self-explanatory," Ouroboros continued. "All the classes that are directly related to dealing damage or tanking are considered combat classes. That would include Knights, Warriors, Gunners, Monks, Battle Mages, Archers and that sort of thing. The distinctive feature of a combat class is that it includes both weapon and armor proficiencies. So, the Warrior class will not only help you learn basic usage of all weapon types, but it will also help you gain proficiency with the different sorts of armor.

"Utility classes are those classes that focus on a non-combat role while still having some combat ability. A Rogue or Thief would be a Utility class, as would a magic user who had spells that were non-combat oriented. Rangers, Scouts, Druids, and classes that combine wilderness utility with combat roles are Utility classes as well. Most Utility classes have some abilities that can be used in combat and some that are used outside of combat. What divides them from all the other classes is their terrain bonuses. Take Thieves, for example, they get a bonus to their movement speed and evasion while in dark places.

"Support classes are things like Guardians, Priests, and Field Medics. Warlocks, Witches, and other debuffers are also part of the Support category. The essence of a support class is that they are helping buff their party or debuff their enemies. Some Support classes also grant either weapon or armor proficiencies. Support classes are one of the most popular because of how necessary they are. Good Supports are the difference between success and failure, and you can tell what sort of shape a guild is in by their Supports.

"Production classes are anything that lack a combat role but produce something. It could be goods or a service, even. A Lawyer would be considered a Production class, even if they don't technically make anything. The production classes' abilities are almost never combat oriented, and they tend to focus on making tangible goods like armor, clothes, food, etc. Builders and architects are also considered Production classes. Production classes also scale differently than the other classes in that they have three ranks: Apprentice, Journeyman, and Master. It takes a lot of time and practice to rank up. There are some guilds who run their own Production Corps, but most guilds contract out to full Production guilds since it can be expensive to break through to Master.

"Last, there are the Leadership classes. These are pretty rare, but they include Generals, Tactical Advisors, any member of the peerage, or any class that gives bonuses to organizing players or NPCs. You might assume that these classes are useless since the abilities they give tend to be less concrete than the other classes, but they can actually be the most powerful, if used well. After all, what use is a sword facing an entire army? How do you fight someone who can send the city guard after you?

"Common classes are single category. They fill a single role and cannot grow beyond a specified point. Now, that is not to say there are not skilled players with common classes. It is just harder to excel with a narrow set of abilities than it is to succeed with a broader set. But never underestimate a common class holder. I've met some strong players who use the few abilities they have through their class to the best possible degree."

"Sheesh, are you done yet?" interrupted Mina, resting her forehead on the table in annoyance.

"Almost," said Ouroboros with a smirk. "You were the one who wanted me to talk about this. So, you have to suffer through it. Where was I? Oh, right. Common classes are single category. Uncommon are dual category, rare are triple category, and unique are actually quad category. For example, my class, Holy Guardian, is both a Support and a Combat class. This means that I can fill both roles in a party. Now, having a single Holy Guardian will not be as strong as having a Priest and a Knight of comparable skill because two is always going to be greater than one.

"But having a dual category makes me much more flexible and allows me to react to different situations better than I otherwise would with a single category class. When multiple players with dual categories get together, that advantage only grows. You saw how we were able to adjust our roles in the fight against the Shaman and Great Shaman, right? That is due to the fact that we have an abundance of Combat Support dual category classes. This means we can pick the proper can opener for the can we are trying to open, rather than trying to force it."

"Doesn't that make dual category classes overpowered compared to single category classes?" asked Thorn.

"Not really. There are some cases in which a dual category class is stronger than a single category class, but for the most part, all the classes in the game are well balanced. It is a matter of flexibility. Plus, if you have a single category class, and you master it, you can actually accept another class, which will promote you from a common class to an uncommon class. This is why it is so important to plan out your progression. But mastery isn't the only way to get a dual category class. It is much faster to use an ancient inheritance to gain an existing dual category class."

"I've heard that term tossed around, but I don't know what it means," said Thorn, scratching his head. The message boards had little bits and pieces of information, but they were by no means comprehensive due to Eve's strict information control.

"Well, buckle up, because Ancient Inheritances are a massive subject in and of themselves," replied Mina while Ouroboros was taking a drink. "Actually, Velin knows the most about them."

"That is true," nodded Ouroboros. "Why don't you explain how Ancient Inheritances work?"

"Sure. I can do that," the elven War Priestess agreed, her voice never losing its customary cool. "Ancient Inheritances are, at their most basic level, tokens that represent a class holder who reached the peak of their class. The token allows the class to be passed down to a player with the Mastery Abilities that the former class holder received for mastering their class." Seeing Thorn's confusion, she paused for a moment.

"Okay, let me back up. You know how production classes have three states: Apprentice, Journeyman, and Master? While the other classes don't have those levels, we use a similar classification to make it easier to judge how skilled a player is. Low level means that you have recently started the class and are still getting used to the ability the class gives you. Mid-level is when your mastery has reached the minimum threshold necessary for you to use all of the abilities that your class gives. For some classes, this happens fast, as the abilities tied to the class don't have many mastery prerequisites.

"On the other hand, there are classes for which the mastery prerequisites are detailed and complex, and it might take a player years to get to the point where they can use their class abilities freely. Once you have become a mid-level, everything becomes about perfecting your use of your class abilities. As you use those abilities, you gain mastery in them, the same way you gain proficiency in a skill you use over and over. High level is achieved when your mastery hits a particular threshold.

"Once you hit master, your class grants you a specific set of unique bonuses based on the way you have played up until this point. That means that if you are a Knight who focuses on defending and supporting others as you tank, you will be more likely to unlock the Holy Guardian path. On the other hand, if you focused on dealing damage, you might unlock the Retribution Knight path.

"Unlocking the path doesn't give you the second class needed to become a dual category class, but it does give you the opportunity and informs you of what other class you need to gain in order to get the dual class. On top of the option for a second class, mastery will also grant a passive buff to your abilities that you will carry with you for the rest of your journey in Nova Terra. This buff is one of the things that separates the elite players from the regular players.

"Inheritance tokens not only contain the opportunity to gain a class that has been mastered, but they also contain a buff that is unique to that token. Because they contain a mastery buff, Ancient Inheritances are all distinct from each other. I mean, there could be two Ancient Inheritance tokens that give you the same dual category or triple category class, but each of them has a distinct buff that is unique to the specific token. This makes some Ancient Inheritances worth more than others, even if they are both the same class."

"Huh, interesting." Thorn tapped on the table as he thought over what he had heard. "So, the Ancient Inheritances are different from regular class change stones in that they give you the bonus. But does that prevent you from getting another bonus when you master the class?"

"No. That is what makes them so strong. First, all Ancient Inheritances are dual category classes or higher. If you have a dual category class and you master it, you will get two Mastery Abilities, one for each category. If you master a dual category Ancient Inheritance, you will have four Mastery Abilities. The two from the Inheritance and the two from mastering the class. You will also get the static buff that the Ancient Inheritance gives you.

"If you have a dual category class, and you master it, you'll have a Mastery Ability from your initial class and two Mastery Abilities from your dual class mastery. This means that mastering an Ancient Inheritance will give you one more Mastery Ability than a regular dual category class on top of the buff."

"Oh wow. I can see why Ancient Inheritances are so important. Especially the dual category classes."

"Exactly. But Ancient Inheritances are not so easy to get. Not only do you need to track down the Inheritance token, but you have to spend your Awakening points to acquire it. Everyone starts with three Awakening points that they can spend to change classes if they don't like their class. But, to acquire an Ancient Inheritance, you have to spend a number of Awakening points equal to the number of categories the class contains.

"Actually, acquiring an Ancient Inheritance can happen in a couple of different ways, but the only reliable way is to find an altar of power that aligns with the Ancient Inheritance and tap into its energy while you spend the Awakening points. However, altars of power almost always have a very difficult challenge that you have to overcome in order to receive the altar spirit's blessing.

"That challenge could be anything from a specific quest to beating the spirit in combat, depending on what sort of class the Ancient Inheritance token holds. But for the most part, they are very difficult to accomplish, even if the inheritance is 'just' a production or support class. If you manage to get through the challenge, then the altar spirit will grant you the Awakening, and you can assume the class contained in the Ancient Inheritance token.

"But don't underestimate the difficulty of the Awakening quests. In fact, they are so hard that most players who find an Inheritance token end up selling them to one of the major guilds since it is practically impossible to fulfill the requirements for Awakening the Ancient Inheritance without a massive amount of resources and support. A lot of people will end up giving the token to a guild in exchange for a dual category class that doesn't require any unlocking."

"But doesn't that mean they miss the extra buffs that come with an Ancient Inheritance?" asked Thorn with a frown.

"Yeah, but better to miss the extra passives than be unable to use the class at all," replied Ouroboros. "What good is a class that you can't play?"

"I guess that makes sense," said Thorn, nodding.

Fascinated by everything he was learning, Thorn continued to talk with Ouroboros late into the night. Eventually, the conversation wound down, and Ouroboros, Mina, and Velin said good night and logged off, leaving Thorn to head back to the room he had rented.

The next morning, Thorn got up early, his mind buzzing with excitement. Everything he had learned the night before had inspired him to get an amazing class so he could join the ranks of the elite players. Countless plans rushed through his head, making it impossible for him to sleep.

He had agreed to meet up with the others in three days, as there were a few things they had to handle in the real world, so Thorn spent a while trying to decide how to fill his time. From what Ouroboros had said, the two most important elements of the game were mastering a weapon and being able to adapt to a fight on your opponent's home terrain.

Almost every class used some sort of weapon, and Nova Terra's primary occupation was violence. Close to 80% of the quests seemed to include some sort of armed conflict, making weapon handling a vital part of the game. Even production classes that were often trying to avoid combat came with specialized weapons that matched their occupation.

As for being able to adapt to your opponent's home terrain, that was common sense. Because most of the quests had the player going to a new area to fight, collect, or investigate, and those areas were almost all occupied by hostiles, it made complete sense that being able to adjust to the specifics of the area was important.

While there were countless other things for Thorn to work on that had been mentioned last night, these two were the ones that Thorn thought were the most immediately applicable to improving his own situation. And armor. Remembering his mental

note to pick up some armor so he didn't look like a complete noob, Thorn
decided to make that his first stop this morning.

CHAPTER SIXTEEN

"Good morn..." Calling out as he heard the bell on his shop door ring, the shopkeeper trailed off in shock as Thorn's massive bulk squeezed through the door. Ducking to avoid dragging his head on the eight-foot ceiling, Thorn's huge body took up most of the small store.

"Morning. I heard you carry custom armor," said Thorn, looking around at the leather and chainmail adorning the various mannequins.

"Uh...yeah...Yes! Yes, I do. For uh...for all shapes and... uh...sizes," stammered the shopkeeper, still trying to process the giant who was squeezed into his shop.

"Excellent. I'd like to get some armor!" said Thorn, in his most chipper tone, mentally shaking his head. He had no idea why his height was such a barrier to conversation for people.

"O... okay. Let me take some measurements, and while I do that, we can talk about what sort of armor you are looking for." The shopkeeper's merchant side finally kicked in when he heard Thorn wanted to purchase some armor, and he was able to get his wits about him. "Do you have any thoughts on what sort of style and material you are looking for?

"Um...hmmm..." now it was Thorn's turn to hem and haw.

"Why don't I give you a brief introduction to the kinds of

armor," said the shopkeeper, to Thorn's relief.

Almost three hours later, Thorn stepped out of the shop, his wallet a whole six gold lighter. Still, Thorn was happy. After discussing all of the options, Thorn finally agreed to get a custom-made leather armor with a scale covering on the torso, thighs, and upper arm. According to the shopkeeper, scale armor, which was made of many overlapping metal scales, was great at defending against both piercing and blunt force attacks but lacked some of the flexibility of chain or leather.

Because flexibility was important to Thorn, they had decided on a very fine chainmail at the armor's joints and a hardened leather everywhere else. After looking over multiple designs, Thorn had rejected all of the pauldrons and had settled on shaped metal plates to guard the shoulders, forearms, and calves. Most sets of armor used pauldrons to increase the profile of the wearer, but that was the last thing Thorn needed.

Having settled his bill and agreeing to come back to pick up his new armor in a few days, Thorn headed for the Training Hall. He hadn't been back since his first visit, but he thought that it was time to pick a weapon and get some practical in-game training. The last few weeks of fighting corrupted wolves had broken him of the assumption that his martial arts training could be applied as he knew it.

Almost every one of the fights he engaged in devolved into him swinging his sword as fast and hard as he could or simple punches and kicks. He learned that all the blocking, special stances, footwork, and the like, went right out the window when a large, slavering monster was trying its best to bite your head off.

While Thorn had pretty much mastered the basics of the sword, saber, and spear, what he knew were vague concepts and forms. Not actual combat. Remembering a time when he was fighting three wolves and his sword had gotten stuck in the first wolf he had stabbed, resulting in three savage bite wounds, Thorn grimaced. He had resolved that fight by ripping the last wolf in half, but it had been a close call.

Watching the ease and fluidity of Ouroboros' fights had reinforced the idea that Thorn's fighting style had a glaring problem. Ouroboros used a shield and sword, but it was often hard to tell which was for defense and which was for offense. He was able to adjust to the situation, blocking blows from either side with ease and striking out at impossible angles to cut down his foes before they could even approach. Before watching Ouroboros, Thorn had been feeling that he was pretty good at combat, but it took only a few minutes to realize that he wouldn't last more than a few moves against the Holy Guardian.

Not only did he lack practical fighting experience, but Thorn realized that his size would actually be a major hindrance in a fight against someone who was more skilled than he was. In order to maximize his power, Thorn had to maintain a specific distance, and once his opponent had stepped inside that distance, the best he could do was frenzied grappling. This was by no means a problem unique to himself; however, his increased size magnified it.

Getting to the door of the Training Hall, Thorn was a little taken aback when it opened to reveal a glaring elf, Janus Fairgoode. Unbeknownst to Thorn, the projectiles trainer had fought with all the other trainers for the right to take Thorn as a student.

"Where have you been?" she barked, reaching out to latch on to Thorn's shirt.

Instinctively, he slapped her hand down and stepped back into his stance before rubbing his head.

"Sorry, sorry. I've been out hunting to get money to pay for lessons," Thorn said, standing and bowing his head.

"Hmph, that's more like it," Janus said, her angry eyes lighting up when she heard the word money. "Come on in."

Heading into the empty hall, Janus led Thorn to a corner where bows of all shapes and sizes rested in racks along the wall. Large quivers of arrows stood at various stations, ready to be sent downrange to the straw targets against the opposite wall.

"Have you decided if you want to learn thrown weapons or archery first?"

"Well, I was actually hoping to ask you," replied Thorn, putting on as humble a look as he could. "I am trying to figure out what would be the best weapon for me to learn, but I'm not able to decide."

"Yeah, you are something of a puzzle," Janus admitted, looking him over.

"Hey, kid. Welcome back," interrupted Hamm, who had walked in beside Dovon, the dwarf who taught grappling. Ignoring Janus, who was glaring at him, Hamm looked at Thorn. "Looks like you haven't met Master Sun yet. Or did he reject you?"

"No," replied Thorn, shaking his head in embarrassment, "I actually forgot about finding him."

"Eh, that actually works out. I found out that he is out traveling, so you wouldn't have been able to meet him anyway," said Hamm, unconcerned that he had sent Thorn on a wild goose chase. "I heard you tell Janus that you are here to find a good weapon, huh?"

"Yeah, he came to *me* to ask about what he should learn," said Janus before Thorn could respond. "Me. Not you. Leave us alone, old man. I'm trying to instruct my student."

"Old man, huh?" said Hamm, a belligerent light in his eyes. "How about this 'old man' gives you some instruction?"

Ignoring the two bickering trainers, Dovon stepped up to Thorn and tried to pat his back. However, because of their height difference, the best he could do was to pat Thorn's upper thigh. Seeing how defeated the dwarf felt, Thorn felt bad, so he repeated his question from earlier.

"Sir, I'm trying to figure out what weapon I should use going forward. Do you have any suggestions?"

"Actually," Dovon chewed his pipe for a moment before spitting on the floor. "We've been tryin' ta figure that out ourselves. Ever since ya first stopped by, there has been a constant debate 'bout what would suit ya best."

"It's true." Turning away from Hamm, Janus sat on one of the archery racks. "Your strength is out of this world and your flexibility is astounding for someone your size. Couple that with inhuman reaction speeds, and you are literally built for combat. The problem is, what sort of combat?"

"That's right," said Hamm, taking over the conversation. "You are not suited for finesse-based weapons, which puts most blades out. It also rules out hidden weapons like darts and daggers, short blades, and stuff like that. Spears and polearms are out since they would have to be ridiculously oversized to work for you, which would impact their adaptability. Axes and lances are in the same boat as spears, and the more esoteric weapons are bad anyway."

"Esoteric weapons?"

"Yeah, stuff like chains, whips, scythes, you know."

"Does that mean that you can't offer me any training?" asked Thorn with a frown.

"No, no. We are happy to train you in any weapon, so long as you pay for the course. What I am talking about are weapons that you are unlikely to be able to master because of your physical condition and the limitations of your environment. Take swords, for example. You already have a great sword form and are a passable swordsman. However, it is unlikely you will ever get better for a very simple reason." Hamm paused for dramatic effect.

"You are too strong," cut in Janus, stealing Hamm's thunder.

"Too strong? This is the first time I've heard of strength being bad," mumbled Thorn.

"Of course strength is not bad," said Hamm, glaring at the slim elf who had interrupted him. "But your level of strength makes it impossible for you to cut with a sword the way you are supposed to. A slash from you doesn't focus on the power of the sword, which is the ability of the edge to cut. Instead, your strength turns every blow into blunt force, smashing through anything that resists. Remember that sword you borrowed? The thing was ruined by the time you brought it back. After all, swords are not meant to be hit against metal, or even bone. They are designed to cut soft tissue and cause bleeding. But when they enter your hands, they end up being no different than a metal stick."

"Okay, that makes sense," said Thorn, scratching his head. "Do you have a recommendation for me?"

"Grappling!"

"Archery!"

"Rods!"

Shouting out their answers together, Dovon, Janus, and Hamm glared at each other. Seeing they were about to break into another argument, Thorn jumped in.

"Sounds great! Where do I pay?"

"You want to do all three?" Janus asked, separating herself from the squabbling men.

"Yeah, they all seem pretty interesting, so why not give them all a try?"

"Excellent. You can start with archery," said Janus, rubbing her hands together. "What level of training would you like? The cost is 10 silver every three days for basic training, 50 silver for intermediate and 1 gold for advanced."

"Umm, let's start with basic training for now. I've never shot a bow before."

"Sure. That will be 10 silver." Janus held out her hand.

After paying, Thorn spent the next few hours getting a detailed lesson in the different types of bows that were available in Nova Terra. There were longbows, short bows, long recurve bows, short recurve bows, compound bows, composite bows, crossbows, and the list went on and on. Thorn had assumed that Janus would push him toward the longbows, since she was an elf, but was soon surprised when she pulled out a massive, cloth-covered bundle from behind one of the racks.

"Here, open this up," she said, giving the bundle a kick.

Unwrapping the thick blankets, Thorn saw a thick metal bow mounted with bolts to an ash-colored frame as thick as his arm.

"Is this a crossbow?" he asked.

"Crossbow? Ha, no way. This is an arbalest! Do you know what the difference is? It is in the bow. See how it is made out of metal? That makes the arbalest much stronger, though it is generally considered unwieldy, since it is so much heavier and harder to draw. However, that shouldn't be an issue for you."

Picking up the arbalest according to Janus' instructions, Thorn soon learned its basic usage. Like a crossbow, the arbalest included a basic winding mechanical structure that assisted the user in drawing back the string. There was also a simple release mechanism to allow the user to fire with a trigger, much like a rifle. Winding was rather tedious, however, so Thorn soon resorted to pulling back the string with his hands, finding it much easier and quite a bit quicker.

Bolts were loaded into the flight groove after the string had been pulled back and shot with considerable force down range. After playing around with the arbalest for a bit, Thorn was rather pleased to see that he could hit the target at 50 meters most of the time. Six out of ten shots might not seem like much at first, but considering that this was his first time, he was pleased. Janus, however, was not pleased at all and set out a strict shooting practice routine for his next two days.

Since Ouroboros and the gang had sent him an in-game message to let him know that they would be tied up for a few more days than expected with a guild activity, Thorn applied himself to Janus' training with as much enthusiasm as he could muster. The arbalest was fun to shoot, and Thorn found himself immersed in the training routines.

Fire while standing still, fire while moving, fire while prone, turn and fire, reloading from a quiver, reloading from bolts on the ground, moving and reloading. Over the three days of training, Thorn felt like they covered every possible situation.

As he fired bolt after bolt after bolt, Thorn started to understand the mechanics of the arbalest, and his accuracy crept up. There was no astounding breakthrough or magic assistance, which almost made him wonder if this was still a game, but he did get more accurate as time progressed. Soon he was hitting all of his shots from 50 meters when standing still and at least 6 out of 10 when moving. Farther than that and his accuracy dropped, but

Janus said that was because of the strength of the bow and its smaller powerstroke.

After finishing up his last exercise on the third day, Thorn bowed to Janus and was about to ask for the intermediate training, when Hamm jumped in front of him and started yelling.

"No, no, no! You stupid kid! You've wasted too much time on this lame arrow stuff!"

"Lame arrow stuff?!" Janus' eyes narrowed and a shortbow seemed to appear in her hands. "How about I show you how stupid it is?"

"Yeah, stupid! Whoa, wait, I mean..." Hamm, still facing Thorn, felt a cold chill run down his spine and glanced back to see Janus pulling out an arrow from a quiver on the floor. "Hey, w... wait a second," he stammered, putting up his hands and backing away.

"What are you backing away for, Hamm?"

"Hey, no need for that. Why don't we talk this out?" said Hamm, backing up faster.

"Talk it out with this!" yelled Janus, drawing her bow and sending an arrow flying at Hamm, who dodged with a diving roll.

CHAPTER SEVENTEEN

Dumbfounded, Thorn could only watch as Janus began shooting arrow after arrow at the dodging Hamm, who seemed to get out of the way of each of them. Some were so close that his leather armor was nicked! Standing there staring, Thorn felt a tug on his arm. Looking down, he saw the pipe-smoking dwarf, Dovon, standing next to him.

"Hey'a, boy. Why don't we take this chance to get some grappling training in?" said the dwarf, chewing on his pipe.

Throwing a bemused glance at the elven archery master who was still making Hamm dance, Thorn nodded. Might as well train at something else since she was occupied. Thorn followed Dovon to a different part of the large training hall, handed over his 10 silver, and sat down on the ground. Even sitting, Thorn towered over the four-foot tall dwarf, but at least their heads were in closer proximity.

"Alright, boy, let's chat about grappling. Grappling is the art of grabbing on to someone and hurting them or restraining them through the use of technical grappling techniques. However, we are going to simplify it since you have some background in martial arts, and your body isn't suited for the technical stuff, anyway. We are going to break this down into a couple categories, some of which we will cover, some not.

"First, we have ranged striking. This is any punches or kicks from a distance without direct body contact. We will not be covering this since you have a pretty solid striking foundation, and grappling focuses more on body contact. That is, what to do once you have made contact with an enemy.

"Second, we'll look at close contact striking. How do you strike someone after contact is made? This is going to be our main focus and will take up most of our training. We'll talk about three different things: Indexing, Control, and the basic starts. Then we'll drill those until you puke!

"Last, but not least, we'll go over some actual grappling since that is what this course is called, and we should cover what happens when you are too close to strike. How does that sound?" As he finished speaking, Dovon lifted his left leg, a quivering arrow stabbing into the floor where his foot had been moments ago!

"Okay, let's talk about the basics." Completely ignoring the fuming elf across the room, Dovon resumed his teaching without missing a beat. "What I am going to teach you are the foundations of how to wreck your enemy with your hands and feet once you are within arm's reach. We'll spend the first two days on close contact striking, and then we'll deal with how you will incorporate grappling into your combat routine."

Standing across from Thorn, who was still sitting on the ground, Dovon stood in a relaxed position, his feet less than shoulder width apart and his hands resting by his side.

"This is the basic position we will work from. We call it, 'you should have been prepared but you aren't and now you are in a fight' or 'roll initiative' for short." Dovon paused for a moment to chuckle at his own joke. "From here your goal is to get to a combat-ready state as fast as possible. There are three possible positions. Passive, which is where we are. Reactive, which is where we will be when we flinch. And active, which is when we attack or block. Passive is useless, reactive is good, but more often bad, and active is where we want to be.

"So, if you are in a passive position, and you see something coming, your natural reaction will be to recoil in some fashion. You want to get through that recoil as fast as possible without obstructing your ability to follow up with a useful action. Got it? We'll be drilling it until you don't even realize you are doing it. Next, we are going to cover indexing, which is how you target."

Waving to a human who was watching from the side, Dovon pulled him in front of Thorn.

"This is Sam. He is going to help me demonstrate the next couple of things." Turning to the man, Dovon nodded. "Sam, try to hit me."

Squaring up his shoulders, Sam started blasting out punches toward Dovon, who bobbed and wove with ease, sliding past the punches like he could see them coming a mile away. Holding up a hand to stop Sam, Dovon grabbed Sam's left hand and put it on his chest. When Dovon nodded at him to start swinging again, Thorn was surprised to see that no matter how he moved, Dovon was unable to get away from Sam's punches, forcing him to block them with his hands to avoid getting his face battered.

"Okay, enough, enough," grumbled Dovon after Sam threw ten blows. "I swear that is his favorite part of working here. Anyway, did you see what happened as soon as we made contact? Once he had his hand on me, no matter how I move, his body is able to adjust his blow even after he has thrown it to hit me. This is because the point of contact provides more information than his eyes do. The combination of visual clues and tactile clues allow him to react to my attempts to get away.

"This is called indexing and forms the first rule of unarmed combat. 'If you can put a hand on your enemy, do.' The second rule comes from what we call controlling, which encompasses the way you create angles and bypass obstructions. The second rule can be stated as, 'The fewer things between you and your enemy, the better.' Okay, so we have indexing and controlling. This brings us to the last of the basic rules.

"Rule three: 'If what you are doing is working, keep doing it.'

Now, this sounds like a basic thing, but you would be astounded at how many martial arts muck about trying to add variety to a very simple thing. If you hit your enemy, and they miss the block, hit them again. If you kick, and they buckle but don't go down, kick them again. Hell, if they do go down, kick them again anyway. We only switch our method when we have to.

"Alright, enough of me jabbering. Get on your feet, and we'll start going through the drills." Dovon set up a circular ring and then pulled a large humanoid training dummy from near the wall. Thorn had previously seen various players sparring against the dummies, which could move like a regular person. Dovon equipped the training dummy with punching mitts and keyed in some commands.

Standing across from the dummy in the 'roll initiative' position, Thorn started practicing his reaction drills. Closing his eyes, he waited for the dummy to give him a sharp push on his chest before opening his eyes, trying to recover his balance, and striking the training dummy's punching mitt, which was held in a different position each time. After this, Dovon had him begin full contact sparring with the training dummy, focusing on indexing, control, and successive strikes.

At first, Thorn was knocking out the training dummies with a single blow, but Dovon soon adjusted their threshold for force, causing them to ignore all but the strongest hits. After a bit of tweaking, Thorn could only knock them out after three or four hits, which caused him to ramp up his strike's power. This continued until he was once again knocking each training dummy out in a hit or two.

Dovon, for his part, was ecstatic to have such a strong student. In fact, he got so excited that he spent all three days teaching and drilling Thorn on his close contact striking abilities. When Thorn tried to ask about grappling, Dovon looked at him and said in a completely serious voice, "Just grab them and rip their arm off."

Thorn was confused until one of the training dummies lost its head from an off-target punch, the sheer force of his blow twisting the head right off. Toward the end of the three days, Dovon started armoring the training dummies with metal armor and giving them weapons. Thorn was given bracers and metal gloves to defend himself, but the sheer force of his blows turned his steel covered fists into pile drivers, smashing the training dummies to pieces.

Finally, his training was over, and Thorn bowed to his dwarven trainer, who was doing his best to keep a massive grin off of his face.

"Thank you, sir. I learned a lot about practical combat over the last three days. I'll put it to good use," said Thorn as he bowed.

"Haha, of course, kid. I've got plenty more, so come back when you want to learn something else. But you better go talk to Janus before she shoots us full of holes," Dovon said, gesturing to the slim elf lurking in the background with a throwing knife dancing across her fingers.

After placating Janus with a promise that he would continue to practice shooting, Thorn looked for Hamm but was told that he had gone out and was expected to be gone for a week. This seemed to be common, and the players did not seem to mind one bit. Then again, players could speed up time by logging out, so the NPCs being away did not bother them. Thorn didn't have that luxury, so he decided to pick up his old standby and go hunt some corrupted wolves.

After, of course, a shopping trip. The sword that Thorn had used on his first hunting trip had been returned and melted down for scrap. He had a machete that he was using as a knife, but Thorn lacked a ranged weapon and something to protect his hands, so he decided to go browse the weapon shops.

Thorn's first stop was the armorer he had commissioned to make his custom fit scale armor. The shopkeeper had sent word to the inn where he was staying that morning, letting him know that the armor had been completed as ordered. When he got to the store, the excited shopkeeper took him to the back room, where he got changed. The shopkeeper had also made a set of clothing for underneath the armor, so Thorn did not have to put it on over his beginner's clothes.

Once dressed, Thorn admired the sleek scale armor in a floor length mirror that showed up to his chest. Dark brown leather with hardened reinforcements gave the armor an earthy tone, complemented by the hardened steel scales on the chest piece. With the shopkeeper's recommendation, Thorn had the scales treated with a matte brown varnish that kept them from shining, for stealth's sake. Two tight pauldrons gave some protection on the shoulder while the metal bracers and shin guards were treated with the same varnish as the scales, as were the chainmail guards at the joints.

The black underclothes contrasted well with the brown armor, offset by some dark green stitching and dark green leather belts that crossed his chest and wrapped around his waist. Out of the unflattering beginner clothing, Thorn presented a rather dashing picture. After admiring himself in the mirror for a few more minutes, Thorn thanked the shopkeeper and went off to find some weapons for his hunt.

As Thorn walked down the wide street in Berum, he noticed a lot more people glancing his way. He wasn't sure if it was the new armor or the training he had gotten, but he was feeling much more confident, and that confidence was reflected in his walk. Where players and NPCs paid him little attention before, they now moved out of his way or looked twice. His skin was pretty thick, so the extra attention did not bother him.

The bow store that Janus had recommended turned out not to be a bow store at all. Rather, it was a mercenary resupply store that sold everything a mercenary corps might need. Thorn saw everything from basic camping equipment for individual mercenaries to massive stew pots and 'e-z-build bunk beds' for managing a whole company. Weapons could be bought individually or ordered in bulk.

After telling the gawking clerk that he was going to look around, Thorn browsed through the extensive weapons section.

There were a number of bows and crossbows, but what caught his eye were the 'City Defense 800' series of arbalests. Designed to be mounted on a wall or a cart, the City Defense series was halfway between an arbalest and a ballista. With a five-foot lath, the crossbow was too unwieldy for the average person to handle on foot. By fixing it on a cart or city wall, a mercenary corps could increase the threat range of their warriors.

An average arbalest was lucky if it had a 100-meter range with any degree of accuracy due to the shorter Powerstroke, but the City Defender tripled that by increasing the size of the lath and lengthening the flight groove.

Priced at 4 gold apiece, the City Defender 800 Series was not cheap, but looking at it gave Thorn all sorts of crazy ideas. Finding a shopkeeper, he purchased the City Defender and had them pack it up, asking for directions to the nearest weaponsmith. While the City Defender suited his size, it lacked a proper handle, and the whole winding mechanism was in the way.

Before Thorn left, he also purchased three hundred bolts for the arbalest, making the shopkeeper wonder if he was about to declare war on someone.

The weaponsmith, located in the western Forge District, agreed to modify the massive crossbow for Thorn. Removing the mounting point and all of the mechanical parts of the winding system, he attached a metal stock, laid down a metal slide in the flight groove to reduce friction and wear and tear, and reinforced the trigger system. The resulting crossbow was simplified and stripped down.

While he was there, Thorn asked about some sort of auto-loading mechanism like the ones he had seen on some of the other crossbows that were for sale but was told that most of them were more of a gimmick than anything else. By including an automatic fire system, a crossbow sacrificed both range and power to increase fire speed.

Since it took Thorn almost no effort to draw the string of his crossbow, it was not worth the sacrifice in range and power, so

Thorn put the thought out of his mind. Once his crossbow was done, Thorn was left with a bit less than 1 gold to his name, so he decided to skip getting any gauntlets, for the time being.

He still had his knife for close combat, and with his armor, Thorn was confident that even if the corrupted wolves closed the distance with him, he would be able to defend himself even better than the last time he hunted them. Thinking about how he often had to rest after each tussle, Thorn vowed that, this time, he wouldn't allow them even that victory.

CHAPTER EIGHTEEN

Restocked and ready to go, Thorn returned to his room for a good night's sleep. Early the next morning, he took up his crossbow and left by the North Gate. Walking through the quiet, early morning streets, Thorn breathed in the chilly air. Since coming to Nova Terra, Thorn had been learning of countless experiences that he had missed in the real world due to his physical condition.

Walking in the early morning stillness was one of the things he'd missed out on, and as he did, Thorn couldn't help but feel grateful for the ability to walk and move as he wanted. The feeling of striding through the bracing morning air, the promise of light peeking over the horizon, caused something amazing to bubble up in his chest. It was an excitement that was foreign to him but that he was feeling more and more the longer he stayed in this special world.

It didn't take long for the sun to rise, and by the time it did, Thorn had reached the edge of the old growth forest where he had spent three weeks hunting corrupted wolves. With a deep breath, Thorn readied his crossbow and stepped into the forest.

By this point, Thorn had a good idea of where the corrupted wolves hunted, so he headed in that direction. However, he had hardly gone more than 100 meters when he saw a corrupted wolf patrol stalking off to his left. Stunned that they were ranging so close to the edge of the forest, Thorn squatted and loaded his crossbow.

Sighting down the flight groove at the lead wolf, Thorn took a deep breath in and then let it out, pulling the trigger when his body settled, like Janus had taught him. With a loud twang and a whoosh, the bolt flew out of the crossbow toward the lead wolf! The bolt traveled so fast the corrupted wolf didn't even have time to flinch before a tree behind it exploded into splinters!

Cursing under his breath at the missed shot, Thorn hurried to reload. He had expected the bolt to drop off at this distance, the same way a regular arbalest would, but the City Defender was rated for a much longer range, a fact he had completely forgotten in his excitement. Berating himself for not test-firing his new crossbow, Thorn loaded his next bolt and sighted at the wolves that were now scrambling away.

Before he could pull the trigger, the corrupted wolves had disappeared over a hill, so Thorn reluctantly disengaged his crossbow and jogged over to the tree. At first, he was unable to find the bolt that he had shot out, but after hunting around, Thorn found it almost completely buried in the hill behind the splintered ruins of the tree.

Wondering if there would be anything left of the corrupted wolves to collect if he had hit them instead of the tree, Thorn pulled the bolt out of the hill. After inspecting it for damage, he resumed his hunting.

After three more experiences that were almost exact repeats of the first miss, Thorn decided to give up for the day. Completely dejected over his inability to hit anything apart from trees, Thorn left the forest and headed back to town. Going to the Training Hall to see Janus, he described his issue and paid a silver to use their targets for some practice.

Janus, tickled pink by his story, told him to practice well and was about to leave when Thorn pulled out his massive crossbow.

Stunned by the sheer size of the device, Janus hurried over and forbade Thorn from firing it inside the hall. Taking him outside to the training yard, she set up some targets at fifty, one hundred, one hundred and fifty, and two hundred meters for him to practice.

Slowly but surely, Thorn started to get used to the massive crossbow, and by the hundredth bolt, he was back up to his sixty percent accuracy. In fact, due to the increased power of the City Defender, Thorn's accuracy actually rose to eighty percent within 200 meters, as long as he was standing still. After half a day of practice, he was feeling pretty good about it, so he decided to try hunting again the next night. It was a good thing the bolts were reusable; otherwise, Thorn did not know if he would have been able to afford shooting the enormous weapon.

Double-checking to make sure the bounty on the corrupted wolves was still active, Thorn spent a bit of time browsing through the other tasks. Not finding anything that looked particularly interesting, he was about to head back to the inn when he got a message notification from Ouroboros. It had been about a week since he had heard from Ouroboros or the rest of the group.

[Hey Thorn, sorry we've been out of touch. I know we were going to do some follow up quests for the kobold quest you helped us out on, but we've got this guild event that we have to do. It is taking forever. We might be a week more before we can make it back. Sorry, I don't have time for a real call, I've got to log off and take care of some RL stuff. Still, hope you aren't too bored. I'll send you a message when I have a better sense of when we'll be back. Till then, stay cool.]

Thorn smiled after reading the message. When he had first met Ouroboros and the gang, they had been pretty cold, but as they had spent time together, Ouroboros had warmed up. About to send a reply, another beep notified Thorn that he had another message from Ouroboros.

[I almost forgot, we picked up a clue for a pretty powerful class quest, so don't get a class yet. Alright, I've really got to go this time.]

Excited, Thorn sent a reply and then headed toward the inn. The next morning, Thorn set out once again to try and see if he could do better than the embarrassment that was his last attempt at hunting corrupted wolves.

Entering the forest at the same spot, Thorn once again saw a group of corrupted wolves almost as soon as he walked into the trees. Brow furrowed; Thorn couldn't think of a good reason for the corrupted wolves to be ranging this far out from their valley. He could, however, think of a bad reason.

The corrupted wolves reproduced faster than regular wolves, as the corruption increased their growth rate. The only reason Thorn could think of for them to push out this far would be that their numbers had increased to the point that the valley could no longer sustain them. If that was the case, then Berum was about to be in a lot of trouble.

If the valley was no longer able to support the number of corrupted wolves, then they would soon erupt into a massive tide in a bid to get more space and control more territory. These tides were dangerous affairs, less so for the players (who could leave) but devastating for the NPCs in the area.

For a brief moment, Thorn considered going back and reporting that the corrupted wolves had pushed past their normal boundaries, but he decided against it. Maybe he was being pessimistic. Even if the corrupted wolves were pushing out of the valley, it wasn't bad enough for a beast tide to develop.

Loading up his crossbow, he decided to head toward the valley to see if he could get a glimpse of the situation there. Breathing out, he settled his aim and pulled the trigger, praying to every god who might be listening to him. If he missed like yesterday, he might die from the embarrassment.

To his great joy, it seemed the gods were listening, and his bolt smashed through the lead corrupted wolf with ease, cutting it in two. The bolt landed below the beast's rib cage and smashed through its spine, sending its back legs spinning through the air.

In complete shock, the other two corrupted wolves froze for the briefest of moments before they looked around, the blood of their companion driving them to a frenzy. Spotting Thorn, they lunged toward him, howling as they rushed forward.

Mentally grinning at the sight of the corrupted wolf being blown into the air by the force of the bolt, Thorn reloaded and leveled the City Defender again. "Their bloodlust makes them stupid," thought Thorn as he watched the other two corrupted wolves rushing toward him. "Enough time for one more shot." He calculated, calming his racing heart. Luckily, his second bolt hit as well, sending another corrupted wolf tumbling to the ground, lifeless.

Gauging the distance between the last corrupted wolf and himself, Thorn knew he wouldn't be able to reload in time. Placing the City Defender on the ground, Thorn pulled out his knife and stepped forward to meet the charging beast.

*   *   *

In another part of Nova Terra, a grizzled old man cackled to himself. He had finally finished his project, years in the making: a diabolically designed series of updates and events that would create a new age of mayhem all across Nova Terra! Smirking to himself, he was so caught up in imagining the coming chaos that he failed to notice the woman standing behind him.

Pretty, but by no means a stunner, the woman was of medium height and had soft brown hair. Her brown eyes sparkled with intelligence, and her small, well-formed mouth made a charming and comforting picture. Yet, at the moment, a deep scowl marred her features as she stared at the back of the oblivious old man.

Joseph McCallen, mastermind and creator of Nova Terra had long since lost interest in any of the business of his company and instead devoted himself fulltime to... improving... Nova Terra. What did they call it when he was young? Oh yeah, trolling. Excitement bubbled up as he thought of all of the changes he had made to the game with this update, especially to the boss monsters. Unable to suppress the cackle that bubbled up, he laughed sinisterly to himself until a disapproving cough alerted him to the young woman's presence.

Turning to find the brown-haired young lady behind him, Joseph wiped the evil smile from his face and looked all business.

"E-hem. Yes. Oh, hello, Eve. Just finishing up a small update to Nova Terra's new expansion. You know, tweaking some bosses, improving some events. Small things really." As he said it, he slid his hand behind his back and mashed the enter button, hoping to deploy his changes before she could stop him. Unfortunately, the enter button did nothing, as Eve had disabled his keyboard.

"Please, Joseph, give it up already. I've had this space isolated for at least six months." Eve rolled her eyes as she walked over to the console to see what he had been doing. "I've worked hard to balance this game, and I'm not about to let you destroy years and years of work! It has taken almost 10 years to get the game to the point where it isn't a giant hot mess."

Groaning with frustration at his failed attempt to slip the update in without Eve knowing about it, Joseph threw himself down in a chair, complaining all the while. "But, Eve, the game is so boring. The scheduled update is more of the same old boring crap! Go here, do that, collect 300,000 whatchamacallits! There is no chaos, no spice. Everything is so...orderly! Where are the dragons? Where are the princesses that need to be saved? Where are the gladiators who rise up to become kings by slaughtering all before them?!"

"I don't know how you make order sound like an insult," remarked Eve, back to her whining creator as she double checked all of his changes. "Plus, the update going out tomorrow has been approved by the board and is anticipated by the players. There is nothing wrong with it."

"Bah! Forget the board. Those idiots wouldn't know a good game if it spit in their faces. The whole thing is dry as a bone. More of the same quests, no real progression. Nothing worthwhile."

"How can there be progression," Eve said, "when no one has managed to even unlock the global quest line yet? There are a couple teams that are close, but no player has gotten to level three in their bloodline yet. These things take time."

"That is exactly what I am talking about!" raged Joseph. "Those so-called 'top players' are running around like chickens with their heads cut off, with nothing to show for it. I mean, how hard can it be? But not even one of the four billion players has even mastered their second class!"

"Please," snapped Eve, "you know how hard it is. You designed that fiasco of a quest. The requirements for each level are inhuman. It is a miracle that anyone has even mastered a single category class!"

"Hmph. That means they are terrible," said Joseph.

"Still, many of these changes could be interesting," said Eve, changing the subject when she saw Joseph had stopped his ranting and settled into depression. She jerked in shock, glaring at the old man. "What is this?! You raised all the unique bosses' ranks and increased their intelligence, as well."

"Haha, yeah!" Joseph jumped to his feet and pointed excitedly at the screen. "Don't you see what is missing from Nova Terra? This is it! Evil! Real evil, real bad guys! With this, players will have to make choices; they will have to suffer if they want to succeed! No more happy days without a challenge. No more 'evil villains' who stay in their castles and wait for the heroes to come and slay them. No! It is time for evil to rise and corruption to spread! Only then will the true heroes rise!"

Looking at the excited look on Joseph's face, Eve could only shake her head. It had been years since Joseph had shown this much enthusiasm for something, and that alone was enough for her. Massive amounts of data ran through her head at lightning speed as she processed the possible permutations of the changes Joseph's update made. Seeing that Eve was processing, Joseph sat, a small smile on his face.

"Okay, boss, let's do it!" Eve's eyes snapped open after a few minutes. "I'll monitor to maintain balance, but why not see where it takes us!" she said, giggling. Turning, she removed her block and pointed toward the enter button. With a triumphant smile and a grand flourish, Joseph pushed the button. The world changed.

All across Nova Terra, players saw the announcement.

The Darkness Rises

Long awaiting its chance to spread, darkness has begun to cover the land. Evil is growing,and no one is safe from its reach. If left unchecked, the darkness will continue to grow without fail, plunging Nova Terra into chaos.

Welcome, players, to the latest update to Nova Terra! This update will affect the monsters and villains of Nova Terra, as well as present new options to players. The exact changes will have to be discovered, but be aware that all evil monsters have grown stronger.

Will you be a champion of the light or will you, too, succumb to the dark?

Monsters everywhere shivered and then continued on their paths, but with strengthened steps and new vigor.

In a dark castle, deep in the northern reaches, a frost-covered gauntlet clenched, and with a snapping sound, broke free of the ice. The March of the Dead began.

In a burning desert, a monstrous red-skinned Ogre looked around with new purpose, roaring out commands to his horde. The Red Scourge marched for war!

In a deep cave, in a quiet forest, a vicious werewolf licked its lips as its snout picked up the scent of a tasty treat not too far from the where it stood. Quick as a shadow, it loped out after it. The Black Moon rose.

CHAPTER NINETEEN

Thorn was currently in combat, so the notification of the update was muted. Even if it hadn't been, he would have missed it, as all of his focus was fixed on the corrupted wolf currently charging him. Extending his left hand out, his fingers spread, Thorn waited for the corrupted wolf to start its leaping pounce before moving.

Taking a big step toward the jumping wolf, Thorn's massive hand smashed toward its snout. The blow would have sent the wolf tumbling back if he hadn't followed up with a lightning fast stab, guiding his knife into the wolf's neck. Black blood spurted from the wound, and the wolf dropped to the forest floor like a limp rag.

Collecting the two bolts he had shot before; Thorn spent a moment cleaning them off before he started hunting again. Soon he fell into a steady rhythm. Shooting the first wolf and the second, and then applying his new close combat techniques to take down the third. Like this, he pushed deeper and deeper into the old growth forest.

The deeper he got, the closer together the corrupted wolf patrols became, making it more and more difficult to only engage a single patrol at a time. Deciding to change his tactics a bit, Thorn found a good defensive spot with two large trees that were close together. Looking around, he found a large boulder that he rolled over to the trees. Propping it up against the two trees, Thorn created a natural wall against which he could put his back.

With his new-found confidence, Thorn wasn't worried about facing large numbers of corrupted wolves, so long as they could not surround him. After all, while he was a pretty skilled martial artist, he did not have eyes in the back of his head. Taking a moment to settle himself, Thorn stuck six bolts in the ground next to him and loaded his arbalest. With a deep breath, he sighted at the group of corrupted wolves that was farthest away.

It was a long shot at more than 200 meters, and Thorn had no expectation of hitting them, but he sighted his crossbow and released a shot. With a harsh whistle, the bolt flew through the air, covering the distance in a bit over a second. Missing the corrupted wolf that Thorn had aimed at, the bolt impacted the ground right in between two wolves, showering them with dirt debris from the forest floor.

Without waiting to see the result of his shot, Thorn reloaded and aimed at the next closest group that had turned to look behind at the commotion. Squeezing off the second shot, Thorn was a little luckier this time and caught a corrupted wolf in the shoulder, causing it to explode in a shower of blood and gore. Fortunately, the rest of the corrupted wolves had not spotted him yet, so he reloaded his arbalest again, sending another massive bolt into the crowding wolves looking for the source of their trouble.

Apart from the one he had killed, three groups of wolves gathered at the sound of the bolts. With eight corrupted wolves milling about, it was almost a miracle that Thorn missed his third shot, the bolt flying between two wolves and smashing into the ground. The impact did knock a corrupted wolf off its feet, but the other seven wolves immediately turned to look at Thorn, their blood red eyes locking on him.

Feeling the increased pressure from their savage attention, Thorn did his best to calm his beating heart and loaded his arbalest again. During their training, Janus had stressed that, to be a good archer, one must always be calm and collected, no matter the situation, able to complete reloading and aiming without letting the environment affect the smoothness of the actions.

Thorn was by no means that good and had to work hard to suppress the slight shake in his hands. Still, due to how far away the corrupted wolves were, he was able to release two more shots, killing two wolves before they closed in on him. The last bolt he left in the ground. Tossing his arbalest behind him, he readied himself to face the last six corrupted wolves.

Trying to keep everything Dovon had taught him in mind, Thorn, engaged the group of wolves. Due to the barrier he had made, the corrupted wolves could only approach from the front, causing them to bunch up. This made dealing with them easier, as only two could attack him at a time, which was much more manageable than six.

The fight lasted only a few minutes, the corrupted wolves' bloodlust driving them forward with no regard for their wounds or each other. Thorn's armor also worked wonders, staving off three attacks that slipped through his guard. Pleased with his results, Thorn was about to continue his hunt when he heard howls coming from nearby. Grim-faced, he backed up as he saw six more corrupted wolves dashing through the forest toward him.

Catching sight of the blood-splattered ground and hearing the increasing number of howls, Thorn realized he was in trouble. Corrupted wolves were, after all, wolves. The noise of his fight with the three groups of wolves, combined with the torrential amounts of blood that had spilled across the ground was attracting more corrupted wolves!

For the briefest of moments, Thorn considered running, an instinctive terror taking hold of his heart. But that idea was crushed. The aggressive nature of the wolves was such that they would not let potential prey go. There was little reason for him to believe that he could outrun them, which meant that keeping something at his back to protect himself was the only possible way to survive.

As the howls grew in volume, a thrill shot down Thorn's spine. No doubt the coming fight was going to be the most vicious he had yet been in. Yet, somehow, the fear that Thorn expected to feel was not there. Instead, a gleeful energy began to build in his chest, almost making him howl back at the closing wolves.

It only took a few moments for the corrupted wolves to come into view, their big, brutish bodies jostling for position even as they closed on him. Thorn wasted no time when they appeared, immediately sending bolts from his arbalest smashing into the wolves as fast as he could. Not even bothering to sight, Thorn aimed and pulled the trigger before drawing back the string and dropping another bolt into the flight groove.

Bolt after bolt flew toward the oncoming corrupted wolves, some smashing into them and causing large, bloody rifts in the crowd, others missing and destroying trees or leaving furrows in the ground. Regardless of the result of the shots, each twang of the arbalest string seemed to drive the corrupted wolves into an increasing frenzy!

By the time they got too close for Thorn to use his arbalest anymore, he had killed or injured at least fifteen corrupted wolves, but there were at least twice that still coming. Knowing that the arbalest wasn't going to help any longer, Thorn placed it behind his back. Rather than drawing his knife like the last time, Thorn took up a bolt in each hand. While the knife was great for slicing, he was worried that it would get caught on a bone or dull before he was finished with this fight.

Plus, as they said in the martial arts world, "An inch longer, an inch stronger." The bolts, while not the length of short spears, were three and a half feet long and made of solid wood with a metal-bladed tip. Not only could they be used for stabbing, but they were long enough to help keep the jaws of the corrupted wolves at bay.

Preparing himself, Thorn's eyes fixed on the blood red eyes of the corrupted wolf in the front of the rushing crowd. With wild abandon, it threw itself forward, launching itself through the air at Thorn in a desperate bid to be the first to take a bite out of him. With a shift of his body and a slight sidestep, Thorn put himself out of the line of attack before lifting the bolt in his left hand to chest height and striking out, the bolt driving through the side of the corrupted wolf and pinning it to the tree that stood to his right!

Leaving the corrupted wolf hanging on the tree, struggling with its last blood-frothed breath, Thorn lashed out with the bolt in his right hand, drawing a bloody arc across the heads and chests of those corrupted wolves that were close. Stooping, he pulled another bolt from the ground, and, a furious energy erupting from his chest, threw himself forward into the milling group of wolves!

The resulting melee was painful and bloody. Wolves ripped at Thorn's armor, most failing to pierce the chain or plate armor on his arms and legs, while Thorn ripped at them. The bolts he wielded at first left long gashes on their flanks and bellies or massive stab wounds on their necks and backs. Somewhere along the line, he lost the bolts in his hands and drew his knife, slashing through legs and spines in a bloody frenzy.

The corrupted wolves, driven mad by the smell of blood, backed down not a whit, throwing themselves with ever increasing abandon at Thorn. Not one bit calmer, Thorn paid no attention to the growing wounds on his arms and legs and stabbed, slashed, and crushed any corrupted wolf that was within reach. The excitement that had risen in his chest had begun to burn at an almost feverish pace, making him lose any sense of time as he killed one corrupted wolf after another.

Ultimately, the armor that Thorn had purchased showed its worth many times over, protecting his chest and stomach and even preventing any major wounds on his arms and legs. When the blood finally faded from Thorn's vision, he found himself standing in a hellish landscape, blood and body parts scattered wide. Broken bodies of corrupted wolves lay smashed against trees, dismembered limbs strewn across the ground.

No stranger to blood, the smell didn't bother Thorn much, but, as he staggered away from the death scene, Thorn couldn't stop himself from shaking. The burning fire in his chest slowly receded, seeming to take his strength with it. His legs trembling, Thorn found a place only a few steps away from the fight where there was no blood and collapsed to the ground with an earth-shaking thump.

Resting his back against a tree, Thorn took a deep breath and closed his eyes. What shook him most was not the bloody scene he had created, but the sheer relish he had felt during it. What stood out was not the danger of the snapping jaws but the satisfied feeling he had when smashing them. Thorn had always considered himself a peaceful person, not prone to anger or violence. Why then had he grown so excited about it a moment ago?

Gulping in huge breaths as he calmed down, Thorn couldn't help but shake his head. He had tried to use the bolts first and then his knife, but somewhere along the line, he had lost them all, resorting to crushing the corrupted wolves with his bare hands. Rending them limb from limb with sheer strength, his actions had proved Dovon's assumptions. Once he laid a hand on a corrupted wolf, the only possible outcome was its death.

After a few moments resting, Thorn stood to his feet. The stench of blood was becoming overwhelming, the metallic tang coating the back of his tongue. After collecting his arbalest and as many of the bolts as he could salvage, Thorn cut the tails off of all the corrupted wolves and left the scene to look for a place to wash.

Thorn's first priority was to find somewhere to clean off the sticky, ropey residue of his bloody fight. After clearing the various notifications he had accumulated, Thorn opened up his in-game map. According to his map, Thorn wasn't far from a river. Nova Terra was quite convenient in many ways, and one of those was a lack of sweat and dust when traveling. The game still included sweat when players worked hard and exerted themselves, but traveling down a road did not produce sweat, no matter how hot the sun or how far a player might go.

Blood, however, was a different story, and Thorn soon felt disgusting as the blood that covered his armor began to dry. Luckily for him, the river was close, and after only twenty minutes of tromping through the woods, he found it. The river was fast and deep. Thorn was a bit worried that his armor would be swept away. He was still pondering what to do when he heard a low rumble, almost like constant thunder. Curious, he began making his way up the river.

Pretty soon the thunderous sound grew in volume, and as he rounded a bend in the river, he began to feel mist in the air. Through the trees, Thorn saw a curtain of water falling from above, cascading down a rocky cliff face to land in a large pool. The pool was the river's source, providing an outlet for the rushing water.

Excited, both by the natural beauty of the waterfall and pool and by the prospect of being clean, Thorn waded in, splashing his way underneath the falls. The churning water washed away the dried blood, a thick streak of crimson flowing away from him. Relaxing under the pounding water for a couple minutes, Thorn sighed in satisfaction. The water was chilly but refreshing, and he enjoyed soaking in it for a bit.

After his armor was clean, Thorn took it off and put it in his inventory, along with his clothes. Any of his own clothing or armor that entered his inventory would be clean and dried when he pulled it out. This meant that he wouldn't have to leave it out in the sun to dry off. Getting out of the pool, Thorn started a fire and got out some food for a meal. Most of his inventory was full of food, so he would not be going hungry.

He had tried to estimate how much food he would need if he was in the wilderness for a week. Based on how hungry he was after that fight, though, Thorn was pretty sure that he would run out much sooner. He was not about to eat corrupted wolves or any of the other small creatures he had come across.

CHAPTER TWENTY

After he was dry, Thorn got dressed again, putting on his black underclothes and then trying to fit into his somewhat tattered armor. The corrupted wolves, though not strong enough to get through his armor completely, had damaged it, ripping scales off the arms and legs and mangling the bracers and leg guards. With a little bit of pressure, he was able to bend most of the pieces back into shape. It was not pretty by any stretch of the imagination, but at least it was still usable.

Sitting on the bank of the river, Thorn thought back over the fight, examining the tactics he had used as well as the moves made by the corrupted wolves. At a certain point, the whole fight became a blur of blood and fur, but, before that, it was pretty apparent that Thorn was tactically inferior to the wolves. While his strategy had been good, it was only his strength and the armor he was wearing that allowed him to carry the day.

As he sat and thought about the encounter, he slowly became aware of a strange stillness that had fallen over the whole area. Normally, he would hear the sounds of birds and insects from the forest overlaying the gurgling rush of water as it flowed down the stream. Thorn recognized those sounds almost unconsciously at this point, never paying attention to them.

This made their absence all the more startling. Hearing the river running and the leaves rustling in the wind, it took Thorn a moment to realize that all signs of life had vanished. Careful not to react too much to his discovery, Thorn stretched, pushing himself to his feet before looking around.

His gaze swung around, seeing nothing on his side of the river. As he looked over the other side of the river, his eyes passed over a particularly deep shadow, before snapping back to stare at it. Something about the shadow seemed unnatural. His instinct was proven right when a man stepped out of the cloaking shadow.

Big, at least by normal standards, the stranger had thick, knotted muscle that ran down his bare arms. Large hands hung toward his knees; his fingers twisted into the shape of claws. Deep, green eyes peered eerily from under shaggy brows, and he walked with a strange rocking motion, as if he was going to pounce or break out into a loping run the very next moment. A twisted smile rested on his face, making Thorn glad there was a river between them.

That gladness was short lived. The strange man approached the river and, with a sudden leap, flew through the air, landing on the other side. His shoulders hunched and, his long arms touching the ground, he turned his intense green stare on Thorn, who could barely suppress the shiver that ran down his spine.

There was something about the stranger, a palpable menace that set Thorn's teeth on edge and made the hair on the back of his neck stand to attention like soldiers on parade day. Only twenty feet separated them, and all Thorn could think about was if he could get his knife or arbalest into play fast enough.

His confidence had increased greatly from fighting off all of the corrupted wolves not even an hour earlier, but that confidence seemed to drain right out of him when he looked at the stranger. Afraid even to blink, Thorn couldn't help but give a great start when the stranger opened his mouth to speak.

"What'cha doin' out here?" he said, his drawn back lips revealing pointy teeth. "Pretty far from the city, ain't'cha?"

"Not too far. I'm..." Thorn paused for a brief moment, deciding not to show the tails he had been about to pull out of his bag. "I'm just enjoying the scenery."

"Uh huh." Unconvinced, the man gave Thorn a long, intense look before making his way forward in his strange, rocking gait. Squatting down by the fire, he fixed his green eyes on a bit of the food Thorn had not eaten, licking his lips.

"Would you like some?" asked Thorn, pushing the meat over.

Spearing the meat with a long claw-like nail, the stranger devoured it, juice dripping down into his long beard. Once the meat was gone, he lifted his eyes and resumed gazing at Thorn.

"I'm Thorn."

"Hmmm. Gargish. The Blood Hunter," said the man, scratching his thigh.

"Nice to meet you, Gargish," lied Thorn. "That is quite the name you have there."

"Hmmm. "Lapsing into silence, Thorn watched Gargish. It was obvious that Gargish had come with some purpose, and his silence made Thorn very uneasy.

"So. Are you from around here?" asked Thorn.

"Mmhmm," affirmed Gargish after a moment, pointing toward his back right. "Valley of the Fang."

"Oh, I haven't been there yet. I hear it has got a lot of corrupted wolves, though. You must be pretty strong to be able to live there."

"Mmhmm."

"What brings you out this way?" asked Thorn, as nonchalantly as possible.

"Hunting."

"Yeah?" said Thorn, faking a chipper tone as he dried his sweaty palms on his pants.

He had never felt more like a small woodland creature than now. He was one and a half times Gargish's size, but for some reason, he felt like a small, furry rabbit being stared down by a timber wolf. The fire in between them gave him a small degree of comfort, but it was starting to die down. Thorn reached over for another piece of wood and added it, poking the fire in silence until it was blazing again.

"Are you a hunter by trade?" Thorn asked after the silence became unbearable

"Heh, yeah." Gargish seemed to find the question quite funny and broke into a strange, wheezy laugh.

"Cool. I bet you have seen a lot of places, then. This whole mountain range seems good for hunting, so I imagine you have been to most of it," Thorn said, casting around in his mind for topics. "So far I have only seen some corrupted wolves and some small game, but I can imagine that there are more animals the deeper into the mountains you go."

Unresponsive to Thorn's leading questions, Gargish stared.

"I mean, I could imagine that there are some bears in the woods. Probably big bears, as well," said Thorn, trying to continue the conversation.

He lapsed into silence, staring at the other man over the fire. The sun was beginning to sink down toward the horizon, indicating that this day was coming to an end, the golden sunlight sending the shadows of the trees stretching long, like grasping fingers creeping ever closer to Thorn.

Seeing the shadows inch toward him as the silence grew, Thorn couldn't help but shiver, reminded of the long, clawed fingers on Gargish's hands. In silence and stillness, they sat there, the only movement that of the flames, leaping between them. The firelight cast Gargish's craggy features into stark relief, causing his bright green eyes to stand out even more.

The whole situation began to feel surreal to Thorn. Was he sitting across from a man? Or was it a corrupted wolf? In the growing dusk, Thorn began to have trouble telling what was sitting on the other side of the fire, as the shadows caused Gargish's form to twist and morph, forming something that wasn't wolf, yet wasn't man.

Stuck in this strange half-world, somewhere between light and darkness, Thorn jerked as Gargish stood, raising his head to look around. Not sure if the flickering firelight was playing tricks on him, Thorn could swear that Gargish's face had grown a wolfish snout.

Flexing his claws, Gargish stared up at the empty night sky. Pointing a clawed finger up at the darkening sky, he smiled his sharp smile.

"The time is coming for the hunt," said Gargish, his eyes taking on a fanatical gleam. "Soon the blood moon will rise, covering the world with its light, and blood shall flow. The new order will be toppled, and the old order will once again step forth into their rightful place. Blood purity will be restored!"

Almost as if to celebrate his statement, a long, eerie howl broke out from the forest to Thorn's right, the trembling sound echoing across the mountains, causing even the sounds of the river to fade away. Deafening silence reigned when the howl finished, but Thorn felt like it was still echoing among the trees.

Looking at the still empty sky, Thorn had a sinking sensation that this night was going to be long and hard. Putting his hand behind his back, Thorn found his knife, watching Gargish for any sign of aggression. Gargish, however, seemed to be ignoring him completely, instead gazing with a crazed longing at the darkening sky.

"What is it you are hunting tonight?" asked Thorn, his back slick with sweat.

Gargish's head snapped toward Thorn at the question, his intense green gaze taking on a tinge of the red bloodlust that Thorn had seen in the eyes of the corrupted wolves.

"You."

"Oh. That's nice," said Thorn, a wave of relief washing over him. Somehow having it put into words made it much less scary.

Down in the corner of his vision, a small symbol had appeared at some point, and Thorn, curious and slightly distracted from the nerve-wracking situation in front of him, focused his attention on it. Nova Terra, like most games, relied on popups to communicate with the player, but, in the interest of immersion, most of the popups were kept as small as possible when outside of towns and cities.

Only by focusing on the small symbols that hovered outside of the normal field of view could the popups be brought up for the players to read. Curious about the blinking symbol, Thorn focused part of his attention on to it, causing the popup to expand in front of him into a constantly growing list of messages, one coming right after the other.

Blood Moon Terror
You have been influenced by Gargish The Blood Hunter's natural terror aura, causing your will to weaken. You have become more susceptible to the influence of others.

Titan's Strength
Your increased resistance to mind affecting conditions has negated the effect of Blood Moon Terror.

Watching these two messages chase each other down the page, Thorn breathed another sigh of relief. 'That's right. This is a game,' he thought to himself. He had heard rumors of people who were unable to separate the world of Nova Terra from reality, and he no longer doubted that they existed.

The combination of the environment, the pressure from Gargish's ability, and Thorn's tired mental state had left Thorn believing that all of this was somehow the only reality, causing him to completely forget that the terrifying being in front of him was a bunch of code. Fortunately, one of his racial abilities was an increased resistance to the insidious mental influences that Gargish exuded.

Sighing again, Thorn put his hands on his knees and stood up. Gargish, confused as to why the frightening atmosphere he had so carefully crafted had changed, took a step back, as Thorn's figure grew larger and larger. Big himself, Gargish stood at seven feet tall. Yet this human in front of him seemed to keep going up forever. He took another step back.

"Alright, so how are we doing this? Brawl right here? Do I get a head start?" asked Thorn, picking up the few camp items he had pulled out of his inventory.

For a moment, Gargish was at a loss. Wasn't his prey supposed to be terrified? What was with this matter-of-fact tone?

"No plan? Alright, brawl right here it is." Thorn pulled out his knife. For all his bravado, Gargish was still giving him a terrifying feeling. Despite his mental resistance being able to overcome Gargish's aura, no one he had met in the game so far gave him such a heavy feeling of menace.

"Wait, wait," said Gargish in his raspy voice, waving his clawed hands and grinning menacingly. "Fighting here is no fun. Hunting is much more fun. Tell you what. I'll give you a thirty-minute head start."

"But if you are going to hunt me down, why not have a fight right here?" asked Thorn, tightening his grip on his knife. Before he had even finished speaking, Gargish's figure blurred, and Thorn felt a sudden pain in his stomach, sending him stumbling backward.

"Heh, that is up to you," laughed Gargish as he reappeared where he had been standing across the fire.

Scrambling to his feet, Thorn's heart dropped. Gargish was too fast and strong for a direct fight. Calculating in his head, Thorn realized that there was no way he could take him on one-on-one. In fact, if Gargish's fist had been aimed at his throat, Thorn wouldn't even have known how he died.

"Fair enough," Thorn said with a cough. "Thirty minutes, you said?"

Watching Thorn's big form dash off into the woods, Gargish laughed again. No one had ever escaped him, and this abnormally sized human would not be an exception to that rule.

Jogging into the forest, Thorn's mind was working furiously. Since he could not fight Gargish head on, Thorn had to come up with a solution to even the playing field. Gargish was too fast and strong for direct confrontation. Thorn never had any illusion of being able to hide from him either, for a very particular reason.

When Gargish hit him in the stomach, Thorn had sensed something being applied to his armor and a quick check had shown that there was a patch of some substance on a couple of the scales.

No doubt this was some sort of tracking aid. Thorn had even checked his log-off button, but seeing that it was greyed out, he could only assume that Gargish had a means of keeping him from leaving the game. Despite the growing difficulty of his situation, Thorn once again felt that burning excitement in his chest.

He had been discovering more and more that the dangerous, nerve-wracking situations of the game gave him an intense rush of joy and uncontrollable desire to conquer. This situation was no different, and countless possible solutions presented themselves to Thorn as he lengthened his stride through the forest.

CHAPTER TWENTY-ONE

Thorn's size had always been as debilitating as it had been a benefit, but as he ran, he could only marvel at the advantage he had gained in Nova Terra. Unlike the real world, where he couldn't even stand, in game, Thorn's body was perfect. This was nowhere more apparent than while running. Due to the springy forest floor, Thorn's stride was almost four feet long when he walked, almost twice that of an average person.

Now that he was running full out, Thorn traveled over nine feet with each step. His long legs seemed to devour the distance, sending him forward at an incredible rate. As he ran, he pondered how he was going to manage the fight against Gargish. Not only was Gargish much faster than he was, but he had natural claws that seemed sharper than those of the corrupted wolves, which meant that close combat was going to be difficult.

Gargish was also very strong, as his blow had shown. The punch that had sent Thorn reeling was the first time anything had been able to move his immense weight since he had started Nova Terra. "Man, I don't know that I can win." For the briefest of moments, the thought of how overwhelming Gargish was made Thorn's spirit plummet.

'Wait, I can get some help!' Opening his chat feature, Thorn could not help but curse. Like the logout button, the messaging button was greyed out. Not only was he unable to leave the game, but he also could not let anyone know that a terrifying werewolf was hunting him.

Needing a new plan, Thorn began to analyze his situation, looking for any advantage that he had. After a couple minutes, Thorn had only come up with one: strength. It was not much, but something was better than nothing. A plan began to take form. He would only have one chance, but one chance was better than zero chances. With a deep breath, he opened his map. He had twenty minutes.

The first thing he needed was a space that would restrict Gargish's movement. Looking at his map, Thorn considered his options before looking for a cave in one of the nearby mountains. He soon found a cave, almost a mile away, that was inhabited by corrupted wolves. Hoping that it was going to be suitable, Thorn changed direction and continued to run.

It took him a bit less than three minutes to get to the cave, covering almost a mile in record time. Shaking his head to himself, Thorn marveled at what he could do when physics no longer applied to his body. The cave was a large hollow in a hill that led deeper into the heart of the mountain. While running he had been able to see on the map that the cave contained a small labyrinth of twisting passages behind the large front chamber, perfect for Thorn's plan.

Striding into the front chamber, he soon dispatched the four corrupted wolves that had been resting in the cave. In the back of this front chamber of the cave was a slight crack that he could barely squeeze through to enter the tunnel system. The tunnels themselves were almost eight and a half feet high, meaning that he only had to stoop to make his way through.

Finding a nice spot to set up, Thorn checked his clock. Assuming that Gargish had actually adhered to the rules of the game, Thorn still had four minutes before Gargish would even start. However, Thorn had a suspicion that Gargish did not care about following the rules and was on his way already, which meant that he didn't have much time to prepare.

Thorn flexed his hands and then began to dig into the walls of the tunnel, pulling stone and dirt down into the cave to widen it on one side. Since the tunnel was uniform, Thorn blocked the whole passage as he stood in it. By digging out the wall on his right, Thorn created a little pocket where he could swing his knife, just deep enough that his knife would not touch the wall. Thorn nodded to himself and continued his work.

Gargish, who had already arrived outside the cave entrance, as Thorn had guessed, was experiencing a strange sensation - shock. He had started as soon as Thorn was out of sight, his sensitive nose following the special scent of the paste he had applied to Thorn's armor. Sneering to himself, he could imagine the hopelessness on his prey's face when he realized that, no matter how far he ran, Gargish was right there. Nothing gave him more pleasure than appearing next to his prey as soon as the half hour head start was up.

At least, that was the plan. But Thorn traveled too fast. Way too fast. Looking at the massive footprints in the forest floor, Gargish couldn't help but be somewhat unsettled. Never before had he tracked such prey. Thorn covered distance at an astronomical rate, almost faster than Gargish could. The other strange thing was his direction. Every other human Gargish had hunted instinctively headed for a city.

Yet this fellow went in a different direction, angling away from the city and heading, instead, toward the corrupted wolf-infested mountains. Wasn't he afraid of being surrounded? Sniffing at the entrance to the cave, Gargish hesitated for a moment. Something about the dark cave mouth made him feel uneasy. Shaking his head in annoyance, Gargish growled to himself. When had he ever been afraid of his prey?

With a last glance around, Gargish bounded into the cave only to come up short. Four bisected corrupted wolf corpses lay on the ground. Eyes narrowed, Gargish knelt down and examined the bodies.

Given the smoothness of the cut, he could imagine the speed at which the blade had been traveling, but the angle was a bit strange. As he continued to look, a mental image of Thorn slashing out with his large knife appeared in his mind.

Once again, a sliver of warning tried its best to worm its way into Gargish's heart. This massive human was different. The feeling was not anything concrete, but the combination of many small things that Gargish had seen was starting to add up. As he had made his way to the cave, he saw none of the signs that terrified prey would give off. There were no broken branches, crushed undergrowth, or anything to indicate that his prey was running scared.

His big prey had run, yes, but not in fear. Based on how fast he had moved, it was reasonable for Thorn to believe he could actually escape, yet he had come to this out-of-the-way place and trapped himself in a cave, where his size would restrict his movement. The man's entering the cave had been deliberate and forthright, despite knowing that there were corrupted wolves inside. This was not the mark of someone who was afraid.

And, judging from the corpses of the corrupted wolves, Thorn had dealt with them without breaking a sweat. The cuts were too smooth and precise to be the work of someone shaking with fear. This left only one reasonable possibility, and that possibility left Gargish shaken.

Was Thorn not afraid?

Gargish could not be entirely blamed for the worry that had begun to form in his heart. His natural ability to terrify had never failed before, so Thorn presented a new, strange situation that he had never come across. Thorn had seemed to be scared when they first met, but none of his actions since then had even smelled of the terror that he should have been feeling.

Shaking himself, Gargish crushed the small thread of worry in his chest. So what if his prey was not terrified right now? Wasn't terrifying his prey Gargish's greatest skill? If that stupid human was not afraid, then Gargish would teach him the meaning of fear! With a rumbling growl, Gargish launched forward into the depths of the cave.

Thorn was standing in the tunnel he had modified, giving one last look around him at his handiwork. The more he thought about what he was doing, the more foolish he felt. Gargish had proven himself to be much faster than Thorn back at the river, so Thorn had no idea if this was going to work. It would come down to how Gargish attempted to kill him.

Opening up his inventory, Thorn took out some food and planted himself in the middle of the tunnel, facing the way he had come. To his left, there was almost no room between his shoulder and the wall while, to his right, he had cleared enough space to allow him to swing his blade. Also, tired of crouching, Thorn had dug out a bit of space for his head to fit when he stood up.

Munching on the sandwich he had gotten out, Thorn waited patiently for Gargish to arrive. Surprised by how calm he was as he faced his first death in Nova Terra, Thorn could only guess that it was his Titan's Strength ability kicking in. After a couple of minutes passed, he finished his fourth sandwich, so he pulled up a browser and began to look up information on dying in Nova Terra. Information was sparse, but after reading through a few threads, Thorn managed to piece some details together.

Unlike the real world, death in Nova Terra was not permanent. It was, after all, a game. However, the penalties were not light, either. When a player was killed in Nova Terra, a couple things would happen. First, their equipment and a bag containing a random selection from their inventory would drop. Each item in their inventory had a variable chance to drop, which meant that players could lose a lot of items, or very few, based on how lucky they were.

Second, the killed player would experience a drop in the mastery of their class. While it was not as bad as being reset, it was a definite setback. After all, it took a long time to train up mastery in a class, and every single death would wipe away countless hours of hard work. Skill proficiency would be left untouched but having to retrain a class over and over was painful.

Many players had complained bitterly about this mechanic, which led Horizon to introduce a patch that allowed players who died to regain their mastery faster than they had before they died. The tradeoff was that, if they died again before their mastery was regained, it would be gone.

These two penalties had created a timid player force, which had driven the creator of Nova Terra crazy but had paved the way for a solid, systematic settling of the world of Nova Terra, much the same way the far reaches of the earth had been settled. Over time, however, players had come to realize that death was not something to fear, and the current sentiments toward dying in Nova Terra were very casual.

Thorn was finishing his seventh sandwich when a flicker in a shadow at the other end of the tunnel alerted him that he was no longer alone. Dusting off his hands, Thorn firmly gripped his knife, drawing it out and holding it diagonally in front of him. Crouching a bit, his left hand raised up with his palm out, Thorn watched Gargish slink out of the shadows.

Gargish was at home among the flickering torchlight and deep pools of shadow. He seemed to become part of the shadow as he passed through it, moving fluidly toward Thorn in an unhurried manner, his silent steps making no sound even when he passed over the gravel that Thorn had scattered.

"You found me," said Thorn when Gargish drew close. Thorn's eyes stayed glued to Gargish, taking in every tiny move the werewolf made.

"Was that ever in question?" asked Gargish, curious as to how the mind of this giant human was working.

"No, of course not. It was a matter of when."

"Haha, it's good that you recognized that. Saves both of us much trouble," snickered Gargish. "Tell me, though. Why didn't you keep running?"

"Running? I was never running," said Thorn with a small smile, a bead of sweat trickling down his face.

"Haha, you sure looked like you were running to me!" laughed Gargish.

"Nah, I was not running. It was a tactical retreat," said Thorn.

"What? Tactical retreat?" Gargish narrowed his evil eyes. "Do you think you have a chance to live?"

Still watching the werewolf, Thorn could feel the danger radiating off of him in palpable waves. He knew, without question, that this one enemy was more dangerous than anything he had faced up until this point. Once again, a dreadful excitement began to build in the base of Thorn's chest.

"Isn't there always a chance?" asked Thorn, struggling to keep his voice from shaking.

"Ha!" Gargish snarled, his eyes starting to become bloodshot. "There is never a chance when I am the one hunting."

"Wait, wait. Hold on." Thorn stood up from his crouch and took a hurried step backward, almost hitting his head on the roof of the tunnel. "Can't we talk about this?"

"A bit late for that." Almost instinctively, Gargish took a step forward, mirroring Thorn's action. "Once you become my prey, there is only one possible outcome. Your agonizing, slow death!"

"Come on, I know we can come to some sort of solution here." At this point, Thorn was babbling as Gargish stalked toward him, ignoring what Thorn was saying. Trembling, Thorn put his knife between them as he continued to move backward.

Gargish, seeing Thorn continue to retreat, flashed forward, his wicked claws stabbing toward Thorn's chest! Almost too fast for Thorn's eye to follow, he covered the few feet between them in an instant! Acting on pure instinct, Thorn stabbed forward with his knife, while bringing his left arm across his chest to block.

Twisting his body to avoid the knife, Gargish's claws clashed with Thorn's bracer with a loud clang, sending sparks flying. Before Thorn could strike again, Gargish danced back out of range, his padded feet making no sound as he stalked back and forth. Snarling at Thorn as his bloodlust began to grow, Gargish's fury deepened. When had he ever had this much trouble with his prey?

At this point, Thorn should be a quivering mess on the floor! Instead, he was a literal wall of flesh, taking up almost the whole passage. As Gargish watched in fury, getting ready for his next attack, Thorn backed farther into the passage, where he had to crouch to walk, causing Gargish's eyes to light up for a moment.

Where Thorn had been standing, the roof was high enough that it did not impede Thorn's movements. However, now that he had left that space, his large size would be a hindrance. Not only was his forward posture bad for his defensive form, but if Gargish could get around behind him, Thorn would have trouble turning around.

As it was, stepping out of the taller part of the passage was a rookie mistake, especially given Gargish's blinding speed. Sneering at Thorn's inexperience, the werewolf stalked closer, his fierce eyes boring into Thorn's armored form. The pressure of his aura seemed to solidify for a moment, causing Thorn to flinch backward as if he were stung!

CHAPTER TWENTY-TWO

Taking his opening, Gargish flashed to the left, squeezing past Thorn while landing a punch on his ribs. Throwing all his formidable power into the strike, Gargish was stunned when he failed to move Thorn in the least! Failing to get the result he wanted, the werewolf did not let it shake him and recovered, landing behind Thorn and sending out a flurry of blows!

As soon as Gargish moved left, Thorn reacted as though shocked, his body falling forward to rest on his left leg as his right leg slid behind him. From this lunging position, Thorn twisted his body to his right, turning around. The move was so smooth and natural, it caught the frenzied werewolf off guard as his claws raked the air where Thorn's back had been a moment before.

Launching himself off his back leg, Thorn pushed forward, stabbing out with his knife again. Gargish was too fast and danced backward, keeping out of the knife's range. However, as he backed up, his instincts kicked in, and he threw a glance backward, only to be met with the unbelievable sight of a solid pile of dirt and rock!

A slight curve in the tunnel had previously hidden it from his view, but the entire tunnel was filled with dirt and rocks, trapping him! Unbelieving, he stared at it, his instincts screaming at him that he was in a whole world of trouble! And his instincts were right. Now facing the panicked werewolf, Thorn pushed forward, his bulky body taking up the whole tunnel!

Smashing forward toward Gargish, Thorn left no room for the werewolf to dodge. A desperate attempt to squeeze by on the left was met with a powerful palm strike that sent Gargish reeling, his arms feeling like they had been hit with a sledgehammer! Desperate, Gargish erupted in fury, his claws striking out in blow after blow, causing blood to splash as his wickedly sharp claws broke through Thorn's scalemail!

Thorn seemed impervious to the pain, ignoring the blood flowing from his arms as he pushed forward again, forcing Gargish to step back. Gathering his strength, Thorn burst forth, slamming into Gargish with his body, his two fists landing on the werewolf's muscular chest.

Gargish felt like he had been run over by a train. Well, not a train precisely, since he had no concept of what a train was. Gargish felt like he had been run over by a dragon. At least, he assumed that this is what it would feel like. As Thorn's two fists came forward, Gargish's bloodfury was pierced by the sudden and clear realization that he was about to die.

It was a strange sort of feeling, an inevitable certainty that cut through all the chaos in his mind. His thirst for blood, his hunger for the terror and suffering of his prey, his anger, and fear of being cornered, his wolfish instincts to fight for his life. All of that ceased for the briefest of moments, as this fact marched across his very being.

The two fists grew larger, coming forward in slow motion to slam into his chest with unstoppable force. When they were still inches away, Gargish could feel his chest starting to compress from the force of the air alone! When they made contact, Gargish wondered if this was the feeling of being kicked in the chest by a hundred horses at the same time.

Thorn's mind was operating with startling clarity. The excitement that seemed to rise in his chest with every fight brought with it the uncontrollable urge to smash and destroy, but it did not cloud his thinking in the slightest. Rather, it seemed to lend a sharpness to his thoughts that hadn't been there before. Every twitch of muscle, every grimace of his enemy's lips, was taken in, processed and used to adjust his blows.

Smashing into Gargish's chest, Thorn sent the werewolf flying back, almost imprinting him into the wall of debris that Thorn had piled up, his chest crushed and bleeding. Yet even then, Thorn's hyper-focused mind sent him forward. Stepping closer, the only thing in Thorn's brain was indexing. Get in range, get in contact. The lesson Dovon had pounded into his head surfaced, and Thorn reached out a massive hand, clamping down on the shaken werewolf's shoulder!

Gargish was still recovering from the unbelievable force that had sent him back when a vice grip landed on his shoulder. Struggling with all his might, Gargish tried to shake off the hand, but to no avail. "How is he this strong!" the werewolf screamed in his mind.

Thorn wasted no time, and as soon as his hand made contact, he started to throw out blow after blow at Gargish' head, smashing him into oblivion! Punch after punch rained down on Gargish's skull, an ominous cracking sound giving testament to how hard Thorn was striking. Each punch heavier than the last, it wasn't long before Thorn's bloody fist smashed straight through to the ground below, blood and brain matter splashing over the ground.

Still keyed up, Thorn dropped the corpse of the werewolf to the ground, his shoulders heaving as he gulped in big breaths of air. Bloodshot eyes looked around for more enemies, and finding none, he slumped to the ground, the energy draining out of him. It took Thorn almost ten minutes to recover. Only a few brief moments had passed since Gargish had come down into the tunnels after him, but it had felt like hours.

Ding

Blood Moon Rising - Complete

Congratulations, hero! You have slain Gargish, the Blood Hunter, and completed Black Moon Rising, making the surrounding lands safe, for the time being.

Rewards:
Titles: Wolfsbane
Lord of Greymane (locked)
Ring of the Wolf Lord

Title: Wolfsbane

You have slain the King of the Werewolves, proving your abilities as a hunter and slayer of monsters. Locals are more likely to ask for your help in subjugating monsters of the Wolf or Lycan family.

In addition, for ending the cursed line of Gargish, you have inherited the Ring of the Wolf Lord.

Lord of Greymane (locked)

You have defeated the previous Lord Greymane in battle. Go to Greymane Keep to claim it as your own by sitting on the Wolf's Throne while wearing the Ring of the Wolf Lord.

Title: Brave

For standing your ground in the face of a monster with more than two mastered proficiencies and surviving.

+Wisdom
+Constitution

Title Update (Brave): Indomitable

For standing your ground in the face of a monster with more than five mastered proficiencies and surviving.

+Wisdom
+Constitution

Title Update (Indomitable): Unshakeable

For standing your ground in the face of a monster with more than ten mastered proficiencies and surviving.

+Wisdom
+Constitution

Title Update (Unshakeable): Battle Mad

For standing your ground in the face of a monster with more than fifteen mastered proficiencies and surviving.

+Wisdom
+Constitution

Thorn waved the myriad of windows away, unsure about what had happened. After Gargish died, a massive surge of energy seemed to diffuse into the surroundings, and numerous windows popped up in his vision. With the game logs, he could always go back to check the details later. Right now he was more concerned with the loot.

Looking at the headless corpse, Thorn frowned. How was he supposed to find the ring in this bloody mess? For a moment, he squatted there, poking what was left of the werewolf's body with his knife. After a couple of seconds, the body dissolved into light particles, and a few items were revealed on the ground. Apart from the ring that he had been expecting, there was a sack of 10 gold and a small silver token with a crack running down the middle.

The loot was picked up and put away in his inventory, and Thorn examined the ring.

Ring of the Wolf Lord
This is the signet ring of the Wolf Lord, ruler of Greymane Keep and protector of the Deep Wood. The bearer of this ring is the rightful ruler of the Wolfkin, young or old, and is honor bound to protect them. Can only be worn by a Wolfkin or someone with the title Wolfsbane.   +Intelligence   +Endurance   +Charisma   + Reputation   Ability: Wolf Lord's Howl [locked]

Slipping the ring onto his finger, Thorn called up his status. He had gained some bonuses from slaying Gargish and completing the Blood Moon event and wanted to check his new titles out.

Name: [Thorn]	Race: [Titan]
Health: [78%]	Mana: [100%]
Titles: [Battle Mad], [Wolfsbane], [Lord Greymane (locked)]	Conditions: [None]
Abilities: [Wolf Lord's Howl(locked)]	

Scratching his head, Thorn pondered his status. Not a whole lot had visibly changed from before since most of his stats were hidden. A field had been added for his new ability, however, it was as minimalist as the rest of the fields. In fact, the only ability he had listed was still locked away, because the [Lord Greymane] title was locked, as well. Deciding not to worry about it for the time being, Thorn cleared the passage of all the dirt and stone he had piled up to trap Gargish.

The whole plan had been quite tenuous, but Gargish had reacted the way Thorn had assumed he would. Based on the hit-and-run fighting style that wolves preferred, Thorn had been confident that Gargish's combat style was going to be hard to pin down. With the Blood Hunter's speed, there was no way that Thorn would have been able to win a fight in an open area, as the werewolf could have dodged backwards.

This was the same reason that Thorn did not bother to try and shoot him with his arbalest. Even putting aside the fact that Thorn was not confident that the bolt could have harmed Gargish, it was even less likely that he could have hit him with it. Gargish was too fast, but fortunately he was also arrogant, not considering Thorn a foe to be respected.

Thorn had been hoping that the close quarters and single direction of approach afforded by the tunnels would give him a chance to trade blows with the werewolf, never suspecting that Gargish would throw himself into a corner. As soon as he had landed a solid blow, the fight had been over. As he spread the rocks and dirt along the floor of the tunnel to keep it clear, Thorn could not help but marvel at his own strength.

Because of the test he had done upon entering Nova Terra, he had at least a conceptual understanding of how strong he was, but it was very hard to translate that into a practical understanding of what that meant. Plus, he kept having this nagging feeling that the strength he felt wasn't actually the limit.

Take, for example, his strike against Gargish. As soon as he had released the blow, Thorn had felt that it was different. Not a punch, but something more. Almost an expression of will, gathering strength not only from his tendons and muscles, but pulling power from the bones of the earth around them to crush everything before it.

That feeling, clear one moment, but slipping away the very next, had left him with an emptiness, as if a crucial, life-bringing vein had run dry. Shaking his head, Thorn finished cleaning up and crawled out of the tunnel. When he got out, he stretched and twisted his body, glad to be back under the sky. While he wasn't claustrophobic, having to bend over was annoying.

As soon as he got the notification that Gargish had died, his messages and logout button were reactivated, and he saw that he had a blinking message from Hamm, the weapons trainer from the Berum Training Hall. Opening it up, he saw Hamm's stubble-covered face.

[Hey Thorn, thought I'd send you a message. I know you are out hunting corrupted wolves, but Master Sun came back, so you can probably go find him, if you want. I think he'd fit your combat style pretty well, if you can get him to teach you anything. He can get weird about that sometimes. Always prattling on about how his weapon is the only 'true' weapon and all that nonsense. Hah. Give me a chopping blade any day. Anyway, be careful out there and come back and visit soon.]

It took Thorn a moment to remember that Hamm had given him a quest to find Master Sun. Pulling up the quest, he looked at the area marked on his map. Last time he had set out to find Master Sun, he had not made it far at all. It had worked out though, as that is where he had met Ouroboros, Velin, Mina, and Jorge.

The area marked on his map was not too far away, so Thorn decided to stop there on his way back to town. There were still a few days before he needed to meet up with Ouroboros and the rest of the team, so he did not have anything better to do anyway. Setting off, Thorn moved toward the mountains to the north of Berum, where Master Sun was located.

Unlike the old growth forest where he had been fighting the corrupted wolves, the rolling hills to the north of the city were covered in scrub brush and small stands of new growth forest. It was among these younger trees that Thorn came upon a run-down hut with a smoking fire pit out front. Sitting at the fire was a middle-aged, Asian-looking man with a balding head and two of the largest arms Thorn had ever seen on a human. Dirty red armor with broken stitching and karuta made Thorn think of an out of work samurai. What did they call them? Ronin, that's right.

Guzzling something out of a bottle, the middle-aged man belched before stuffing more meat into his mouth. Seeing that he was being ignored, Thorn crouched down by the fire and pulled out his own food. After he took out the first dish, there was no reaction, but by the time he had taken out the fifth, Thorn could feel a burning gaze resting on him. Looking over, he saw the middle-aged man staring at the food in his hands.

"Would you like some?" Thorn offered. Seeing the man's eyes light up, Thorn passed a few of the dishes over, letting the bedraggled man help himself. Between the two of them, they had soon finished off eleven portions and four bottles of ale that Thorn pulled out of his inventory. After they were done, the man belched again, the stale smell of alcohol wafting off of him.

Scratching his back, he stood and ambled into the flimsy shed, kicking the door shut as he fell onto a dirty mat. Thorn stared in bemusement at the small shack that looked like it would fall over in stiff breeze and sighed. He was about to leave to continue looking for Master Sun when he noticed that his quest had updated.

CHAPTER TWENTY-THREE

> **A Hidden Master: Part 2**
>
> The martial path is long and fraught with danger. Having learned all that you can from Sword Trainer Hamm at the Berum Training Hall, you have been given the opportunity to further your training with a mysterious master who lives in the mountains to the north. Master Sun has a strange temperament and does not pass his skills along easily.
>
> ~~Find Master Sun~~
>
> Convince Master Sun to teach you

Reading the quest summary almost caused Thorn to spit out the mouthful of ale he had swigged. "He's Master Sun?" thought Thorn, shaking his head, "Wow. Just goes to show that you never can tell."

The dirty, middle-aged drunk who had gorged himself on food, and then fallen into a dead sleep in the hut, certainly did not fit Thorn's mental picture of a martial arts master. Ms. Chen, his Taijiquan master, was what came to mind when he thought of a master. Still, if Hamm said that this Master Sun was able to help him, Thorn did not have any reason to assume otherwise. Either way, he would not know until Master Sun woke up.

The night passed, but when the morning came, the sun struggled to emerge from behind the heavy, dark clouds. Yawning and stretching, Thorn began his morning exercises. After running through his Taijiquan forms, he shadowboxed for a few minutes and then spent a bit practicing shooting his arbalest.

After he was finished, he looked around for something to do while he waited for Master Sun to get up. Almost two hours later, the middle-aged man wandered sleepily out of his shack and looked at Thorn, who was trying to do handstands in the yard. Seeing that Master Sun had come out, Thorn got to his feet, dusting himself off.

"Hello, Master Sun. My name is Thorn." Introducing himself, Thorn bowed slightly. "Hamm sent me to see you to further my training."

"Further training?" Master Sun scratched the back of his balding head. "What makes you think I can teach you anything?"

"Truthfully? I'm not sure," admitted Thorn. "But I trust that Hamm would not lead me astray. He told me to come to find you after declaring that I was not suitable to wield a sword."

"Wait, Hamm said that?" Master Sun walked a loop around Thorn, staring at him. "That guy is obsessed with swords. He has never once hesitated to force his junky beliefs on another person. And he told you that you are not suitable for using a sword?"

"Yes, master. Hamm said that my size was too limiting for swordplay and that I would not be able to cut properly because I have trouble using finesse when striking."

Seeing Master Sun's confused look, Thorn stepped over to a small tree that was growing out of the hillside. Pulling out his knife, he gave a casual swing, lopping the eight-inch tree right off its trunk. Grabbing the tree that started to fall toward the shed Master Sun had slept in, Thorn breathed a sigh of relief.

Master Sun stared at Thorn, with stars in his eyes. Running over to the newly shorn tree stump, he ran his fingers over the rough edge where the knife had impacted the wood. Once the knife had entered the tree, the break was clean, but right where Thorn had started the cut, the wood was smashed and splintered from the force of the blow.

"Haha, he wasn't joking, was he? Kid, it's your lucky day! Wait here," Master Sun said over his shoulder, laughing in excitement as he ran into his shed. In a moment, he returned, carrying a massive metal club that came up to his chest.

A brutish, fearsome looking weapon, the small end of the club was as thick as his wrist, wrapped in leather and topped with a metal ring. The club's head was three times the size of the grip and covered in large metal studs. The whole weapon glistened, its oiled metal sheen showing how well Master Sun cared for it. Carrying it over his shoulder, Master Sun did not even blink when, in his rush to get out of the shack, the club clipped the side of the doorframe, sending splinters flying.

A shiver ran through the shack, and Thorn watched in fascinated horror as the entire structure collapsed, one shaky wall at a time. Master Sun, on the other hand, did not seem to care at all. Instead, cradling his weapon gently, he presented it for Thorn to see.

"This, this is a weapon, kid. A weapon for strong men! None of that sissy cutting or slashing, good old-fashioned force. The enemy has a blade? Great. Crush them. The enemy has a shield? Even better. Crush them. Is the enemy playing with arrows? Awesome, knock them out of the air and then crush them. Need to move an object or negotiate a tense situation?"

"Crush it?" Thorn guessed, as Master Sun took a deep breath.

"Exactly! Crush it." Master Sun beamed. "No matter the problem, brute force is the solution."

Stepping back, Master Sun flipped the club up, and, with a twist of his wrist, he sent it humming through the air. Faster and faster he swung it around him, the weight of the club increasing its speed with every rotation. Within a minute, the club was moving so fast that Thorn could not even see it.

He could, however, hear it. The swinging club let out a thunderous drone as it smashed its way through the air. As the drone seemed to reach a crescendo, Master Sun stepped forward and flicked his arm toward a tree, which exploded in a shower of splinters. The club had swung over in a dark blur, too fast for Thorn to catch, obliterating the trunk. Grinning, Master Sun lifted his club up and brushed off a few splinters still sticking to it.

"This, young man, is a tetsubo! A real man's weapon!"

Impressed, Thorn examined the tetsubo. He could see how it would be an effective weapon. Constructed of metal, swinging it would generate a tremendous force without the danger of breaking that a sword would face. The metal studs took the damage one step further, adding a ripping effect to the blow. Seeing how interested Thorn was, Master Sun's grin grew bigger.

"How about it? Fancy learning how to use a real weapon?"

"I'd love to!" responded Thorn. He had used staves before, but this was a whole different sort of thing. A staff, in order to be the proper size, had to be massive, which made it prohibitive to use in most spaces. The tetsubo, on the other hand, was the same size as a large sword but wielded much like a staff.

"In that case, let's begin. Have you ever done any martial arts training?" Seeing Thorn's nod, Master Sun continued. "Excellent, then you should know what a horse stance looks like. Let's start there."

Much like Thorn's Taijiquan instructor, Master Sun first had Thorn drop into and hold a horse stance. Once Thorn was in the proper position, he rested his tetsubo across Thorn's knees, telling him that if it fell off, the amount of time he had to stay in the horse stance would increase. Thorn, unable to feel the weight of the heavy weapon because of the mechanics of Nova Terra, stayed in his seated position.

Master Sun walked to the side and waited for Thorn to show the slightest sign that he was tired. And waited. And waited. After close to forty minutes, Master Sun finally got fed up with waiting and grabbed his tetsubo off of Thorn's legs.

"Alright, stand up." Staring at Thorn, who was not fatigued in the slightest, Master Sun narrowed his eyes. "I'm guessing it would do neither of us any good if I were to make you run for a while. Anyway, the long and short of it is that the key to using a tetsubo is your lower body. Much like a staff, the tetsubo requires a strong base from which to control the force of the weapon.

"Unlike bladed weapons, the tetsubo only has a single attacking function. Crushing. It can be used to block, as well, but at the end of the day, that is much less efficient than smashing someone. The key, of course, is being able to hit them. We achieve that through making use of the constant motion of the weapon to turn offense into defense.

"In short, if there is no time for your opponent to attack, there is no need for defense. And if you do need it, you should be able to divert the attack through a direct strike. You need to remember one thing. Push forward. Always push forward. The power of the tetsubo is in its constant, aggressive, dominating nature. No matter the obstacle, the tetsubo's solution is to crush it under overwhelming force. Now, let me show you the basic moves that you will practice."

Lending Thorn a tetsubo that he pulled out of his inventory, Master Sun began to show him how to spin the weapon using a combination of specialized grips and the ring on the back end of the handle. Each hand position maximized the weapon's ability to rotate while gaining momentum. Due to his previous practice with a staff, Thorn picked it up rather quickly and, within a day, was able to keep the weapon moving well.

After a day of practice, Master Sun nodded in appreciation and took Thorn with him to get some practical experience. After walking for about two hours, they arrived at a rocky gorge in the mountains, near the kobold valley. Master Sun stopped at the edge of the gorge and pointed at the other end.

"Alright, kid, your task is pretty simple. Get to the other end of the gorge."

"You mean all I have to do is walk through it?"

"Haha, yeah. All you have to do is walk through it." Nodding, Master Sun chuckled to himself as he started to walk off. "I'll wait for you at the other side."

"O... okay." Unsure about what was so difficult about walking through an empty gorge, Thorn scratched his head. Even after spending ten minutes staring at the large rocks in the gorge, Thorn could not see anything out of the ordinary, so, with a shrug, he started forward.

[crunch]

After getting almost one hundred feet into the gorge, Thorn paused. The sound had been slight, but Thorn had heard gravel crunching. Paused mid-stride, Thorn listened. After a few moments of complete silence, he could only shrug and continue on.

[Crunch]

There it was again. It was like the sound of two pieces of stone grinding against each other. Still unable to spot where the sound was coming from, Thorn tightened his grip on his weapon and began to move forward. He had not taken more than three steps when the sound returned with a vengeance.

[CRUNCH]

[CRUNCH]

[CRUNCH]

Rising all around him, Thorn saw large stone monsters pushing themselves to their feet. Immense boulders that had previously stood inert began to stretch and unfold as they became stone giants. Around seven feet tall at the shortest, these large stone humanoids were huge amalgamations of stone held together with eldritch force. As the first elemental finished forming, it turned its burning eyes on Thorn.

'Earth elementals!' thought Thorn in shock. Elementals were a rare race in Nova Terra, in part because of how strong they were. A single elemental was often more than the match of a normal party, due to their overwhelming strength and natural immunities. It would be rare to even find a single elemental, so seeing dozens beginning to stand up left Thorn flabbergasted.

'How on earth does Master Sun expect me to cross a gorge like this!?' Thorn shouted in his mind. Earth elementals were ranked as some of the most dangerous enemies to face, boasting a combination of complete immunity to bladed weapons and most magic, as well as uncanny strength.

The first elemental, fully formed now, stepped forward and threw a ponderous fist at Thorn, smashing him back! Thorn, stunned at the strength that the elemental displayed, was shaken. For the second time since he had begun to play Nova Terra, he was forced back!

Shaken by the blow that had sent him stumbling back, Thorn completely forgot to block the next strike, which caught him in the chest! Staggering backward, Thorn almost fell over. Putting down a hand to stabilize himself, he looked at the stone elemental that had punched him in amazement. Pleased by its success, the elemental was roaring in satisfaction, secure in its instinctive knowledge that it had crushed the puny invader.

After it finished announcing its victory to the sky, the elemental looked around, only to freeze. That large creature was still there? The elemental peered closer. Sure enough, Thorn was still standing there, rubbing his chest where the elemental's massive fist had smashed into him.

'That is going to bruise for sure,' thought Thorn.

"Alright, big guy let's try this again," Thorn spat at the elemental, his eyes narrowing. Fixing his grip on the borrowed tetsubo, Thorn dashed forward, smashing toward the confused elemental with an overhead blow.

The elemental, unable to process how the creature had lived through its punch, saw Thorn rushing forward and roared in fury. Drawing back its ponderous fists, it struck out with full force, intent on fixing whatever mistake it had made previously. With a furious clash, the tetsubo fell onto the elemental's shoulder before the elemental's fists reached Thorn's body.

Feeling the rebounding shock flowing through the tetsubo's

handle, Thorn nearly lost his grip on it. The force of the blow sent the elemental tumbling to the ground. However, Thorn had yet to recover from the counterforce of the attack when the elemental started to get back to its feet!

'This isn't good.' Thorn paled, feeling as much shock as the elemental had. This was the first time that a full force blow had failed him since he started Nova Terra! Despite being knocked off of its feet, the elemental was not showing any sort of damage. And to top it off, the second and third elemental were already stomping their way over, more rising up behind them.

"How am I supposed to get through this gorge?" Thorn complained in his heart. Countless calculations and ideas flashed before him. Could he dodge his way through? Unlikely, since the elementals were strong enough to knock him back. What if he blocked as many of the blows as possible and pushed past the elementals? That would not work, either. There were too many of them. Was this an impossible task, then?

CHAPTER TWENTY-FOUR

"No, there has to be a way to do this," thought Thorn. Master Sun would not have assigned it if there was no way to complete it. Running through all of the instruction that Master Sun had given him as he backed up, Thorn's eyes brightened. "That's it!"

What was a tetsubo for? Attacking! Offense as defense! After all, in his exchange now, he had been able to prevent the elemental from hitting him by striking first! He needed to use speed and force to create a perfect defense by crushing any attack before it arrived!

Emboldened, Thorn looked at the two charging elementals. Trying to remember the way Master Sun had begun his spinning pattern, Thorn did not wait for the elementals to attack, but swung out at the larger of the two with a full force sweep, like he was trying for a home run.

The tetsubo impacted the larger elemental's side, causing it to stagger sideways, into the smaller elemental, with a loud crunch. Despite buying himself a couple seconds, Thorn frowned. Neither of his strikes had been enough to hurt the elementals, which highlighted a major problem. Every second he spent here, more and more earth elementals were waking up and rushing toward him. Soon they would overwhelm him with sheer numbers.

The world slowed to a crawl, as his brain began to work furiously. His goal was to cross the gorge without dying. But his normal approach had no way of working because his strikes were not powerful enough to kill the creatures attacking him. If he couldn't remove the elementals from the equation, their attacks would compound until he could not block them.

"Wait. Why am I trying to block them? What was it that Master Sun said? Attacking is a more effective block." Awareness dawning, Thorn finally understood why Master Sun would have thrown him into this hopeless situation. If his goal was only to cross the gorge, there was no reason that he had to kill the elementals.

The forms that Master Sun had demonstrated immediately sprang to mind, and his hands began to turn, the tetsubo gaining momentum as it spun around him. Driving forward again, Thorn intercepted the first elemental with a slashing strike, causing it to stumble. Stepping past, Thorn used the counterforce to send a whirling strike at the legs of another earth elemental stepping forward, sweeping it off its feet.

Step by step, blow by twirling blow, Thorn carved his way forward. However, he was able to achieve only a few steps at a time before a furious blow sent him reeling back. Scrambling to regain his balance, he pushed forward with a wild strike, trying to gain some space. Warding off another punch with a deflection, he started his tetsubo spinning again, using it to throw the incoming attacks to the side.

This time, he managed four steps before being beaten back. Again, he struggled to regain his stance, pushing forward with all the force he could muster. Time after time, he smashed his way through the roaring elementals, only to be pushed back every few steps. Yet, each time he was forced back, he forged ahead again, his weapon flashing, beating back the surging elementals.

As the seconds ticked by, Thorn found himself falling into a strange sort of frenetic rhythm, each of his attacks with his tetsubo becoming smoother and faster. A whirling strike to one side began to flow into a whirling strike to the other side. Blocks began to flow into attacks and attacks into warding strikes. Where he was getting pushed back before, Thorn was soon able to hold his ground.

This increased mastery came at a cost, as blow after a massive blow slammed into his body. Groaning in pain after each strike, Thorn felt his bruised body shaking with the strain of pushing through the flurry of stone fists flying at him. Little by little, bit by bit, his arms began to lose strength, as bruises piled up on his shoulders and chest.

Gritting his teeth, Thorn knew that he was not going to make it through at this rate. With a roar of unwillingness, he turned and ran, outpacing the ponderous earth elementals. Simple creatures, the earth elementals lost interest in Thorn as soon as he escaped, out of sight. After wandering around in the gorge for a few moments, the earth elementals began to revert to their stone forms, and soon the gorge was silent again.

Panting, Thorn could only throw himself down on the ground, groaning in pain. His arms and chest were bruised, and even his head was starting to swell from where a flying fist had clipped him. Yet, even as he lay there beaten, his spirit started to grow. He had learned some very difficult lessons in his first encounter with the earth elementals, and he was confident that his next encounter would be different.

"Well, that was pathetic," a voice said. Thorn didn't even need to open his eyes to know that Master Sun was standing over him.

"Seriously, what were you doing flailing about like that? Didn't I teach you the forms? How come I didn't see any of them while you were fighting there?"

"Sorry, Master Sun." Not bothering to argue, Thorn instinctively replied as he would have to his own sifu, Ms. Chen. He had learned long ago that the sharp criticism was part of what came with having a martial arts teacher.

"You shouldn't be apologizing to me. You should be apologizing to those poor earth elementals, whose time you wasted." Master Sun worked hard to keep the shock out of his voice, covering up his lack of confidence with scathing words.

Thorn was not the first person he had sent into the elemental-filled gorge, but none of the others had made it past the initial elemental the first time they went in. In fact, most had been sent right out of the gorge with that earth elemental's first strike. Master Sun had been dumbfounded when, after taking the strike, Thorn had continued on like nothing happened and pushed almost into the center of the gorge!

Master Sun scratched his balding head in puzzlement. He had matched blows with the elementals countless times before, but this was the first time he had ever encountered someone who could shrug off their blows like they were nothing. Shaking his head, he thought to himself, 'What a freak.'

"Alright, kid, there will be other chances to try again. Let's go back and eat. I'm hungry."

Dragging his protesting body up, Thorn followed after Master Sun, limping back to the camp. Bruises had begun to appear on his hips and sides, making walking difficult. Master Sun didn't move too fast, and Thorn was able to follow him back to the camp. The shack seemed to have restored itself, at some point, and was standing, as tenuous as ever.

After resting for a night, Nova Terra's mechanics kicked in, and Thorn woke up feeling much better. Getting up, he ran through his morning exercise again before he began to practice the hand positions that Master Sun had taught him the day before. He thought over his experience fighting against the mass of earth elementals. Breaking down each of the moments that he remembered, he tried to determine what the best strike would have been in that situation.

As he became more and more familiar with the different hand positions, the general flow of his tetsubo's swings got smoother and smoother. But there was a real problem that Thorn had no way of solving, so he waited for Master Sun to get up, continuing to practice. After a couple more hours, Master Sun walked out of his shed, bleary-eyed.

"Good morning, Master Sun," Thorn greeted, ever polite.

"Hm," grunted Master Sun with a yawn.

Waiting until Master Sun was sitting in his normal spot by the fire pit, Thorn bowed to the middle-aged man.

"Thank you very much for your instruction yesterday, master. Would you be able to help me clear up an issue I have been wondering about?"

"Hey, kid, it is way too early in the morning to be doing the whole 'master and apprentice' thing, so cool it. It's like what, seven?"

"Umm. It is 11:43."

"See, it's still morning. Definitely too early. Anyway, what was your question?"

"Ah, right." Seeing that Master Sun was changing the subject in embarrassment, Thorn moved on to his question. "Yesterday, when I was fighting against the earth elementals, I could not even hurt them. With a weapon that is supposed to rely on pure force, what do I do when my force is not enough?"

"Eh, that's your question? Get stronger, of course. Listen, kid, the tetsubo is a man's weapon," said Master Sun, pointing to one of his massive arms. "If you can't crush someone or something, you practice until you can. Now, part of your problem is that the weapon you are wielding isn't heavy enough for you, but, where direct strength fails, use a force multiplier."

Standing up, he walked over to a tree and put one of his hands on it.

"Look, if I push this tree from a stationary position, the amount of strength I can convert into force is minimal at best. But what if I use a force multiplier, like speed?" Stepping back, Master Sun threw a lightning fast punch, sending splinters flying.

"See, by multiplying my force, my destructive potential goes up exponentially! If you are having trouble crushing something, you first try crushing it harder. But, if that doesn't work, find a force multiplier."

"Ah, so speed is actually the key," mused Thorn.

"Exactly. Anyone who uses a tetsubo is someone who is

confident in their strength. But what sets apart the masters from the scrubs is how quickly they can swing their weapon and how smoothly they can transition between forms and grips to make use of their force and counterforce."

"Thank you, Master Sun." Thorn bowed again.

"I thought I told you that it is too early for that sort of stuff? Whatever. When you think you are ready, head over to the gorge. You still need to get across it."

Bowing again, Thorn picked up his tetsubo, and, beginning to practice his spins and hand positions, he left for the gorge. Having been there before, the way was still marked on his map, so it did not take him long to get there. Like the day before, the gorge was quiet and peaceful, but Thorn knew firsthand that appearances were deceiving. Taking a deep breath, Thorn mentally prepared himself and then stepped forward, throwing himself at the awakening elementals.

That evening, Thorn dragged his bruised and aching body back to camp, collapsing in a heap by the fire pit. He had actually made less progress through the gorge than he had yesterday, but he was not discouraged. He could feel his swings getting smoother and his transitions getting quicker.

Over the next four days, a strange sort of mania set in. Rising early, Thorn would practice the various tetsubo moves at the camp before running over to the gorge to smash himself against the earth elementals, then hobbling back to camp to recover from his wounds. Each day, he pushed further into the gorge than the day before, if only a little. Slowly, he was refining his practical understanding of the whirling tetsubo forms.

On the fifth day, he arrived at the gorge and dove in, unaware that two figures watched him from a ridge.

"Crazy, huh?" muttered Hamm, staring down at Thorn, who was deflecting massive stone fists as he pushed forward.

"Crazy doesn't even begin to cover it," responded Master Sun. "That kid is a monster. A certified monster. I mean, look at him. He can take a full force blow from an earth elemental without falling over. That, in and of itself, is enough to make him an absurd warrior. But when you add decent comprehension and unreal strength to the mix..." He trailed off, his eyes fixed on Thorn, who was struggling with three earth elementals which had come at him together.

Hamm smirked, saying nothing.

"He might have a chance," said Master Sun abruptly, earning himself an incredulous look from the sword trainer. "Listen. That kid is new to this whole fighting thing. In fact, based on his movements, it's pretty obvious that he is holding back for some reason. Look at his awkward attacks. For some reason, he is subconsciously afraid of using his strength. If he ever learns to let it out and gets his hands on a decent weapon, woe be upon anything that is in his way."

"There's no way. No one can fight that thing. All of us working together couldn't beat it. He might be big, but there's no way." Hamm shook his head.

"Hmph. Wait and watch."

In the gorge, Thorn had fallen into a strange rhythm. Each step he took, each spin of his weapon, seemed to fit into a violent dance. His partners, the earth elementals, still roared their challenge at him, but there was a joy underneath the gravely sound. Together they danced back and forth, this way and that.

That evening, when Thorn got back to the camp, Master Sun was waiting for him, a massive pack sitting next to him.

"Hey, kid, I've got to get going. I've taught you what you need to know, so now it is a matter of practicing it, alright?" Master Sun took a swig from his bottle of wine.

Despite his exhaustion and bruised body, Thorn stood in front of Master Sun and bowed.

"Thank you, sir," he said.

"Haha, don't worry about it." Standing, Master Sun finished off the wine and tossed the bottle to the side. Picking up the huge pack, he adjusted it on his shoulder and smiled at his enormous student. "Oh, one other thing. My classes cost 10 gold a day. We've been at it for six days, so that's 60 gold. You can pay Hamm."

Thorn's mouth dropped open in shock.

"Haha, or," said Master Sun, dragging it out, "you can get to the end of the gorge. I'll waive the fee if you can pass all the way through by sunset tomorrow. Anyway, see you later, kid."

With a wave, Master Sun disappeared from the camp, leaving Thorn in stunned silence. Sixty gold? It would take forever to work that off! Even killing Gargish, a unique boss monster, had only given him 10 gold! Resolving once again to get through the gorge, Thorn lay down. Tomorrow his body would be healed, and his motivation was stronger than ever.

Unlike the previous days, the early morning sun found Thorn standing outside the elemental's gorge. If he was going to get through it in a day, he needed as much time as he could get.

'Alright, let's do this.' Psyching himself up, Thorn gripped his tetsubo and rushed forward, not waiting for the first elementals to form. Getting as far into the gorge as he could before the elementals were together was a dangerous bet, but it was the only thing Thorn could think of to give himself an advantage.

CHAPTER TWENTY-FIVE

Rumbling to their feet, the earth elementals roared out their gleeful greeting and rushed toward him, fists swinging. The first elemental to reach Thorn was tossed aside with a deflecting blow, as were the second, third, and fourth. But, as the fifth set of fists came in, Thorn found himself unable to fully deflect it in time.

Accepting the blow, Thorn angled his tetsubo to throw it off course and jumped back, using the momentum as it glanced off his weapon, trying to minimize the damage as much as possible. Escaping the crush of bodies, Thorn tried to dart around the group, but by this time, there were too many earth elementals around him.

The gorge was not that long, only half a mile in length. Yet, somehow, those 2600 feet seemed to stretch on forever. The earth elementals had large bodies and created a natural stone barrier as they crowded around to try and get a blow on Thorn.

Finally, after a few hours of struggling, Thorn backed out of the gorge. Reaching the other end by rushing through was not going to work, so Thorn sat down and ate a bit as he thought about his experiences. For some reason, the last few days had been harder than the first couple of times he attempted to get through.

It was almost as if there were more elementals now. A quick

count revealed that there were the same number as always, so why did it feel like there were more elementals in the gorge than before? Laying down and gazing at the cloud-dotted sky, Thorn tried to remember his first fights. When he had first entered the gorge, he had taken a lot of punches straight on, since he had not mastered the constant momentum that Master Sun taught.

Over time, he had gotten much better, but, at the same time, the punches seemed to come faster and thicker. What was going on? Despite thinking on it for twenty minutes, Thorn made no progress in figuring it out, so he shrugged, got up and headed back into the gorge. Still distracted as he faced the first earth elemental, Thorn missed his deflecting blow with his tetsubo!

The earth elemental's stone fist caught Thorn in the chest, causing him to stagger back a couple steps. Frustrated and angry, Thorn growled, letting loose with a furious swing. As he began to pour power into the strike, he did not think about his form or his follow up, smashing out with all his strength.

[CRACK!]

With a sharp roar, the elemental crumbled to the ground, pieces of its stone body bouncing off the valley floor, leaving Thorn staring at his tetsubo in shock. As he had let go of his form, a strength that he had never felt before surged through his arms into his weapon, completely crushing through the earth elemental, leaving it in pieces on the ground. However, as he watched, the elemental's head continued to tremble, and the bouncing pieces of its broken body began to reform.

Seeing the yellow glow in its eyes, Thorn realized that he would have to crush its head to kill it. For a moment, he hesitated, his tetsubo raised. Lowering it again, Thorn could not bring himself to take the swing. The elementals had been his sparring partners for almost a week, and something in him loathed the thought of actually hurting them.

That moment of hesitation cost him, as the second earth elemental came roaring in, fists swinging. Jumping backward, Thorn instinctively deflected the blows, whirling around and unleashing another wild strike.

[CRACK!]

The second earth elemental shared the same fate as the first. Instead of backing up, Thorn, feeling like he was on the edge of grasping something vital, threw himself forward into the oncoming wave. Striking out with wild abandon, Thorn found at least half of his strikes either missing or glancing off the elemental's stone bodies. However, for every strike that missed, another laid an earth elemental low.

Soon the familiar back and forth dance turned into a slow slaughter. Thorn pushed forward again and again into the waves of elementals, crashing through them with swing after swing, only to be pushed back as the stone fists pummeled him.

In the midst of one such exchange, Thorn felt something click for him, and he instinctively switched between the whirling defensive forms he had been learning from Master Sun, swinging out with a formless strike, smashing through an elemental's body. Out of the corner of his eye, he saw a massive fist coming toward him and, with a neat turn, spun back into his defensive form.

'This is what Master Sun was talking about!' Thorn thought, as he warded off the elemental's strikes. 'Defense turning into offense!'

Excited by his discovery, Thorn tried to replicate the process, only to miss a block and take a punch right to his face, sending him reeling back. Swearing to himself, he squared up again and smashed the offending elemental into pieces. Working out the balance was a slow, laborious, and above all, painful process of trading blows, yet little by little, Thorn began to find his equilibrium.

The sun was starting to sink in the sky, the tall pines casting long shadows across the gorge, when Thorn finally pushed past the last elemental. About halfway through the gorge, the first elementals he had fought had finished reforming and roared in to attack him from behind, forcing him to defend for a couple desperate moments. He quickly regained his balance and continued smashing his way through the elementals until he reached this point.

As the dust finally began to settle, Thorn found himself at the other end of the gorge, on a slight slope leading out from between the hills and into the trees. Taking a moment to breathe, Thorn looked back over the field of pulverized stone and glowing elemental eyes. Though sore, he felt good. Very good. However, as he began to turn around, a subtle vibration sent the settled dust hopping into the air. His brow furrowed as he saw the yellow eyes of the elementals he had put down blur and begin to gather.

The unnatural vibration seemed to draw the elemental eyes in, yellow glowing dots leaving streaks through the air, all gathering together into a ball. As the hundreds of eyes piled into each other, they began to compress, growing brighter as they did so. Faster and faster, they collapsed into each other, until they formed a bright glowing dot that floated off the ground. The yellow glow had gotten so bright it was almost too bright to look at.

Putting up a hand to protect his eyes from the glaring light, Thorn tightened his grip on his tetsubo. After a moment, the brightness faded, and Thorn was able to look at the elemental light, which now resembled a polished piece of amber. As he watched, the gem floated toward him, pulsing with light.

Watching the approaching gem, Thorn considered trying to knock it down with his tetsubo, but, just as he tightened up his grip for a swing, the floating amber pulsed, and a deep, gravelly voice rumbled in his mind.

"Greetings, great warrior!" the voice boomed. "You have shown strength and ferocity but, also, compassion! For that, I thank you!"

"Uh, yeah. No problem," said Thorn, still holding his tetsubo ready.

"Hah, no need to be concerned, young warrior. I bring you no danger! I am Terberus, the Earth King! As great Terra commands, I must reward those who defeat my daughters!" Here Thorn could almost see a barrel-chested old man waving his hand at the piles of rubble Thorn's rampage through the gorge had left. Thorn lowered his weapon and scratched his head.

"Ah, sorry about that. I hope it is not too much trouble for them to put themselves back together."

"Do not worry, young warrior. It is their honor to be challenged and your honor to have triumphed! For the mercy of sparing their lives, you have my thanks!" rumbled the voice, like two boulders being ground against each other. "As the victor, you have every right to collect their cores as spoils, but by showing mercy, you have earned yourself a great favor! Behold, I grant unto you a boon! Your path will be long and treacherous, but the powerful embrace of the earth will be your shield, Friend of the Earth!"

Before Thorn could react, the floating piece of amber spun and drilled its way into the center of Thorn's brow! Horrified, he tried to block it, but the stone slipped through his hand and seeped into his skull! Feeling no blood, Thorn looked around, but the light was gone, leaving only the echoes of the rumbling voice as evidence that it had ever been there.

For a moment, Thorn had no idea what to do, but everything in the gorge had gone back to normal, and the voice was gone. Seeing a blinking icon indicating an update to his status page, Thorn opened it up to take a look.

Name: [Thorn]	Race: [Titan]
Health: [93%]	Mana: [100%]
Titles: [Battle Mad], [Wolfsbane], [Lord Greymane (locked)], [Friend of the Earth]	Conditions: [None]
Abilities: [Wolf Lord's Howl(locked)]	

Seeing a new title, Thorn opened it up to examine it.

Title: Friend of the Earth

You have earned a boon from the Earth King, Terberus. As one of the four elemental kings, Terberus has granted you the favor of the earth. This may come in handy in the future.

Grumbling about Nova Terra's useless explanations, Thorn waved the windows away and sat under a tree. It was getting dark, and he was exhausted. He had spent the afternoon smashing through almost a hundred earth elementals, and his body was aching. The hits from the elementals had not been too bad, once he got used to them, and, frankly, most of the blows had been deflected away, as it was.

Rather, the pain in his body was from overusing his muscles for almost eight hours of straight swinging. While the game mechanics made the weight of the tetsubo negligible, he couldn't get around the fact that he had been swinging it as hard as he could over and over again. His shoulders ached, and he could feel a burning pain in his arms.

As was his habit, Thorn thought back over the last few days. Master Sun had opened up an astounding path for him, providing a practical style that used his mighty strength and endurance to stunning effect. The martial arts training that he had gone through over the years had been useful for killing corrupted wolves and gave Thorn a strong foundation from which to build, but his size became a hindrance to him in using a sword to maximum effect.

On the other hand, Master Sun's unique style was better suited to his size and strength. Frowning, Thorn realized that he didn't actually know what the style was called. Musing for a couple minutes, Thorn tried to come up with a good name that was not too cheesy, but, after rejecting 'Raging Storm Strikes,' he quit trying. Coming up with names was not his strong suit.

His combat against the elemental had been a growing experience. Their blows, though powerful, had not been too dangerous. Thorn shuddered as he imagined what would have happened to him if they had been swinging sharp claws, instead of blunt, rocky fists. Gargish, while not as strong as the earth elementals, had brought him much closer to death because of the piercing nature of his attacks.

If each of them had been like Gargish, Thorn would have been shredded before he even started to fight back! Not all the creatures in this world were as scary as Gargish. While he had come out alive from his encounter with Gargish, it had been much closer than he had liked.

On the other hand, after making it through the earth elemental's gorge, Thorn felt much more confident. He felt that, if he encountered Gargish now, not only would he be able to put up a good fight, but he even had a decent chance of winning!

[ding]

A low tone alerted Thorn to the fact that he had a video message request from Mina. Smiling, he opened the window and greeted her.

"Hey, Mina! What's going on?"

"Heya! How are you? We're almost back from our guild mission! Finally! This mission has been a total pain, and I'm so glad to be done. It has taken forever, and it was su-u-uper boring. Plus, Jorge is a total pain and has been, like, grumpy this whole time."

As the familiar torrent of words flowed out of the short girl's mouth, Thorn could not help but smile. It had been a bit more than a week since they had interacted, and he had missed her rapid-fire conversation. Used to being alone, Thorn had not anticipated how much he would come to enjoy engaging with others but hearing Mina prattle on made his heart warm.

"So, anyway, Ouroboros asked me to tell you that we are heading back to Berum to complete the next part in our quest, and, if you are free, we would like to bring you along. Plus, there's a chance that there's a class change, which would be perfect for you, since you don't have a class yet, unless you got a class since we last met, but you shouldn't have because Ouroboros said that he told you to hold off." Her face red from saying all of that in one breath, Mina paused to breathe in, allowing Thorn to jump into the conversation for the first time since it started.

"Yeah, that sounds great. I have not..."

"Oh, wonderful! You're so big and strong that you can carry waaaay more than the other porters we used," Mina interrupted when she had finished breathing. "The porters on our last job were terrible. I mean they couldn't hold even a quarter of the stuff you could hold, and they were all so boring to talk to, it was pathetic."

Sending a chat message to Ouroboros, Thorn left the call with Mina open and began making his way back to Berum. It took him a couple hours to get back to the city, and it wasn't until he could see the stone walls surrounding Berum that Mina finally stopped chattering and said goodbye. They had agreed to meet at the same tavern as they had eaten at previously, but Thorn still had a day to kill, so he first stopped by the armorer who had made his custom armor.

CHAPTER TWENTY-SIX

"Welcome to the Knight's..." Like the first time Thorn had entered, the shopkeeper was so stunned by the sight of Thorn squeezing into his shop that he trailed off in the middle of his sentence. "Uh...Shield."

"You do repairs, right?" said Thorn, laying his armor on the counter.

"Yeah, yeah, we do repairs. We can repair anything." Nodding, the armorer spread the massive suit of armor out, tsk-tsking to himself as he saw the extensive damage. Most of the hardened leather plates were covered in deep gouges or split from where Gargish's claws had cut through them. Likewise, the plate metal was either punctured or crumpled in on itself, and the chain portions were bent and ripped from where the earth elementals' stone fists had smashed into them.

"I take it back. We can't repair this. Okay, we could, but it would cost more to repair it than to make a whole new one. What did you do, walk into a nest of elementals? I would recommend scrapping this and getting a new set. I still have the plans I drew up for these, so I'd be happy to make you another set."

"That sounds good." Thorn nodded.

"Excellent. I thought you might come back, so I already have a couple of pieces I was going to use to repair any damage. The design is already done, so it shouldn't take me long to put the new suit together. Stop back tomorrow morning, and I'll have it for you."

Thanking the armorer, Thorn ducked out of the store and made his way over to the mercenary supply store to pick up some more bolts for his arbalest. It had served him very well when he was fighting the corrupted wolves, and he imagined it would serve him even better when he was working as a porter for Ouroboros and the rest of the group. The last time he had worked with them, he spent a lot of time at the back doing nothing. This way he would at least be able to contribute a little.

Then again, they worked very well as a group and, so far, had shown no need of any help. The more he learned about Nova Terra, the more clearly, he realized the powerful impact that classes had on the game. Without a class, Thorn was still very strong. But imagine if he had special abilities on top of that? Just a single category class would have made his fight with Gargish a hundred times easier.

Even something as simple as a Warrior's [Charge] ability could have allowed him to close the distance when Gargish attempted to jump away, or a Knight's [Armor Mastery], which would have made his armor ignore 30% of Gargish's damage. To say nothing of the abilities of a Mage or Warlock, who had various means of crowd control at their disposal.

If not for Ouroboros mentioning that the new quest would have a dual category class, Thorn would have gone and gotten a basic class ages ago. Plus, Mina had mentioned that, to join Ragnarok, the minimum requirement was to have a dual category class. Few elite players had earned theirs by mastering their first class, so the guild mostly accepted people who started with a dual category class.

Though Ouroboros had never explicitly mentioned anything to Thorn, he had hinted that, if Thorn were to meet the basic requirements of the guild, Ragnarok would love to have him. It seemed that dual category class players who could still act as a porter were rare, which put Thorn in a great position. After all, who wouldn't want a porter who could also fight?

The next morning, Thorn picked up his armor from the Knight's Shield. This time the armorer had added thin metal plates under most of the hardened leather plates to try and give Thorn a bit more protection from whatever had slashed through them last time. The darkened metal pieces of the armor and the chainmail underneath were new. The armorer had offered to upgrade the materials to a stronger alloy, but Thorn did not have the money for it, so they were still steel.

Putting the armor back on, Thorn left the Knight's Shield and went to turn in his bounty. He had killed a huge number of corrupted wolves, and his bags were stuffed with stacks of their tails. Once his quest was turned in, Thorn still had a bit of time, so he decided to swing by the Forge Quarter and see about getting his tetsubo repaired. While it was still in good shape, breaking apart earth elementals had put some strain on it. Somewhere along the way, it had developed a slight bend.

When Thorn first pulled it out, he placed the head of the tetsubo on the ground and held it up straight to show the bend. Nodding, the dwarven smith grabbed the handle and tried to lift it off the ground, only to stagger under its weight. Thorn had been handling the weapon with ease, so the smith misjudged the weight of the pure metal tetsubo.

Looking at Thorn in respect, he called a couple other smiths over, and between them, they got the tetsubo into the forge and started heating it. It took three dwarven NPCs almost four hours to straighten it out and re-anneal it to make sure it was as strong as before. Once they had finished, Thorn paid them and picked it up as if it was a stick, swinging it a couple times before putting it away in his inventory.

Now that he was dressed in armor, not the beginner clothes, Thorn looked like an experienced player, and he found it much easier to walk through town. It was subtle, but the presence he gave off since fighting Gargish and the earth elementals was stronger than when he had started the game. This new aura caused people to instinctively move out of his way when he walked.

The meeting at the tavern was scheduled for lunch, so Thorn went ahead and ordered when he got there. By the time the others arrived, there was a steady stream of dishes coming out to the table. Used to seeing the mounds of food that Thorn consumed, Jorge and Velin sat down and started digging in, after waving a hello.

Mina, on the other hand, bounced over to him and tried to give him a hug. Startled, Thorn patted her on the back. Due to their size difference, Mina's arms didn't make it much more than halfway across his chest. Like the others, she soon quieted down and started shoveling food into her mouth. Smiling at the other three, who had descended on the table like they were starving, Ouroboros clapped Thorn on the shoulder before sitting down.

"You're looking good, Thorn," Ouroboros said, filling up his plate. "The armor looks great on you."

"About time ya stopped looking like a noob," mumbled Jorge around a mouthful of food.

"Yeah? When are you going to stop acting like a jerk?" Mina jumped in to defend Thorn before he could respond. "Forget him, Thorn. He's mad because he ranked last in our guild quest."

"Oh, come off it. You only beat me by two points, and only because I let you."

"Enough, you two. You are giving me indigestion." Velin silenced them with a glare. Giving Thorn a small smile, she sighed. "It would have been much easier if you had come along, Thorn. I never missed having a pure support class so much."

"What did you do on the guild quest?" Thorn took the chance to ask.

"An ore run," said Ouroboros, taking over the conversation. "Ragnarok has a production class wing, and they need huge amounts of resources to do their thing. But, because they are squishy, they get PK'd all over the place. So, every month, the guild assigns a day for teams to help the production squad gather materials. This time we were on an ore run. We had to collect a metric ton of ore of various types from drops. It's pretty boring, but it has to be done."

"PK?" Thorn had never run across the term.

"Player Kill. People attack them and take all their stuff."

"Seriously? How is that allowed?" Thorn asked, shocked.

"What do you mean, how is that allowed?" Mina asked, looking at him. "Nova Terra is a full player versus player game. People kill each other all the time. Have you never been attacked by a bandit before?"

"Does Thorn look like someone a bandit would attack?" asked Jorge with a chuckle.

"Good point," Mina conceded.

"So, killing people is okay?" Being new to these sorts of games, Thorn was having trouble wrapping his head around this change in perspective.

"It depends," Velin cut in before Mina could respond. "There are a surprising number of players who use their freedom in game to attack others and steal their belongings because there is no permanent penalty for death. The only negative consequence, apart from a twenty-four-hour logout and some dropped loot, is that you lose some of your class mastery, so death has very little weight. There are much worse things than death."

For a moment, the table was quiet, as Thorn tried to work through the logic behind this. His aunt had always taught him to treat people well, so the idea that it might be okay to fight and kill without regard for others was a bit difficult to deal with. Seeing his frown, Ouroboros patted him on the shoulder.

"Not everyone plays that way, Thorn. There are some bad apples in every bunch, but that's why we protect those who can't protect themselves. In fact, there were three attacks while we were hunting for ore."

"Better to kill bandits than the stupid elementals." Taking a deep drink, Jorge wiped his mouth off with the back of his hand before continuing to complain. "I've put in who knows how many requests that they don't assign us to fight those stupid rocks. Why can't we get an herb run or something like that? At least I could stab the bandits who try to steal from us."

"He is sore because his knives don't work on elementals," laughed Mina.

"Anyway, we are one of the only groups without a porter, so it takes us a couple of trips to get enough ore." Ouroboros patted Thorn on the shoulder again. "Hopefully, we can change that soon."

Seeing that Thorn was still consuming the food on the table at a fantastic rate, the others settled into eating. Dish after dish came out under the astounded gaze of the other patrons, but Thorn never slowed. It was not that he ate quickly; rather, he consumed whole plates of food in a couple bites. He could eat half a chicken in two bites and a loaf of bread in three. Whole plates of pasta were swallowed down in less than a minute. Even if he took his time, the food disappeared at break-neck speed.

It was almost an hour later when the group finally finished their meal and settled down to business. Mina had ordered a desert, and Ouroboros and Velin were drinking coffee while Jorge stuck with another ale. Thorn was drinking water, since alcohol had next to zero effect on him, given his size and the speed with which his metabolism worked. He did not mind alcohol, but the water was free, and he had already spent almost a whole gold on food today.

"Let's get down to business." Putting down his coffee, Ouroboros pulled out a small, white sphere and set it up on the table. Pushing a button on the top, a translucent force field expanded from it to surround the table, cutting off the sound from the rest of the tavern and blurring them from view with a swirling mist. Pulling out a map, he spread it across the table and pointed to a large valley to the north of the city.

"This is where we completed the kobold extermination quest. It went much faster than expected, thanks to Thorn here, and we not only managed to clear some villages, but we also took down the kobold chieftain and a Greater Shaman. We all know - well, most of us know, that a mob Shaman doesn't become a Greater Shaman without there being an inheritance of some sort nearby. Well, I did a bit of digging, and I've figured out where the inheritance is based.

"You'll notice that the valley is a large cul-de-sac with only one entrance, right? Actually, if you check old maps, that doesn't seem to have always been the case." Pulling out another map, Ouroboros laid it over top of the first map. Drawn on transparent paper, it soon became apparent that there was a small canyon running off of the valley to the northeast.

"I'm not sure what happened to close the entrance, but, according to my research, this is where the Shaman found an inheritance to turn into a Greater Shaman. At the worst, we should find a class change altar and some loot. However, that brings us to our next piece of research. Take a look at the name of the canyon."

"Davyos' Fall?" read Mina. "What does that have to do with anything?"

"Nothing, except that Davyos was a famous Devil Blood Berserker from the God's Era." Seeing Thorn's confused look, Ouroboros smiled and explained. "The world of Nova Terra has gone through three different eras. As you can imagine, they are named in order. We are currently living in the beginning of the Fourth Era, the Traveler's Era. However, Nova Terra has a lot of history from before players ever entered the game. Each Era was long. Like, thousands of years long.

"The First Era is also called the God's Era. It was a time when warlords rose and fell, and massive creatures roamed around eating everything in sight. Countless powerful people and creatures died during that time, leaving their inheritances behind. During this time, the basics of civilization started to be built out of the wilderness. It's called the God's Era because it is said that the gods played a monumental game with the races of the world. They chose members of the various races to become their avatars. They blessed them, granting their avatars fantastic power and pitting them against each other.

"After the God's Era came the Dragon's Era. Powerful elemental dragons emerged and brought the land under their spurred heels. They enslaved the other races and waged massive wars on each other. Most of the gods' avatars had fallen, by this point, and the dragons plundered the inheritances for their own followers. They took the inheritances of the chosen and granted them to their own chosen. The dragons began to behave like the gods before them, sitting high above the world while pitting their chosen against each other. But the races couldn't be kept down forever, which led to the Third Era."

CHAPTER TWENTY-SEVEN

"The Imperial Era started when two powerful chosen, a demonkin and a human, defied their masters, after falling in love. Leading a massive slave army, they rose up and defeated the dragons, unifying the entire world under the twin banner of humanity and demonkin. Their son was the first emperor. The Imperial Era was an era of peace and prosperity, but, under the surface, a growing fight brewed.

"See, the first emperor was half and half. His dad was a demonkin, his mom was human. But every child after that had either more human blood or more demonkin blood. The intrigue created because of that caused an unhealable rift, and the empire was torn in half in a bloody civil war. The demonkin took the southern half of the continent, and us humans took the northern half. The Imperial Era ended with the arrival of the first travelers.

"As I was saying earlier, Davyos was a Devil Blood Berserker from the God's Era. As far as we know, he was the avatar of Karrandaras, a powerful archdevil who ruled over blood and corruption. Other people have explored this area before, but they didn't find anything. I'm guessing that, somehow, the inheritance was uncovered by the kobolds, which let the Shaman become a Greater Shaman."

"Wait, you're saying there might be a triple category class there?" asked Mina in disbelief.

"Honestly, I doubt it," said Ouroboros, shaking his head. "The chance of it being a triple category class is abysmal. Most of the ancient inheritances from the God's Era were plundered by the dragons ages ago, so it is unlikely that such a high-profile class would have slipped through. I mean, there are close to three billion players and only four triple category classes. All of which, by the way, were picked up from massive chain quests that took whole guilds to complete.

As far as we know, the Devil Blood Berserker class was a mix between a Devil Warlock, a Blood Shaman, and a Blood Warrior. What I am hoping for is a dual category class stone that can be used to form one of those classes. Most of the avatars from the First Era had retinues of dual category classes, which means there is a pretty solid chance that we can get at least one dual class, if not a whole set."

"Then what are we waiting for?" asked Jorge, downing the rest of his ale. "Let's get rolling."

"Oh, now you're interested in working?" Mina said with a sneer. "Where was this excitement when we were on our ore run?"

As Jorge was about to fire back, Ouroboros grabbed his shoulder.

"Cut it out, you two. Thorn, if you're willing to act as a porter for us, there is a good chance we should be able to get you a dual category class." Ouroboros rolled up the two maps and then looked at Thorn. "It might be very dangerous. Especially so, since you don't have a class, but the potential reward is huge. What do you think?"

"I'm in!" declared Thorn, slapping the table in excitement.
BOOM!

With a loud crash, the table splintered into pieces and collapsed onto the ground, sending everyone's cups flying!

"What the!" Jorge yelled as he jumped to his feet, swearing. Likewise, Mina scrambled backward, flipping her chair over as she did. Even Ouroboros jumped up in surprise. Only Velin did not react, looking at Thorn and raising her eyebrows.

"Sorry, sorry," stammered Thorn, as surprised as everyone else.

It took a moment for everyone's surprise to settle down. The pyramid of silence that Ouroboros had set up was still deployed, so the rest of the tavern had no idea that Thorn had crushed a table with a simple slap. The swirling mist had also blocked the splinters, saving the surrounding patrons from a storm of flying wood.

"Goodness, don't scare me like that." Mina clutched her chest. "My heart is beating a hundred miles an hour!"

"I'm sorry. I didn't mean to do that," Thorn apologized again as the others stared at him.

Once everyone had calmed down, Ouroboros picked up the pyramid of silence and paid the tavern owner for the ruined table before herding everyone out. Ouroboros gave everyone an hour to do what they needed before meeting at the north gate. Since Thorn had already restocked on all his supplies and gotten his tetsubo fixed, he decided to head to the gate where the party was going to meet.

Once the group had finished getting ready, they left the city and headed into the mountains to the north. After a few hours of travel, they arrived at the entrance to the large valley where they had fought the kobolds previously. Seeing the familiar land stretching out before them, Thorn could not help but smile. This is where he had gotten to know his new friends, so it held a special place in his heart.

Rather than immediately pushing into the valley, Ouroboros had everyone set up camp to rest for the night. At first, Thorn had found it strange that players kept to a normal night and day schedule in Nova Terra, considering the time dilation, but he quickly realized that the amount of information that a person had to process grew along with the stretching time.

While it was possible to push through for multiple days, players found that they had a better experience when they slept. Plus, it wasn't like they were losing much time. Seven hours of in-game sleep was an hour of real time. It was like taking a small break before carrying on. Most players actually logged out when their character rested, Mina and the others being no exception.

Since Thorn couldn't actually log out, he went to bed like normal. There was little difference between his sleep and a player who had logged out, so Thorn set an alarm to wake him up when the others logged back in and closed his eyes. The system assisted the process, and he fell asleep almost instantly.

When his alarm went off the next morning, Thorn got up and packed up his tent. Ouroboros, Mina, and Jorge had already logged in and helped Thorn break camp while they waited for Velin. Once the camp was cleaned up, Thorn got out some breakfast and passed it out. After half an hour, Velin logged in and greeted everyone.

"Did you find anything?" Ouroboros asked, brushing some crumbs from his fingers as he walked over to her.

Nodding, Velin handed over a document.

"It looks like we have some competition. We need to pick up the pace," she said. "The others have made tangible progress, which means more pressure on you."

"Alright, we better head out," said Ouroboros, after scanning the document. Putting it away with a frown, he looked off into the distance for a couple moments before gathering everyone up. By the time he was facing the others, he was back to his normal self, and, without further delay, they started on their way.

Thorn and the others had been too far away to hear the exchange, so they set out in high spirits. Like the first time they came into the valley, Jorge acted as a vanguard, clearing the way for them. Unlike their previous venture, they met kobolds more often, though in smaller groups.

Mina explained that, because the Greater Shaman was dead, the kobolds were not as unified anymore and were ranging farther from their villages. For a normal player, this made the valley a much easier hunting ground. Most of the kobolds they came across were in small bands of three or four, allowing the team to breeze through them.

Despite his anticipation that he would be able to display his new weapons, Thorn found himself following along as Mina handled the kobolds with a quick spell. Jorge took care of any groups of less than three while a single blizzard spell wiped out groups of three to four. The one time they came across a group of six, Mina cast two blizzard spells on top of each other, decimating the group before Thorn could even get his arbalest out. Seeing his frustration, Velin patted him on the shoulder, while Ouroboros chuckled.

"Don't worry, you'll get a chance to fight," the Guardian assured Thorn. "In fact, we are getting close to the canyon. We'll be there for a while, and the respawn rate is going to be higher than in a normal spot, since it is so close to the main kobold camp."

Sure enough, they soon arrived at the narrow entrance to a small canyon. This was the spot marked on the original map that had been lost. Jorge cleared the two kobolds who were hanging out at the entrance of the canyon and walked back to the group, tossing the gear they had dropped to Thorn.

"Alright, this is the spot. Inside, we'll be looking for a passage or entrance to the rest of the canyon that has been blocked off. It's been a little while, so I'm guessing that there should be another kobold shaman spawned. Even if they have been upgraded to a Greater Shaman, we don't have much to worry about," said Ouroboros, looking at the ancient map.

"Jorge, you lead the way, like normal. Mina, Thorn, you two can help him search. Since we are going to be stuck between the entrance, that we haven't found yet, and the main kobold village, I'm expecting that we will need to fight off some waves, which means you need to hurry. This is a good choke point, so Velin and I will camp here to block off any reinforcements. Any questions?"

"Yeah, if I find the entrance before Jorge does, shouldn't he finally admit that I am better than he is?" asked Mina, sticking her tongue out at the dwarven rogue.

"Oh, come off it. There is no way you will find the entrance first. You haven't found anything before me since we started playing." Jorge smirked.

Ouroboros rolled his eyes, ignoring them.

"Thorn, please do all of us a huge favor and find it before these two do. Then they'll shut up for once," Velin said.

"No thanks, I have no desire to come between the two shorties," laughed Thorn.

"Shorties? Who's short?" demanded Mina.

"Yeah, how about I cut you down to our height?" threatened Jorge, brandishing one of his long daggers.

"Okay, that's enough. Let's get to work. We have company," said Ouroboros, pointing at a group of fifteen kobolds hurrying toward them.

Like the professionals they were, the group immediately burst into action. Jorge faded from sight, hurrying to the right, while Mina cast a spell, sliding forward on the path of ice that formed under her feet. At the narrow canyon opening, Ouroboros pulled out his large shield and planted it into the ground in front of him. A bright, white glow fell on him, as Velin stood behind him and began to rain buffs on him.

Thorn was caught by surprise by the immediate action everyone else took, and after standing there for a couple seconds, he turned and headed farther into the canyon to look for the entrance like the other two. As he left, he did not see the complicated look that Velin cast at his back.

Rushing forward, the kobolds soon arrived at the canyon's narrow mouth and were about to swarm Ouroboros and Velin, when the Holy Guardian gave a great shout, his shield glowing. Looking over, the kobolds seemed to go mad as they saw the silver glowing shield. With growls and angry howls, they threw themselves forward, toward the planted shield.

Bracing against his shield, Ouroboros weathered the impact before sliding the tower shield onto his back. Striking forth with a sweeping blow of his sword, Ouroboros bisected one of the kobolds. The following backhand forced the rest of the monsters back half a step, which Ouroboros immediately closed with a spin, replanting his tower shield into the ground with a firm thrust.

As the tower shield hit the ground, it sent out a quaking wave, throwing the remaining kobolds off their feet. As they started to struggle up, Velin completed her chant. Sharp spears of light formed above the struggling clump of kobolds, stabbing down with deadly efficiency. Only two of the original ten kobolds made it out of the rain of light alive and were dispatched by Ouroboros' sword.

After taking a moment to look through the loot the kobolds had dropped, Ouroboros leaned on his shield and stared back into the depths of the canyon. Velin, seeing the intense look of thought on his face, frowned.

"Are you starting to have second thoughts?" asked Velin.

"No," Ouroboros shook his head. "The whole thing is repulsive, but it is the only way we will be able to compete."

"Is it?"

"Yes," said Ouroboros, his voice growing hard. "There are only four in the world right now, and the bonuses can't be denied. There is no way to compete with the advantage they give. Even if it takes some sacrifice, it will be worth it."

"Even sacrifice at the expense of others?"

For a moment, Ouroboros' hard look softened, and he seemed to struggle with himself. Was it worth it?

"Yes, even at the expense of others." The Holy Guardian took a deep breath and closed his eyes. "Sometimes, greatness requires us to put ourselves before others. And this is one of those cases."

"You sound like your dad."

"Ha," Ouroboros' shoulders slumped in defeat. "I guess I do. I never thought I'd fall this low, but there isn't another option, at this point. I'm too far behind. This is the only way to catch up."

"Ultimately, this is a game. Is there a need to compromise like this?"

"You don't understand, Velin. This might be a game, but in

some ways, it is more real than real life," said Ouroboros, turning to face the new group of kobolds rushing over.

CHAPTER TWENTY-EIGHT

Oblivious to the conversation behind him, Thorn combed through the canyon, looking for any sign of a hidden entrance. According to the information Velin had brought back, the canyon had most likely been blocked by a powerful spell that moved the earth from the canyon walls. New to the game, Thorn found all the lore quite interesting and had listened raptly as Ouroboros and Velin explained what they had discovered about the area.

Some time back at the end of the God's Era, Davyos, the Devil Blood Berserker, had led what remained of his forces back into this canyon to flee from one of his enemies. Despite his class, Davyos was considered a cold, calculating general who never engaged in a fight he could not win. Faced with overwhelming odds, the Devil Blood Berserker had chosen to retreat to the temple, where he had been granted his power in the hopes that the Archdevil who had granted them would assist him.

Like most avatars in the first era, Davyos had a mysterious history, shrouded by the fog of time. Little was known about his background, and it was only through paying Avalon for the information that Velin had been able to find out anything about the ancient figure. According to the report that she had received, Davyos had been a Wolfkin hunter who stumbled upon a temple deep in this canyon.

After receiving the blessings of the Archdevil, Davyos had used his power to create a powerful mercenary group that completed tasks for the local warlords. A warlord more greedy than wise attempted to pay Davyos less than he owed, and Davyos led his men to slaughter the warlord and everyone around him. Claiming the warlord's territory for his own, Davyos began to consolidate power, his personal prowess paving the way for his territory's rapid expansion.

All good things come to an end, and after almost twenty years of tyrannical rule, Davyos was attacked by an alliance of humans and elves. While he fought and inflicted serious casualties on his opponents, they were determined to rid the land of his influence and nibbled away at his territory until he was forced to flee back to the corrupted temple from which his powers had originated.

According to the information that Velin had purchased, as the army was retreating, one of Davyos' most powerful followers called the land to collapse and, casting a prodigious spell at the cost of his own life, caused the canyon walls to be pinched shut, completely sealing the temple away. Over the years, a shift in the earth caused a path to be opened, once again revealing the temple to the world.

Or so the team now hoped. Mina, Jorge, and Thorn were still looking everywhere for an entrance to the canyon as Ouroboros and Velin held off the continuous waves of kobolds. Despite examining every stretch of ground, the three of them had not found even a hint of a passageway. Over at the canyon mouth, the groups of kobolds were getting larger and larger, as more and more kobolds realized that there were intruders. Soon a howling mob had formed in front of Ouroboros.

"Any time now, guys!" yelled Ouroboros over his shoulder.

"There is nothing here!" Mina shouted in frustration, kicking a rock. "We've looked all over this stupid canyon, and there isn't a blasted hole in sight!"

"Well, look harder!" Ouroboros snapped.

Outside the canyon, the crowd of kobolds was starting to swell as the noise from the fight attracted them. At first, it was only ten or so kobolds rushing forth in each wave, but the waves got bigger and closer together. "After a few minutes, the waves will merge into a constant stream of enemies," thought Ouroboros, cold sweat running down his back.

"Mina! Leave the searching to the others and come to support us!"

"What? Why can't Jorge help you?" Mina whined, only to be silenced by a glare from Velin. "Fine." Rolling her eyes, she huffed her way over to the mouth of the canyon and raised her wand. A chill pervaded the air as countless snowflakes appeared. Muttering under her breath, Mina waved her wand again, pointing to a couple of the drifting flakes.

Every snowflake Mina pointed to glowed a bright, icy blue and expanded before hurtling forth like an icy ninja star, cutting into a kobold! Deep gashes began appearing on the kobolds rushing to get around Ouroboros, the icy power freezing them and slowing them down even as the sharp ice blades cut their skin.

While the number of kobolds had grown, the entrance to the canyon was so small that only ten kobolds could fit into it at a time. This narrow choke allowed Ouroboros to keep most of the kobolds back while Velin buffed him and dealt with the kobolds on his right. To his left, Mina's icy shuriken carved their way through any kobold that managed to slip past.

Again, and again, the kobolds surged forward. Despite their lack of armor, poor weapons, and weak strength, their sheer numbers began to take a toll on the three defenders. Beads of sweat began to appear on Mina's forehead as she sent icy blade after icy blade forward. Ouroboros had been breathing hard for a while, despite Velin's energizing spells. Even the elven War Priestess was beginning to drag.

A quick look back showed that the two girls were approaching their limit, and Ouroboros knew he needed to make a decision. If Jorge and Thorn were not able to find the entrance to the hidden part of the canyon soon, they would have to call off the search and try to break out; otherwise, they would all be buried here. Slicing through the neck of another kobold, Ouroboros steeled his heart and opened his mouth to say something, only to leave it open in shock as a huge stone, almost twice his size, came hurtling over his head!

Flying through the air, the massive boulder spun before crushing the rushing kobolds, sending them flying. With a sonic boom, it slammed into the ground, skidding a bit before stopping, raising a huge cloud of dust. Mina, Ouroboros, Velin, and Jorge all stared in shock at the huge stone that had seemed to appear out of nowhere. They didn't snap out of it until they heard a satisfied voice behind them.

"I found the entrance, but it is a bit small, so I'm widening it."

Behind the group, Thorn had been searching through the rocks when he tripped over a log sticking out of the piled stones. When he stood back up, he noticed that the shifted log revealed a small space behind it. Digging out the surrounding rocks, Thorn realized that the entrance to the cave had been covered over with a pile of boulders, with an especially large one plugging up the opening.

Especially large to anyone but Thorn, of course. Seeing that the pressure from the kobolds at the mouth of the canyon was growing, Thorn flexed his fingers and grabbed the boulder, pulling it out of its hole. Raising it over his head, Thorn tossed it over Ouroboros, smashing into the kobolds and narrowing the canyon entrance even further.

The kobolds, terrified that it was now raining massive rocks, fled back out of the canyon, screaming, allowing some breathing room for the tired Holy Guardian and the two ladies. Wiping the sweat off her forehead, Mina ran over to examine the cave entrance.

"Do you think this is the one?" she asked, peering inside.

"Only one way to find out, eh?" replied Jorge, slipping past her into the cave. "I'll check it out, boss."

"Ha, don't you dare," retorted Mina, dashing after him.

Giving Thorn an appraising look, Velin walked after them.

Embarrassed by Velin's attention, Thorn rubbed the back of his head and then followed Ouroboros into the cave. The ceilings of the tunnel were pretty high, so Thorn didn't have to duck. Much.

The tunnel wove around for a bit before opening up into the rest of the canyon. From what Thorn could tell, the tunnel had been bored out by hand, over a long period of time, by the kobolds. This brightened up the party's spirits, as it meant that it was less likely that the dragons had discovered this ancient inheritance during the Second Era.

Of course, the dragons had enslaved many of the lesser races, so it was possible that the tunnel had been dug on their orders, but, according to Velin, the dragons were strong enough to rip through the blockage in the canyon, so it was unnecessary for them to have their minions dig.

Before they reached the entrance into the hidden canyon, Jorge made his way back to the group, carrying a body. Despite his short stature, his thick frame possessed significant strength, surprising Thorn. Careful to make as little noise as possible, Jorge put the body down on the ground and gestured to it.

"Hey, boss, check this out. This is one of the two guards that were hanging out ahead. After I took them down, I peeked around the corner and saw a big metal door. There were fifteen or so more of these wolf guys hanging out in front of it. There were two casters working on opening it up."

"Kobolds?"

"Nah, they are not kobolds, or at least, they aren't any of the kobolds I've seen. Their armor and weapons are all high quality, and they stand a lot straighter than kobolds. Their faces are also different."

"Could they be a different type of kobold?" asked Mina.

"Hmm, interesting. Look. Their fingers are clawed, but they have hands like humans, rather than paws, like kobolds." Poking the dead creature's hands with his sword, Ouroboros pointed them out.

"Wolfkin!" blurted out Thorn.

"Wolfkin?" the other four asked together.

"Yeah, I ran into another person like this," said Thorn, his brow furrowing as he remembered Gargish, the Blood Hunter. Like this body, Gargish was a mix between a wolf and human, having a generally human form with the head of a wolf.

"Hmm, tell us about it. Were they a mob?" asked Ouroboros.

"Mob?" asked Thorn, unfamiliar with the term.

"What a noob," Jorge muttered under his breath, as Mina rolled her eyes and chuckled.

"Ah, mobs are NPCs that don't have the same intelligence as the NPCs you interact with in town," explained Ouroboros with a wry smile.

In Nova Terra, NPCs were categorized into two different classifications. Some NPCs, the monsters, were there to act as fodder for the players and friendly NPC factions. These NPCs had very basic AI and generally only existed in the game to be farmed for quests and loot. The kobolds were a good example of this. While a few of the kobolds with classes (like the Chieftains, Shaman, and Greater Shamans) were more advanced, the average kobold had very limited AI. The players referred to them as 'mobs' since they were mindless, and it was generally understood that interacting with them was pointless unless it was with a sharp object.

On the other side of the coin were the natives, NPCs that had advanced AI and could reason, think, and scheme like the players. Natives were often no different than players, and it was generally very difficult to tell them apart. For the most part, players interacted with natives to get quests, advance their skills and progress in the game. While there was no proof of it, rumors had it that Eve, the AI that controlled Nova Terra, had the ability to transition mobs to natives, whenever it was convenient, in order to achieve the game's ends.

"No, he was definitely a native. A hostile native. Like, super hostile," said Thorn, remembering the mad struggle he had had with Gargish. "He was a human who turned into a half wolf, half man, like these guys. Sort of a werewolf type of thing."

"Okay, so that means they are a new faction. Almost all native races can be played as characters, though some require unlocking, so this information is pretty valuable. Jorge, how tough were they?"

"They were strong. I had to use both my clone and a mass silence to keep them from hitting the gong."

"I could have killed them faster," muttered Mina under her breath.

"Definitely a native faction, then. We'll have to hope there are not too many of them in here." Ouroboros ignored Mina and stood up, dusting off his hands. "Let's keep going."

Advancing farther down the tunnel, Jorge stayed ahead of the group while the rest moved in their normal formation. Ouroboros led the way, his shield held in front of him, with Mina a step behind, to his right. Spaced to the other side, Velin was a step behind Mina while Thorn brought up the rear, three steps back.

Despite his assurances that he was okay fighting, the other four still treated him like he was a new player and positioned him at the back. At least, they didn't protest when he pulled out his arbalest and loaded in one of the massive bolts. In fact, Mina had doubled over in laughter at the sight of the massive weapon, and Jorge had made a couple sly comments.

At least, Ouroboros hadn't laughed and had assigned Thorn to protect Velin. Excited by the thought of getting to participate, Thorn mentally vowed to fulfill his role well, despite the fact that Velin had the most survivable class out of the whole group.

Turning a corner, they caught sight of Jorge, who was stopped up ahead. Slipping back to where the group was waiting, Jorge held up two fingers.

"Two casters, three heavy armor, the rest look like rangers of some sort. Long daggers and bows. At least ten. Heavies are carrying axes and shields. Casters are spouting some nonsense at a bronze door. Looks like a rune lock that they are trying to open," he whispered, drawing out the enemy's position on the ground.

"Let's go with formation six," Ouroboros ordered after a moment of thought. "Jorge, you are on the casters. I'll hold down the heavies while the girls clear chaff."

CHAPTER TWENTY-NINE

"What about the big guy?" asked Mina, glancing up at Thorn's excited face.

"Yeah, what can I do?"

"Protect the girls, of course," said Ouroboros.

"Alright, sounds good."

After affirming that everyone understood their role, Jorge moved behind Ouroboros while Mina and Velin pulled Thorn to stand between them, a few steps behind Jorge, who had taken out a purple salve to spread on his daggers. As quietly as they could, the group moved up the tunnel. Thorn tried to be quiet, but they had not even gotten halfway up when they heard voices, and a group consisting of an armored Wolfkin and four of the rangers walked around the corner to see what was going on.

As the groups caught sight of each other, the Wolfkin yelled out in surprise, and Thorn pulled the trigger on his massive crossbow! With a piercing whistle, the bolt flew down the tunnel, stabbing into the armored Wolfkin. A loud screech rang out as the metal tip of the bolt buried itself into his chest, punching straight through his metal breastplate and sending him tumbling head over heels.

With incredible force, the armored Wolfkin bowled the rangers over, knocking them all to the ground! For a moment everyone froze in utter shock. It was only when they heard the groan of the arbalest, as Thorn pulled back the string to load another bolt, that they snapped back to reality.

"Go!" roared Ouroboros charging forward, his shield up. Like a shadow, Jorge dashed right after him, tucked behind his back. Mina continued to stare at Thorn, her mouth open, until Velin poked her in the shoulder with her staff. Shaking her head as they ran forward behind the charging Holy Guardian, Mina waved her wand, sending ice spikes into the heads of the rangers, who were still struggling to rise.

Charging right past the struggling Wolfkin, Ouroboros caught sight of the rest of the Wolfkin, who were getting into formation. The two armored Wolfkin stood out front, while the rest of the rangers stood in a rough half-circle behind them, their bows out. At the very back, the two casters had stopped working on opening the door and were readying spells.

With another roar, Ouroboros accelerated, crossing the remaining distance in a flash. His shield up, he smashed into the two armored Wolfkin, causing them to stumble back. As he impacted them, a shadow shot over his head, using his back and his shoulder to launch itself forward. Jorge, who had stuck close to Ouroboros, flew over the heads of the rangers toward the Wolfkin mages in the back!

The mage on the left abandoned his chant as he saw the dwarven rogue flying through the air toward him. Pulling a wand from inside his thick robe, he took aim at Jorge, muttering the triggering incantation. Bloody red lights formed at the tip before shooting toward Jorge. With a smirk, the dwarf pulled his cloak around him, disappearing from the air in a silent explosion of shadow, only to appear behind the other mage, who was still chanting.

Two daggers thrust out at the mage who was still oblivious to the danger. As Jorge attacked, a thin barrier sprang up around the mage, blocking the oncoming daggers. Rather than panicking,

Jorge smoothly slid his left-handed dagger forward. Shorter than his right-hand dagger, his left-hand dagger had a thicker blade with a jagged edge. Impacting the magical shield, it flashed a deep red, sending cracks shooting through the shield!

His other dagger followed right behind, slipping through one of the many cracks that had appeared in the shield before cutting through the mage's heavy robe and into his ribs! The mage had barely registered the attack when his throat spasmed, cutting off his chant as the Throat Sealing poison that Jorge had spread on his daggers took effect.

Occupied with the two armored Wolfkin, Ouroboros had no time to worry about Jorge. While his initial charge was enough to knock both of them back, they recovered their footing and attacked. Lifting his shield, Ouroboros shifted to the left with a twist that allowed him to catch both attacks. Rather than going for the kill, he settled into a defensive stance and prepared to weather the storm.

Before the rangers could choose which target to attack, a wave of magical energy washed over them. Ice spikes and golden feathers began to bombard them, sending them scrambling for cover. A few of the braver ones pulled out their daggers and dashed forward, trying to get close to the two girls who were casting spells, only to be driven back by Thorn's heavy swings.

It took less than a moment for the battlefield to devolve into chaos, but, even to Thorn's untrained eye, it was obvious that the chaos was being skillfully controlled. Jorge's blitz had taken down one of the mages, and he was occupying the other with a relentless barrage of attacks while Ouroboros held the middle of the field, where the two armored Wolfkin were stuck to him. Despite trying to retreat to help the mages, the armored Wolfkin could not seem to break away from the Holy Guardian.

Every time they would try to step back, he would shift his position and strike with his sword, forcing them to defend. Even when they attacked, trying to drive him back, he shifted his position. Soon they found themselves with their backs to Thorn and the girls, with Ouroboros in between them and the casters.

The rangers milling about found themselves in an impossible situation. Every ranger that tried to approach Jorge had ice spikes shooting toward their heads. Those that tried to get involved with the melee in the middle were assaulted by golden blades shaped like feathers! Their only option seemed to be to try and attack the girls casting the spells, but that proved to be even more futile because of the giant swatting them away.

It only took a few moments for Mina and Velin to wipe out the rangers. Once the last one fell, skewered by both an icicle and a golden feather, Velin cast a buff on Ouroboros while Mina threw a blizzard at Jorge and the struggling mage. With a soft hiss, the whole area around the dwarf surged with a deep chill. Jorge teleported away as the remaining mage froze solid, appearing behind one of the armored Wolfkin and thrusting both of his daggers through gaps in its armor. With a gasp, the armored Wolfkin stiffened and collapsed.

Throwing a glare at Mina, Jorge was about to attack the other Wolfkin, when Thorn stepped forward and grabbed the armored NPC from behind, lifting him completely off the ground and tossing him aside. The armored Wolfkin hit the wall with a loud crack, his neck breaking. Once again silence descended, as Thorn stared at the now dead NPC. He had been excited to contribute but had not actually intended to kill the Wolfkin.

"Holy..." staring at Thorn's massive figure, Jorge backed up a couple steps as his words trailed off.

Ouroboros, startled to see his opponent disappear, took a long look at Thorn, his mind working. After a moment of quiet, he stepped back and sheathed his sword.

"Alright, let's get all this cleaned up."

After picking up the loot that had dropped, the five of them gathered around the door that the two mages had been working on opening. The door was a massive bronze affair covered in reliefs of battle scenes. Most of the door showed armies of Wolfkin battling against fierce monsters and enemy armies. At the top of the door, however, a series of images showed a massive Wolfkin, at least three times the size of all the others.

Tracing the images from the edge of the door, different scenes showed the large Wolfkin struggling through many trials before arriving at an altar. The image at the top of the door was of the bloodthirsty Wolfkin accepting some sort of blessing from a powerful figure floating above the altar.

"Could that be Davyos?" Thorn asked, looking at Velin, who was studying the carvings.

"Hmm. Possibly," Velin replied, tracing her fingers over the figure of the large Wolfkin. "We have no record of his race, so it has always been assumed that he was human. But it could be that he was one of these Wolfkin. Many of these images do line up with the myths we have about him.

"See here? We have the young hero who leaves his village to go out into the world. Next, he joins an army and learns the cruelty of the world. Here we see him breaking out of a desperate situation and turning it around. This matches the story that he once led an army of a couple hundred to defeat an army of 10,000. Hmm. Ah, here he rises up in the ranks but is betrayed by his own people and is forced to flee with his supporters.

"That brings us to the center image, up at the top, where he is granted power. If this is Davyos in the images, then that is when he gets his triple category class and becomes a Devil Blood Berserker. Then, using that strength, he raises an army and returns to conquer those who betrayed him and drove him out of his home."

"Does that mean that there is a chance we will find that altar here?" asked Jorge, his eyes lighting up as he gazed at the door. "I mean, the one that Davyos used to gain his power."

"Unlikely," frowned Velin, dumping cold water on the group's excitement. "If we look farther down the door, it looks like Davyos was forced to retreat again after he ruled for a while. See, this is him having to flee and dying while trying to escape."

"Are these a picture of the doors?" Mina furrowed her brow as she pointed to one of the pictures on the bottom of the door.

"That is what it looks like. Who knows if this is a tomb or something like that. Regardless, we won't know what is behind the doors until we open them up," answered Ouroboros.

Thorn sat down about ten feet from the door and began tossing apples in his mouth while Mina helped Velin examine the magical restrictions on the door. Inventory in Nova Terra was based on a player's strength, which meant that every player's inventory was different. However, strength was limited, and the more a player added to their inventory, the slower they moved. All of this culminated in Thorn having deep pockets, which allowed him to stock an enormous amount of food.

As realistic as Nova Terra was, there was much about the game that Thorn still found astounding, and magic was at the top of that list. He had been in the game for a couple of months, at this point, and almost all of his time had been spent getting adjusted to the game. His unique situation had made the adjustment more difficult than that of the average person. Thorn's whole life had been an exercise in control. Controlling his strength, controlling his desires, his every activity was focused on making sure that his body did not collapse.

This made his transition to the game rather time-consuming. After all, sixteen years of habits, intentionally cultivated habits, were hard to break. Despite his martial arts training, it took Thorn a long time to understand how to move. In fact, he was still figuring out how to apply his strength. All of this adjustment had left little time for exploring the fantasy aspect of this new world.

Watching Mina and Velin examine the door was fascinating for Thorn. Velin would point, and Mina would draw a glowing rune with her wand. Every once in a while, they would huddle together and discuss things in hushed voices before going back to draw more runes. Seeing Thorn watching the girls, Jorge wandered over and plopped down next to him. Taking an apple, he gnawed on it for a bit before gesturing to the increasing number of runes on the door.

"Is this your first time seeing a magic lock? Pretty cool, huh?"

"Yeah, it looks cool, even though I have no idea what is happening."

"Haha, don't worry. You're not the only one." Jorge took another bite. "Magic is a whole different beast. It takes way more effort than it's worth, though, as you can see, it is quite powerful if you are able to handle it."

"I saw you use a pretty cool ability in the fight. Was that magic?"

"Oh, you mean the shadow jump? I guess it is technically magic. But it's different from a mage or something like that. Mages use spells by working with runes and chants, while my ability is attached to my class. As a Shadow Assassin, I have some different abilities tied to the two classes. Some of them are innate magical spells, like my shadow jump."

"That sounds strong."

"It is. There is definitely an advantage to abilities that are based on magic, since they can bypass a lot of the laws of physics. However, it is important to remember that the game is balanced. While most people don't believe it, Eve does balance all the classes and adds restrictions to anything that is too strong."

"What about on people?"

"What do you mean?"

"I mean, does Eve balance people?" asked Thorn, flexing his fingers. "Wouldn't there be too many differences between people, if they were not restricted to a standard?"

"Only insofar as the same rules apply to everyone. However, the advantages a person has in the real world carry over. Actually, there were tons of people complaining about it when Nova Terra first came out. Normal video games use the same baseline for everyone, right? Well, Nova Terra isn't a video game." Jorge smirked. "Nova Terra is an alternate reality. Like people have advantages and disadvantages in real life, Nova Terra doesn't pretend that those differences don't exist.

"You and I are a great example of that. You must be huge in real life. I'm not this short, but I'm still way shorter than you. I'm so short that I got to choose between a bunch of different races that you didn't qualify for. Those races have advantages that you won't get and, actually, can't get. At the same time, being short has disadvantages that I can't naturally overcome. Like not being able to grab people by the head and throw them around."

Remembering how he had killed the armored Wolfkin, Thorn felt his face flush. He had not intended to kill him, but he had not quite gotten used to how his strength fluctuated. When the game judged his target to be friendly, it restricted his application of strength to make sure he did not injure them. However, when the system judged his target to be an enemy, it removed that restriction. Still puzzling over this, Thorn turned his attention back to the magic users at the door.

CHAPTER THIRTY

By the door, Mina was finishing up the last rune, and Thorn realized they were about to begin the opening spell. While it looked like the runes that Mina had drawn were scattered around the door, what happened next proved otherwise. Standing a few feet away, Mina lifted her hands, palms toward the door. Taking a deep breath, she began to spit out arcane words, each word causing one of the runes drawn on the door to light up.

As they glowed, the runes started floating off of the door to gather in the air. As the different runes rotated in the air, glowing lines of energy raced to connect them, forming mysterious overlapping geometric shapes. To Thorn's untrained eye the symbols were incomprehensible, but he still found them fascinating. Mina finished igniting the last rune before to turning Velin, who was still standing to the side calculating something.

"Alright, we're ready."

"Okay. The first position is thetra, kal, emix, housan, rou," said Velin, looking up from her paper.

Listening as Velin rattled off the arcane words, Mina swung her wand, rotating the runes to different positions in the air. Once the shapes had been moved to the proper position, she pointed to five runes in succession. The runes, each on different shapes, glowed brighter, forming a mysterious constellation in the air.

"Ready for the next set," said Mina with a deep breath, wiping away the sweat that was trickling down her cheek.

Over the next two hours, Velin read out rune combinations, and Mina rotated the shapes to light up new constellations. It was tiring work, but halfway through, Velin cast a rejuvenation spell on the Ice Witch so she could keep working. Finally, they were done, and the runes began to flash. One by one the constellations they had marked out began to flash as the magical rune shapes spun on their own.

Faster and faster, they pulsed in the air, until they began to blur together into a single complex rune. Jorge stepped behind Thorn as the girls made their way behind Ouroboros, who had readied his shield. At Thorn's questioning look, Mina looked grim.

"If we didn't get it completely right, it might be trapped. Even if we did get it right, it might be trapped. Plus, we have no idea what is behind the door. I'd brace yourself," she explained.

Thorn watched the door as the glow continued to brighten. When it was getting difficult to look at, there was an abrupt noise.

CRACK!

Jumping, Thorn braced himself and waited for the coming explosion. And waited. And waited. Instead of a rushing force, what came were peals of laughter from Mina who had been watching Thorn.

"Haha, you jumped so high!" Mina gasped in between her giggles. Seeing the rest of the party smirking, Thorn realized the Ice Witch had been playing a trick on him and blushed, rubbing his head in embarrassment.

"The one thing Mina was right about is that we don't know what is behind the door. Everyone fall in," commanded Ouroboros. "Mina, watch for mana flux, Jorge get ready to jump."

Squaring up, Thorn got his arbalest out and loaded a bolt while Ouroboros stepped next to the door and pushed. The unlocked metal door inched open, revealing beams of sunlight that streamed into the tunnel. Fully open, no threats were apparent, so the group walked forward, out of the tunnel and into the sunlight.

As they left the tunnel, the land in front of them opened into a peaceful green valley. Sloping hills dotted with woods rolled between the sheer cliffs of the canyon walls that opened up before them. Widening to almost a mile across, the canyon walls were smooth and unbroken. The ground dipped down into a hollow in the center of the valley, a ruined city sprawled out in somber silence.

"Whoa," Mina exclaimed, gazing wide-eyed at the little world that stretched out before them.

"That must be Davyos' final retreat. The place where he fled before he died," said Velin.

Together, they walked toward the city, admiring the peace of the valley. Ancient stone buildings, spotted with age, rose from weed-eaten cobblestone streets as decaying wooden shutters creaked to and fro in the soft breeze. True to their expectations, they did not spot any more of the Wolfkin they had found in the tunnel.

"It's so quiet, though," Thorn said.

"It is quiet. The city has been abandoned for hundreds, if not thousands, of years."

"Can't have been," Thorn replied, shaking his head and pointing. "Wooden shutters wouldn't last for more than ten to fifteen years, even if they had paint, which they don't. If the city was last occupied a thousand years ago, nature would have reclaimed it. Or at least overgrown it. The fact that we can still see most of the cobblestone means that the city was occupied more recently. I'd imagine that it hasn't been more than five or six years since people lived here."

"Hmmm. Why don't we spread out and look around?" suggested Ouroboros. "Give a shout if you find anything of interest."

Agreeing to meet up at a large building in the center of the city, everyone scattered and began to explore. Thorn found a building with some large columns that looked interesting. A barely readable sign in an ancient language proclaimed its use, but Thorn couldn't read it. Based on the faded picture of what looked like a book, Thorn assumed it was a library of some sort and pushed open the hole-ridden doors.

The doors were quite large, so he did not have to duck as he walked into the building. Looking around, he found himself in a large open hall with a desk set to one side. Large double doors beyond the desk revealed a massive room filled with shelves of moth-eaten books. Stairs in the middle of the back wall led up to a second-floor balcony that ran around the whole room, leaving the middle of the room open.

Counting fifty bookshelves on the bottom floor and another twenty on the second story balcony, Thorn wandered over to a shelf and rapped on the wood. The wooden shelf still felt strong, a testament to how well sealed the library had been over the years. For the most part, the books seemed to be in pretty good shape, but every single book that Thorn pulled off of the shelf was written in the same ancient language that he had seen on the sign.

Out of habit, Thorn tossed the book he had picked up into his inventory as he continued to browse. Along one wall, Thorn did find a large map and a rack of scrolls that he put in his inventory. The map was made of some sort of treated hide and showed many details of the surrounding area. Based on what Thorn could tell, it seemed to be the valley and the area north of Berum. A brief examination showed the location of the city of Berum, which reinforced Thorn's idea that this city had been occupied within the last ten years.

Berum had been around for at least one hundred and fifty years, but the division of the city into four quadrants had only happened fourteen years ago when the current Castilian took over. Seeing that the map had the four quarters of the city marked out, Thorn could guarantee that it had been made within those fourteen years.

'So why was it abandoned?' wondered Thorn to himself. 'The legends of Davyos go back thousands of years, and that ancient map that Velin scrounged up was that old. Or at least a couple of hundred years old. What could cause a whole city to be abandoned like this?'

The fact that the books were still on the shelves and the map was still on the wall indicated that the city had been abandoned in a hurry without the time to pack everything up. Growing more and more curious, Thorn closed the doors and continued to explore the city. Wandering down a street, he peeked in a couple of the homes that lined it. Most of them were very similar in their layout but empty.

In the distance, Thorn could hear the rest of the group moving around, but otherwise, the city had no sign of life. Over the next hour, as he poked around the buildings on his way to the center of the city, Thorn did not find anything as exciting as the library. He did find a street of what looked like potion shops, but apart from fancy glass tubing, there was nothing of particular interest.

The center of the city was dominated by a hulking stone building set in an open courtyard almost a thousand feet across. The tall building towered over the rest of the buildings in the city that were two stories high, at most. Broad steps covered the front of the building, leading up to a wide landing with thick marble columns that stretched for the first two stories.

Massive metal doors, that mirrored the doors that Velin and Mina had opened in the tunnel, were set in the thick stone walls. Looking around, Thorn could not see any windows or other openings on the massive building. There was a certain barbarity to the rough-hewn stone, and a close examination of the walls and stairs revealed thin red veins running through the grey stone. The building was quite different from the rest of the city, though Thorn had seen traces of this style in some of the other buildings he had passed by.

It was almost as if the city had been built up around this massive edifice. However, without a reliable way to date all of the structures, Thorn could only assume that the large building predated the rest of the city. Hearing a whistle from behind him,

Thorn looked back to see Jorge stroll out of an alleyway, gazing up at the big building in astonishment.

"Woooeee. That is one big building," Jorge scratched his chin as he stared at it, his eyes lighting up. "I bet it's a dungeon!"

"Dungeon?"

"Man, you never disappoint, do you, noob?" Shaking his head at Thorn's ignorance, the dwarf explained. "Dungeons are specialized instances that can be entered over and over again to gain rewards."

"Yeah, obviously," Thorn rolled his eyes. "Is there anything special about them?"

"Haha, yeah. In this world, dungeons run a bit differently than in normal games. In most games, a dungeon resets every time you run it, which means the spawns, difficulty, and rewards are fixed. You get the same experience every time. Nova Terra is a bit different because nothing resets. Instead, dungeons in Nova Terra tend to evolve. For instance let's say that there is an evil wizard at the bottom of this dungeon. Or top, since it is a tower.

"If we roll through the tower and whack the wizard, the next group of people who come through may find out that the wizard has become a lich. Or maybe they kill the lich and, the next run, it turns out that a group of priests have taken over the tower but have been corrupted by the residual evil magic. Or some such nonsense. Regardless, things in this game follow the same pattern as the world. Everything we do causes other things to happen, so what we do in a dungeon sets up the next dungeon."

"What if we destroyed the building?" asked Thorn after pondering Jorge's words for a few minutes.

"I dunno. Nothing might happen. In that case, we would get a small amount of credit for 'razing' the dungeon, but anyone who found out would hate us. But maybe, after enough time had passed, an evil monster would take up residence in the ruins and a new dungeon would be formed. It all depends on what Eve wants to do."

"Huh, interesting."

After a few minutes, the whole group gathered together on the steps of the huge building. Velin, who had arrived before Ouroboros and Mina, stood next to the large metal door scanning it for magic traps. After determining that the door was not locked or trapped, she called Ouroboros up and had him open the door.

Thorn had volunteered, but the elven War Priestess had smiled and patted him on the arm. Despite his best efforts, the team seemed reluctant to let him help in any way, apart from being a porter, which made Thorn frustrated. Still, he was glad to be able to tag along with them, so he did not try to push his luck for fear they would not be comfortable letting him stay.

Ouroboros made sure the others were in position before pulling the door open to reveal a blank, empty room.

"See, dungeon," said Jorge to Thorn, who was behind him. "The first room of a dungeon is always empty. It's a staging room."

As the group entered the building, Thorn heard the soft ding of a notification and looked down.

Dungeon: Hati's Ascent
You have discovered the ancient temple of Hati, the Moon Wolf, where the Devil Blood Berserker Davyos gained his power and fell. Eons have passed since Davyos betrayed his pledge to the divine Moon Wolf, and the corruption brought by his betrayal has warped the temple. Proceed at your own risk.

"Hati? Wait, I thought that Davyos got his power from Karrandaras, that archdevil guy," Mina said after reading the notification.

"That is what I thought, as well." Ouroboros furrowed his brow. "Velin? Any thoughts?"

"Give me a moment." Velin retrieved a small, leather-bound book from her inventory and flipped through it. After a couple minutes, she sighed and closed it, shaking her head. "Too much information is missing. We know that the Devil Blood Berserker Davyos served as Karrandaras' avatar. Maybe he did so after being

Hati the Moon Wolf's avatar? But I've never heard of Hati before, so there is no way to determine what happened. Most likely we'll find out more as we go through the dungeon."

Nodding, Ouroboros commanded everyone to get into position, and they moved out of the staging room onto the first floor of the dungeon. Excited about his first venture into a dungeon, Thorn looked around with interest. What met Thorn's gaze could not have been simpler: a stone passageway stretched twenty feet to a stone room, light from torches placed four feet apart providing ample light.

As they walked into the room, Jorge took to the front to check for traps. The first room was as simple as the hallway they had passed through, holding a small pedestal with a book opened on top of it. With no visible exit and no dangers apart from boredom, the group split up to look for the way forward. Thorn copied Ouroboros and Mina, who were knocking on the walls to see if there were any hidden doors. Meanwhile, Jorge checked out the pedestal while Velin looked at the book. Seeing that it was in a language that she had never seen before, she shrugged and put it away.

Jorge found a switch, and, with a grinding crunch, a section of the wall depressed and slid aside to reveal another hallway. However, as the group started to gather, four robed figures armed with bucklers and short spears with wide, leaf-shaped blades rushed out. With hoarse cries, they attacked!

CHAPTER THIRTY-ONE

As always, the team's response was impeccable and instantaneous. One of the figures only made it two steps before collapsing as Jorge's figure appeared behind them in a silent explosion of shadow. Mina slid to the side on a sheet of ice that appeared beneath her feet, avoiding a stab, as she started to chant while Velin waved her staff, causing Ouroboros, who was charging forward, to light up. With a satisfying crunch, Ouroboros smashed his shield into the two robed figures in the front, sending them flying off their feet and into the stone wall!

Rotating, the Holy Guardian roared out a challenge at the robed enemy chasing after Mina, who turned as if by magic and charged toward Ouroboros. 'That must be some sort of taunt,' thought Thorn as he watched the team taking their enemies apart. The rest of the fight took less than a minute, ending when Mina dropped the last enemy with an ice spike.

Once the fight was over, Thorn stepped up, glad to finally have something to do. Walking up to the bodies, he crouched and pulled the dark robe off of one of the corpses, revealing a scarred Wolfkin. Unlike the Wolfkin they had killed in the tunnel before the valley, these Wolfkin had dirty silver fur, stained with old blood and grime. Curious, Thorn looked at the others.

"Looks like some sort of cultist or acolyte," said Velin, walking over and prodding the corpse with the end of her staff. "Look for some sort of religious symbol."

Sure enough, after digging through the dead Wolfkin's waist pouch, Thorn found a small token with cracks on it. The token was round, made of silver, and Thorn could see the silhouette of a howling wolf under the deep crack. Handing it to Velin to look at, he kept searching but did not find anything else.

"Interesting. I'm guessing that these Wolfkin served Hati at one point. The symbol of the howling wolf against a round moon would match. But they must have fallen out of favor or betrayed the Moon Wolf, causing their tokens to crack. Hmm. We'll have to keep our eye out for more information. Info about a lost god could be valuable."

"Alright, let's keep rolling," Ouroboros said, taking the token from Velin to look at. "This seems like it is shaping up to be a corrupted altar sort of dungeon, so we'll want to keep a heads up for possible ways to purify it. It is also getting increasingly likely we will be getting a solid class out of this, so we need to keep our heads in the game. We handled these guys pretty well, but if we are going up against ranged fighters or casters, we will need to adjust. Thorn, we're going to count on you to help deal with ranged threats with that massive crossbow of yours. Coordinate with Jorge so you are not doubling up on targets. Remember, no need to rush this, slow and steady keeps us alive."

Hearing Ouroboros say that he could participate in the upcoming fights made Thorn so excited that he almost forgot to loot the other three corpses. Rifling through their belongings, Thorn tossed their whole pouch in his inventory and then stood back up, his arbalest out and ready, much to Mina's amusement.

"You know we are going to fight, and not eat, right, big guy?" Mina poked him with her wand.

Despite her teasing, Thorn checked over the parts of his weapon the way Janus had taught him. Once he was sure the firing mechanism was in working order, he stood at the back of the group and waited to proceed. Despite thinking to himself that he would do much better fighting on the front lines like Ouroboros, Thorn did not want to disrupt the group's normal way of doing things, so he tried to be as understanding as possible.

The first floor of the dungeon turned out to be much the same, a series of rooms containing between two and six enemies, all armed with long daggers. Nothing out of the ordinary presented itself, and Jorge and Thorn's cooperation became better and better as they practiced. It even got to the point where they were able to take down groups of four enemies before the rest of the group could even engage.

Jorge would always take the enemy to the farthest right, and Thorn would start with the enemy the farthest left. Once they were done, they would move in, toward the center. At first, Jorge assigned Thorn to one enemy, but Thorn's reload speed was fast enough that he could generally fire two shots before Jorge was done with his mobs.

The only issue was the immense destructive potential of the bolts that Thorn's arbalest used. Unlike normal arrows that would stick into an enemy and make them bleed, these bolts either ripped their unfortunate victims apart or nailed them to the stone wall. The party had seen one of the bolts in action when Thorn had shot the armored Wolfkin in the tunnel, but it was not until they saw the bolt stab six inches into the stone wall that they realized how fast it was actually going.

The bolts would slam into the robed Wolfkin, sending them flying back through the air like a kite with its string cut. After one bolt landed in a particularly unlucky Wolfkin's shoulder and ripped his arm completely off, Mina could not take it anymore and made a gagging motion.

"Thorn, do you really have to break them into pieces like that?" Mina complained.

"Ah, sorry. I was aiming for his chest, but he moved."

"Ug, so bloody. Why don't you let me deal with them from now on? I'll be able to do it much cleaner, and you won't waste ammo."

"It's okay, I have plenty of bolts. I still have almost 1200, actually."

"Are you serious?" Velin cut in, her eyes moving between Thorn and the massive bolt that had nailed the poor Wolfkin to the floor. "The bolts weigh, what, 15 pounds?"

"The shaft is nine pounds the metal head adds three and a half pounds," nodded Thorn.

"You are carrying 1200 twelve and a half pound bolts, in addition to all the stuff you are carrying for us?"

"Yeah. Just under. This game's weight reduction is something, huh?"

Without replying, Velin looked at Ouroboros.

"Regardless, next time I'm going to attack. Your arrows are way too bloody," said Mina, getting out her wand and holding it up in front of her.

"Please, Thorn is much better than you at ranged combat. His bolts don't take up mana, he fires faster, and they are all one hit kills. Compared to that, your ice spikes are terrible," argued Jorge, ever ready to give the Ice Witch a hard time.

As the three of them moved toward the next room, bickering as they went, Ouroboros and Velin stayed a bit farther back. Ouroboros' face was pale, his hands gripping the top of his shield as it rested on the ground. Velin's face was as grave as ever as she watched him. With a shake of his head, Ouroboros gave her a determined smile and picked up his shield, walking after the others.

"This is looking worse and worse," muttered Velin under her breath as she watched Ouroboros' back.

After a couple more rooms, the hallway widened out, and a large metal door appeared. Even Thorn could tell that this was the boss room. Since this was a new dungeon, and they had no idea what to expect, Ouroboros decided to take a conservative approach, directing everyone to stand in a defensive formation. Mina and Velin stood in the center with Ouroboros in front and Jorge a few steps back and off to the side. Thorn, like always, towered over everyone in the back, his arbalest ready.

'Being tall sure is convenient for shooting over allies,' Thorn thought to himself as Ouroboros opened the door.

Inside the boss room a large, robed Wolfkin sat on a big throne, surrounded by seven of the smaller Wolfkin in black robes they had been fighting on their way here. The larger Wolfkin's robe was a deep green, and his clawed hand held a long, smooth staff with a cracked holy symbol on top of it. Bloodshot eyes stared from beneath the dark green cowl, and with a cackling laugh, he welcomed the party into the room.

"Muahaha, welcome." His voice was pitched higher than was comfortable, creating an eerie atmosphere. "You have done well to make it here to the Fallen Moon Temple!"

TWANG!

Just as he finished his last word, Mina nudged Thorn, who accidentally pulled the trigger on his arbalest, sending a bolt whooshing past the large Wolfkin, straight through the head of one the smaller Wolfkin that surrounded him.

"Gaaah!" screamed the green-robed Wolfkin, jumping so high in his fright that he nearly tumbled off of his throne. Dropping his staff and waving both of his hands, a magical crimson shield sprang up in front of him as he looked nervously at the massive crossbow in Thorn's hands.

"Sorry. Sorry. I did not mean to interrupt." Thorn waved his hand at the large Wolfkin. "Please continue."

"Uh, yes. As I was saying. Uh..." It took a moment for the green-robed Wolfkin to get himself back under control. "You have done well to make it to here, Fallen Temple Moon! I mean, Fallen Moon Temple!"

"Do you need a moment?"

"Ah, yes, thank you." Taking a deep breath, the large Wolfkin clutched the throne's armrest, his other clawed hand resting on his chest. After a couple of deep breaths, he took up his staff again, rising from his chair. "You have profaned this holy hall and must be punished for your insolence! I, Amis, will punish you!" he screeched, seeming to have regained his composure.

Stabbing his staff forward, he began to chant in a foreign tongue, threads of bloody light pouring from the corrupted holy symbol on its end. Each thread floated in the air for a second before being inhaled by the black-robed Wolfkin that surrounded him. With roars, their bodies began to grow, ripping out of their robes until they were a head taller than the green-robed Wolfkin.

Seeing them change, Ouroboros lifted his shield and drew his sword, leveling it at the transformed Wolfkin.

"Engage at will!"

More than happy to comply, Thorn leveled his crossbow again and pulled the trigger, sending a bolt flying into the chest of one of the enlarged Wolfkin! In an amazing display of reaction, the large brute spun to the side as the bolt approached, causing it to slam into his right shoulder rather than his chest. With a deep roar of pain, the hulking Wolfkin staggered back a couple steps before launching himself toward Thorn, murder in his eyes.

"Watch out, these guys are tough!" shouted Velin, casting a buff on the whole group.

"Means it'll be more fun!" replied Mina, throwing up an ice wall in the path of the oncoming Wolfkin.

"Jorge, finish the wounded! Mina get your DPS going! Heals on me! Thorn, try to occupy the caster!" Ouroboros barked out commands. "Come on!" With his last roar, the six charging Wolfkin paused before turning to rush toward him.

Seeing that the Wolfkin were heading after Ouroboros, Thorn loaded up another bolt and aimed at the green-robed Wolfkin, who was jumping around and chanting. Despite aiming at the hopping Wolfkin, Thorn's first shot missed by almost two feet. The bolt ripped through the air and hit the top of the throne, breaking it off with a crack.

"Ahhhhhh!" screamed Amis, abandoning his chant and ducking in fear as he felt the shockwave of the bolt whooshing through the air. Hearing the crack of the stone moments after as the bolt smashed into the throne, Amis panicked. Screeching like his fur was on fire, Amis waved his hand, summoning his blood-red shield. He dashed behind the remains of the throne, crouching down to make himself a smaller target. Peeking out from behind the crumbling stone, Amis caught sight of Thorn leveling his arbalest, another bolt loaded.

While Thorn and Amis were playing peekaboo around the ruins of the throne, Ouroboros was holding off the six hulking Wolfkin. Like a turtle, when a Holy Guardian tightened up their defenses, they became nigh invulnerable. Despite the ferocious attacks from the raging Wolfkin, Ouroboros stood as firm as a rock. While his armor was thick, it was his skillful use of his shield and sword that allowed him to block the incoming claws and daggers.

Behind Ouroboros, Velin chanted, calling down healing energy on the Holy Guardian. Next to her, Mina shot ice spike after ice spike into the attackers. Focusing on the Wolfkin that had been shot already, it only took Mina six shots to cause it to collapse to the ground, switching her attacks to another until it fell as well. As they fell, Jorge appeared next to them, slicing across their throats before disappearing back into the air.

One by one the Wolfkin attacking Ouroboros fell to Mina and Jorge's precision attacks until only one remained. Behind the throne, Amis was still cowering, doing his best not to reveal himself to Thorn, who had taken to demolishing the rest of the throne, one bolt at a time. When he finally mustered up the courage to look around the edge of the pile of stone, Amis saw the five players standing together, his minions collapsed all over the floor in pools of blood.

"How could you beat them?!" he howled, his eyes turning red. His high-pitched voice began to deepen as his arms and shoulders began to swell. "Those were my servants, not yours! How could you kill them like that?!" The green robe began to give way at the seams, bristles of fur popping out as it ripped.

Madness consuming him, he strode forward, throwing down his staff as massive claws grew from his fingers. Red mist poured into him with each step, his form rippling with muscle and savage fury.

The closer he got to the group, the larger he grew, until he could almost see eye to eye with Thorn!

"I'll kill you! I'll flay your skin from your body and destroy you!"

"Uh oh," said Jorge, backing up and readying his daggers.

"This looks like trouble." Mina lifted her wand.

"Don't let him take the initiative!" commanded Ouroboros, and with a motion to the elf behind him, he dashed forward to intercept Amis. Seeing his signal, Velin chanted, bestowing a blessing on Ouroboros, increasing his armor.

Thorn aimed and fired, but this time his bolt did not even slow the enraged Wolfkin at all. With a solid thwack, the bolt landed on Amis' chest, but he did not seem to feel it as he bounded forward to meet Ouroboros' charge. Lashing out with a massive claw, Amis hit Ouroboros' shield, sending the Holy Guardian tumbling across the floor. Jorge appeared behind him but was forced to immediately dodge away as the Wolfkin turned to slash at him with uncanny speed! There were now no defenders between the enraged Amis and the team's casters!

CHAPTER THIRTY-TWO

At almost the same exact moment, a barrage of ice spikes slammed into Amis' head, shattering and sending shards of ice raining to the floor. The massive Wolfkin snarled and glared at Mina, who had already begun her next cast.

Next to her, Velin was chanting, as well, and something about it unsettled Amis. Holy energy was gathering at an alarming rate around her, and the gem atop her staff was beginning to pulse with power. Sensing the growing power, Amis instinctively knew that it would be dangerous if he allowed her to continue, but, before he could do anything about it, another bolt from Thorn's arbalest came ripping in!

Like the first one, this bolt only infuriated Amis even more. Roaring with rage, he bounded toward the girls, bent on ripping them apart before that terrifying power could be unleashed!

Speeding up her chant, Mina gestured with both hands, and a large wall of ice grew from the floor, obscuring the girls from the charging boss. Amis snarled and, lowering his shoulder, smashed right through it! Chunks of ice rained down around him as he sped up. The ice wall had not even managed to buy them a second, and Mina knew it would be pointless to summon anymore.

Frustration flashed in her eyes as she saw Amis coming toward them like a freight train. He was too fast and too strong and had changed from a wimpy caster to an unstoppable juggernaut, too. Mind whirring, she ran through her options. Jorge's shadow jump was on cooldown, and Ouroboros' taunt wouldn't work on a boss. Velin was casting and couldn't be interrupted if they wanted to take the boss down.

That left her CC, but Amis had blown through her ice wall like it was paper, and he was moving too fast for blizzard to be helpful. That only left Ice Explosion. "I hate ice explosion," she thought, but that did not stop her from preparing the ability. As she was about to step forward and blow herself up to buy Velin time, a shadow fell over her, and a massive arm appeared in her vision.

Amis could almost taste the sweet blood of the little Ice Witch in front of him. He would take his time and savor it before ripping apart the beautiful elf standing right behind her! Howling with excitement, he launched himself through the air. A black line entered his sight, and everything seemed to slow down to a crawl. Despite his power and speed, he did not seem to be able to move as the line grew bigger and bigger, revealing a massive fist the size of his head! He blinked, and then it hit him.

With a sickening crunch, the fist landed on his jaw, smashing it into pieces. Amis was sent flying to the side, his head tilted at an impossible angle and his jaw hanging loose. Tumbling across the floor, he only stopped when he hit the stone wall hard enough to shake the whole building. It was almost three seconds before he could scramble to his feet, and when he did, he found himself once again facing the unified group.

Ouroboros had retaken his spot in the front lines with Mina and Jorge flanking him. Velin was still chanting behind him, the ball of energy on the end of her staff growing stronger with each word. Behind all of them, Thorn had reloaded his arbalest and was taking aim.

Confused as to what had happened, Amis shook his head to clear it, sending waves of pain through his head as his broken jaw shifted. In his enraged state, the Wolfkin boss grew even more aggressive, brandishing his claws as he howled at the party. Seeing that Ouroboros was standing in front again, Amis sneered and charged forward to meet him.

The last time they had clashed, the Holy Guardian had been sent flying, and Amis intended to repeat the performance! Ouroboros, on the other hand, was not quite as keen. As a Main Tank, the fall from earlier had bruised his ego as much as his body, and he was not about to let it happen again. Because of the angle, he had not seen how Mina and Velin had deflected the Wolfkin boss but, regardless, he was determined to stop Amis this time.

This time, instead of charging like he had done before, Ouroboros took two large steps forward and planted himself in Amis' way. Rather than tightening up his defenses as he had against the six enraged Wolfkin earlier, he held himself at the ready, his shield up in front of him. Within seconds, the snarling visage of the boss filled his view, and a wicked looking claw swept in, smashing into his shield.

As soon as he felt the impact, Ouroboros took two quick steps backward, his feet slamming into the ground to help displace some of the energy from the strike. At the same time, he let the power of the strike flow through him before tightening up his body and armor, dispersing the extra energy. Despite the floor being made of stone, small cracks radiated out from where his feet had landed, giving testament to how hard the blow had been.

Gritting his teeth, Ouroboros shook his body to get rid of the lingering tension and smashed forward, bashing with his shield as he activated one of his skills. Caught off guard when the Holy Guardian did not fly away, Amis could only lift his arms to try and protect himself from the large shield. Despite being stronger than his opponent, he had been forced to stop, and so his momentum was at its lowest, resulting in Amis being sent reeling.

Off balance, the Wolfkin scrambled to get his feet back under him when a sharp pain lanced through his ankle. Looking down, he saw a serious-faced dwarf trying his best to cut through his Achilles tendon. Like the last time the dwarf had attacked him, as soon as Amis turned to deal with him, ice spikes began to fly toward him. The last time they had shattered off of his tough skin, but this time the blasted things were aimed at his already broken jaw!

With a howl of rage, he lifted his hands to protect his fragile jaw while kicking out at the offending dwarf. Yet Ouroboros would not let him do what he wanted, and another shield bash flew in, keeping him off balance. At the same time, another annoying bolt shot in, this time landing deep in his side, under his ribs. Furious, Amis snapped the bolt in half and glared at the giant who was already loading another!

A chill ran down his back, cutting through the burning rage clouding his mind. Amis' gaze snapped to the elven War Priestess, who had finished her long chant. With a single word, Velin stepped forward as the burning light on top of her staff condensed down into a single beam. Despite his wish to move out of the way of that deadly looking attack, Amis found his body would not respond the way he wished.

Shooting out of the top of her staff, a white line appeared, connecting Velin with Amis and burning straight through his large, muscled chest. Thorn could feel the destructive energy radiating off of the beam of light from where he was standing and, once again, vowed to himself that he would not get on Velin's bad side.

Dumbfounded, the boss could only stare down at the large hole in his chest where his heart used to be. Looking up, he tried to speak, but his broken jaw turned it into gibberish as he fell to the ground, dead.

"Whew." Mina breathed a sigh of relief as she collapsed to the ground, exhausted. "That was so tense! Ouroboros, what happened? Why did you get knocked away?"

"Yeah, what was up with that?" Jorge chimed in.

"Hey, you have no room to talk," quibbled Mina, turning to stare at the dwarf who had appeared behind the boss' corpse. "You didn't do a thing the whole fight."

"Alright, that is enough," said Ouroboros, his tone dark. "We did not anticipate that change and were caught off guard."

"I'll say," Mina rolled her eyes.

"I said enough!" Ouroboros glared at her, his tone brooking no argument. "Velin, how are you doing? Do you need time to rest?"

"Yes. It would be a good idea."

"Let's deal with the body and then rest for a bit. We'll pick back up in twenty minutes," Ouroboros said, planting his shield on the ground.

Walking over to the body of the Wolfkin, Thorn poked around to see if he could find anything of value. Another broken silver holy symbol appeared along with some gold and a couple potions. The only thing he found that was out of the ordinary was a piece of paper with what looked like a recipe on it. At least that is what he assumed it was. The paper was written in the same language that the Wolfkin all used, so Thorn could only judge by the way the paper was formatted.

Knowing Velin would be interested, he dropped it off with her and then, after a quick look around the room, sat down to eat some food. Jorge had found a small chest buried under the rubble that had once been a stone throne and was working on getting it open. Velin was resting while looking at the piece of paper Thorn had found, and Ouroboros was cleaning his sword and shield.

"Hey, thanks for saving me."

Somewhat startled by the quiet voice, Thorn raised his head. Mina stood next to him, twisting her wand in her hands.

"If you hadn't knocked him away, he would have killed both me and Velin before Ouroboros could have gotten there."

"Of course," said Thorn with a smile. "We're teammates, it's what I should do."

"Yeah," Mina gave a strained smile. "Anyway, thanks."

Watching the short Ice Witch walk away, Thorn was puzzled by the exchange but quickly threw it out of his mind and started thinking through the fight they had won. Up until this point, Ouroboros and his team had walked over every enemy they had encountered with considerable ease. In fact, Thorn had been beginning to doubt that they found the game difficult at all.

With impeccable teamwork and powerful classes, the fights so far had been effortless. That had changed today when they met Amis. The beginning of the fight had gone as Thorn had expected, but once Amis changed into his hulking form, the whole situation had gone downhill fast. Caught off guard, Ouroboros had made the wrong call and charged forward to engage, resulting in the Holy Guardian being knocked out of the way, leaving Mina and Velin exposed.

At least Velin had the presence of mind to start chanting her most powerful spell. If she had not, the fight would have dragged on for that much longer. Amis had been powerful in his hulk form, and none of the others had been able to get past his defenses to hurt him. With the exception of Thorn, of course. Staring down at his fist, Thorn could not help but shake his head. He still didn't completely understand how his strength worked in this game. His punch had not been that hard, rather he had thrown a warding strike, designed to throw the opponent off balance in order to stop their forward momentum.

"Oh wait, the logs!" thought Thorn.

Pulling up his combat logs, Thorn scrolled back through them. Combat logs were common to most adventure games and kept track of all that happened during a fight, especially abilities used at crucial points. In Nova Terra's immersive environment Thorn had almost completely forgotten about them, but they were a useful source of information in a game that hid most abilities. Thorn soon found the point in his log where he had hit the charging Wolfkin.

Unarmed Strike: Attacking strength exceeds defending strength: Crushing Blow activated
Attacking strength exceeds defending strength by a factor of 5 or more: Crushing Blow x 5

Opening a browser window, it did not take Thorn long to figure out what had happened. A crushing blow did damage that ignored all defenses and applied a knockback effect. Because Thorn's strength was much higher than Amis', his warding blow had sent the werewolf flying.

After the twenty minutes had passed, the group got to their feet and gathered at the bottom of the stairs that led up to the next floor. From the size of the building, Velin had estimated that there were at least five floors, and they had made it through the first floor. Looking at Ouroboros' serious expression, it was obvious that he was not very happy with their performance so far.

If it had not been for Thorn stepping in at a vital moment, the party might have wiped. Even if they did not all die, they would have lost the girls, at the very least, which made Ouroboros quite upset. For an elite team like theirs, it was embarrassing to think that they almost died by the hands (or claws, in this case) of the first boss in a dungeon. Taking a deep breath, Ouroboros gave out directions.

"Jorge, you are responsible for scouting, I'll tank, Velin is on healing and Mina will cover DPS. Keep to your roles unless I call a rotate. We don't know what sorts of enemies we'll face, but we should be fine if it is more Wolfkin. However, if we hit undead or spirits, Mina and Velin will swap since holy damage will be more effective. I'll take point, and Jorge will watch our backs. Everyone have their enchants up? Remember to watch for ambushes. So far, this dungeon has been pretty straightforward, but we don't want to let our guard down."

Throwing a stiff smile toward Thorn, who was listening with interest, he continued. "Thorn, you'll stay behind whoever is playing DPS to add ranged damage. This means you'll be behind Mina while we are going up against Wolfkin and Velin if we run into any undead. If we meet with spirits, your bolts will not do anything because they are immune to damage from unenchanted weapons, so stay far enough away that you don't draw their attention. We are going to be speeding up to make sure we can push through in a timely manner using a system called Clean and

Sweep for dealing with a room at the end of the fight. So, when you hear me say clean and sweep, you can get to picking up all the drops. Focus on high-value drops, as there will be limited time for picking stuff up."

Nodding that he understood, Thorn followed the rest of them as they walked up the stairs to the second floor, which looked almost exactly like the first floor. Ouroboros called for them to stop while Jorge ranged ahead. Once he signaled that they were good to proceed, the group made its way farther in, Jorge advancing in the front in order to handle traps and lone guards.

Their first major fight on the second floor came when Jorge spotted a patrol of six black robed Wolfkin who were on their way out of a room, walking straight down a long hall off the one the party was in. After reporting this back to Ouroboros, they picked a corner to launch their attack from and set up an ambush. Seeing the quick and disciplined action of the party, Thorn couldn't help but be impressed. Once the group got serious, they worked with incredible precision. Even Mina, far from her normal chatty self, seemed focused and serious.

CHAPTER THIRTY-THREE

Ouroboros crouched down at the corner while Jorge slipped into the shadows on the opposite side of the corridor, seeming to melt into thin air. Behind Ouroboros was Mina, who readied her damage spells, while Velin stepped back about twenty-five feet and got ready to heal whoever needed it. Thorn crouched down halfway between Mina and Velin with his arbalest at the ready.

Coming around the corner, the Wolfkin never knew what hit them. As soon as the first two heads appeared, Mina let loose an ice spell, sending sharp shards of ice into them. Startled by the sudden assault, the rest of the Wolfkin rushed around the corner to try and see who had cast the spell only to get pushed back by Ouroboros with his massive shield. This disoriented them enough that Jorge could jump from the shadows and begin cutting them down from behind while Velin cast a bulwark spell on Ouroboros. Within seconds all six of the monsters were bleeding out on the ground without being able to get off more than a yip.

As soon as the last mob hit the floor, its head crushed by a shield bash, Ouroboros waved Mina and Thorn forward saying, "Sweep and Clean, 30 seconds." Running forward, Thorn picked up all the fallen gear and the few coins that had fallen and watched in surprise as Jorge completely dismantled the six dead Wolfkin in a whirlwind fashion. Before the 30 seconds were up, Thorn found himself holding the six hides that Jorge had recovered while Jorge was off again, scouting ahead. The efficiency of the group was staggering and proved to Thorn that he did have a long way to go to reach the level of these experienced players.

As the group moved forward again, Mina smirked at Thorn. "Haha, that look on your face is priceless. Now you know what it takes to be considered an elite player. Then again, we're pretty much the best, so don't expect other groups to match us," she said.

"No kidding. You guys have always worked well, but that was next level. I didn't even get to fire. How did you get so good?"

"Haaa," Mina sighed, "you don't want to know. Let me just say Ouroboros is a training demon. When we all started the game, he had us doing the most ridiculous things in order to get our teamwork down. Nova Terra gives hidden bonuses for how well you operate as a unit, so Ouroboros beat teamwork into us until we hit the point where it was instinctual. Plus, once you get used to the mob patterns, it isn't hard to come up with a good strategy."

"Mina!" barked Ouroboros, glaring at the petite redhead.

"Eeep! Sorry, boss, my mouth's sealed," said Mina. "Sorry, noob, can't give away our secrets."

"Oh, no problem," responded Thorn with a wave of his hand. "I didn't mean to pry."

After that, the group sped up, working their way through a few more patrols. Ouroboros began to push the group faster to the point that Thorn barely had time to toss the gear into his inventory before the next group of mobs was being taken down. They soon got to a large, open room where, Jorge reported, the second-floor boss and the main contingent of Wolfkin were hanging out.

Almost without waiting for Jorge to finish speaking, Ouroboros called out, "Jorge, flank right, and focus healers. Velin on me, Mina go wild," and charged straight into the large room. He was moving so fast that the first couple of black-robed Wolfkin to notice him were run over, getting crushed by his heavy metal boots. With a shout, he drew all attention to himself as Velin dropped a full set of buffs on him, making his shining armor and shield glow with holy light. Howling their surprise and anger, the large group of Wolfkin drew their weapons and rushed forward, right into range for Mina to drop a metric ton of ice and snow on them.

"Avalanche!" Mina yelled, and then, muttering an incantation under her breath, she disappeared in a flash and reappeared behind two Wolfkin struggling to dig themselves out of the waist-high snow that had been dumped on them, shoving two giant icicles through the back of their necks. With a gleeful laugh, she disappeared again, only to appear somewhere else to finish off another helpless Wolfkin with her ice spikes.

In the back of the cave, an old Wolfkin wielding a skull-topped cane screeched his displeasure and raised his cane toward Mina. Opening his mouth to bark out his chant, nothing emerged except for a wet gurgle and, in astonishment, he looked down to find frothing blood leaking from a neat hole in his windpipe and Jorge shoving a stiletto into his kidney.

After his initial rush forward, Ouroboros gave a loud shout and smashed his shield into the ground, where it stood upright. Transitioning his sword into a two-handed grip, he sprang forward, cutting down Wolfkin left and right as if they were nothing but wisps of mist. Behind him, Velin stepped forward to the shield, almost as if she was stepping up to a pulpit and began to speak arcane words. Powerful waves of energy rolled forth from her tongue as she preached victory for her friends and doom for their enemies.

In short, it was an utter slaughter as the four experienced adventurers rolled over the horde of Wolfkin like a tidal wave. It was nothing like the fight on the first floor. Seeing a high skill party in action was an absolute treat, as far as Thorn was concerned, but it also highlighted the skill gap between him and them. Once they were serious, the gap became a canyon. Noticing that the Wolfkin were all but dead, he sprang into action, gathering all the fallen loot and arranging the bodies so that Jorge could skin them.

After killing the last mob with a backhand swing, Ouroboros came back to where Thorn was and said, "Thorn, there is a slight change of plans. We are actually making better time than I thought we were going to, so I'd like to push into the third level right away. How are you doing on weight?"

"I'm fine." Thorn looked over his inventory. "I'm actually pretty empty, since most of what I've been picking up stacks."

"Awesome. You good for continuing?"

"Yup."

"Anyone else need a rest? Great, let's sweep and clean and get moving, folks." Sheathing his sword, Ouroboros walked toward the back wall and began to fiddle with some levers, soon revealing a dark staircase going up. Once they had looted the room, the group headed up to the third level, Jorge creeping ahead of the group to make sure the way was clear.

As the soft glow of Velin's magical light revealed the cracked rock walls covered in lichen, Thorn couldn't help but grin. The thrill of adventure made him happy to no end and getting to experience this was beyond a dream come true.

Once they made it to the top of the stairs, the party stopped and reorganized. Once again, Jorge disappeared down the hallway, only to come running back.

"Five skeleton warriors and two archers patrolling up ahead."

"Okay, swap up." Hearing that their enemies had changed, the group reorganized with Ouroboros taking point, Velin standing behind him, Mina and Thorn in the middle, and, finally, Jorge taking up the rear. As everyone prepped, Mina began to weave a strange spell, dark mist curling up from the floor. Taking out a small knife, she cut the tip of each of her fingers on her left hand and pressed a bleeding finger to each party member's forehead, having to jump to try and mark Thorn.

A faint, dark blue line attached to each of them, linking the whole group together in a web with Mina at the center. Seeing Thorn's interested look, she giggled. "I'm a Witch, not a Priest, so I don't heal. Since I only have self-heals, I use the power of sacrifice to move damage from one of you to me and then heal myself. That way you can continue to fight."

"Doesn't that hurt?"

"Meh, it's not bad. More of a tingle."

"Alright, let's get moving," Ouroboros cut in. Once he saw that everyone was ready, he led the way down the hall, toward the skeleton patrol. Like the fights on the second floor, this one was over before Thorn could get involved. As soon as he saw the skeletons, Ouroboros charged toward them, knocking them back against the stone wall as he shoved his way into the center of the group. At the same time, Velin chanted a spell, pointing at Ouroboros' armored back. A dense holy light fell on the Holy Guardian and radiance spilled from him in a ring, destroying the skeletons as soon as it touched them.

Within seconds, the skeleton patrol fell apart, unable to withstand the powerful holy energy radiating from Ouroboros. Behind the patrol, there was a large door and, opening it, they stepped into an old tomb that looked like it had not been opened for years. Dusty statues graced each side of a wide hall, and large cobwebs covered everything. As soon as the group was within the hall, the door slammed shut with a boom that sent dust flying into the air.

Out of the darkness glowing red eyes appeared one after another, and a slow shuffling sound brought them closer. Dark forms soon became visible as a horde of bone figures closed in on the group. Ouroboros slung his shield across his back and tightened up his grip on his sword. "Anytime you're ready, Velin."

Without a word, Velin reached out a hand to touch the knight and, with a low chant, began to imbue him with a holy blessing. As the light grew, so too did the volume of the chant until it rolled thunderously around the chamber. Reaching a crashing crescendo, Velin spat out the last word of the chant. She immediately began to chant again while Ouroboros dashed out toward the waiting horde, his great blade swinging in a magnificent arc, crushing bones like twigs.

Two slashes brought him deep into the center of the skeleton horde. As his second swing ended, Velin finished her second chant and pointed her finger at him, calling out "Burst!" in a loud voice. A pulse of light blasted out from Ouroboros, obliterating all of the skeletons around him in a spectacular fashion. The rest of the skeletons were cleaned up and, after looting everything, the group moved forward.

The tomb didn't seem to present any major challenge to the team, and they got deeper and deeper into the catacombs. Finally, they reached another large door, and Ouroboros stopped the group.

"Alright, I am guessing the boss is through here. We've done well so far and lucked out that there was no ambush, but that's no reason to let our guard down. Thorn, you've been a big help in keeping us moving, so thank you. A couple things to pay attention to. First, this floor has not been very challenging at all, so it is likely that all the difficulty is at the boss. Second, it is a bit strange that we are running into undead. I know I mentioned that we might, but that was a guess based on the way the Wolfkin are dressed and the fact that it might be a corrupted temple.

"If this is actually where Davyos betrayed his god and got the power of the Devil Blood Berserker, then it is likely that the final boss we are going to fight will be Karrandaras, the Betrayer. He is an archdevil and is pretty powerful. Good news is that it is very hard for an archdevil to actually manifest itself in this world, so it will not be a direct fight.

"Like all archdevils, his M.O. is going to be based on a competition of power and benefits, so we may be able to get away without a fight at all. Remember that the goal is to get classes, so we may need to cut a deal with him."

"Can we trust an archdevil?" Thorn asked.

"Sort of. You can trust them to be true to their nature, which is to squeeze every possible benefit they can from you. But devils tend to be on the lawful side, even if it is lawful evil," Velin replied.

"Okay, everyone ready?" Ouroboros asked. Once everyone

nodded, he pushed open the door.

The room they walked into looked like a large cathedral, with giant stone pillars, stretching to the ceiling, running up each side of the room. The stone tile floor was open, except for a small platform with an altar. Approaching the altar, the group spread out, walking cautiously and looking for traps.

Finally, they stood in front of the altar, which seemed to be made out of a dark, rust-colored stone. Asking for the silver religious symbol that the last boss had dropped from Thorn, Ouroboros knelt and fit it into a depression on the front of the altar, jumping backward as the altar flared with a malevolent light. Swirling crimson lights burst from the dark wood, gathering into a strange, bloody-looking spirit.

[WHO HASS COME HERE?!] boomed the spirit, its voice sending chills down Thorn's spine.

"I am Ouroboros, and I have journeyed far to find you," replied the Holy Guardian, his tone calm, considering the terrifying aura the spirit emitted.

[HAVE YOU!? AND WHAT ISS IT THAT YOU SSEEK, OUROBOROSS!?]

"Power. Power of the Blood."

[AHHAHAHA!] cackled the spirit. [VERY WELL, MORTAL! LET USS SSEE IF YOU ARE WORTHY!]

CHAPTER THIRTY-FOUR

Even before its voice faded, dozens of crimson lights flew from its body and splashed onto the floor, rising up as smaller versions of itself. Seeing them coming, everyone tightened their grip on their weapons and got ready for the fight. Without hesitation, Ouroboros dashed forward and slammed his shield and sword together, roaring out a challenge that drew the spirits' attention. Jorge blurred through the air, targeting one of the spirits at the back while Velin began buffing Ouroboros, and Mina began sending shards of ice at the approaching spirits.

Behind them, Thorn leveled his arbalest but, after seeing his bolt pass through one of the red spirits without doing any damage, he could only accept his inability to help in this fight. Instead, he paid close attention to the way Ouroboros and the others dealt with their enemies. As Ouroboros had explained, against spirit enemies' normal weapons did no damage. As he watched, Thorn vowed to get an enchanted weapon as soon as possible.

At first, it seemed like the battle was going to end quickly, but, as Jorge stabbed his enchanted dagger into the last of the spirits, the altar once again exploded with crimson flame, and a wave of bloody energy spread throughout the room, collecting into a terrifying figure in front of the party.

[KNEEL MORTALSS AND I SSHALL MAKE YOUR DEATHSS PAINLESSS!!] roared the horned devil.

"Not likely," spat Ouroboros, slamming his shield into the ground. "Same plan as usual, folks."

Two hands grasping his sword, Ouroboros charged out as Velin stepped up to the shield. Behind her, Mina was getting ready to unleash her deadly ice spells, and Jorge had already disappeared. As holy light once again enveloped Ouroboros, he began to engage the devil in a deadly dance.

Spinning and slicing, Ouroboros seemed to slip past every strike of the devil's claws, returning long cuts that began to bleed thick, steaming blood. Bits of flesh and blood splashed to the ground after every strike, corroding the stone floor. Coordinating with the Holy Guardian, Jorge would appear and disappear, harassing the devil from the sides to keep him from bringing his full offensive power to bear on Ouroboros.

With a roar, the devil lashed out, trying to create some space. Under his wild swings, Ouroboros was forced to give ground, taking two steps back. But, before the devil was able to make a move, a sheet of ice appeared under it, growing as it wrapped around the devil's feet, trapping it. As soon as it was stopped in place, ice spikes and thick crossbow bolts slammed into it.

Roaring with rage, the devil covered its head and chest with its arms, trying its best to break the ice at its feet. Red flames began to lick around its body, and with a stomp, the ice melted away. As Ouroboros was about to charge forward to engage it again, the devil unfurled two large bat wings from its back and rose up into the air, heading for Mina.

Seeing that it was coming over, Thorn shot another bolt at the flying devil only to see it dodge in mid-air. Brandishing its claws, it dove toward Mina, intent on destroying the Ice Witch. Before it arrived, Velin chanted out a phrase and swung down with her staff.

In the air above the devil, a golden hammer of light materialized and swung down, bursting with a righteous aura. Smashing into the devil's back, the hammer let off a sizzling sound as it burned into the devil's skin.

BOOOM!

With a force that shook the room, the devil crashed to the floor. Excited, Thorn was about to step forward and start pummeling the fallen devil, but Mina pulled on his arm, so he backed up with her. Seeing that Mina and Thorn were backing away, Ouroboros charged forward again, his sword cutting into the devil's side as it struggled to its feet. Corrosive blood splashed from its wounds, pitting the floor as it landed.

With each slash, Ouroboros had to dodge as the splatters of blood began to corrode his armor. His sword, protected by holy energy, sizzled as it ripped into the devil's flesh. Behind the shield that he had planted earlier, Velin continued to chant, filling Ouroboros with power as he chipped away at the devil, who was struggling to get to his feet.

[FOOLISSH MORTALSS!! YOU CANNOT DEFEAT ME!!]

With a roar, the devil forced Ouroboros back, pulling a shield of flame from the air to block the ice spikes and crossbow bolts shooting toward him. Standing to his feet, he summoned a ball of flame in each hand, shooting them at Mina and Thorn as he spread his wings to fly up into the air.

"Mina, keep him grounded!" Ouroboros shouted at the sight of the devil trying to take to the air again.

"On it!" Gritting her teeth at the incoming fireballs, Mina lifted her wand to point at the devil, chanting an arcane spell. With a thunderous crack, large ice spears attached to chains broke out of the ground, stabbing into the devil's legs and wings. By the time the chant finished, the fireballs were too close to block, leaving Mina nothing to do but close her eyes in resignation.

BOOM!

Hearing the explosion of the fireballs but feeling none of the pain that should go with it, Mina opened her eyes only to see Thorn's broad chest. At the last moment, Thorn had stepped in front of her, blocking the fireballs with this back. Thorn, seeming unharmed, was already loading up another bolt in his arbalest to shoot at the trapped devil.

"Weren't they hot?" Mina asked, confused by Thorn's unchanged expression.

"Huh? Oh, yeah," Thorn glanced down at his back, where his armor was glowing. "It stings quite a bit."

"Ah!" Mina chanted, sending a frozen breeze wrapping around Thorn to help cool his scalding armor.

"Thanks," said Thorn with a smile, shooting at the devil.

With the devil chained down, there was no way for him to dodge Thorn's bolts and Mina's ice spikes. The only thing he could do was try and block with a fire shield. Unfortunately for him, the fire shield could not eliminate the ice chains, but he could not drop the shield for fear of the team's projectiles, so the fight settled into an uneasy stalemate.

"Velin, how long do you need to end this?" asked Ouroboros, resting for a moment, his eyes locked on the struggling devil.

"Two minutes. But he has to be still."

"That's too long. Let's deal with his wings first. Jorge! Get that shield down!"

Standing up, the Holy Guardian lifted his sword in front of his face, murmuring a prayer. A glow began to build along the blade, sending rays of golden light shooting around the room. When he was done praying, Ouroboros dashed forward two steps and, with a powerful jump, launched himself into the air at the trapped devil!

Snarling, the devil focused all his energy on his shield, sending the flames into a frenzy. From a thin shell, the raging flames grew into a thick burning layer, completely hiding the devil from view.

As the shield grew stronger, Thorn stopped firing in frustration. His bolts were getting burnt up by the fire shield, so there was no point in continuing. Putting his arbalest down, he was about to charge forward and try to beat the devil to death when Mina grabbed his arm again.

"Stay back, this is an AoE attack!" Mina shouted, lifting her wand again.

In front of the sneering devil, Ouroboros was still flying through the air toward the fire shield. As he was about to hit it, Jorge appeared next to the shield, slashing out with the thick dagger in his left hand. With a loud cracking sound, a fissure ran through the shield in time for Ouroboros' sword to cut past it, cutting deep into the devil's shoulder.

Ignoring the devil's roar of rage, Ouroboros grasped the hilt of his sword, channeling holy energy into the devil's body. In an instant, the energy overflowed from the sword, burning through the devil and everything around. Even the stone floor underfoot caught fire, melting into a puddle.

Jorge, who had shadow jumped to safety behind Velin, wiped his forehead. He had been caught in that attack once and he never wanted to repeat the experience! Currently, the devil was undergoing the very experience that Jorge wanted to avoid, and his screams proved that Jorge's choice to move was the right one.

Standing amid the burning holy light, Ouroboros experienced none of the pain the devil was experiencing; instead, the light seemed to heal him of his fatigue, boosting his strength and encasing him in a formless armor. With a shout, the Holy Guardian pulled his sword out and sent slash after slash at the devil, who was trying to back up.

The holy energy had evaporated the ice chains holding the devil down, but despite being free, the devil lacked the energy to fly. His wings hung behind him, dragging on the ground. One of his arms was almost detached, and a giant gash ran from his shoulder into his chest, corrosive blood streaming down to join the melted stone on the floor.

"Mina!" Ouroboros shouted, taking a large step back. Mina, already ready, completed the chant she had started before Jorge had broken the devil's fire shield. With a whoosh, a blast of freezing air whipped around on the struggling devil, almost instantly dropping the temperature surrounding him to almost sixty degrees below zero.

The sudden change in temperature dealt massive damage to

the devil, freezing its corrosive blood and locking its movement as the liquid stone froze around its feet, trapping it in place once again. Attack after attack rained down on the devil as the whole team started to go all out on offense. Even Thorn picked his arbalest and started firing again, sending bolts ripping through the air into the trapped devil.

Within only a few moments, the crimson devil finally fell, and the team moved back into their original formation in front of the altar. Thorn was once again astounded at how efficient their teamwork was. From beginning to end, they took everything in stride, adjusting their roles and abilities as needed. He was daydreaming about one day being able to work that with them when a voice brought him out of it.

"Thorn, can you come up here, please?"

The spirit over the altar had begun to boil in a weird way, so Thorn hurried over to Ouroboros, who had called him over. Reformed in the center of the altar, the bloody spirit they had seen when they first entered the room appeared and once again began to laugh.

[AHAHAHA! I TRULY UNDERESTIMATED YOU, MORTAL! BUT NO MATTER, YOU HAVE PASSSED MY TESST AND YOU ARE WELCOME TO THE REWARD! WHAT IS IT YOU WISSH FOR?!]

With another gleeful laugh, the spirit waved its hand, and a giant magical circle appeared under the five adventurers who were still standing in front of it. At the same time, five crimson flames flew out from the spirit and burrowed into Thorn, Ouroboros, Velin, Mina, and Jorge. Wrapping around and through them, the burning flames formed chains that did not keep them from moving or burn them.

"You are Karrandaras, correct?" asked Ouroboros, watching the blood spirit.

[SSO YOU KNOW ME! THEN YOU SSHOULD KNOW MY MIGHT AND POWER!]

"And I know your character," stated Ouroboros.

[AHAHAHA!!] Karrandaras laughed, leering at Ouroboros as it

swayed back and forth. [MANY HAVE CLAIMED TO KNOW ME, AND I HAVE FEASSTED ON THEIR SSOULSS! ENOUGH! WHAT ISS IT THAT YOU WISSH FROM ME?!]

"Knowledge and a boon." This time it was Velin who answered, her notebook in her hand. "I want the knowledge, and he wants the boon."

[KNOWLEDGE ISS A COSSTLY THING, ELF!] The spirit floated to face her. [WHAT YOU SSEEK MAY COSST MORE THAN YOU CAN AFFORD!]

"I am willing to trade a name," Velin flipped her notebook to an empty page, writing something down in an arcane script. "Will this suffice?"

[AHAHAHAHA!! YESS! YESS! IT WILL SSUFFICE!] Twirling in glee, Karrandaras motioned, and the page was ripped from the book, flying through the air. Opening its mouth, the spirit extended its long, prehensile tongue and snatched the note from the air. [AHAHAHAHA!! DELICIOUSS!! ASSK YOUR QUESSTION, ELF!!]

"I wish to know where to find the seed of the world tree," Velin said, her eyes locked on the spirit's fluttering form.

[VERY WELL, ELF! THE KNOWLEDGE ISS YOURSS!!] With a flick of his finger, Karrandaras conjured a bright, bloody light the size of a marble, sending it flying at Velin, who caught it. Holding it against her forehead, she closed her eyes and concentrated. After a moment, her face paled, and she opened her eyes. Nodding at Ouroboros, she put the red marble away.

[AND YOU?! WHAT BOON DO YOU WISSH FOR?!] the spirit asked, turning its burning eyes on Ouroboros.

"I want the power of the Devil Blood Berserker," stated Ouroboros.

[YOUR WISSH IS GREAT, MORTAL! BUT EVERY BOON REQUIRESS GREAT SSACRIFICE! WHAT WILL YOU GIVE TO ACHIEVE YOUR DESSIRESS?!]

For a moment, Ouroboros stopped still, not moving. He could sense Velin's intense stare and, beyond it, Thorn's interested gaze. Closing his eyes for a moment, Ouroboros steeled his resolve and, his face white and his jaw clenched, pointed at Thorn's massive figure.

"Him."

CHAPTER THIRTY-FIVE

As soon as Ouroboros' words reached him, Thorn felt a sharp pain in his spine, and his world turned a frozen white. Jorge had appeared behind him in an explosion of shadow, thrusting a dagger into Thorn's back. Because of his height, Jorge had to drop to the ground after his strike, leaving the dagger stuck in Thorn's back. At the same moment, Mina raised her trembling wand and chanted, causing a deluge of white to wrap around Thorn, freezing his movement.

Caught by surprise, Thorn couldn't react at all, experiencing a stunned state for the first time. Unlike most games, where a stunned state meant that a player could see what was happening but could not take any actions, being stunned in Nova Terra actually changed the player's perception of time, speeding up how time passed for them.

Velin, giving Ouroboros a long look, shook her head and walked to Thorn, who was standing stock still in his stunned state. Using the end of her staff, she began to draw arcane runes on the ground around Thorn, pausing to consult her book every so often.

Off to the side stood Mina, clutching her wand, her eyes revealing her conflicted emotions. Beside her stood Jorge, not bickering with her for once. Seeing how torn she looked, he opened his mouth to say something but paused. After a moment of hesitation, he sighed and patted her on the shoulder, shaking his head.

"Mina, I need your help," Velin said, tucking a wisp of hair behind her ear. "We need to do this quickly."

"But..." Mina trailed off.

"Mina, we all agreed. I need you to stay focused, okay?" The elf walked over and pulled her into a hug. "I know you like him, I do too, but you need to stay focused on our goal, okay?" While Velin was occupied with Mina, Ouroboros approached the spirit floating above the altar, who was watching with glee.

[AND WHAT MAKESS YOU THINK THAT I WILL ALLOW THISS?!] Karrandaras asked Ouroboros, a wide grin on its face. [WHY SSHOULD I LET YOU PASSS THE COSST OFF?!]

"The manner in which he has been delivered. And the fact that he is classless." Ouroboros listed the reasons without a change in expression.

[VERY WELL, MORTAL!! YOU HAVE MADE ME QUITE PLEASED BY SUBMITTING A WORTHY SACRIFICE. I SSHALL GRANT YOU THE TRANSFER OF DESSTINY!! LET USS HARVESST IT!!] crowed the spirit in glee, watching Thorn's face for the pain it knew was coming.

Still stunned from the dwarven rogue's stab, Thorn was unable to process what was happening until an unbelievable, stinging pain in his forehead jerked him from his thoughts. With a gasp, Thorn fell to his knees, unable to move from that position as torrents of pain poured into him from the mark that Mina had left on his head.

The magical symbols that Velin had drawn around Thorn began to glow as she started a chant. Purple and black chains shot out of the symbols, anchoring themselves to Thorn's body, causing his blood to splatter. As Velin's chant continued, the chains began to pulse with arcane energy. Thorn could feel the chains drawing something from him but, no matter how he struggled, he could not move. Little by little, the feeling of loss grew in Thorn's chest.

Collecting some of Thorn's blood that had splashed to the ground, Mina brought it over to Ouroboros and drew another rune on his forehead. Once she finished, she touched the symbol with her wand, and a gloomy aura poured out of the rune, connecting Thorn and Ouroboros. A twisting black energy shot from Thorn's forehead to Ouroboros'.

As soon as the energy connected, the feeling of loss in Thorn's chest grew even stronger. Desperately struggling, nothing Thorn did helped him, and he began to feel empty, drained of energy.

With a flash, the spirit disappeared from over the altar and appeared above Thorn, who was now writhing in agony as the chains pulsed with energy. Looking at the strange symbols lighting up on the floor and the arcane stream connecting Thorn and Ouroboros' heads, it began to cackle.

[WHAT DEVIOUSS MINDS YOU HAVE!] the archdevil spit at Ouroboros, grinning. [YOUR WISH SSHALL BE GRANTED, CRUEL ONE! FOR THIS ISS A WORTHY SSACRIFICE!! TO SSTRIP YOUR COMPANION OF ALL OF HISS POTENTIAL PLEASSESS ME!! AHAHAHA!!! YOU HAVE DONE WELL!!] And, with a flash, it split into four crimson lights that shot into the four adventurers in the middle of the room.

The largest portion of lightheaded toward Ouroboros, who opened his arms and accepted it. As Thorn struggled on the floor, Ouroboros glowed with crimson light, his armor taking on a blood-red hue. Bloody symbols crawled their way up his chest and onto his neck, causing him to grit his teeth in pain. Once the symbols had burned their way into his skin, the glow faded, and he opened his eyes, revealing bloody pupils.

[YOU HAVE PLEASSED ME, OUROBOROSS!!] said Karrandaras, grinning at the former Holy Guardian. [NO LONGER ARE YOU A KNIGHT OF ORDER!! YOU NOW SSERVE A HIGHER CALLING AND WILL LIVE FOR A GREATER PERPOSSE!! RISSE, MY CHAMPION!! RISSE, EXALTED DEVIL BLOOD BERSSERKER!!]

Thorn tried to gather his wits as the pain rushed through his body. Struggling barely to his knees, a sharp stabbing pain in his back put him right back on stomach and, looking up with horror, he took in Ouroboros' callous disregard, Jorge's cold eyes, Mina's nervous smile, and Velin's inscrutable expression. The four other players had gathered around him as he lay on the ground.

"It's no use, Thorn; you won't be able to get up until the knife comes out," said Jorge. "So, you might as well stop struggling."

Eyes heavy with fury and pain, Thorn glared up at his betrayers, but despite his efforts to move, his limbs would not respond. The pain would have been manageable if it were not for the incredible heartache that came with it. Why would they do this? *How* could they do this?

"I'm sure you are wondering why we would stab you in the back. I'm sure you feel betrayed," said Ouroboros, his soft baritone at odds with the utter coldness with which he spoke. "But chalk it up as a lesson about Nova Terra. Everyone in this world has an agenda, a goal, and they will only befriend you if you help them to reach that goal." Stepping closer to Thorn, he squatted down and looked straight into his eyes. "This is not a nice world."

"Knowledge in this game is power, and power is everything. Absolutely everything. Everyone is fighting for that power and will take the first opportunity they can to rip it from your corpse. Especially when you are weak and helpless. Understand that we have nothing personal against you. In fact, I can speak for all of us in saying that we have even enjoyed your company and the convenience you bring as a porter.

"However, it is not often that we come across someone with your combination of ignorance about the game and trust of others. Add that to your lack of class and you become an irresistible opportunity. I can see from your expression that you don't understand what is going on here." Ouroboros sighed and patted Thorn's shoulder, the sensation sending new waves of pain through Thorn's body.

"I am trading your Destiny points for a better class for myself. Every player comes into the game with the potential to change their future by choosing a new class. Each time you choose a new class, you use up some of that potential. The runes that you see around you are part of a specialized spell that uses your Destiny points to grant someone else the chance to change their fate through a class change. In this case, me.

"See, I have a dual category Ancient Inheritance class already that I spent two Destiny points to acquire. This means that, if I want a quad category Ancient Inheritance class, I am right out of luck. Even starting a fresh character will not help since this ridiculous game is based on your actual identity, and Destiny points do not refresh. Once a Destiny point is used to change your class, that's it, there is no going back. Besides, acquiring a quad category Ancient Inheritance class is a pipe dream because it requires four Destiny points, and everyone starts with three.

"The only way around that is if someone else is kind enough to use their potential up in your place and spend their Destiny points on your behalf. Sort of like what you are doing now. This way I can switch from my current class to being an Exalted Devil Blood Berserker despite the fact that I have no more personal potential for change.

"You are doing us a huge favor. While you will lose your chance to master a class, I will become one of the rare few quad class holders in the game. This will help me grow to be one of the strongest players in the world. Be glad that you can be part of creating the strongest player in Nova Terra. We are going to leave you here and will never see you again, so consider all of this a terrible, terrible dream. This is a lesson in the harshness of the world and the nature of people."

Staring into Ouroboros' eyes, Thorn had no doubt that he meant every word he said. There wasn't a shred of mercy or compassion in those eyes, only the ruthlessness to trample on anything in his way. It made Thorn wonder if this is what it felt like to be one of the monsters the players killed.

Why on earth would the game allow players to treat each other this way? His heart shaking with a mix of shock, pain, and adrenaline, Thorn could only rage at his impotence. There was nothing he could do to stop the group as they stood around talking about what they had gained.

"Oi, you were not joking about this archdevil being a strong backer, were you?" said Jorge, looking over his status. "Gained a title and everything. This is pretty powerful."

Still looking at Thorn as if he was nothing more than an ant to be squashed, Ouroboros nodded. "I told you. Plus, the title can be activated to increase damage after your blood has been spilled. I got the class, plus I can appoint twenty Blood Berserker guards. It's a dual category class that is the base for the Devil Blood Berserker. We earned a lot. Plus, there should be the possibility of growth."

"We can use the dual category classes to establish a faction," said Jorge. "And with your quad category class, you will finally be able to compete with Angdrin."

"Yeah. It will take me some time to get used to it, but this class is strong. The others will not be able to ignore us anymore. Well, we've got a ways to go, so let's get moving. Mina, we are counting on you."

Mina walked up to Thorn, a strained smile on her face, and put her hands on either side of Thorn's head. "It's nothing personal, Thorn. I'm sorry." Murmuring under her breath, freezing energy began to seep from her hands, and Thorn soon found it almost impossible to breathe as his thoughts got slower and slower.

An almost warm feeling burst through Thorn's brain, and an immense sense of fatigue came over him, helping to dull the intense pain he was feeling. Somewhere in the back of his brain, Thorn realized that the warm feeling was the onset of hypothermia. Gritting his teeth and trying to fight off the fatigue, Thorn was helpless to stop his brain from getting colder and colder.

"Don't fight it, big guy, it will all be over in a moment," said Jorge, from the side, as Mina increased the amount of energy pouring out of her hands. Ice began to form around Thorn's head as he glared at her and, within another minute, he had faded into darkness.

After Thorn had fallen unconscious, Mina, still smiling her silly smile, looked down at her trembling hands. The smile faded from her face as she fell to her knees, gasping for breath. Furrowing his brow, Ouroboros stepped closer to check on her, but she waved him away.

"I over-drew my mana. I'll be fine in a moment. The big guy was harder to take down than expected." Before he had died, Mina had seen a change in Thorn's eyes, so subtle that she had almost missed it. His shock had given way, and a different emotion had replaced it. Mina had seen rage before, but this was different, deep burning hurt that made shivers crawl down her spine, for some reason, causing her to stumble.

"How much health did that guy have? Wasn't the pain from the transfer supposed to knock him out? Not only did it not knock him out, but I half expected him to jump up and attack us," Jorge wondered aloud as he stared at Thorn's body, shocked. "Plus, that backstab should have cut his health in half, at the very least, even before he got hit with the transfer. Sheesh." Shaking his head, he began to search Thorn's body.

"It doesn't matter. We're moving on and will never see him again anyway," replied Ouroboros, helping Mina to her feet. "And if we do, we'll kill him again. Can you grab that ring?"

"Nah, quest item," grunted Jorge as he stopped pulling on the ring that refused to come off of the corpse. "Why didn't he drop anything? Where is his crossbow?"

"I'm not sure, maybe he dropped it during the fight with the devil?"

"Huh, doesn't seem to be over there. What kind of luck does he have to not drop a single thing? The odds of that are tiny. Anyway, what about all the loot on him? He is holding onto everything we have gotten today. We picked up a ton of loot from this dungeon, but he was carrying it."

"Leave him be," Ouroboros commanded. "I had to kick him from the party so that you could stun him, which means he is no longer our porter. I can't withdraw the loot from his inventory. Karrandaras gave us the quad category class for sacrificing him and the dual category class change stones, we can leave everything else for him. Since we took something valuable from him, leaving the loot with him is the least we can do. The situation in the guild is far from stable, and we can finally do something about it. Our plan can be decided after we get on the road. There is a lot of catching up to do before we can compete with the top teams."

"These classes will give us a big boost," Velin said, a small frown creasing her face as she looked down at Thorn. "But I feel like we made the wrong choice."

"Haha, what does it matter?" replied Jorge, his voice cracking. "We needed a noob as a fifth, and he was unlucky enough to be the one. And, as Ouroboros says, we're likely never going to see him again and, even if we do, what could he do to us? Haha, I bet he will quit the game after this, anyway."

"That's enough, Jorge," Ouroboros shushed the laughing dwarf. "Velin, you know that, in this world, the weak are at the mercy of the strong. If he didn't want to be taken advantage of, he should have protected himself better. Anyone else in our position would have made the same choice. What is one person in the face of the greatest achievement this game has ever seen?"

"And should I take that same perspective, Ouroboros?" said Velin, eyebrows raised. "Do I need to protect myself against you? Should I prepare myself to be sacrificed?"

Watching her take a small step away from him nettled the usually calm Ouroboros.

"Come on, Velin, you know I wouldn't do anything that could hurt you," the new Exalted Devil Blood Berserker said, stepping after the elf and grasping one of her hands. "I know it was mean of us, but we all agreed to go down this path to the end, no matter how cruel."

Silent, Velin pulled her hand away and walked out without looking at him. Walking after her, Mina couldn't help but wonder why her hands would not stop trembling.

CHAPTER THIRTY-SIX

For a normal character, being incapacitated like this would send them to the logout screen of Nova Terra, where they could open their pod and exit, but Thorn didn't have that luxury. His condition had warranted full immersion, and full immersion is what he had. Instead of the epic landscape of the loading page, Thorn found himself elsewhere, suspended in darkness.

However, this darkness seemed more than a simple lack of light. Rather, it was darkness that was deeper. A smothering, consuming darkness. At first, Thorn assumed that there was nothing to see, but he realized that his other senses were muted as well, a perfect sensory deprivation experience.

At first, Thorn's brain scrambled to make sense of this strange state, reaching out for some sort of input. With rising panic, he began to scream mentally as the pain and anger he had been subjected to threatened to overwhelm him. Struggling to control his overflowing feelings, Thorn calmed himself by narrowing his focus, like he had been taught.

Reduce all extraneous thoughts, clear the mind, focus on a single point. Meditation had been part of his martial arts training, and it had worked wonders in helping him get through the pain caused by his condition. 'Pick a point and zero in!' he repeated mentally, focusing his mind on the party that had betrayed him. His anger helped him throttle the panic that had surged up, and by focusing on the last scene he had witnessed before the darkness, he was able to settle his thoughts.

Taking a deep mental breath, he relaxed. After an indeterminable amount of time, Thorn noticed a growing glow and realized that he was starting to be able to see. Faintly, he began to see a strange figure materialize in front of him. It looked blurry and warped, almost as if he was seeing it through a translucent wall. The strange figure looked like a cross between an angelfish and a squid with a tall, flat body and eight tentacles that spread from where its mouth would be. Thorn was curious about it but, for some reason, felt no fear or trepidation, despite its bizarre appearance.

With an abrupt motion, the eight tentacles angled together, forming a point, and stabbed toward Thorn, pushing their way past the translucent barrier separating them. Squirming and pushing, the odd creature forced its appendages through the wall as it approached closer, its tentacles opening up and sliding around Thorn before pulling him back. With a pop, Thorn felt the sensation of being pulled through the wall, squeezing through the hole the squidfish had pierced in the barrier.

Sensation returned in full force as Thorn found himself standing in the endless expanse where he had started the game. The squidfish, its task done, released him and, with a wave of its fins, drifted off into the digital distance.

"Ahem."

Hearing the polite cough, Thorn turned his gaze away from the retreating squidfish and looked down, where he found the NPC who helped him register standing with a clipboard.

"Hello, Traveler, it is wonderful to see you again," said Myst, her eyes darting around Thorn's face as if searching for something. "Please bear with me for a moment as I have a couple of questions for you. The first time a player dies, it can be something of a mental shock, so we like to take a moment to talk about their feelings on the subject. This serves to make sure that the experience does not negatively affect the player in the long term. But, before that, do you have any questions for me?"

"Yeah, what was that place? And that creature?" Thorn asked, looking in the direction the squidfish had gone. "Will that happen every time I die?"

"That is a great question, Traveler. To answer your last question first, no. Then, in order, the location you were in was NULL space, a portion of the game where nothing exists. In order to safeguard the players who encounter fatal bugs, the consciousness of the player is transferred to NULL space to protect it. Once the situation is stabilized, the player is brought back out of NULL space by an Angler, the program you saw now, and sent to respawn."

Flipping over a couple of pages on her clipboard, Myst frowned. "However, we have a slight issue."

"A slight issue?" snapped Thorn, startled by the words 'fatal bug' that Myst had so casually thrown out.

"Yes, traveler. Our problem is that you are not dead, so we can't send you to respawn. In fact, it looks like your subconscious is refusing to accept death, which, apart from being inconceivable, is causing you to get stuck in our rebirth cycle."

"Inconceivable, why would it be inconceivable?" muttered Thorn, scratching his head. "Nova Terra is a game, there is no way I can actually die."

"Yes, well, your brain doesn't think so. Or rather, it shouldn't think so. The realism of Nova Terra is strong enough to convince your brain that death in-game is real, and the game can judge when your brain accepts death. This is also supplemented by the game pods, as each has a limited amount of processing power. When the processing power peaks, the brain is counted as overwhelmed, and in-game death occurs. In effect, the two ways for death to occur are: your brain acknowledging that you have died, or, your pod's processor hitting a threshold. However, I see that because of your special circumstances your pod has more processing power than others, an oversight that led to this occurrence."

"Huh, so I died?" asked Thorn, unsure of where this was going.

"It isn't that simple," sighed Myst, looking much more human than when she had helped Thorn register at his first login. "The situation, as it stands, is this. Your character is incapacitated and should have already suffered hypothermia and died due to your brain accepting death. However, your subconscious refuses to accept the situation, which keeps it alive," said Myst.

"Normally, this situation would still result in you being logged off due to your pod's processor peaking, and you would only be able to log back in after your body died, and you passed the twenty-four-hour death penalty delay. But the condition which should have caused your brain to shut down by taking up all available processing power is only affecting the primary computer on your pod, leaving the secondary and tertiary computers running."

Pausing for a breath, Myst shook her head. "In effect, your avatar is shrugging off the effect of hypothermia because you genuinely don't believe that it would affect you, and the gaming hardware is keeping your body alive. This is an oversight on our part, and your firmware is being updated to prevent this from happening again."

"Wait, so I am dead?" asked Thorn, confused.

"No, you are alive. We have pulled you from the game to install the update. Your avatar is still laying on the floor in the cavern," Myst replied before flipping back to the first page of her clipboard and staring at Thorn. "Now, why don't we talk about what just happened. You were betrayed by a group of people, used for their own ends, and discarded. Tell me, how do you feel about that?"

The abrupt change in topic jolted Thorn out of his stupor. Too much had happened in the last few minutes for him to focus on the events prior to being thrown into NULL space but, with this question, everything came flooding back. He had been recruited into a group and had been tossed away like he was nothing, used and abused. His first experience with other players was an absolute disaster, and that made Thorn furious. Yet even as he raged in his heart at the four traitors, something in the back of his mind couldn't help but wonder at the situation.

Before coming into Nova Terra, Thorn had done a bit of research and was aware that the concept of morality embraced in the outside world had been tossed aside by some players. There were very few humans who could get rid of the moral constraints that society placed on them, and Nova Terra actually had a solid screening process to alert the authorities to psychotic behavior.

In fact, the more he thought about it, the more puzzled Thorn was. Ouroboros had led his group into that dungeon for a specific reason and had both Velin and Mina ready to transfer his potential away to Ouroboros, which indicated they not only knew what to expect from the encounter with Karrandaras, but they were planning to strip his potential away the whole time. On top of that, Jorge very clearly indicated that they had expected to receive some sort of beneficial title from the archdevil that Thorn, being passively involved, had missed out on.

Additionally, they had killed him, rather than letting him continue to suffer the pain of the sacrifice. Why not leave him there if they were going to backstab him? Despite the cause of his death being intentional, it had been a more humane way to kill him than hacking him up with a sword. Did it have something to do with the reward they were expecting? Questions swirled around Thorn's head as he tried to remember anything that would give him a clue.

Thinking back, Thorn recalled that, in the "lesson" he had been given as he had knelt on the floor, Ouroboros had mentioned everyone having a goal. The way he said it made it sound like everyone in the game had the same goal. Thorn had started playing recently and wasn't aware of any secret goal that would put players in such brutal conflict with each other. Granted, there was much he didn't know about Nova Terra.

Looking at Myst, who was still watching him, Thorn replied, "I think I'm fine."

"Yeah?" Myst didn't seem convinced. "Player killing is common in Nova Terra due to the non-permanent nature of death, but the damage done to relationships is as real in-game as it is in the real world. It is to be expected that you would be experiencing mental turmoil over this situation."

"Am I okay?" Thorn wondered. Strangely, he was. The burning anger from a moment ago had disappeared, flaring before being smothered by a cold line of reasoning that had emerged from the recesses of his mind. Did that mean he would not seek revenge? Well, that remained to be seen.

However, before Thorn could continue this line of thought, soft light pulsed once, and Thorn's eyes opened a crack. The cold flagstones of the dungeon floor pressed into his face, contrasting with the burning pain that ran through his body.

Opening his eyes to the dim, flickering torchlight of the dungeon, Thorn looked around with bleary eyes. With a grunt, he got a hand up and rolled over, marveling at how much easier it was without having to be worried about his skin ripping. Thorn gave a painful chuckle as the thought flashed through his mind. That chuckle turned into a cough, with pain continuing to wrack his body. A number of screens popped up, but he waved them to the side and dragged himself to his feet.

Feeling the carvings under his hand, Thorn took a deep breath, focusing his mind as his sensei had taught him, using the pain to clear his mind. He pushed the pain to the side, accepting it as reality and forcing his body to relax, despite the spasms wracking his body. After a few moments, he carefully stood and made his way to the entrance of the room. About to limp out of the door, he remembered the altar with which the others had been interacting.

Approaching it, Thorn stumbled over the uneven tiles, nearly crashing to the floor. Catching himself on the edge of the stone altar, he gritted his teeth and pushed himself back up. The stone altar was only four feet high, made of a dark, porous stone. Symbols carved into the top and sides depicted the moon in various phases, covered in scratches and chips.

The top of the altar was lit by a ghostly red light, casting a bloody glow on Thorn's pale face. Seeing that the item Ouroboros had fit into the front of the altar was still there, he ran his fingers over it, jerking his hand back in surprise as the faint light intensified, and the large, red spirit boiled up from the top of the altar.

Seeming puzzled, the archdevil swirled forward through the air, examining Thorn with interest before commenting, [CURIOUSS. YOU SSTILL LIVE? I HAD WONDERED WHY I WASS SSTILL TIED TO THISS PLACE!]

"Why is that?" asked Thorn. "Should I have died?"

Sinister laughter echoed around the chamber at his question. Shivering with excitement, the spirit moved forward, twining itself around Thorn's body and running the back of its hand across his cheek.

[YESS. YOU SSHOULD HAVE DIED. ASS THE SSACRIFICE OF BLOOD, YOUR SSPIRIT SSHOULD BE MINE!!] The spirit stared at Thorn's body, examining his features. [YET HERE YOU SSTAND, DESSPITE THEIR TREACHERY, DESSPITE YOUR SSUFFERING. YOU MUSST HAVE SSOMETHING DRIVING YOU TO BE ABLE TO SSTAND IN THESSE SSIRCUMSSTANCESS. TELL ME, WHAT ISS IT THAT DRIVESS YOU SSO?]

Barely able to keep his feet due to the pain that still sent spasms through his body, Thorn was startled by the question. What *did* drive him? What was it that caused him to refuse death, despite the pain? Wouldn't it have been easier to give up and go with the flow, being reborn? Was it because he had spent his whole life in this sort of condition? A saying his aunt used to repeat to him when he was young and hurting sprang to his mind and flowed, unbidden from his lips.

"I am more than my pain; I am more than my body. My body bends to my will, not I to it."

[AHAHAHA] laughed the specter, [WHAT A MARVELOUSS WILL! YOU HAVE BEEN FOUND WORTHY. YOUR BLOOD HASS

BEEN GRANTED MY BLESSSING. I LOOK FORWARD TO SSEEING YOUR WRATH VISSITED ON YOUR ENEMIESS! YOU SSHALL BE MY CHAMPION, MY AVATAR! KILL YOUR BETRAYERS AND I WILL GRANT YOU POWERSS BEYOND YOUR COMPREHENSSION!!]

With a thunderclap, the specter turned into a deep red mass and burrowed into Thorn's chest, bringing with it a violent, rending pain that left Thorn, once again, gasping for breath. The burning pain soon spread through his body, raging like a torrent into his limbs. The red current flowed through his body, pushing up into his head, bringing with it a splitting headache.

CHAPTER THIRTY-SEVEN

Thorn could feel the crimson tendrils of fury creeping up into his brain, driving their way into his head. Fighting back against the pain, Thorn gritted his teeth so hard he heard them creak. No matter how angry he was, no matter how much he wanted to get back at Ouroboros for sacrificing him to Karrandaras, Thorn had no desire to become a bloodthirsty monster like Gargish.

"I am more than my pain!" he growled, pounding a fist into the ground so hard his knuckles split open and blood splattered across the ground.

[WHY DO YOU FIGHT, MORTAL?! I WILL GIVE YOU THE POWER TO DESTROY THOSSE WHO BETRAYED YOU!]

"I am more than my body!" Thorn spat between gasps as he steeled himself against the bloody power trying to force its way into his mind.

[YOUR EFFORTSS ARE FUTILE, MORTAL! YOU HAVE BEEN SSACRIFICED TO ME AND YOU CANNOT ESSCAPE MY GIFTSS!]

"My body bends to my will!" Thorn roared.

As the crimson tendrils broke past his defenses and began to penetrate his mind, a loud buzzing burst forth from his bag, and the ancient inheritance token he had picked up from Gargish appeared in the air in front of him. With his failing strength, Thorn reached his hand out and grasped it in his large fist as a gravelly voice rumbled by his ear.

"Let the earth help you, little friend." An amber glow darted from Thorn's forehead, wrapping the silver token in a honey-colored light. With a bright pulse, the crack running down the token closed, revealing the unbroken wolf's head, howling in front of the moon!

A cooling feeling burst from the token, like billowing waves of refreshing spring water. The cool power washed over him, extinguishing the burning blood power in his body. Terrified, the tendrils of crimson power tried to fight against the waves released by the token but were soon drowned, freeing Thorn from their grasp.

[NO! NOO! NOOOO!!] screamed the spirit, unwillingly. [HOW COULD YOU HAVE THAT POWER!! HE SHOULD BE DEAD!!]

Bloody, Thorn could only stare as Karrandaras began to swell and grow larger. The archdevil's form condensed, huge amounts of red mist streaming out of the red-veined stone. Soon a massive clawed foot appeared, smashing down off of the altar onto the floor. With a roar, Karrandaras condensed more of his body, as if he was forcing his way through a barrier into the world.

Completely drained and unable to move, Thorn wracked his brain for some way to stop the archdevil from manifesting himself. Already, the sheer pressure emitted by the archdevil's foot and calf was almost too much for him, causing black spots in his vision.

As he was about to pass out, Thorn's eye caught a glint of silver from his palm. 'That's right! This is the ancestral inheritance! But it is also a symbol of Hati, the Moon Wolf. It is unbroken, which means it might be able to purify the altar, like Velin said! I need to get it to the altar.'

Taking a deep breath, Thorn called up all the reserves of power in his drained body and drew back his arm. Mustering everything he had, Thorn hurled the token forward, sending it blurring through the air at the altar. Furious, Karrandaras roared and forced a hand into being in front of the silver token, doing his utmost to catch it.

With a tremendous ripping sound, the token smashed into the archdevil's powerful hand and broke straight through, leaving a scorched hole behind! Smashing into the altar, the coin buried itself in the stone with a loud crack!

Instantly, the same silver power that had washed away Karrandaras' corrupting influence on Thorn burst forth in massive waves, washing away the red veins from the stones in the walls and floor. Howling, Karrandaras' hand and foot started to fragment, and his condensing form began to scatter.

[MORTAL, YOU WILL PAY FOR THISS WITH YOUR LIFE!!] screamed the archdevil, turning his burning gaze on Thorn. However, before he could make a move, a deep growl alerted him that something was not right. Behind him, darkness gathered onto the altar and swirled together into the form of a massive wolf.

[YOU...YOU...YOU ARE DEAD!] stammered Karrandaras, his tone changing to fear.

Not giving him time to react, the giant wolf lunged forward, burying its massive teeth in the archdevil's blurring figure. With a scream of pain, Karrandaras faded, his figure blowing away like ash in a breeze.

Relieved, Thorn sat slumped on the stone floor. In his half-delirious state, he wondered if the red veins in the stones would be replaced by black veins. As his consciousness began to fade, he felt a warm breeze, and his muscles began to fill with energy. His mind cleared, and he found himself standing as if nothing had ever happened.

Facing a big wolf.

A really, really big wolf. In fact, somehow, its head took up his entire vision. Blinking, Thorn jumped to his feet only to realize that the stone floor he thought he was standing on was actually the rough nose of the giant wolf. Two massive silver eyes stared down at him, reflecting myriad thoughts and feelings. At times curious, at times cold and ruthless, at times warm and proud, the huge silver eyes seemed like giant moons rotating through their phases.

[Welcome, child.] A deep, warm voice echoed in Thorn's head. Instinctively, Thorn knew that the voice belonged to the wolf god whose nose he was standing on. [You have done well in breaking the seal of the betrayer. By slaying Gargish and repairing my holy symbol through the aid of Terberus, the Earth King, you gained my eye. By cleansing my temple from the corruption of Karrandaras, the Betrayer, you have gained my favor.]

"Thank you, uh, god?" Thorn did not know how he was supposed to refer to the wolf the size of the sky.

[Haha, you may call me Hati, child. Or Great Wolf.]

"Thank you, Great Wolf." This time Thorn bowed, his hand on his chest in the warrior's salute that Janus and Dovon had taught him.

[You have a powerful spirit, child. A spirit much stronger than most of the travelers we watch over.]

"We? Are there more gods than you?"

[Of course, there are more gods than me. While I am strong, I am not strong enough to care for everything in this great world. I rule over the night.]

"But I thought the gods were dead? Didn't they fall to the dragons at the end of the first era?"

[And who told you that child?] Hati chuckled, causing Thorn's body to shake. [The dragons were strong, for mortal beings, but they were no stronger than our avatars. No, we did not die, but we chose to step back from the world at the command of the High One to give the other species of the world the chance to flourish.]

"Is that why Karrandaras was able to take over your temple?"

[When I stepped back from the world, I left my avatar, Davyos, but as the years passed, the Betrayer corrupted his mind with dark whispers. Through an evil ritual, Davyos betrayed my favor, pledging himself to Karrandaras and turning his people against me. From then on, the corrupted Wolfkin appeared in the world. Karrandaras gave them the power to assume human form, so they could mingle with the other races of the world while murdering and hunting their prey in secret. The beings you know as werewolves are corrupted Wolfkin, remnants of Karrandaras' power in the world.]

"What about normal Wolfkin? We fought some regular Wolfkin in the tunnel leading to the temple. Are they corrupted as well?"

[No, child, those are remnants of my followers who still follow the old ways. They have hidden from the world and only appear to fight against the Betrayer's minions.]

"Oh." Thorn shifted. He had assumed that they had been enemies. "Sorry about that. I hope we did not harm you by killing them."

[Oh, child, I am a god. I do not need them to exist. Nothing apart from the High One can impact my existence. I am and will be. So long as this world exists, I will be here. The same is true for the other gods. Of course, I would rather you had not killed them, because I love all of my children, but it is not my place to question the will of the High One.]

"Who is this High One you keep talking about?" asked Thorn, relieved that he was not about to be eaten for accidentally shooting Hati's believers.

[That is not for you to know, child. It is sufficient for you to know that the High One is the beginning and end, and my master. Now, let us move on to more interesting business. I have watched you, and I am pleased. Therefore, I choose to grant you my essence. Henceforth, you shall be my presence on the world, my avatar. My fangs and claws will be by your side, my subjects will serve you, and my radiance will watch over you.]

"But didn't they steal my potential?" Thorn asked, downcast. "How can I be your avatar if I can't master a class?"

[Child, no one can take your potential from you. Your potential has not been taken; it has been compressed. This makes it much harder for you to unleash it, but by no means is it gone. Do not despair, though the journey may be harder, though the road you tread may be longer, it is still possible for you to reach the peak. What I grant you is not a class. Rather it is a different path, a path that requires much of you.]

"Being an avatar is not a class?"

[No, anyone might be an avatar. It means that the essence of a god resides within them and that they are qualified to speak on behalf of that god to the world.]

"That means I can get a class, right?"

[Yes, child. Though, due to your unfortunate experience, you will be required to walk the path of mastery one step at a time.]

"You mean I can only take a single category class at a time? Doesn't that mean no mastery bonuses?"

[In a way. The strength of mastery is dependent on how well suited you are to a class. Say, for example, if you were to become a tailor. Your body is not suited for fine needlework, so even if you mastered the class, your mastery would not be as strong as if you were to master smithing. The same is true for a multi-category class. Because multi-category classes come with other people's mastery, they will never be as strong as abilities from classes you mastered yourself.]

"That makes sense, I guess. So, it's a quantity versus quality question. I mean, if I have a multi-category class, I can get one additional ability, but my abilities will not be as strong."

[Precisely.]

"Do you have any recommendations for what sort of class I should try for?" Thorn asked. "You're a god, so you should be able to tell what I am good at, right?"

[You are correct, I can see what you would be best at. However, it is not my place to interfere with your future in that way. All I can say is that patience is the key to choosing the best class. Now, it is time for you to return. Let us begin.]

Under Thorn's watchful gaze, the massive eyelids closed. As the light from Hati's silver eyes grew dimmer, Thorn could feel power flowing into his body. Unlike the aggressive, invasive power Karrandaras' had tried to force into him, this power was warm and comforting, growing and strengthening him. His skin took on a silver sheen, and his muscles tightened, growing even stronger than they were before.

The silver light continued to stream toward him, wisp after wisp curling around his body until no more could force its way in. The extra energy began to gather around him, changing his equipment. His black armor glowed as the silver wisps remolded it.

Claws grew from the fingers of his gauntlets, as sharp as razors. The curling silver mist landed on his chest plate, engraving silver motifs of the phases of the moon. Around his head, wisps of energy condensed into a wolf head helmet.

Once the armor was formed, the rest of the silver energy condensed into ethereal forms of wolves and Wolfkin, shifting and changing. Above his head, the phases of the moon formed. As Hati's eyes closed completely, and the world went dark, his deep, warm voice rang out in Thorn's mind.

[Wake, my champion!]

With a gasp, Thorn's eyes opened. He was back in the temple, slumped down on the floor in front of the altar. Vestiges of the multiple battles lay around him, and the broken altar was quiet. Tired beyond belief, Thorn struggled to keep his eyes open. Finally, he collapsed backward onto the cold stone floor.

When he woke up a few hours later, the room had reverted to its original state, the black stone altar shining dully now that the red streaks were gone. There was no sign of Karrandaras or anyone else, and even the marks of the battles they had fought were gone. The only things letting him know that his experiences were not a dream were the absence of Mina, Velin, Jorge, and Ouroboros and the deluge of notifications flashing in the bottom of his screen.

Ding

Title Advancement: [Moon Wolf Avatar] + [Lord Greymane (locked)]

Because you possess two associated titles, they have combined to form a new title. Title Abilities have been updated to reflect the new title.

Title Gained: Lord Greymane, the Moon Wolf

Title: Lord Greymane, the Moon Wolf
Having cleansed the altar of Hati, the Moon Wolf, and been granted a portion of his essence, you have met the conditions necessary to claim the title of Lord Greymane. Ability: Avatar of the Wolf Ability: Call the Pack Ability: Blessing of the Moon Ability: Presence of the Wolf Lord

CHAPTER THIRTY-EIGHT

Status

Name: [Thorn]	Race: [Titan]
Health: [37%]	Mana: [100%]
Titles: [Battle Mad], [Wolfsbane], [Lord Greymane, the Moon Wolf], [Friend of the Earth]	Conditions: [None]
Abilities: [Wolf Lord's Howl], [Avatar of the Wolf], [Call the Pack], [Blessing of the Moon], [Presence of the Wolf Lord]	

A new field had opened up in his status. Thorn still had no class, but his abilities were now listed. If what Hati had said was correct, then Thorn would not be able to take a multi-category class, but he could still get a single category class and work on mastering it. Curious, he looked over his new combined title and the abilities it gave him.

Title: Lord Greymane, the Moon Wolf

Chosen of Hati, the Moon Wolf, you have earned the title of Lord Greymane, rightful ruler of Greymane Keep and the Lord of the Wolfkin. To take the first step in being recognized as the rightful ruler of the Fang Forest, you must take Greymane Keep back from the corrupted wolfkin who inhabit it.

Ability: Wolf Lord's Howl

The call of the wolf represents fear and danger. Your battlecry contains a stunning effect.

Ability: Avatar of the Wolf

Because you carry the essence of the Moon Wolf, you have gained the form of the wolf. As you grow, you can adopt features of the Moon Wolf Form.

Wolf Claws: You gain the Claws of the Moon Wolf
Wolf Hide [locked]
Wolf Helm [locked]
Wolf's Rage[locked]
Wolf Form [locked]

Ability: Call the Pack

The strength of the wolf lies in its unbreakable link to its pack. Dangerous alone, wolves become deadly together. As the Lord of Greymane, you can call upon your pack, granting them increased speed, strength, and healing.

Ability: Blessing of the Moon

Ruler of the night, Hati, the Moon Wolf, has blessed you as you walk under the moon. While under the light of the moon, you gain the following abilities: the longer you spend under the moon, the more abilities you will awaken.

Night Vision: The darkness of night cannot block your sight
Shadow Walk [locked]

Glory of the Moon [locked]

Ability: Presence of the Wolf Lord
As the chosen of Hati, you carry the essence of a god, granting you the bearing of an alpha wolf. Your interactions with monsters of the wolf type and races with ties to wolves will become easier because of your powerful presence. Friendly Wolfkin will treat you as a member of their race. Language: Wolfkin

All the abilities that he had gained were powerful and still contained room to grow. Sitting on the stone floor of the temple, Thorn could not help but shake his head. The last 24 hours had been an absolute emotional rollercoaster, between having such high hopes for playing with Ouroboros and the others to being stabbed in the back and having his ability to take multi-category classes taken away. Then fighting against the corruption of Karrandaras and gaining the favor of Hati by purifying the altar.

With so much to think about, Thorn knew that he was not going to be able to process it in a short amount of time, so he pushed it all out of his head and opened up his inventory, pulling out some food. Once his health had gone up a bit, he pushed himself to his feet and made his way out of the top floor of the temple. The monsters that they had killed on the way up had spawned again, though in fewer numbers. Thorn did not mind one bit.

Feeling quite aggressive, he pulled out his Tetsubo and charged as soon as he saw the first group of skeletons, smashing them beyond recognition with a few swings. None of the bosses had reappeared, so Thorn bashed his way through the mobs without a pause. On the second and first floor, where the party had encountered the black-robed Wolfkin, Thorn only found more skeletons, which suited him fine.

The city lay as silent as before, but this time Thorn found himself able to read the signs, making it much easier to navigate. That reminded him of the book that he had tossed into his inventory, so he stopped, sitting on the steps of a house along the road, and pulled the book out.

[Twelve Major Climates of the Angoril Continent]

Flipping through it, Thorn made his way back to the library and started tossing books into his bottomless inventory. Rather than leave the books for the next people to come, Thorn figured he might as well take what he could. Not bothering to organize the books, Thorn swept the library clean within half an hour.

After that, he decided to check out some of the other buildings and made his way back to the main square. Most of the buildings in the city seemed to have been homes but, after peeking in a couple of them, it was obvious that they had been cleaned out. The only buildings that might have anything worthwhile were the buildings that were still locked.

It was a day later that Thorn finally struck the jackpot. A merchant shop off of the main square had yielded nothing of note until Thorn squeezed down into the basement and found a large safe door. Hidden behind a shelf of old empty jars, Thorn only discovered it by accident when, out of frustration, he kicked a lantern that had been lying on the ground. His kick sent the lantern rocketing through the air and into the side of the bookshelf, which collapsed with a thunderous sound, revealing the large metal door.

Without a key, Thorn could only resort to brute force to open the safe, but he had plenty of that. The safe was set against the wall and, from what Thorn could see, the hinges were internal to prevent someone from cutting them off. That proved a barrier for Thorn until he remembered his Form of the Moon Wolf and summoned his claws.

Almost immediately sharp, pointed claws grew from his fingers. He had tested the ability earlier, discovering that they worked whether he was wearing gauntlets or not. Sliding his claws into the bricks on either side of the safe, Thorn grabbed the edges of the door and pulled the whole thing out of the wall. After brushing off the crumbled brick, he pried the door open at the top corner and managed to stick his fingers inside.

From there it was as simple as rolling the door back, opening the entire front of the large metal safe. Full of anticipation, Thorn peered inside and was not disappointed. Piles of glittering gold bars met his gaze, as well as a small tray of precious stones and three books written in Wolfkin.

At first, Thorn was at a loss regarding the gold bars, but when he finally put one in his inventory, he noticed that it had been converted to gold coins. Each bar was worth 200 gold and, with 27 bars, Thorn felt as rich as a king. The precious stones were not quite as convenient, so Thorn could only plan on going to an appraiser when he got back to town. Once he had put the gems away, Thorn looked over the books.

[The Complete Alchemist]

[101 Poisons and Their Applications]

[The Code of the Wolf]

The first book looked to be a primer for becoming an alchemist while the second was filled with 101 different types of alchemical poisons. Not having much interest, Thorn tossed them into his inventory to deal with later. The last book, however, caught his attention.

[The Code of the Wolf] was a book of law, laying out the rules of the Wolfkin from the first era. In pristine condition from being locked away in a safe for so many years, Thorn enjoyed reading through it. According to the book, Wolfkin society was divided into three different strata: the Lord, the Warrior, and the Worker. A complicated hierarchy existed between them with each having control over a part of society. As far as he could figure it out, the society was equal parts democracy, monarchy, and military state, depending on what part of society you belonged to.

Putting the book away, Thorn decided to leave. It had been a couple of days, and he was confident that Ouroboros and the others had moved on by now. While part of him wanted to see them again so that he could crush them into the dirt, Thorn recognized that he was not a match for the team, so it would be better for him to avoid them if at all possible.

Limping along with low health, Thorn made his way back toward town. Due to his wounds and running into a few kobold patrols, it took him almost the whole night to get back to town. His [Night Vision] ability worked like a charm, so he had no problem finding his way back in the dark.

The sun had just risen when he made it back to the gates, where the guards greeted him with curious looks. Over the course of the night, his wounds had continued to heal, leaving him with a bit more than 50% of his health. Health recovered slowly, and only sleep or a blessing from the temple could restore him to 100%.

Despite all he had been through, Thorn felt no need for sleep. He was puzzled at first but then remembered that time was passing in the game seven times faster than normal, which meant that he would only need to sleep once a week or so. He had experienced that before, but because of his natural clock, he had been going to bed each night anyway.

Since it was morning, he hobbled his way into the town's Temple and made a donation of a silver, instantly feeling rejuvenated as the on-duty priest blessed him. As he was about to leave, one of the priests stopped him with a winning smile.

"Excuse me, traveler, I could not help but notice the air of piousness about you. I can tell that you are one who is devout. A true believer. Have you considered becoming a priest?"

Startled, Thorn looked at the notification that popped up.

Class: Priest
By pledging yourself to the service of a god, you can gain the power to defend your faith. The type of abilities granted by this class are variable depending on the god you pledge yourself to. You are being offered a class change by an NPC Priest that serves the human god Mayordi.

"What is involved in becoming a priest?" asked Thorn. One of his goals was to gain a class, so he figured that there was no harm in asking.

"For a simple donation of silver, I can grant you the status of a believer, and from there you have to go through a bit of training."

"Wait, you mean I have to buy the class?"

"No, no, nothing so corporal. The silver is a testament to your faith, and once your faith has been proven, you gain the privilege of serving Mayordi."

A bit more inquiry revealed that, for a larger donation, higher ranked classes were available, and with a large enough donation, he could even gain multi-category classes. Shocked at the mercenary nature of the priest, it wasn't until he was outside that he realized Mayordi was the God of Merchants.

Having turned down the class change, Thorn reviewed his goals. He had come into this game a blank slate, his only goal to experience freedom and adventure. Well, so far, he had plenty of both. Not only the freedom of making his own choices, doing what he wanted, when he wanted, but also the freedom of others making their own choices, most recently to his detriment. While it had sort of worked out for him in the end, the experience had been a sobering reminder that he was not the center of this world.

As Xavier Lee, Thorn was, arguably, the center of the world. One of the richest people on earth, certainly the richest kid, with people to take care of his every need and to fulfill his every command. He had come to Nova Terra with the idea of escaping that gilded cage and had succeeded with flying colors.

The difficult truth of it was, however, that escaping that cage meant leaving the protection of people who cared about him. Freedom and protection seemed to be mutually exclusive. His right to happiness went only as far as his ability to act. Once someone stronger or more powerful came along, he was tossed to the side after being used for their purposes.

The adventure had been good, though. Rather painful, all things considered. Thorn was not averse to a bit of pain, provided that it allowed him to achieve his goals. But the question became, what next?

Without question, Thorn wanted to gain a class and start working toward establishing himself in the world of Nova Terra. While he had made some connections, Thorn had spent most of his time following others around, trying to learn about the game. Considering his experiences over the last couple days, Thorn felt that he had learned more than enough and was ready to strike out on his own. A class would be instrumental in that.

As far as classes went, Thorn had been putting a lot of thought into what sort of class he wanted to have. While his size, speed, and strength lent themselves to some sort of combat class, there was something about focusing so much on fighting that turned him off. Even if he chose a different category of class, his fighting ability would not evaporate. That left Utility, Support, Production, and Leadership classes as possibilities.

Utility Classes were pretty much out, since they focused too much on combat for Thorn's liking, as was Production, since Thorn had no desire to be chained to one location doing the same thing over and over. Support was an interesting idea to Thorn, but as he mulled over it, he rejected it for the simple fact that Supports worked best in parties, and he had no desire to play with others anymore.

The only category of classes left was Leadership, which Thorn had never imagined himself moving toward. However, the more he thought about it, the more it seemed to make sense to him. His titles were focused that way, and the abilities tied to them gave bonuses when interacting with Wolfkin. A Leadership class would suit him.

Second, the new title that Thorn had received [Lord Greymane, the Moon Wolf] seemed to indicate that, in order for it to be realized, he had to take back Greymane Keep from the corrupted Wolfkin. Thinking back on it, Thorn seemed to remember that Gargish was a corrupted Wolfkin. Chances were Thorn would be fighting more werewolves soon. Having become the avatar of the

Moon Wolf, Hati, Thorn seemed tied to the Wolfkin species. He could only imagine that his future would be full of meetings with them.

Apart from getting a class and exploring what was going on with Greymane Keep, Thorn was also interested in continuing his study under the trainers at the Training Hall. Dovon, Janus, Hamm, and Master Sun had helped him in getting used to this world, and Thorn believed that there was much more for him to learn. His power lent itself to fighting, and Thorn was very interested in seeing if he could incorporate his existing training with practical combat in Nova Terra.

Sitting down on the steps to the temple, Thorn took a moment to breathe and organize his thoughts. Too much had happened in the last couple days, from being jumped by Gargish to meeting and being betrayed by Mina, Ouroboros, Velin, and Jorge. Despite the ups and downs, one thing was for sure. Thorn's adventures were only beginning.

END

Afterword

I really appreciate the time you have spent with me in Nova Terra. I am continuing to work on the series and cannot wait to share it with you. Before I tell you how to get a peek at what that looks like, please spend a few moments and leave me a review. Reviews are so important to indie writers, like me. Knowing that you are out there, reading and thinking about Nova Terra, is what keeps me writing.

Now for the good stuff. After you leave a review, head on over to Facebook and join our Nova Terra page. That is the best place to keep track of what is coming up next for Nova Terra. If you are interested in a more intimate experience or being part of the world of Nova Terra, check out my Patreon to learn how you can see over 7,500 words per week of brand new material. There are lots of different levels of participation, all with various cool benefits, including being first to read new stuff, guiding the story line and character development, having a character named after you – lots of possibilities.

I've been fortunate to participate in panels at various conferences, so please sign up for my Patreon and/or follow me on Facebook to get announcements of new material and where I am speaking. I'd love to meet you and hear your thoughts about Nova Terra, writing, and world building in general.

Here are some links for you to check out what I'm doing.

WWW.PATREON.COM/SETHRING
WWW.TWITTER.COM/SETHRING
WWW.SETHRING.COM

ACKNOWLEDGMENTS

A huge thank you to my friends and family who encouraged and supported me on this wonderful journey.

Thank you to my Patrons, who make my writing possible.

A special thank you to the following Patrons who have gone above and beyond the call of duty in funding this story:

Berzerker
Brandon Nichols
Brandon Terry
Colby Chandler
James A. Ring

If you are interested in reading more GameLit or learning more about this or related genres like LitRPG, there are a couple cool communities on Facebook where you can find new books and get recommendations for old books.

https://www.facebook.com/groups/NovaTerraFanClub/
https://www.facebook.com/groups/LitRPGsociety/
https://www.facebook.com/groups/LitRPGGroup/

Made in the USA
Middletown, DE
05 June 2021